A FANNY FULL OF SOAP

NICHOLA McAULIFFE

A Fanny Full of Soap

The Story of a West End Musical

OBERON BOOKS
LONDON

First published in 2007 by Oberon Books Ltd.

521 Caldonian Road, London N7 9RH

tel 020 7607 3637 / fax 020 7607 3629

info@oberonbooks.com / www.oberonbooks.com

Reprinted 2007.

A catalogue record for this book is available from the British Library.

Cover illustration by Andrzej Klimowski

ISBN: 1 84002 744 4 / 978-1-84002-744-0

Printed in Great Britain by Antony Rowe Ltd, Chippenham

A Fanny Full of Soap is a work of fiction, and all characters, names and incidents are entirely fictitious. Any resemblance to the name, character or history of any person is coincidental and unintentional.

Acknowledgements

Thanks to all at Oberon Books led by James Hogan and Charles Glanville.
To my patient editors Dan Steward and Will Hammond,
and to Andrzej Klimowski for the cover illustration.
To Nicki Van Gelder of Conway Van Gelder Grant,
Virginia Wilde of Equity, Richard Powles of Farrer & Co.,
Peter Wilson of Theatre Royal, Norwich,
Mary McAuliffe and Don Mackay for their support and strength.
Finally, a special thanks to the Famous Marji Campi
whose Fanny it was.

Acting and prostitution have a lot in common. Both require you to do what you love, with whom and when you don't want to do it. For money.

In both, there is physical or mental intimacy and intensity – however brief and one-sided.

The main difference is the length of engagement.

OVERTURE

The Country Wife

ONE

David was embarking on a bout of foreplay when he insisted we go to Phyllida's for Christmas. I would have preferred his mind to be entirely focused on the stimulation of my pleasure centres, but her darling old husband had died, leaving her with six labradors who were only marginally younger and marginally less smelly than he had been, and David thought we ought to make the effort.

I couldn't argue; one didn't argue with David, even when he was naked but for an excitedly distended pair of underpants. He had a militarily precise way of putting one in one's place. My place being somewhere between the blind mole-rat and the bonobo.

Of course he hadn't considered that when he'd got me 'up the duff', as his father put it, and 'done the right thing by the ghastly little trollop'. David had a remarkable appetite for unsuitable sex. Or at least sex with unsuitable partners. Oh, I wasn't genetically suspect, but the truth was David had inseminated an utterly unsuitable mother for his line because I had compounded the sin of being lower middle class by being an actress. A television 'star' and 'celeb'.

The words *star* and *celebrity* had become grubby with overuse by then, but for a while I was a favourite with the tabloid press, and, to a certain extent, the public. David always found it excruciatingly embarrassing when I was accosted by affectionate old ladies in the street wanting my autograph. At least, I thought it was embarrassment; perhaps it was envy.

Anyway, it was hoped his family's genes would all but obliterate mine. Certainly they'd be gone by the next generation. Everyone was politely regretful, as though David had been somehow caught out. This was only made worse when, shortly after the birth of the son and heir, I landed a regular part in a daytime soap about police vets and promptly became a national icon for saving a kidnapped sniffer dog. The story ran for weeks and I was all over every newspaper, even mentioned at Prime Minister's Questions. It was more than fifteen minutes of fame, and David detested it.

But a standing cock knows no conscience, as my friend KT always says. He also said he couldn't believe anyone in this day and age could have been stupid enough to fall pregnant and go through with it. *Fall pregnant* – extraordinary expression. As if I'd tripped on a badly laid kerbstone and torn the hem of my virginity.

Poor David. My husband. Small, neat, dapper; dirty blond hair and a shy smile. That vulnerable half-smile that attracted maternal instincts like wildebeest to a waterhole. An absolutely old-fashioned gentleman. Sweet, charming, diffident. And a gold-plated bore with a borderline personality disorder. Well, all right, if I was such an astute judge of character, how did I come to be married to him in the first place and pretty soon have WELCOME embroidered in large letters across my forehead? Quite simple, really: I was desperately, madly, blindly in love and my brain was disengaged. The wheel was spinning but the hamster had long since passed on.

I was absolutely defined by the men in my life until comparatively recently. I'm not saying that's an entirely bad thing; it saves wear and tear on one's intelligence and it never occurs to you to wear trousers rather than wax your legs.

But, as Shakespeare might have said: I run before my Volvo to Sainsbury's.

Christmas. Phyllida lived, still does live, in a rambling, ersatz stately home in Gloucestershire. Not quite within hunt distance of royalty, but exclusive nonetheless. She was a Phethean by birth. I'll quite understand if this impresses you with the same force as discovering she uses skimmed milk, but apparently in these circles of middle-class rurality, a great deal could be learned from a name.

The Phetheans had loose connections with the Bosanquets and were directly descended from William IV and Mrs Jordan. But then so is a crowd big enough to fill Wembley stadium.

David was frightfully impressed with her. She had married the 27th Baronet, Sir Tristram Fyvie, when he was 67 and she 33, and had become Phyllida, Lady Phethean Fyvie, lest her ancient name be lost, like her husband's upper set the first time he introduced her.

I thought her a strikingly plain woman, far too long in the gum. Blue eye-shadow, no mascara, as is the way of women who wear Hermès scarves and pearls with wellies. I can only imagine her desire for his title was as great as the deterioration in his eyesight. Late onset diabetes, apparently. She never seemed particularly fond of him, and when he slipped into a twilight world peopled by 'big women' and 'bloody Irish stiffs', she gave him less attention than she gave to any one of the spoiled dogs already mentioned.

This pack of sleek black labs surged and ebbed around her, shared her bed and infested every chair and sofa in the house. I loathed visiting, as I always came away with enough shed hair to knit a yurt and smelling like a 1970s sheepskin coat. But David always said:

'Poor dear Phylly.' No, he didn't say it, it drawled out of him, pulling the left corner of his lower lip out of alignment rather than disturb the stiffness of the upper. 'She must be desperately lonely, darling.'

Darling – that was suspicious; I was usually Lumpy, or Kipper Feet or Old Pudding.

'I think it would be a fine thing to take Christmas down to her this year. First one alone. Be difficult for her.'

I could never work out why he spoke like a 1940s Guards captain. He was at least a foot too short to join the Guards, years too young to have done national service, and the closest he'd been to a parade ground was waiting for a bus outside the territorial army barracks when the Land Rover was being serviced.

David was a forensic anthropologist. Only in his forties, but the dryness of the bones he worked with had dessicated his soul. He was ancient and I had become old to accommodate him. So successful was I that, had things not changed, I would soon have been mistaken for his mother. Or, more probably, nanny.

Anyway, Christmas.

I was of course and as usual left to buy, plan and prepare the entire event. David Carved The Turkey – and all my efforts paled before the sheer beauty of his feints and passes with a newly steeled carving knife.

We drove down to Gloucestershire on Christmas Eve in my ancient Metro. Originally known as the Flying Bidet, it was now so old it was the Venerable Bidet. David had wondered if we should take the four-wheel-drive or his classic Mercedes tank, but he wanted to drink and wouldn't trust me with the Merc since I'd driven it twenty miles in top gear with the handbrake on. Easy mistake to make. And I wouldn't drive the Discovery without an HGV licence. So Bidet it was: my faithful friend who'd never liked the cold and, in car years, was about 85.

The turkey wobbled about on the back seat like a nodding dog with my home-made Christmas pudding and my painstakingly iced Christmas cake – just a drop of Quink blue ink out of my school Osmiroid to make the white icing whiter; thinking of my father with tears in my eyes as I recreated the flowers and trails he'd taught me when I had to stand on the upturned washing-up bowl to see onto the table. Sprouts, chipolatas (a dozen for us, two dozen for the dogs – all organic), potatoes, breadcrumbs, brandy, champagne, wine and dinner-party crackers, guaranteed to yield gifts over which we'd squabble after the port... And us crammed in the front seats with our knees wedged under the dashboard.

We arrived at dusk. David disappeared into the house with Phyllida, airily saying how much he needed a drink and he'd unload the car later.

I did it. Alone. No help and in the dark.

In those days, last Christmas and a lifetime ago, martyrdom born of guilt was my preferred mode of dress. Comfortable. Like a bra that's lost its wires in the wash.

While they started on the gin and tonics in front of the log fire surrounded by tail-waving labradors, I put everything in the pantry, and that which didn't belong in the pantry in the larder, and the rest in the fridge. I laid out my stall, happy in my unassailable domestic superiority, accompanied by an ancient brown and white spaniel – so old its rear end stayed still while its front walked round it. Its watery eyes, tired after a lifetime of looking up for food and love, gazed unfocused into a bone-filled past at ankle level. The poor old thing was far too frail to compete with the rough young dogs next door.

I put a bit of bacon in front of him. His nose, more by a process of elimination than smell, guided his mouth to it. His tongue hoovered it over his gums and slotted it into a space where teeth had once been. He sucked at it contentedly, chin resting on outstretched paws.

When I was satisfied the kitchen was familiar to me and that I could face Christmas morning with confidence, I joined David, Phyllida and the pack in the living room. It was beautifully decorated – Dickensian, with its large tree dripping with sentimental fancies. In fact, there was nothing in the Victoria and Albert Museum shop that was not hung, propped or nailed up in this room. I felt like Cook going above stairs for the festive sherry. I was even more acutely aware of my position as I reached out to take my drink from Phyllida. Her long pale fingers only just touched my raw red ones, but I saw them like a close-up, on widescreen. Why wouldn't my nails grow like that? Where her hands tapered elegantly away, mine came to an abrupt end, like coal shovels. Hands like navvies' feet. Capable, the nuns had said.

She sat down. Either side of her, dozing black dogs. David, brightly flushed by the nearness of the fire and the strength of the gin, I supposed, sat in a high-backed club chair, all leather and brass buttons. Every other raised surface was covered in dog.

I sank to the threadbare rug which was masquerading as an antique kelim, forced my legs to cross as they had in the infant school hall for assembly, and murmured that I always sat on the floor. David and Phyllida continued their conversation, neither inviting me in nor purposely excluding me.

One of the dogs farted.

Silent, deadly and level with my face. By the time it drifted as high as Phyllida's nose it was dilute enough to be laughed at, but on the floor I was as afraid to inhale as if it had been phosgene gas.

'Oh, Winston. You naughty dog. Really. Stinky creature!'

I dipped my toe into the conversational stream: 'That's a nice name for a dog. What are the others called?'

Phyllida was pleased with the question – unlike when I asked where the turkey dish was (she didn't have one) or how many saucepans there might be without nameless encrustations in the bottoms.

'Well, Nora…'

Nobody called me Nora.

'…The little one behind you is Peter, next to him is Geoffrey, here are Rose and Ruth, and those two are Fred and Winston.'

I flopped a velvety dog ear, exposing its pink insides: 'After Churchill?'

'Good Lord, no. Silcott. They're all murderers.' *God, how stupid was I? Of course…* 'Dahmer, the Wests, Lee…and Sutcliffe.'

Phyllida looked at me as if I were a C-stream woodwork reject when I laughed a little too loudly and said my friend KT had two dogs called Eta and Ira, and that he wanted to get a third and call it Rouge.

Phyllida politely asked why, though I could see she had no interest in the answer.

'Because,' I said, with a slightly desperate vocal flourish, 'the first two are named after terrorist groups, and he wants to be able to go on the heath and shout, C'mere Rouge... Khmer Rouge...'

Not long after that I said goodnight.

They were overly solicitous and polite as I closed the door on the Christmas-card scene and plodded up the stairs, knowing I had made a fool of myself. David had given me that gentle, patronising look he usually reserved for occasions when I'd had two glasses of wine.

My face was glowing red in the hall mirror. The old spaniel staggered out to join me, hoping perhaps for another piece of bacon, or maybe it just wanted me to chew the bit it had. Did I see sympathy in its moth-eaten old face?

I should have liked to go to midnight mass, but there was no Catholic church in the village – the locals still had fond memories of Henry VIII and most had just the one eyebrow.

As I climbed higher up the stairs the air grew colder. And colder. I had only stayed in the house in summer before and had not then noticed the complete absence of radiators, gas heaters, or even one-bar electric fires, above ground level – where the old spaniel stayed, having absent-mindedly wet the hall rug.

The frost had formed pretty patterns on the bedroom window. Inside. My breath clouded the air and died, defeated by the bitter cold. I switched on the electric blanket, which would, I calculated from its position and meagre width, eventually singe one buttock each of a double occupancy. I couldn't bear the idea of taking my clothes off, but thought it might be marginally less painful if I did so and got straight into a hot bath.

I crept into 'our' bathroom, which was about a furlong from the bedroom. The window was open. After ramming it closed, or as close to closed as would still let a stiff breeze through, I stood shuddering and staring down at the bath, like some bedraggled cat waiting for rescue from a perpendicular roof. The bath was the size of Windermere and constructed from off-cuts of the Forth Road Bridge. My mind went back to third-form maths: 'If a man spends two days filling a bath at the rate of four litres a second but there is a hole in the side of the bath and the diameter of the hole in the side of the bath, *etc. etc.*' My answer was always, 'Why doesn't he buy a new bath?' But it was clear to me in that bleak midwinter you'd need an Icelandic geyser to combat the chill of the enamelled iron.

I'll have a shower instead, I thought.

I turned the handle: immediately a gush of steaming water rushed out of the single brass tap. I pushed the lever across and the Niagara hurled itself up the coils of sprung copper. And then it encountered the shower head. A dribble of water forced its way past a century of limescale and formed a puddle beneath. The only way I was going to get warm would be to run round under the holes trying to get wet.

I gave up and went to bed.

There are few things less welcoming than damp sheets steaming in the heat of an electric blanket. The sweat on your bottom is only condensation; the droplets forming between once-pert breasts, fabric conditioner.

Mercifully, I was asleep when David came up. He never liked to risk my being awake in case I required intimacy. Or worse still, servicing. However, if he required that same intimacy, he was a fine and considerate lover, showing the same good manners that dictated he should open a door and allow the lady to go first. He asked permission to visit my bed. The light was always switched off. He never slept with me. And I never questioned him. I had learned, though, that if I made the first move, indeed any move, he was repelled.

TWO

I woke on Christmas morning to find David in his usual position when circumstances forced us to share a bed. He was stretched out, ramrod straight, on his side, facing away from me. Sound asleep, his head was propped up on his right hand, which was improbably and uncomfortably bent back under its weight. The precarious balance he'd found, as if sleeping on a razor blade, was disrupted every time his wrist gave up the struggle and his head pitched forward. It was pulled back into place on its blood-starved plinth time and time again, and yet he never woke.

I wanted to get up. I wanted to use the lavatory, but the thought of the cold walk to our bathroom persuaded my strained bladder to endure another five minutes. The sheets were still clammy and the ice was filtering the weak sunshine through the window.

It was so cold in the bathroom I couldn't face removing all my coverings – nightie, dressing-gown, socks and cardigan – so I had what my aunt used to call a lick and a promise, though her version apparently involved sitting on the draining board, having a rub down with a Welsh flannel. They were like ordinary flannels, only red and hard enough to descale a kettle.

In the kitchen, where the dogs slept close to the warmth of the hot water pipes, I made a cup of coffee and settled down with the runner beans. At home we'd had a wonderful machine for doing runner beans: cast iron, green-painted and with a delicate wooden end to its solid winding handle. I loved to assemble it and screw it hard to the deal table, then feed through the topped, tailed and stringless beans. Perfect angled slivers, eaten in a bowl with vinegar.

David wouldn't let me use it; he said it was unhygienic.

Phyllida barely acknowledged Christmas until she'd taken the dogs and David for a run up a hill as steep and slick as a playground slide. I stayed in the car. Hers. A large and properly mud-spattered four-wheel-drive assault vehicle. I think she would have preferred me to stay close to the Aga, but I'd peeled everything that needed peeling and I needed a break from the Turkey From Hell.

Well, in fairness, it wasn't the turkey's fault. I'd covered it in sacrificial butter, wrapped it in bacon, created a tent of extra wide foil around it and was manoeuvring it into the oven, when I encountered a set-back. The oven was neither wide enough nor deep enough to accommodate the baking tray on which it sat. I tried it at an angle. I tried it tilted slightly on its side. It would not go in. Phyllida looked at me as though I was unable to surmount a one-bar jump on a Grand National winner. I said weakly:

'I don't think it's going to fit…'

David looked up from a fascinating article in Dog Breeders Weekly: 'Oh, come on Nellie, you're just not trying.'

I wanted to say: *Look here you stupid prat, short of using a jar of Vaseline and a brick hammer, there's no way this turkey is going into this apology for an oven.*

Instead I said: 'Maybe on a different tray…?'

Phyllida nodded towards the pantry. 'Have a look in there, you might find something.'

I knew they were both wondering what I was for. I could see it in their averted faces. Their patrician profiles politely set against stupidity. They were embarrassed for me. I could feel myself getting red again, tearful, homesick for my childhood. I stayed in the pantry just a little longer than necessary before I came out, confidently carrying a smaller, less suitable tray.

'I'll try this,' I announced brightly to the empty room.

Phyllida and David had gone outside to look at the early-flowering clematis. No doubt she'd give him a cutting and I'd have to nurture it until he put it in pride of place against the south-facing wall, where he knew I was short of space.

The turkey was wedged into the oven, breast and thighs touching the sides. Erotic words for stuffed, dead flesh. Neither of the botanists seemed to care and, frankly, had I been offered a large sherry, I wouldn't have either.

I sat in the back of Phyllida's four-wheel-drive with the ancient immobile spaniel, watching my husband gambolling like a puppy up an incline I couldn't have enticed him up if I'd been standing at the top wearing nothing but stockings, suspenders and an England cricket cap.

Woman to handsome young man: 'I've got an itchy pussy.'

Young man to randy woman: 'I'm sorry, I don't know anything about Japanese cars.'

I smiled and repeated the joke to the spaniel. It didn't laugh. Maybe it was deaf.

Phyllida and David ran back as if they were in a Senapod commercial. The dogs piled in and over me. Phyllida and David sat in the front, talking and laughing, giving up on me when I kept saying 'Pardon?' over the noise of the engine and the panting of dogs.

Back at the house we changed out of our wellies and Barbours and into our Christmas Day clothes.

Phyllida, though I hated to admit it, buffed up well. She had a strong bone structure and, rare in her breed, a chin that didn't look as though it had been lost in a riding accident. A fine dusting of powder, that, on a lesser face, would have looked like the finishing touches to a Bath bun, completed her make-up. She was the picture of English womanhood in all its equine loveliness. Yes, in certain lights she looked like Desert Orchid, but to the aristocracy that is as silicone breasts to a chav.

We exchanged gifts by the tree and it really was a lovely picture: the long drawing-room windows framing the snow-covered lawns, the exhausted dogs steaming in front of the log fire, the glistening tree, and the choir of King's College singing 'Silent Night' in a key so high the dogs winced.

Phyllida's gifts to me were a fridge magnet, a black velvet handbag filled with jasmine-scented bath requisites and a cast-iron Friesian cow doorstop. Having sniffed and commented appreciatively I could only assume that in Taiwan the scent of jasmine resembles that of sump oil.

To my husband she gave a Penhaligon's travelling aromatherapy candle with matching leather case and a silver corkscrew. I waited for his reaction. He beamed. He chuckled. He dimpled. He kissed her stiffly on both cheeks.

He did not say: 'What sort of raving queer do you take me for?' As he would have done to me. He did not discard the gifts immediately to pour himself a stiff scotch and soda. No: he nursed them in one hand while sipping champagne, pink and smiling. This was how he must have looked on Christmas morning when he was five.

The binoculars I gave him, capable of focusing on a gnat in the next county, were examined, appreciated and placed on a side table. But I knew he liked them. He'd written down the specifications so I'd get the right ones.

Phyllida seemed genuinely to appreciate the devore wrap I had taken hours to choose and a month to pay for. She thanked me and kissed David. Did I imagine her to linger just too long by his off-side cheek? Did I really see a tip of pink tongue flick out against his shaved skin? I felt myself going brick-dust red with guilt at my suspicious mind. David was always telling me off about it.

I slipped away to take the turkey out of the oven and put in the parboiled potatoes and curling parsnips. I pulled back the foil from the heavy bird. Its back was perfect, golden between the strips of bacon, but where it had been wedged against the oven walls it resembled coal.

The plump legs were charred bones; the rounded stuffed breast, flattened slate. I finished off my champagne in one gulp. Never mind, I thought: cover it in holly, no one'll notice.

The old spaniel watched my every move through a veil of cataracts. He seemed to be regaining his youth, and even tripped up one of the larger, more greedy dogs when they hurtled into the kitchen ahead of Phyllida. She beamed at me; I felt like curtsying.

'Nora, darling, you're such a treasure. Such a wife!'

David followed her into the kitchen, which was now so much mine I felt their presence an intrusion.

'Anything I can do, darling?'

Under normal domestic circumstances I'd have murmured an affectionate if slightly patronising 'no', pushed a wisp of hair from my eyes and pressed on, lacking only a wrap-over pinny and a Celia Johnson accent. Come to think of it, I often saw my life in black and white, a mist of nostalgia obscuring the nastier bits. But on this occasion I said:

'Yes, David, could you carry through? Phyllida doesn't seem to have a trolley.'

How sad was my life? My trolley, the trolley less of a hostess than an empress, represented a victory over the Blood of the Bosanquets.

Phyllida and David giggled. 'Of course, Eleanor, but wouldn't it be more sensible to let David carve the bird first? Save the sprouts getting cold.'

'Not too keen on sprouts anyway, so they can go in now for all I care.'

David's jibe at my sprouts was like a slap. I knew he was simply grandstanding for Phyllida, but it was a lie. On our first Christmas Day together he'd ravished me on the granite kitchen work surface, causing me to turn the sprouts down. Sprouts shared a rare and fondly remembered moment of sexual adventure and were one of the few things that held us together.

I busied myself with warming plates and decanting chipolatas into dishes. 'Do you think the dogs would like theirs now, Phyllida?'

I missed the look of pity she exchanged with David but felt it.

'Whatever you think best.' She may as well have said, 'You're mistaking me for someone who cares.'

I nodded decisively: 'Yes. I think now. Then we can enjoy ours in peace.' What on earth was I twittering on about? The spaniel looked up at me. I thought I saw sympathy in those old eyes. But sympathy and greed can look very similar in the canine face. I distributed sausage meat and gravy among the rockery of dog bowls.

Phyllida, after much fussing and clattering, produced a battered serving tray commemorating various milestones in the Queen Mother's life. David ceremoniously placed the turkey on it. In doing so he dislodged the holly.

'Oh, hell....you've burnt it.'

'Well, it didn't fit,' I said defensively. Phyllida averted her gaze, unwilling to be involved in a minor domestic dispute during which the handsome, clever husband showed great patience and calm while facing the spectacular stupidity of his wife. David sighed. That infuriated me. I huffed. 'You try getting a size fourteen turkey into a size ten oven.'

It seemed a sensible thing to say at the time.

David carried the 'charred chicken', as he now amusingly took to calling it, into the dining room and placed it at the head of the richly polished mahogany table.

Phyllida carried in the vegetables and sat at the opposite end of the table, leaving me in the middle like a child home for the holidays.

She looked fantastic, like some English painting from the 18th century. There was no electricity in her dining room, but candle flames danced in the wall sconces and the silver chandelier. The crackling fire was burning pine branches among its sturdy logs. The dogs lay down and a Mozart piano concerto played from hidden speakers. In her tall-backed antique chair, with her fine English hair haloed round her long face and her faded lavender eyes shining in the candlelight, she looked, not beautiful, that would be too easy a word, she looked like the spirit of England, an antique countess in delicate colours. Something within her glowed and it looked to me like a light from the past. As if a Gainsborough lived.

My own reflection in the gilded-over mantel mirror seemed coarse by comparison, my much-envied olive skin dull and dark, my wide mouth and tilted eyes too big, altogether too much, too vulgar. Too obviously sensual.

David was carving the breast meat now. A lock of his hair fell forward, shining in the soft light. Phyllida stood up unhurriedly, apparently arranging and distributing the potatoes. Her hands moved languidly. I was pouring her a glass of wine when she did it; she must have thought I wasn't looking. She *must* have; surely she couldn't have had such contempt for me, such disregard for my feelings? Her left hand, glowing with her marital diamonds, reached across and brushed my husband's hair back into place. He looked up and gave her the briefest and most boyish of his armoury of smiles. The killer smile. The smile he broke my heart with. With which he broke my heart.

'So what are you going to do with yourself while David's in South America?'

Phyllida was putting three roast potatoes and two boiled on each plate. Why three and two? Was it an aesthetic decision or personal preference?

'Oh, I thought I'd go back to my Spanish classes. I can go into the intermediate group now. I took the examination at the end of the last course and did quite well. So I can go on. To intermediate.'

I saw my words falling into uninterested ears. Phyllida said, 'I'm surprised you don't want to work. Aren't you actresses supposed to be desperate for an audience?'

'David doesn't believe in working wives.'

I spoke too quickly, too sharply. Her only reply was a lifting of her eyebrows and what may have been a smirk. 'Oh, so you're not, what is it you call it? Resting?'

David laughed. 'Nora's been offered a job in the New Year. It's a vanity project some American couple are doing.'

'It's a salsa musical about a famous Costa Rican family, actually. The producer's wife has written it.'

I sounded ridiculously prim.

'Of course she's not going to do it, are you Nellie?' David was utterly dismissive. 'All that jigging about after all these years? She'd probably be invalided out after a week. Of course, talent doesn't count these days, it's just whether the great unwashed know your face. They only asked her because she used to be on the "telly".'

He put the word in quotation marks, like tongs, to keep it at a distance. Phyllida laughed.

'They felt my name might help, yes.'

David sighed at my lack of humour. We ate in silence. I think I was the only one who found it awkward. Eventually Phyllida rested her knife and fork, took a sip of her wine.

'This is delicious, Eleanor, you must tell me how to make the stuffing.' The silence had been appreciation. She smiled at me, then turned to David. 'So what exciting thing are you doing next?'

David mirrored her pose. 'I'm off to some Godforsaken clearing halfway up the Amazon where they've found a mass grave. An entire Indian tribe apparently, wiped out by a logging company. That's the theory anyway, they need me to go over and try to shed some light on the remains and the manner of death. Sounds an awful place, riddled with chicken-eating spiders they say. Should be quite interesting but we'll be out of contact for quite a while. No mobile phones there, only a sort of antediluvian radio apparently. Can't e-mail, and I'm told the project can't afford a sat phone.'

'That'll be hard on you, Eleanor.'

'Oh I don't mind,' I lied. 'I'm used to it.'

Phyllida smiled at me. 'Good. Good girl.'

I looked away from her and something caught my eye.

'Er...Phyllida, that dog the spaniel, it doesn't look well.' Actually it looked dead, but I didn't want to be over-dramatic. I needn't have worried, as the effect was electric.

Phyllida screamed. The living dogs all barked but the apparently dead spaniel was noticeably silent.

'Oh God, oh God! Call the vet. Eleanor, the number's by the phone!' She grabbed the dog and started pummelling it. I thought for one horrible moment she was going to give it mouth to mouth. Its back legs moved. It seemed to have gone into spasm.

Mary the Mother of Jesus couldn't have been more excited at the appearance of Gabriel. 'He's alive! He's alive, David! Eleanor, what should we do? You must know what to do. You saved that sniffer dog.'

For all her earlier condescension she, like most of the television public, thought actors were what they played.

'Call the vet,' I said. She looked at me as if I'd refused life-saving treatment.

'No, wait! David you must drive me, Eleanor phone and tell him we're on our way –'

'But it's Christmas night –' I didn't add that, as the spaniel would still be dead in the morning, we could put it in the freezer and finish dinner.

She was now hysterical: 'David, you're not insured to drive my car, we'll have to go in yours, fetch a towel to wrap him in. From the cupboard. Quick.'

She lifted the limp corpse onto the dinner table. I didn't think it entirely hygienic, but she was now reciting a litany of reassurance to the other dogs, none of which would have been remotely interested in the arrival of the Grim Reaper himself, unless he'd been handing out fillet steaks.

David came in with a beach towel. Tenderly they swathed the little body, leaving its dry snout and glazed eyes visible above the words MARINA DEL REY SAYS HAVE A NICE DAY.

Phyllida, now cradling the dog in a caricature of maternal care, followed David out into the unfriendly night. As I stood watching them drive away, the other dogs, disturbed by the panic, crowded behind me. They now seemed genuinely worried and upset. I shepherded them into the sitting room where, reassured, they reinfested the furniture, but one, unable to settle, followed me out to the kitchen and spent some minutes sniffing at the spaniel's last damp patch.

I phoned the vet, who was remarkably sanguine. He said he'd go straight to the surgery but as it was thirty miles from Phyllida's he'd probably be there before them. Thirty miles? David was driving a dead dog thirty miles? He'd moaned about driving me to the doctor at the end of the road when I broke my arm.

I removed the pudding from the top of the Aga. Uncontrollable lump of scrap iron. Give me a gas cooker any time. With an eye-level grill.

In the dining room I sat down amid the wreckage and noticed with no emotion that the spaniel had been finally incontinent on the table cloth. That I would leave to Phyllida. The food contaminated by the odour of death and loosened bowels I emptied into the bin.

I turned on the television in the kitchen. Less than five minutes later I turned it off. I wanted to be at home: Mum and Dad with a pillowcase full of brilliantly wrapped presents; thick winter pyjamas; red ladybird dressing-gown and my rabbit-eared slippers. But all that was as dead as the dog.

I didn't want to cry. I really didn't. But walking into the hall, up the stairs and into the bitter cold bedroom I did. Fully clothed, I crawled under the candlewick cover and switched on the electric blanket. As I fell asleep I saw the old spaniel's sympathetic face and felt, in my slough of self-pity, the loss of a friend.

THREE

Boxing day was a picture postcard of stark black trees and soft white snow. The air seemed denser, the sounds sharper and the world less harsh. The view from the bedroom window was so beautiful I almost forgot the cold, but when I got out of bed, bitter reality hit me again, as did David's absence.

His side of the bed was so undisturbed I almost expected to see a glitter of frost on the pillow. The house was silent. Snow-silent. I thought I'd be greeted by stretching dogs and early morning scratching when I reached the bottom of the stairs, but there was nothing. Tinsel on the tree moved gently for no reason. Through the windows, footprints of birds in the snow led nowhere.

I opened the kitchen door and saw the desolate remains of Christmas night. Congealed cranberry sauce adhered to the once-proud sprouts, held fast in calcified bread sauce. The brilliant snow-light lit up motes of dust settling on every surface. I filled the kettle then searched for a radio, suddenly desperate for the sound of voices.

Then I saw it. Actually I almost tripped over it. It was laid out on the kitchen floor.

The dead dog.

Maybe it wasn't dead, maybe it was just sleeping. I squatted down beside its beach towel. No obvious breathing. I poked it gently with a rolled up newspaper. Dead.

There was a dead dog on the kitchen floor.

'He's there so the other dogs can learn about death.' I hadn't heard Phyllida come in. 'There you are, dogs! Go see! Nothing to be frightened of.'

The dogs dutifully if reluctantly wandered over to sniff the corpse. It didn't take them long to realise that this hadn't come out of a tin and it wasn't covered in chocolate and so, though dead, was not food. It was remarkable how quickly they saw it was, in fact, a dead dog. And, reluctant to be reminded of their own mortality, they turned in a tide of tails and legs, stampeded to the doorway, and almost crushed the runt of the flotilla in their panic to get back to the living room.

'Are you going to bury it?' I tried to sound nonchalant.

Phyllida looked stern. 'Him. Stanley still has the dignity of his sex and his name.'

From what I could see of his undercarriage, Stanley hadn't had the dignity of sex since he was a puppy.

'Would you like a cup of tea?,' I asked.

'Yes... Where's David? We must get over to the hunt meet. Every year we think it could be the last one, but so far we've out-foxed the antis. Out-foxed, d'you see? Ha ha.' She had to help me with the wordplay as I was obviously as thick as bathroom sealant. I laughed obligingly. 'You'll come of course.'

'Of course,' I answered, wondering whether to empty the mould out of the pot or just put the bags into mugs. 'Have you just got back? Do you know where David is?'

Although she looked away, busying herself with a hundredweight bag of dog biscuits, her reply was seamless. 'We got back hours ago. He must have slept on the sofa to save waking you.'

A few minutes later I went upstairs to put on another thermal vest and heard David singing in the bathroom. Gilbert and Sullivan. Then I saw Phyllida had left her bedroom window open again and the arctic wind was howling unimpeded into our room. I reached in to close the door and saw David's socks on the floor by the bed.

Two limp black socks, with what looked like a regimental crest on the ankle. I'd bought them from a shop in Jermyn Street before seeing KT in a matinée of Jack and the Beanstalk. It was an all-star cast and he'd been quite exceptional as the back end of the tap-dancing cow. I must have been in shock, as all I could think of was the front end sitting on its own lap then crossing both sets of legs.

'What are you laughing at?,' asked David, coming out of the bathroom.

'Oh nothing... When did you come to bed last night?'

'You were snoring. I slept on the sofa. Came up when it got too cold.'

'Ah. Right.'

I wasn't sure of the etiquette when one's husband's socks were lying under another woman's bed, so I didn't say anything. As I'd said nothing when I saw Phyllida's intimacy with his hair. I didn't want to think about it, or the other lies that might be found under Phyllida's bed.

We were all frightfully bright and jolly as we piled into the Toyota Land Grabber, leaving the dead spaniel in the middle of the kitchen floor. My main concern was that, as the kitchen was the only warm room in the house, the thing might start going off before we got back. David and Phyllida didn't seem to care, though, and sat in the front chatting and giggling while I winced in the back under a riot of slobbering dogs.

At the hunt meet, Phyllida and David climbed out looking like fashion plates from Horse and Hound. I fell out of the hatchback like a bewildered asylum seeker. We walked down past a variety of mud-spattered Land Rover variations to the village square. The road was icy but the locals didn't slip; neither did David. I gripped the overgrown hedgerow as my legs parted like a turkey wishbone.

On the village green, six or seven solid-looking horses were standing and circling, ridden by solid-looking English women whose voices bayed louder than the pack of hounds. Plates of mince pies and mulled wine in plastic cups were being offered round by ruddy-faced villagers. PLEASE TAKE HOME YOUR LITTER, requested a discreet sign on a rustic front gate.

Phyllida was in her element. David and I stood back while she worked the crowd with seven black labradors on a remarkable selection of leads, including a bit of old rope. She was greeted, kissed and marvelled at until the crowd parted to allow a massive grey gelding through. From it a ruddy-faced woman of about 55, with the sort of bosom the Empire was built on, greeted Phyllida as if hailing the Queen Mary in Southampton:

'Phylly! M'dear! That pup you sent me's a cracker. We've trained him up into a real champion. Bloody fine working dog that.'

'Damn, I forgot to send you his papers. I'll do it first thing.'

'No hurry, Phylly, I might ride over after New Year and let you see him. This the new man in your life?'

As she shifted in her saddle to get a good look at David, I noticed the stitching on her jodhpurs had given way, allowing putty-coloured lumps of thigh to strain towards the daylight. Her jacket gaped slightly as she moved and I saw she had a considerable overlap of stomach resting on her saddle.

'He's my husband,' I said.

The woman looked as surprised as if the dray horse she was sitting on had suggested she go on a diet.

'Oh, I am sorry.'

I was completely unsure, as she'd intended me to be, whether she was sorry for her mistake or sorry he was my husband. Then she inspected me more closely, leaning down and staring at me. Finally she jabbed a leather-clad finger in my direction.

'I know your face.' She strained, as with a reluctant bowel movement. 'Haven't you been on the television?'

I mumbled *yes*.

'Don't know your name. What have you been in?'

Other people were beginning to look across at us. I shrank and shrugged.

'Well, I didn't like it anyway. Daytime rubbish if I recall.'

She exchanged a look with Phyllida and flicked the horse into a lumbering trot. More horses and riders eased their way into the throng. One was a young girl on what looked like a pony, or rather it looked less like a vast, badly stuffed sofa than the others. Everyone was greeted loudly and enthusiastically. Still smarting from the *'weren't you on the telly'* incident, I asked, 'So have they not seen each other for ages?'

Phyllida didn't look round as she answered, but continued to wave and smile at the new arrivals. 'Probably all met up on Christmas Eve, everyone goes to all the parties. It's what we do in the country.'

'Ah.' I nodded.

We stayed for another half an hour, until the horses, hounds and riders finally trotted off. I wondered if, with the increasing number of urban foxes, we might soon see the Inner-City Hunt, a lot of hoodies in dodgy BMWs shooting up the gardens of Tottenham and Streatham. I smiled.

David was glowing like a born-again bucolic.

'That was terrific, Phylly. I only wish Nellie and I could move out here. I'm sick to death of London.'

'Nowhere to get a packet of cigars and a pint of milk at three a.m. round here,' I muttered. David and Phyllida laughed, at me or with me didn't seem to matter anymore.

Back at the house I prepared lunch, stepping over the spaniel every time I had to visit the pantry or larder. Finally, after cold turkey, baked potatoes and various pickles, Phyllida announced:

'I think it's time to bury Stanley.'

We observed a moment's silence, then David said, 'I'll help you.'

Phyllida's eyes filled with tears. She put her hand over his. 'Thank you. Thank you so much.'

It was an emotional moment and one that I did not feel equal to, so I washed up while David tenderly lifted the body which, now rigor mortis had worn off, was floppy and remarkably heavy. I could see the difficulty he was having with it and how much easier it would be to pick it up like a sack of coal instead of a sleeping child. David finally gathered it up and Phyllida laid her hand gently on the dog's thin fur. For some reason, this quiet intimacy hurt more than the socks.

'We should think about going before it gets dark, David,' I said. 'The roads are wet and if they freeze again they'll be lethal.'

Like the look David gave me.

'After all, you've got to get packed up for South America, find your passport, oh, and you promised to fix the fence where the ivy has pulled it over before you go.'

I sounded desperate, pathetic and unattractive, but there was nothing I could do about it.

'I'll put our stuff in the car while you bury Stanley and, if it's all right with you Phyllida, I'll collect my husband's socks from under your bed.'

My voice was shrill. They turned to look at me. I faced them, defiant, brave and unafraid. Phyllida didn't even have the grace to look guilty. I wanted to hit her.

'Well?,' I said. 'Is that all right?'

'Fine,' said Phyllida, 'I was going to wash them first. Stanley, unfortunately, purged himself at the end, all over me. David gave me his socks as I had to take mine off. And my shoes. Unfortunately it's made a bit of a mess of your car too. I was going to give it a clean out but if you're in a hurry to go...' She trailed off, then gathered herself: 'Don't worry about Stanley if you have to go, David. I'd hate Nora to be put out.'

David didn't even look at me, he just carried the dog outside. Phyllida followed. My face was burning. I had to keep moving, to try to get away from myself. David couldn't despise me as much as I despised myself, but I knew the contempt he felt. He hated my jealousy but I couldn't help it.

I snatched up anything that was ours, shoving everything into boxes and bags. From the kitchen to the sitting room to collect our presents.

I stopped dead in the doorway.

On the sofa was a rumpled blanket and an indented cushion. On the floor, open, the book David was reading about mitochondrial DNA.

Through the long windows I saw David digging, with Phyllida by his side, like Lowry figures against the snow. I knew David would be apologising for me, explaining my irrational behaviour. Telling Phyllida about all the things I'd imagined over the years, all the women that in my mind he had trailed through our bed.

I turned away from the window and cleared up, folding the blanket, collecting our things. I didn't hear David open the door.

'How could you? Eh? How the hell could you? You've ruined Christmas. Phyllida's desperately upset. And me…? Well, I've had enough of you and your fantasies. I'm just glad I'm going away. I've decided to go a couple of days early. Can't stand the idea of being around you, frankly. And listen, Nora,' – *Nora*? – 'you've got this month to think about your behaviour, because I'm telling you, one more, just one more demonstration of this ridiculous jealousy and we're finished. Understand?'

I nodded dumbly, unable to say anything in my defence.

'Right. I'm going to clean out the car. Phyllida's not going to see us off, she's too upset, she's going to stay down there with the dogs till we've gone.'

'But I'd like to apologise.' I sounded as I had when I'd accused Susan Williams of stealing my sweetie money then found it in my school coat pocket.

'I don't think that would be appropriate at the moment, I really don't.'

He turned and left the room – and me, empty. I wanted some living thing to reassure me, to understand why I was so frightened of losing David. I saw the old spaniel's face. I was projecting Buddha-like understanding onto a dead dog and my self-esteem was zero. I needed help but had no idea where to find it. I resolved to try therapy after the holiday. I resolved to be a better wife. I resolved to lose a stone and look like Julia Roberts. But when I got out to the car, I simply resolved to keep my mouth shut until we got home and even then not say anything until David gave me permission. Had I had some sackcloth I would have run up a nice little frock, filled it with ashes and cleaned David's shoes with my prostrate body.

FOUR

David sat in the driver's seat staring straight ahead. I put the bags and boxes in the back as quietly as I could, afraid of his volcanic anger. Before I'd pulled the seatbelt across, he was reversing into the drive. In the distance, Phyllida was throwing sticks for the labs, a pile of brown earth marking Stanley's grave. She didn't look round as we drove away.

The drive home was quiet and uneventful. The country dozed in front of old films behind windows filled with twinkling lights. David didn't speak and I didn't dare, despite my overstretched bladder.

He parked the car outside the house and ratcheted the handbrake. He did it on purpose, it was a sort of aggression towards me. He'd have much preferred to push me down a flight of stairs but, being a gentleman, he subverted these desires into car rage. I'd seen him rip windscreen wipers from their anchors. But only when faced with my irrational suspicions. And only from my car.

I'd tried St John's Wort and acupuncture, but I still saw David as a magnet for women of a certain age and texture. Women whose bodies were plump and pale with round breasts neatly iced with pink nipples. Females who smelled of Yardley soap.

We were at home before he finally spoke.

'I'm off first thing. I've ordered a cab to take me to the airport.'

'I'll take you.' I abased myself, it usually worked. 'I'd like to, really. To make up for…well, you know.'

I could see from his face he wasn't going to make this easy. When he was in this mood, nothing less than slaughtering a goat on the front lawn would do.

'No, I don't know, Eleanor. Perhaps you'd like to tell me.'

'Well…to make up for being a bit, well, um…'

'The words you're looking for are neurotic and jealous, Eleanor. As well as unbelievably stupid.'

There'd recently been a woman who'd belted her sleeping husband with a cricket bat, fetched an eight-inch carving knife from the kitchen, run back upstairs, plunged it into his chest, locked the bedroom door and gone to Scunthorpe for the weekend. She pled self-defence and was acquitted. I wondered if…but no. I loved my husband and, after all, humiliation didn't really hurt. It only felt as if it did.

'I don't mean to be, David. I'm sorry.' No reaction. He really wanted the whole nine yards of penitential crawling. 'Would you like a cup of tea?'

'No.'

'Coffee?'

'No.'

'Hot chocolate?'

'Shut up.'

'Yes, sorry, of course. Mm.'

While he packed, I busied myself with the kitchen, admonishing it for getting untidy, tenderly soaping the cabinets, making friends with my neglected saucepans. There was one particular favourite that had a red rose sticker on it, the emblem of the manufacturer, but I liked it so I'd left it on the shiny aluminium. I always thought it looked like an England player with the national flower curved over its swollen chest. To punish myself I scrubbed the rose off. A bit of an empty gesture, as David didn't see it and wouldn't have understood if he had.

Looking back, over the rim of a well-filled glass, I have no idea who that woman was, but at the time, being a doormat at least conferred on me some use. I was standing on a chair dusting the light bulbs when David came into the kitchen.

'What are you doing, Eleanor?'

Windsurfing, David, what does it look like?

'Oh, just polishing the light bulb. It was a bit grubby, with us being away and all.' I trailed off under his withering stare. I knew what he was going to say.

'You are so anal, Eleanor. You really should get help. Don't bother to get up in the morning, I'll be off early, cab's coming at four-thirty, flight's at eight.'

'I'll drive you – Heathrow, is it?'

'I'll get a mini-cab. Look, just go to bed. I'm going to stay up, do some work. Goodnight.'

'But David,' I trotted after him, 'when shall I see you?'

The living room was dominated by his luggage, two soft-sided grips, his laptop and a small bag containing money, passport, tickets.

His sunglasses, camera and the binoculars I'd given him for Christmas were on the table, ready to be packed.

'I said, when shall I see you?'

David, pouring himself a large scotch, shrugged. 'When the job's finished. Probably about three weeks, maybe four. Time for you to get your attitude sorted out.'

How many more times did I have to say I was sorry?

'I'm sorry, David, I really am.'

'Sorry simply isn't enough, Eleanor.'

Funny, that: I didn't think it would be. His mouth had taken on the look of a compressed chipolata. I was dismissed, to go to my bed and consider my position.

I was deep in a dream when the alarm, converted into the tones of an ice cream van by my subconscious, went off. The dream seemed so real, the feeling it left so deep. I had dreamed I was in love, a huge, operatic love, and what filled my whole chest with warm golden syrup was that I was sure I was loved in return. I desperately tried to stop the fading of the dream into the solid winter darkness. I closed my eyes again, tried to get back into the pictures that seemed so real, except... except I couldn't see his face. I could feel his skin and his arms round me, I knew his hair was soft, I could feel his whole body, but no matter how I tried, I couldn't make his face appear. I knew it wasn't David; this man was like a bear, while David was a whippet. All nerves and sinews.

There was a bang downstairs. The front door. I grabbed the clock, turned on the light: four-twenty. The cab was early. He'd gone.

I ran downstairs and out to the front gate. The red of the mini-cab's brake lights glowed as it turned the corner. Never mind, I had the house to clean from top to bottom and I still had some tidying up to do in the garden.

The binoculars, camera and sunglasses were still on the table. I had an excuse to chase David, to make up before he went.

I threw on a jumper and trousers. Sadly, I wasn't liberated enough by urgency to neglect bra and pants. I had once left off underwear, desiring the perfect denim-clad bottom, and caught my pubic hair in the zip, leaving a small but noticeable bald patch.

Maybe I should call the mini-cab firm, get them to radio the driver to say I'd meet David at Heathrow. No time. If I drove through the housing estate on the other side of the main road I could catch up with them.

I took the Mercedes and with screeching tyres roared up our quiet cul-de-sac. Collecting wing mirrors as I raced through the narrow streets, bouncing over speed humps, I tried to drive like an armed robber – but saw from the speedometer I was barely doing thirty. I even had my hands at ten-to-two on the steering wheel. I did take one corner a bit too fast and immediately braked when the binoculars fell off the passenger seat onto the floor.

Then I saw it: a Speedicabs Peugeot estate. I tentatively pushed down on the accelerator as we raced round the one-way system at Vauxhall. The car ahead lazily waltzed across the white lines; I stuck rigidly to the pattern of lane discipline that I'd learnt for my test fifteen years before.

The traffic lights on the north side of the bridge were changing. For the first time I didn't look at the river, didn't say hallo to London as I crossed its main artery. The cab went through the amber light, turning left onto the embankment. I sat at the red with not enough courage to drive on, despite the empty streets.

I reached for the mobile to call the cab firm, call David… Then I saw my phone quite clearly on the hall table and David's beside it: no good up the Amazon. Up the Amazon, where the prophylactics prowl… The words of a song. What song? Where did my brain find that snippet?

Flash! I'd screeched satisfyingly away from the lights and passed a speed camera at sixty-five. My proudly held clean licence would now be that of a criminalist. But it would be worth it, worth three points or more to catch David and make up.

They were visible ahead again, so I eased off the accelerator. I knew it was the cab, as its rear was dented and it seemed to have been painted by a Bolivian dwarf, the bright rainforest colours fading to beige at waist height. I followed at a reasonable distance, having decided simply to drive into Heathrow behind them and jump out of the car with David's forgotten belongings, at which he'd embrace me and cover me with grateful kisses.

I was smiling, giggling, anticipating our happiness and the warmth of our reconciliation when the signs for Heathrow first appeared. We drove past the first one. Not surprising, as it was for cargo. The following signs, the ones that made me smell holidays and suntan oil, prompted me to move into the inside lane. But the cab didn't, it stayed in the centre lane moving at a steady eighty-five past the airport.

Maybe there was another way in, a mini-cab driver's slip road all but hidden from public view? I didn't worry. Why should I?

After another ten miles on the M4, I did begin to worry. No, I began to panic. I reached into the glove compartment for the chocolate. An avalanche of Maltesers, M&Ms, hazelnut whirls and organic slabs cascaded onto the floor. I leaned across, desperately grabbing for comfort, and swerved, almost joining some indifferent sheep in a small field. The chocolates were on the floor by the passenger door. With the binoculars. Could I reach the umbrella on the back seat? Hook a packet across with its handle? I wanted chocolate more than I wanted world peace.

I had an idea. Leaving my right foot on the accelerator I lifted my left foot up and over the handbrake, toe pointed like a greyhound's nose. Cramp set in and I narrowly missed two hedgehogs and a blown out tyre.

I was howling in agony when the cab indicated left. With both eyes closed in pain, I'd missed the signpost and didn't know where we were. We drove down endlessly quaint and rural roads punctuated with small supermarkets and petrol stations. I think I knew where we were going, but refused to recognise the landscape in the same way I'd refused to believe the depressing result of the pencil test. How well an HB can be held under the breast determines the amount of droop… I found I could accommodate an army boot.

Reality, like cow pats, was something I'd always tried to avoid but, looking round, I realised I was metaphorically standing in one the size of a mini-roundabout.

The cab stopped at the gates of a large ersatz stately home. I drew into a lay-by some way off, knowing what would come next. And it did.

A tidal wave of black labradors surged round the cab as David got out. He'd barely paid the fare that could have bought a new dishwasher, when Phyllida appeared like that plump goddess standing on a soap dish. Venus rising from the dogs. Her normally restrained pre-Raphaelite hair was loose, not only round her shoulders, but also now round David's. Her tight English tongue seemed to have disappeared down his throat like an egg-laying alien.

He didn't seem to mind. In fact he appeared intent on eating her face – his right hand kneading her bottom like dough. While the driver took the bags out of the boot, David pushed her back against the gatepost, seemingly with his groin, a part of his anatomy I'd never thought would apply enough pressure to crease linen. He finally pulled away from their kiss, like Dyno-Rod withdrawing from a recalcitrant drain. He and Phyllida grabbed his bags and positively skipped into the house.

⌒~≋≈≋⌒

I sat in the car for eleven hours and only moved then because I'd eaten all the chocolate. Even my bladder was in shock.

Watching the house until it was dark, I'd seen nothing but the milkman and a couple of field mice, but when the moon came out, illuminating the already beautiful scene and transforming it into fairyland, David and Phyllida walked out into the garden. They carried glasses of champagne. Both wore silk dressing-gowns.

I knew they must be in love because it was three below zero.

Phyllida's left leg was visible. Long in the thigh and short in the calf. A young oak of a leg.

This was my moment to confront them, but what could I say? My husband obviously preferred women he could climb up.

I unfolded myself from the car and limped over to the gate where I paused for a moment to allow the blood to find my feet. Then I marched determinedly to the front door, ready to reclaim my husband from this dreadful misunderstanding. Ready to forgive. I passed the living room window, not intending to look in. But I did.

It's an odd thing watching your husband make love. Especially on a narrow chaise longue. The whole exercise looked like a precarious Victoria sandwich. The delicate, golden chaise, the creamy white filling of Phyllida's flesh and the brown upper layer of my husband's back and braced legs.

I suppose I'd never realised how rabbity he looked, with his bottom going up and down so fast it was almost a blur. It reminded me of a wildlife film I'd seen on the Discovery channel. He was approaching some sort of climax, because he arched up and was in danger of losing his purchase; luckily Phyllida's rider's thighs clamped him in place. I wondered if she, like her dogs, locked onto the male's member.

His ecstasy revealed her upper body and I saw that though my breasts might accommodate an army boot hers could easily conceal a small battalion.

Exhausted, David collapsed on top of her and, like a vast amoeba, she enveloped him in her glistening pseudopodia.

I walked away and was sick by the car. All that chocolate no doubt.

I knew where the fault lay as I drove home. It was in me. Had I been a better wife, less jealous, David wouldn't have felt it necessary to turn to Phyllida for comfort.

But, said the voice of reasonable feminism, *you were right. He was unfaithful.*

Ah, said the doormat, *maybe he wasn't until I was unreasonably suspicious.*

By the time I unlocked the front door, my mind was made up and calm. I took an unopened bottle of brandy upstairs and put it on the bedside table, moving quickly so as not to allow further thought. From the bathroom I brought bottles of aspirin, packets of ibuprofen, a dozen old sleeping pills and a bottle of cough mixture that shouldn't be taken while operating heavy machinery.

I was ready for the ultimate sacrifice. The purest show of love. The final act of a woman for her man. I was about to kill myself so David could be happy. If I loved him truly, so my logic went, I wouldn't want him to suffer. Suicide seemed the right thing. The generous thing. The one thing that would make him love me.

But just to make sure, I'd leave a note.

I prepared the paper, my best, with rose petals faintly pressed into the linen. An envelope lined with pale tissue. Then the pen. Mont Blanc, wide-nibbed, blue-inked:

My Darling David,

I have just seen you with Phyllida and although the sight hurt me deeply I can only imagine the pain I must have caused you to make you turn to her for comfort.

My darling, I forgive you. I hope you can forgive me and accept this gift of freedom I give you. I love you and will always love you. Now I shall watch over you forever. Be happy my love, it's all I've ever wanted.

Your Eleanor

I folded the stiff paper and put it in the envelope. Licked it, stuck it down. Wrote his name on its faintly lined face. The romance of it made me cry. A tear blurred the final 'd'. It was all perfect, utterly perfect.

Wearing my prettiest dress – a rather fussy high-necked affair, possibly Laura Ashley – I put on make-up and arranged myself on the bed. I opened the brandy, poured some into the poppy-painted, Lakeland mail-order glass on the bedside table, then realised I may not be found for several weeks.

The idea of becoming a distended bag of bodily fluids being removed by men in contamination suits didn't fit into my image of a demi-sec Ophelia, so I wrote a note to KT saying I was dead and to come round quick before I started to go off.

It took me twenty minutes to find a first class stamp, but I thought second class might not arrive till after the weekend, by which time I might well be past my best, even with the central heating turned off. Thinking of that, I turned the boiler to zero, threw on an overcoat, and popped round to the post box.

On my return I rearranged myself on the bed, swallowed the pills and drank the brandy while crying maudlin tears, before passing out and passing on.

FIVE

The Bells of Hell go ding-a-ling-a-ling, for you but not for me...

I was dead. I was in hell. The bells rang in the abyss where my head used to be. The Devil was looking at me; his eyes flamed, his tongue flicked out and stung my hand. I didn't want to be dead if this was dead.

I didn't understand. I was a good person, I should be in heaven. I wanted the long white frock and the halo, the harp and the ambrosia. This wasn't fair, it wasn't right, this was the wrong sort of dead. I wanted the warmth of everlasting life, not cold damnation and the gnashing of teeth.

I lashed out at the Devil, slapped his face and knocked the phone off the bedside table. It lay on the floor talking:

'Nellie, you daft cow – are you there? Pick the bloody phone up. It's KT. What's the matter with you? Are you dead?'

I leaned towards the handset and fell off the bed.

'Ow, my elbow. I bashed my elbow. Oh... Oh, my elbow... Oh... heck, that hurts, oh, sugar that hurts...'

The reverberations of pain were still rippling through me when I picked up the phone.

'Oh shut up, you silly mare!' said KT. 'It wouldn't hurt if you was dead would it?'

I always thought he sounded more like a South Wales queen on the phone than face-to-face, but that just wasn't possible. Kevin Talfryn Jones, otherwise known as KT, was as Welsh as it was possible to be without being a geographical feature, and as camp as it was possible to be without being a tent.

'Hallo, Kevin.'

'Oh, don't call me that, it's far too butch. So... I got your letter but I couldn't come straight round cos I'm doing my roots and I don't want to look brassy...'

'Heaven forfend,' I mumbled.

'Anyway, you're not dead so there's no harm done, is there? You're all right, are you?'

I wasn't sure. Everything seemed to be throbbing.

'I don't know. My eyelashes hurt.'

'Hangover, love. You're dehydrated, that's what. Get some water down you, I'll be round later.'

He'd rung off before I could react.

What day was it? If he had my letter I must have been out cold for about 36 hours. I wasn't dead. I was pretty sure about that and, having had a glimpse of it, I was quite relieved. God surely wouldn't welcome a badly dressed suicide.

I vaguely remembered switching off the heating.

I tried to get up, but could only crawl into the bathroom, where I hauled myself up onto the loo. In the mirror my face appeared to need ironing, and I had the imprint of an ear on the inside of my right arm.

As I showered I came to the conclusion that the brandy had knocked me out before I could swallow enough pills to finish me off. David wouldn't have been surprised.

My ineptitude was still depressing me when the doorbell rang. KT had a set of keys but always rang before he used them. He was opening the door as I reached the bottom of the stairs.

'Hallo, love. Feeling better?' He looked at me. 'God, you look like Quasimodo's hump.' Pause. 'Cup of tea then, is it?'

He bustled into the kitchen. I followed him slowly, not because I was reluctant but because my muscles were like kapok.

'Where's your teabags? Oh, here they are. Poof's or lorry driver's?'

I was too slow to reply.

'Come on love, Earl Grey or PG Tips?'

'Oh, just ordinary please. Milk, no sugar.'

KT snorted. 'You'll have two sugars and like it my girl.' He bustled up the tea, bustled me into the living room, sat me down, then, dipping a biscuit in his tea, said, 'Well?'

Only KT could invest that one word with such Biblical enormity.

I took a deep breath and unfolded the sorry tale of Christmas past to him. He nodded in all the right places and grunted encouragingly.

He had a young face, blue eyes, blond hair. His features were regular but not striking. His teeth were small and his mouth cherubic. His body was well proportioned, a dancer's figure, slim and supple. Part by part, KT was no different from the majority of the boys filling the stages of musicals all round the country. Except as a walloper, he was geriatric, but there was something of the faun or satyr about him, ageless and magical. Where others had blood, he had mercury.

'It's not right, you know, Nellie. Killing yourself. You always upset someone, even if it's only the poor bugger that has to put you in the body bag. So? What now?'

The question was lightly put but I felt the weight of it.

'I don't know... I suppose I ought to go back down to Gloucestershire, face it out. But I can't. I'll probably wait a day or two and try the hose from the car exhaust.'

I expected him to say something. He didn't.

'I just can't think of any reason to go on living. David's been everything to me. I couldn't live without him.'

KT didn't look at me when he spoke:

'I didn't think I could live when my Simon died, but there was panto, and three shows a day in a cow skin focuses the mind a treat. All you worry about is if the front end had a curry the night before.'

I wanted to say: that was different, this was worse; but Simon had died a lingering death from variant CJD, finally deranged and doubly incontinent, but KT had loved him enough to stay.

He read my thoughts.

'You can't compare pain, Nell. But I'm telling you, killing yourself isn't the answer.'

'I don't see any alternative. I won't be able to live with him and I can't live without him. I couldn't survive. I don't know how anymore.'

KT stood up, inspecting the hideous and hideously expensive Lladro figurines David's mother had given us. Abruptly he stopped and squatted down in front of me.

'Take that job, girl.'

I looked at him with not a clue what he was talking about.

'That salsa musical. Do it. Even if it's only to wind up David. Show him you've got your own life. You don't need him.'

'But it's not true. I do.'

'Don't be twp girl –'

'What?'

'Twp. Welsh for stupid.'

'I thought Welsh for stupid was English.' I smiled. Couldn't help it. The moment for dying was gone.

'You've only stayed with David to be close to Arthur.' My stardust baby. I smelt his new skin. 'But he's not here, girl, and even when he is, he treats you worse than David does. He couldn't wait to get away from you.'

I looked at the carpet: there was a ball of dusty fluff. Where had that come from? When I spoke I could feel my throat tight and aching. KT was right, my son despised me for my weakness.

'He'll be back in six months.'

David had insisted he was sent to an international school in Seattle. At first reluctant to leave his boarding school, he was now so happily independent he'd made it clear he wanted neither to return nor for his despised mother to visit. David was proud of him.

KT put his hand on my knee.

'You got a choice. Stay a victim or take control of your life.' He paused, trying to gauge my reaction. 'Take the job.'

I had one last try at negativity.

'It'll be too late, they start in two weeks.'

⁘

It was that odd half-life period between Christmas and New Year and there was only a frighteningly efficient harpy working the phones at my agent's office. As usual she barked her greeting, then anticipated everything I wanted to say, irritated at my slowness. She called the casting director while I hung on, watched by KT.

The ex-soap star who'd been cast was suddenly unavailable due to a fracas during which she'd thrown up over a bouncer, accused him of rape and broken his leg with a scaffolding bar. She was likely to get a custodial sentence as it was her fourth offence in six months. The job was mine if I wanted it.

I should have been thrilled, liberated, excited. But I hadn't been on stage for years and all I could see was David on top of Phyllida in the snow-filled moonlight.

ACT ONE

The Wild Duck

SIX

It was a chicken pox of the soul. The itch to phone or confront David drove me mad as the hours crawled past. I paced the house, then just a path from the sofa to the fridge. If an orgasm used up the calories of a boiled sweet, I figured misery was worth at least two chocolate éclairs and a tub of Ben and Jerry's.

Six days before rehearsals, KT came round.

'Bloody hell girl, you didn't have that many chins on Friday.'

I looked in the mirror: there was barely space for my face in it.

'I am not starting rehearsals with you looking like Jabba the Hut.'

It took a moment to sink in.

'What do you mean, *you* are not starting rehearsals?'

He looked...well, smug wasn't sufficient a word for the expression of mischievous satisfaction that spread across his face like melting butter.

'You know Karl? Flossie? The choreographer? Well, he's offered me dance captain.' The Gauleiter of the Twirlies. No worse than diving with sharks, but not an easy job.

'How come? I mean, you're a bit long in the bum for twirling, aren't you?,' I said, as he opened the fridge and started throwing cakes into the bin.

'Cheeky bitch. I'm in the first flush. Anyway, Flossie's choreographing the non-salsa stuff and the salsa specialist doesn't speak English. So I'm coming in. To translate.'

'You don't speak Spanish.'

'God, you're picky.'

He lobbed a full packet of chocolate HobNobs in the bin. I winced. What was I going to dunk in my hot chocolate? I needn't have worried: that followed the biscuits less than a minute later. He beamed and held up a limp lettuce.

'Listen girl, your body's a temple. Pity it's starting to look like the Taj Mahal. Get your coat. We is going shopping.'

It took self-control, a padlock on the fridge and a laxative enema to get me looking like a leading lady in time for the read-through.

49

Corseted in jeans, and more nervous than a woman has a right to be of anything but childbirth, I left the dubious cocoon of David's world...

I knew that the rehearsal room, in a part of London used by police for riot practice, was unlikely to be a glittering mirror-lined palace, but the grim gulag with its door sprayed DARREN IS A PEDO was worse than I'd imagined.

Inside was a crumbling hall reminiscent of where I'd briefly been a Brownie. One session prancing round a toadstool had sent me home complaining of child abuse.

To the right was a suspiciously stained concrete staircase; on the left, the green room, a large kitchen area with foam-lined banquettes at one end. I knew they were foam-lined because their dingy nylon covers had rotted away in places, allowing the filling to protrude like a beer-gut through an inadequate shirt.

The hall was full of stage management making tea, dancers flexing their elastic limbs and musical theatre luvvies screeching. Conversations meant to be overheard.

'Did you hear about the boy in Chitty Chitty Bang Bang? Got his dick stuck in a shower head?'

'No!'

'Yeah... And it was nailed six feet up the wall.'

A woman with a red slash of a mouth and cheese-cutter cheek bones looked up from her mobile.

'Oh, you must be Eleanor –'

'Please – Ellie or Nellie.'

'Oh aye, right. Anyway, I need to measure you.' She paused, looking at my figure like a plumber considering a blocked U-bend. Finally, not trusting herself with any comment, she said, 'Do you need to have gold earrings or can I give you any old crap?'

She was small, Scottish and spoke with a Marlboro Red clamped in one hand and a cardboard bucket of double espresso in the other. She saw me looking at them.

'Well there's no point in taking drugs unless you can feel them working, eh? I tried them low-tar Silk Cut once, gave myself a hernia sookin' on them. Oh, sorry, I'm Morag – the designer, wardrobe supervisor, costume mistress… I tell you, I'll be sticking a broom up me arse and sweeping the floor in a minute.'

The floor could certainly have benefited. You had to be grateful for dust mites – without them the place would have been knee deep in dead skin. As it was, bolls of hair and dust eddied across the floor, occasionally catching on the splintered surface. I was thinking about ringworm when a girl with café-au-lait skin and the hips of a racing snake introduced herself.

'I am Glenda from Cuba.' I tried not to look surprised. Maria, yes; Coromoto, possibly – but Glenda?

'Glenda?'

'Yeah, my mother went to Wales when she was pregnant.'

I didn't get the connection for a moment. 'Oh yes.' The light dawned on me. 'Owen Glendower.'

She looked casually contemptuous, as only exceptionally beautiful black women can. 'No. It means valley.'

Now I was completely lost. 'You mean Glen?' I hazarded.

'*Si*,' she said pityingly.

'That's Scotland.'

She shrugged. 'Whatever. Oh, and this is God.'

God?

'Dios, my name is Dios.' I didn't ask where his mother had been but there was no question that this was a deity of some sort – six feet tall, perfection in body and face, with the casual assurance of the Latin lover. God and Glenda: proof that with the rest of us the Creator was just practising. He stared deep into my eyes. 'I am going to make you dance salsa like you make love.'

Reluctantly, with a slab of cold pizza after?

Thankfully, at that moment the director came in. When I'd originally met the producer – pretending to David I was volunteering in an Oxfam shop – the director had been a flabby Californian in a headscarf. The Daily Telegraph obituary column would have described him as 'a confirmed bachelor'. David would have had him shot. The producer, foaming with excitement, had done the introductions.

'This is Ricky Ricky, our great director. Greatest director in Los Angeles. He has – how many awards you got Ricky?'

The pudding face dimpled. 'Eight.'

'Oh, for what?' I enquired, unaware that LA was a centre of theatrical excellence.

'Commercials. Yeah, I do…eggs, cola, pretzels. My latest was for running shoes, you may have seen it. It went mega in Europe. England is Europe, isn't it? Look up my website, rickyricky.com.'

Luckily a couple of days later my agent rang to say Ricky had been offered a Pontiac ad and was suddenly unavailable. Heaven forbid the Pontiac should have run him over.

His replacement was British, the staggeringly beautiful director of a raft of plays and musicals, for whom a string of famous actresses had thrown themselves off bridges. He had broken hearts, wedding vows and hymens all over the country and, seeing him up close for the first time, I could see why.

Past his fabled best now, he looked like a fine building in need of some refurbishment. He was tall and slim, almost Asian in build, with the most extraordinary face. The perfection of its proportions, the angle of cheek bone to chin, the size and shape of the dark eyes, the delicacy of the flawless profile – were simply breathtaking. It was difficult to look at him without staring. Time had left its grubby fingerprints under his eyes and in the lines from nose to mouth, but they only made him more attractive. As did his soft, curved mouth, drawn carefully over butterfly teeth, which caused him to pout slightly unless he was smiling, which he was now.

At me.

Into me.

'Eleanor, I'm Dan, Dan Cawdron. I'm so glad you're doing the show. I've always wanted to work with you.'

Ah, the smell of bullshit in the morning.

KT came up behind me. 'That's a well-trodden path girl. Don't you go blackberrying down it.'

I tried looking stern and superior. That Nellie was long gone, replaced by Nellie the wife and mother. KT tutted.

'I know your fanny better than you do, and right now it's twitching like a dog's back leg.'

The memory of bonking Richard III in my dressing-room came back. The company manager walked in. We chatted. He went. Then I saw the used condom on the dressing table between my false eyelashes. But that had been when I could still pull more than the curtains in David's living room. Those days were gone.

The director's slow smile made me wish for one last chance.

My fantasy was shattered by the door being thrown open by the producer and his wife, the writer. He nodded and gave a newsreel wave; she followed like a geisha as he strode across the middle of the hall, greeting the world.

'Hi, everybody. Hi. Are we late? Pardon me. We didn't mean to be late.'

To call them plain would be unfair. These two had fallen out of the ugly tree and hit every branch on the way down. But they were in no way similar. Where he was extraordinary, she was dull. Built with the flexibility and angularity of an ironing board, she was in her uniform, as I came to know it, of polo neck tucked into belted chinos with catalogue plimsols on her entirely flat feet. Her neck was disproportionately long, her jaw Hapsburgian and her eyes, of an indeterminate slurry colour, were hidden by vast glasses that covered a great deal, but not enough, of her face. Her hair, the same colour as her eyes, was clean. That was all you could say about it. She loped behind her husband with an apologetic droop.

He, on the other hand, was more than the sum of his physical ugliness. He was squat, wearing a square tweed jacket, anti-fit jeans on anti-fit legs and a baseball cap on what was obviously a bald head of around seventy years of age. His right hand, a short square appendage used for emphatic stabbing movements, held a ridiculously large, unlit cigar, the end of which was wet with saliva and fraying onto the floor around his feet.

But it was the face that fascinated. His wide, thin-lipped mouth opened in a tongue-filled slit, revealing no teeth up or down. The effect, added to his round, brown reptilian eyes, yellow skin and seemingly boneless face, was that of a frog – with no hope of transformation.

KT whispered: 'That's what happens when you let ugly people make love.'

Dan stood up to make the customary speech of welcome and intent, but before he could speak the producer approached and grabbed his shoulder, holding Dan at arm's length.

'Daniel, Dan, may I have some input here?' He didn't wait for the answer but went on in an American accent that could have scoured a sink. 'I think most of you here will have heard of me. I'm Izzy Duck.'

He paused for applause which didn't come.

'And I've decided to put my forty years experience as a Broadway Producer behind this great script.'

He had an upward inflection at the end of each sentence which, along with talking as fast as a football rattle and waving a foot-long, unlit cigar around, discouraged interruption. There were looks of frank disbelief on almost every face.

'And I'm proud to say, this great show was written by my wife, Viola. Say, Viola, stand up.' He started clapping, sticking the cigar in his mouth.

'He looks like a rottweiler having a shit,' said KT, loud enough to be heard by the actor sitting next to him, who was just raising a mug to his lips. The coffee in his mouth shot out of his nose, to KT's obvious delight. Izzy continued, oblivious.

'Not only do we have the finest musical written since Oklahoma!, with a score to rival West Side Story by the great Ildefonso Campi…' A tall, Antonio Banderas type, sitting at the director's table, took a little bow while Izzy restoked his lungs. '…But also we have the greatest salsa players here in the shape of Jimmy Fuentes and Samson Quarenton.' The musicians smiled, almost as if they knew where they were. 'Now I wanna tell you Brits about the clave beat. The beat of salsa. Jimmy?'

The percussionist started to tap drums in front of him.

'These are the cajones,' declared Izzy. 'That means boxes.'

'Cojones,' said KT. 'That means balls.'

'Say what?,' barked Izzy at the innocent looking KT.

The beat Jimmy set up was odd, all off-beats. Izzy Duck, a senile uncle at a bar mitzvah, raised his hands above his head, clicking his fingers.

'Hear it?,' he shouted over the drums. 'Five beats. Just like your iambic pentameter in Shakespeare.' He shuffled in rhythmic ecstasy. Eyes were averted, but this was a man impervious to embarrassment. 'My wife Viola loves Shakespeare. She's named after one of the characters.'

'Caliban,' whispered KT. I snorted.

'Bless you,' continued Izzy, without taking breath. 'She read his plays when she was a child, and this piece is Shakespearean in its breadth and brilliance.'

We waited for the under-cutting irony. There was none. The ego had landed in the Elephant and Castle. Izzy was on a roll.

'I believe we have a genius here in our director, Dan Cawdron. I've been to his theatre in Edgware.' He paused for effect. Those that knew where Edgware was looked impressed; most looked like stunned fish. 'And can I say this?' His question was, as we would come to learn all his questions were, rhetorical. 'Dan Cawdron is the greatest story-teller in theatre today. He also won an Olivier Award for his own great musical Pope Paul and the Mou Mou.'

'Pol Pot and the Mau Mau,' said Dan.

'And you know, Dan?' He turned to him like the US President to the leader of an insignificant third-world country. 'You know how we're going to have a West End hit?'

Dan took a breath. Izzy went on, jealous of the oxygen.

'I tell you how we're going to have a West End hit, pal. You gotta get in touch with your inner perfection.'

The rest of his interminable and incomprehensible welcoming speech was lost after this. The suspicion that we were in the hands of a lunatic was forming in some minds. The minds that remained empty were those too blank or personally ambitious to contemplate independent thought.

When Izzy Duck finally sat down, he received loud applause. Like performing seals, actors clap anyone who feeds them. Dan stood up to do his speech before we lost the will to live. And I settled back to observe Viola Duck.

Her plain face was suffused with adoration as she watched Dan standing before his company, clad as always all in black, hands spread in general benediction. Briefly he turned his all-inclusive smile on her. She ducked her long pale face into her script, placing her nose almost on the page as she peered over her glasses. She must be almost blind, I thought. Shame. Bless her... Mind you, to sleep with Izzy Duck you'd have to be blind. I looked round at the company to take my mind from wickedness.

Next to KT sat Lee, the coffee drinker, a genetically modified truck driver in a too-tight T-shirt over a soft chest punctuated with nipples of abnormal prominence. No amount of exfoliation or depilation could feminise the basic package, which he'd tweezed, plucked, squeezed and perfumed. The hormones within remained resolutely masculine, to his obvious disgust. His long nails caressed his slight paunch and his lips pursed in impatience. He burned to perform, and I could see from the sweep his long-lashed eyes made of the room, he didn't see any competition, though he'd smothered me in compliments, and his own humility.

Beside him the soubrette, neither leading lady nor juvenile, was being vivacious. Plump, over-dressed and defensively made-up, her mouth, in repose, was as tight as a cat's sphincter. Tight with disappointment and the proximity of elusive stardom.

In a room full of novices and old-timers who'd traded ambition for regular work, these were the most obvious West End Wendies: performers who bandied the word 'unprofessional' as if it was syphilis, but never applied their extreme intolerance to themselves. David would have dismissed them with a wordless sneer.

His entrance into my mind excluded all other thought for a moment: our first kiss, roses on Valentine's Day…memories, now contaminated, of lust and duty.

Around me scripts were being opened. Jimmy and Samson played, at Izzy's insistence, a salsa riff which was jarringly alien to my ears, clamped so long by David to Radio 3.

All roads led to David.

We clap. Jimmy shrugs and reconnects to his iPod. Izzy announces his masterwork.

'Ladies and Gentlemen, I give you the World's Greatest Salsa Musical… The Merchant…of Venezuela!'

It didn't take long to realise it wasn't just the title that was a turkey.

I hadn't bothered to read it, thinking I'd never do it, and by the time I said yes, money had become more important than the immortal prose. Now here I was, creating the role of Guadalupe Arias, a fabulously wealthy Venezuelan diamond-dealer. Played in an accent thick enough to grout tiles, I thought I might get away with it.

'No! Please! Noh that sonn! Noh the sonn of the nightingales,' I cried with convincing pain. Not so much a musical Arkardina as an Hispanic Madam Arcati. But the image of a comedic dragonfly emerging from its melodramatic carapace was quickly dismissed as I stumbled through speeches Bletchley Park would have been hard pushed to decipher. I looked round the room to see if anyone else was as baffled as I was.

Now, it's not often the producer is reduced to tears by more than the weekly returns, but Izzy was sobbing into what seemed to be a duvet cover. Viola's tale of latino greed and tragedy had moved him to a tsunami of tears.

The coffee drinker and the soubrette, encouraged by his sobs, sang their numbers with more passion than accuracy, and the read-through finished with another speech from Izzy, this time to tell us we were the greatest hand-picked cast ever assembled for a masterpiece. We applauded again and broke for lunch.

'Oh, Eleanor.' It was the soubrette. 'I'm Susan. I saw you in that show at the Wyndhams. Wow! I just thought…um…well, I've got some fab salsa CDs, all the best singers, and a couple of DVDs as well. Would you like to borrow them? I mean it's such a different discipline, isn't it?'

'Well, yes, thank you Susan. That'd be great. Very kind.'

'Kind my arse,' said KT as she waddled off, satisfied. 'Anything to get in with you.'

'Don't be nasty, KT. She's just trying to be friendly.'

KT sighed largely and, lighting a Superking, changed the subject. 'Well, the script's a load of bollocks, isn't it? But Dan's made many a Prada handbag out of worse sow's ears…'

'Oh, it's not that bad.' This was my only family now, so I was determined to err on the side of the angels. 'Just needs a bit of work on the structure.'

'So does Brighton Pier.'

KT and I stood outside the back door of the rehearsal room, admiring the landscape. A thin strip of garden ran the width of the building. An old enamelled bath contained a vast cockroach. Actually it was probably only a beetle, but anything with more than two legs is either a roach or a chorus line.

'Hi. May I join you?' Izzy's tone, only moments ago that of power-mad American general, was now that of an oft-rejected child. I felt sorry for him. Perhaps the bluster was just that; underneath he was as unsure as the rest of us.

'Of course.' We made room on the edge of the bath.

The cockroach made a dash for the plug hole. He'd summed Izzy up quicker than we had. Izzy didn't perch beside us but paced up and down. KT and I prepared for small talk, but where three were gathered together, Izzy saw an audience.

'Say, Eleanor, I'm going to show you the image. The poster, flyers, ads, the whole works. Your agent wanted billing; I said no, no.' He clamped the cigar between his unseen teeth while he reached into his bag. 'Above the title, I want for her. You know we coulda had Judi Dench, Meryl Streep. But they can't do what you can. You're better. And younger.' Not to mention cheaper and more desperate. 'See? Whaddyathink?'

He held up a poster – of a salsa dancer and a palm tree – which could politely be described as *naif*. The palm tree appeared to be growing out of the dancer's head. I arranged my face into admiration. KT didn't bother:

'Bloody hell! Who designed that? Withenshawe Comprehensive?'

Izzy looked astonished. 'You don't like it?'

'You're never going into the West End with that, are you? It's naff beyond belief.'

I held my breath. Izzy had already sacked eight directors, four stage managers, five general managers and a bloke from Rank Xerox who he thought was in the chorus – one twirly more or less wouldn't matter.

'Viola, Viola, come here.' His wife came over, looking like a defeated question mark.

'Yes, Izzy.' She leaned on the 'i', filtering it through a diphthong.

'Viola, honey, KT here doesn't like the poster.'

Her eyes widened in tearful fear behind her glasses. 'Oh, really? Oh, well. I didn't know what to do, we couldn't find an image. I mean, if you have an idea, sure, let's use it.'

KT appreciated being asked. These people were putting their own money into this project, they should be protected. They looked at him helplessly.

'Well, I'll tell you what, why not go to De Kuyper's? They do all the big West End shows. They're the best in the business.'

Viola, despite her stiffness of body, squirmed. Her voice rose in pitch and whine. 'We did. We went to them and they did nothing – they just wanted our money.'

KT and I looked stunned. Almost every iconic show image was theirs, but Izzy simply battered us with reasons why he knew better.

'I been a part of Broadway for thirty years, I know class and they ain't class. They may do stuff here, Lloyd Webber maybe, but he's had his day. Did we have to find our leading lady in a call centre?'

I was beginning to understand how the Indians must have felt under the Raj. KT smiled his most disarming smile and said, in his broadest Swansea accent: 'You is as mad as a bag of ferrets, aren't you?'

I saw anger settle on Izzy's face. For a moment I thought KT would be picking up his P45. Then Izzy opened his frog mouth and honked. It was as close to laughter as he could get.

'Mad as a bag of ferrets? I like that. It's funny. You're a funny man, you know that?' He poked KT in the chest to show how serious he was. 'And you know what? I know funny.'

Izzy was still repeating 'ferrets' when Ruby, the stage manager, who favoured a single red earring and lycra cycling shorts, called Viola and Izzy in for a production meeting. Viola followed Izzy, twittering, 'Why ferrets? Are ferrets funny?'

'Poor dab. She's so dim she couldn't light up a fridge,' said KT, with affectionate contempt. 'I'm going over the greasy spoon. Coming?'

Aware of the dimpled fat still wobbling beneath my baggy rehearsal clothes, I declined. Once alone, I regretted my decision, as my thoughts were immediately colonised by David.

I'd seen a couple of telephone boxes outside. I could phone Phyllida's – maybe he'd answer, I might hear his voice. I'd already worked out that if rehearsals were scheduled in the usual way I'd have at least a day off during the week, as my character disappeared for a chunk of the show. I could drive down there and…

I stopped myself going over again the well-thumbed snapshots of the confrontation, anger and forgiveness that would be followed by David and I living happily ever after in deeper understanding and more profound love. If wishes were horses, beggars would be riders. Who'd said that? An actor whose life was lost in a brandy bottle.

Forcing myself to walk past the phone boxes I headed for Tesco. Organic grapes and a copy of the Daily Mail. Back. Past the telephone boxes.

In the rehearsal room there were comments about my choice of reading matter. I was shocked, I hadn't even considered the Independent or Guardian. David didn't approve of them.

Clutching my lunch, I sat outside with the cockroach, enjoying the pale sunshine and watching the early flies which swarmed over the creeper-covered arch by the door. Hanging from it was a wooden plank on which was painted THE LAST CHANCE SALOON. Did I see the same sympathy in the cockroach as I'd seen in the old spaniel?

Just as I was beginning to think chocolate would assuage my longing for David and the comfort of my living room, Dan came out, rolling a cigarette from a small, black, leather pouch. His hands moved with lazy dexterity.

'Mind if I join you?' He had a slight accent. Yorkshire maybe. I'd once had a dalliance with a Yorkshireman who thought erogenous zones were in Lancashire, hence his reluctance to go anywhere near them.

'Yes, please, sit down.' I indicated a paint-spattered chair. 'How was the production meeting?'

He smiled conspiratorially. 'Well, Izzy's got some interesting ideas.'
'Like?'

'Well…' He lit his roll-up. 'He wants you to look like Maria Montana.'

It took me a moment to take this in. Maria Montana was six feet tall, built like Marble Arch – and black. She also had the taste in costumes of a colour-blind interior decorator, and had spent a lifetime making vulgarity an art form.

'But, I'm, well…' I knew I was whimpering, but couldn't control myself. I wanted to look soignée, sophisticated and, above all, slim. 'I'm five-foot-five with no neck and a short waist. And most of all…I'm white.' That threw him. 'I mean, I can't wear anything too, well… I'll look like a failed transvestite.'

Dan was enjoying himself. 'Izzy and Viola also want you in shoulder pads, a false bust and padded hips for the final scene where you kick over the traces and appear like a new person.'

'Who? Widow Twankey? Do they expect me to black up as well?' Morag overheard this as she joined us, scrabbling for a Marlboro.

'God, that man's a nutter.' We didn't have to ask who. 'It's the sales and he'll no give us any money to buy costumes. He expects me to pay with my credit card and he'll pay me back. He's got two chances of that: nain and fuck-all.'

We considered this, not knowing what to say, except, 'That's outrageous.'

'He says that's the way they do it on Broadway.' She paused. 'Away and shite. Does he think I've just come up the Thames on a banana-boat?'

Dan turned his *'lie down and let me lick this tin of condensed milk off you'* look on me.

'Eleanor, you're the leading lady. We need your help.'

'But Dan, I –'

Any excuse not to get involved. But as I spoke, I remembered how infuriated I'd always been at actors who moaned and whinged but never stood up for anything for fear of…what? Getting a reputation as difficult? Not being employed again? I knew what was right and I had to do it.

I knew that the moment I saw Dan lick his bottom lip. I wondered how he felt about Marmite as I followed him into the Duck's lair.

Izzy was pacing back and forth, barking into his mobile phone: one, I later found out, of three. Dan signalled to him that we'd wait. We went into the stiflingly hot, smaller rehearsal room, where Jimmy's drums were now set up next to an upright piano, at which sat, next to Sampson, a long-limbed woman in her forties, dressed incongruously in hip-anchored jeans and a cut-off top over unfettered but plainly much used breasts.

Her short, curly hair was an indeterminate auburn rinse and her face a collection of good features made imperfect but more interesting by British dental work and sun-damaged skin. She stood up and greeted me with outstretched hand, a fine freckled brown hand. The overall impression was of striking attractiveness and open good nature.

'I'm Karen Tyler, the musical supervisor. Hallo.'

With her wide open smile and patently old-fashioned manners, I almost expected her to say, 'Golly gosh, isn't this ripping?'

'Are we in the way, Dan? Only Sampson's trying to teach me to play salsa.' She laughed. 'Absolutely impossible I'm afraid. I'm making an absolute horlicks of it.'

The composer, Ildefonso, who was sitting in the corner, came to her defence. 'No Karen, you're wonderful. So talented. I can't imagine to do the show without you.'

She turned scarlet at his soft voice and softer eyes. It was definitely a golly gosh moment.

'Um… They don't use the gerund in Spanish as much as we do,' she murmured, as her cheeks warmed the room.

Izzy broke the mood.

'Hi, guys. You want to see me? I was just doing publicity. You know we're going to have the BBC here in a coupla days. That okay with you, Dan?' He didn't wait for the reply. 'You know the BBC doesn't do this, we're going to have five minutes, prime-time. It's because we're a great show. They know that and they want to be the first to get it.'

Who was going to tell him the London local news always covered West End openings? Or that the trick was to get them to come just before first night in the West End, not week two of rehearsals in the Abu Ghraib of South London?

I tried to approach the subject subtly.

'Oh, I'm surprised. They usually come closer to opening. Mike must have a lot of publicity lined up if telly are coming in so soon.'

Izzy waved his wet cigar. 'Mike Kominovsky's gone. I didn't like his style. He just wanted my money, but he didn't wanna do anything for it.'

And there was me thinking Mike hadn't been at the read-through because he was grooming the Dalai Lama for I'm a Celebrity, Get Me Out of Here! Izzy had sacked a PR genius and replaced him with the spotty adolescent who'd been up and down with his mobile so often

KT named him the Bouncing Bogbrush. In the next few sentences, Izzy revealed his recipe for long life, the way to make a million dollars overnight and the size of his swimming pool. I realised why Morag looked so stressed: everyone was working against the clock and Izzy was behaving as if Einstein's theory of relativity was the rehearsal schedule.

I took a deep breath.

'Um, Izzy. I'm just a tiny bit worried.'

Izzy was all attention. 'Eleanor, you're my star. I don't want you worried.'

'Well,' I went on with just a hint of Bette Davis. 'Morag's found some fabulous dresses for me and they're half-price in the sales but –'

'– you being as tight as a duck's arse we cannae get them.'

Luckily Izzy didn't understand Morag's accent. She went on in something closer to what Izzy recognised as English.

'Aye, and we've to get 43 pairs of shoes sent over from Italy. There are 68 costumes in all, as well as the shirts for the band and all the understudies' costumes.'

'And apparently, Izzy,' I fluttered, 'there's no money.'

Izzy was relishing being the centre of attention, of our pleading.

'Sure, there's money, Eleanor, I'll have my accountants let Morag have – how much you need?'

Morag didn't miss a beat. 'Five thousand for now.'

Izzy rounded on her as if she was a shoplifter.

'I give you the money, okay. But I want receipts for every last thing. When we did this show before, in Costa Rica, I gave money, you know? I didn't get a thing for it. I want receipts and results. On my Broadway show the costume budget was two million, you know that? I want Eleanor to look that good. You understand?'

Morag was just starting to tell him it was five grand, not five loaves and a couple of haddock, when Viola slid into the room. Her martyred voice was barely audible, translating what Izzy had just said.

'We've had such bad experiences, Morag. We don't know who to trust. We had a director, before Dan, he'd done Shakespeare but we sacked him and now he's threatening to sue us. He says he wrote the script!'

I thought it unlikely anyone from the RAC, let alone the RSC, would want The Merchant of Venezuela! on their CV, but I resisted saying so.

'It's so upsetting.' Her eyes may have filled with tears, but it was difficult to see through her all-covering glasses. I reassured her about Dan, even though I didn't know whether he'd done time for rape, murder or embezzlement. Suddenly I was her friend.

'Oh, Eleanor.' She had a way of making everything sound as if she was speaking through a migraine. 'You know we've mortgaged our house for this. But, you know, in Costa Rica everything's so corrupt. We wouldn't pay off the surveyor so he valued it at half what it's worth.'

I looked shocked and I wasn't acting. 'What did you do?'

'We had to go to the banks.'

Alarm bells deafened me. Had these people any idea how much it cost to finance a West End musical? I'd seen vanity projects before where the producer developed palsy in his cheque-writing hand as his savings ran out. As soon as I could, I found Dan and told him what had been said. Again, the warm reassuring smile.

'She saves the bread rolls from the hotel breakfast for lunch, too. But you know she's a millionaire Texan oil-heiress, don't you?'

'No, I didn't. So why doesn't she have plastic surgery?'

'Where would they start?'

'True. Are you saying the money's secure then?'

'Absolutely. No problem. The bond is lodged for Plymouth and they've got plenty of time to put the West End bond in place. Don't worry.'

So why did they have to go to the banks? The question nagged at me. The bond would cover our wages for two weeks if the show folded. But looking, or rather falling, into Dan's eyes, I had faith it wouldn't.

'Eleanor, this is their dream and I think we can make dreams come true.' As one whose dreams usually turned into nightmares, I looked doubtful. 'They're a funny couple but, well, I feel sorry for them. Let's show them not everyone is out to shaft them. I'm sure they'll lose the paranoia if we involve them in the creative process.'

Swimming in those Aegean blue eyes, I could believe anything.

EIGHT

A week later my head was wrapped in cling film while the wig-maker traced my hairline with a Mr Men felt-tip pen. I looked like something out of Alien Nation.

Contrary to Izzy's wishes, we'd decided to make me look like Elizabeth Taylor. To bring that off, I'd have to be lit through a gauze the consistency of vinyl cushion floor, but we were optimistic the black wig and clever make-up would transform me into the Glamour Queen of Salsa, and not a ringer for Lennox Lewis, which seemed to be the Ducks' idea of impossible chic.

I looked at my reflection, and the confidence that had been building ebbed away, leaving me beached on the shingle of my own inadequacy. What was I doing? No one was going to mistake me for Jennifer Lopez's sister. I looked more like Trinni Lopez's mother.

Smiling, I thanked the wig lady. She was whippet-thin and beautifully made-up. Perhaps she'd like to play the part? I trailed back to the rehearsal room with my confidence so low I almost called David, but as I reached for the mobile it rang.

'Hallo?'

'Eleanor, where have you been I've been trying to contact you for days.'

'Phyllida?' I stopped dead in the middle of a zebra crossing.

'Oi, you stupid tart, put it in forward or reverse!'

I waved my apology to the irate taxi driver and ran to the kerb. 'Is that you, Phyllida?'

'Of course it is. Now Eleanor, are you listening?'

'Er…yes.' Was this it? The admission? The *'Eleanor, David's asked me to tell you…'*

'Good. David's e-mailed me.'

'He's what?'

'E-mail, Eleanor.' She sighed. 'He said you didn't do technology. He wants you –' She was in a hurry. Maybe her conscience was pricking. I interrupted her.

'Why didn't he phone me?'

There was the briefest pause. 'No phones. He found an internet café.'

'In the Amazon?'

'Oh Eleanor, really. Anyway, he wants you to put anti-freeze in the Mercedes – London's due for snow. You'll do that, won't you? Oh, there's someone at the door, I must go. Bye. Don't forget, will you?'

'But Phyllida –'

Too late. I stood staring into nothing. Anti-freeze? Maybe I should drink it.

'Give us a smile, beautiful, it may never happen.'

Beautiful? From a Big Issue seller. Ah, the kindness of strangers.

———

Dan was justifying his reputation as an Olympic-standard turd polisher when I slipped into the rehearsal room. He was crocheting Mrs Duck's ramblings into something, if not Shakespearean, then certainly entertaining. The plot was still ludicrous, the characters ridiculous and the dialogue as buoyant as a lead parachute, but under Viola's adoring gaze it was improving.

'Ah, Eleanor, we've missed you.' He caressed my arm, at once protective and possessive. Was that the moment I fell in love with him?

Susan the Soubrette saw the gesture and looked as if she'd swallowed a wasp. Dan's appreciation and her jealousy would be a poultice on the boil of my abandonment. And, for medicine, the rivers of alcohol consumed during company 'bonding' sessions after rehearsals were better than the waters of Lethe.

'That's near Edinburgh, isn't it?,' said KT. 'Down by the docks?'

'Lee-*thee*. What you drink to forget.'

'You don't want to be doing no forgetting till you're ready to do forgiving. Anti-freeze? You want to get some curry powder.' He looked at me over a pint of Bloody Mary. 'If you forgive that husband of yours this side of Alzheimer's, I will slap you so hard.'

We were in the pub where Izzy preached interminable homilies to anyone who'd listen: increasingly few, as people dived into lavatories or out of windows to avoid him. In rehearsal he'd pace up and down barking into his mobile, commanding the world with his unlit cigar until we closed the door on him as if he was an incontinent puppy. At tea-break, though, he'd be on us, demanding attention.

For the first three days he'd come into the room, as he thought, unobtrusively. A piranha in a goldfish bowl would have had more chance of going unnoticed. Even his silence was loud, but not as loud as his 'Dan, Dan, may I have some input here?'

Unable to interrupt Izzy's monologue about the dark side of human nature being released by the show, so relieving the audience of their baser instincts, we listened politely. Dan mentioned that it was a musical comedy, and undiluted rape and pillage were unlikely to raise anyone's spirits, let alone a laugh.

'They said the same about Showboat,' Izzy cried triumphantly. 'Inter-racial relationships. Black people and white people. That's miscegenation!' He paused, doubtful. 'Say... You have that here in England?'

The next day he came in with three complete strangers and forced an impromptu concert for this triumvirate, who turned out to be Turkish Cypriot waiters and not, as Izzy thought, delegates from the Costa Rican embassy. But the last straw was when Izzy had half the cast in a recording studio making a hip-hop version of Lee's number to sell the show to gay clubs. Lee, the coffee drinker next to KT at the read-through, was in heaven. By the time he got back to the gulag, he'd fantasised a platinum album and a solo on the Royal Variety Show. Unfortunately, Dan knew nothing about it.

In the pub at the end of the first week, Dan was drawing on a roll-up and sipping his lager and lime, into which someone had stuck a plastic chrysanthemum.

'Izzy's just a child with a toy-box. Problem is, we're the toys.'

'The problem is,' said Morag acidly, 'that wee shite's the producer.'

Dan was about to reply when Glenda and God came in. Every head turned. They moved with the grace of big cats, so perfectly made they looked like another species. Glenda immediately draped herself over Flossie, the non-salsa choreographer, while God got the drinks in.

'So, Dan,' I said, 'what do you think we should do?'

He didn't reply. He couldn't. He was looking at Glenda like a five year-old at Hamley's Christmas window. Megan pursed her lips.

'Och, for Christ's sake, get him a drip tray. Oh, sorry, God,' she said, as he handed her a large vodka tonic.

Dan's look of unrequited longing didn't fade. 'You know,' he said, 'If a show goes tits-up, it's customary to nick anything that isn't nailed down.'

'Yes,' we chorused.

'Well, I'm having Glenda.'

Hearing her name, she languorously turned towards him.

'Hi Dan. Okay?'

Under her great doe-like gaze, Dan, always so articulate, gibbered, grabbed his drink and almost put his eye out on the chrysanthemum. Glenda pouted.

'He doesn't like me,' she said quietly to me.

'On the contrary,' I replied. 'You're so beautiful he doesn't know what to say.'

She looked across at him, a mischievous smile curving her perfect, full lips. 'Oh yeah...iss natural.' And he was dismissed with fond satisfaction.

I consoled myself with the thought that she had no conversation and she'd bore Dan rigid, as she was nothing more than a beautiful but empty skin. Who was I kidding? The only part of him that would be rigid in her company wouldn't be discussing Proust's cake recipes.

Dan, who was charmingly unaware of his own physical perfection, had no difficulty talking to Viola, and overwhelmed her in the same way Glenda overwhelmed him.

'I shouldn't worry,' KT whispered to me. 'He won't shag that, not even to get the show on.'

'He's shagged worse for less,' I hissed back.

'Ooh, saucer of milk for you, my gell.'

Izzy was nowhere to be seen. Perhaps Viola had persuaded him to leave us alone – or perhaps he'd been raped, murdered and dumped in a ditch. Either way we were happy. She listened in a trance of adoration while Dan explained his plans for restructuring her script, which still looked like the Bridge on the River Kwai before Alec Guinness took over.

Back in rehearsal after the wig-fitting, Lee was in full flow:

'Dan, darling, I just think I need a number, I mean I know we've got the duet, but it doesn't establish my character. A solo would do that. The audience just won't know who I am.'

Dan was more dismissive with this irrepressible self-promoter than I'd so far seen him. 'Lee, if you're wearing a gold sequined catsuit, no one will be in any doubt about not only who you are but what you are.'

Everyone laughed, including Lee, but I saw a sliver of malevolence cross his face. I could understand Dan's terseness; Lee's contributions were invariably laced with a desire to turn the production into a Shirley Bassey floor show, with himself as Shirley Bassey.

'Dan, I've been in musical theatre for fifteen years.' Twenty actually, but that would have given away his age. 'And I can tell you, we need something spectacular here, where the first act sags. Doesn't it, Eleanor?'

Lee was looking to me for support. My years with David had taught me to be placatory. I realised married meekness had reduced me to defensive passivity. Perhaps this new self-awareness would make me a better actor, but in musicals introspection was as rare as a Trappist auctioneer – and about as useful. I called on the extrovert in me to confront Lee's insatiable quest for lebensraum, but David's wife mumbled:

'Sorry, I don't know, I was having a wig-fitting. But I'm sure we'll do whatever's best for the show.'

The other me kicked her.

The bruise was still aching when I joined the dance call, where I looked like a member of the Douglas Bader Formation Troupe. God finally lost patience with me as KT, holding my hand, went over the steps that a theatrically dyslexic snail could have mastered in ten minutes.

'Eleanor! *No puedo trabajar contigo!*'

'What did he say?,' I asked, my face setting into a truculent scowl.

'He say he can't work with you,' said Glenda helpfully.

'Well, tell God,' I snapped, 'that he is definitely mistaking me for someone who gives a fuck.'

I was sorry God had to be the first to meet the old me, but I was glad to have her back.

<hr />

Back at home, Mrs Doormat twittered with worry:

I shouldn't have snapped.
I shouldn't have walked out.

What will people think?

And: *Bugger, I've run out of wine.*

I opened the bottle of champagne David had brought back from Odessa. More likely Oddbins, I now realised. Luckily KT called round before I'd finished the first glass.

'I thought you'd be on the business end of a bottle. Do you have any idea how many calories are in that?'

I was defiant. 'Not as many as in these chips.'

KT was delighted; he threw himself on the sofa and turned on the television. 'Oh, tidy. Champagne and chips, my favourite. Don't you dare pour me a drink, my gell.'

Two bottles and two thousand calories later, we'd blamed my hissy fit on PMT, God, and my complete inability to prance about like the brief Brownie I'd been when skipping round that bloody toadstool.

'Scarred me for life that Brown Owl did. Mind you, the only ballet class I went to was worse: "You're all bumble bees flying in a summer garden." I flew straight into a plate glass window and broke my nose.'

'What happened?'

'It got a great laugh.'

KT was soon reassuring me and leading me drunkenly through the choreography that had been such a problem.

'I don't know why you can't do it, you daft cow. Susan picked it up right away.'

'I'm too intelligent. The instructions have to go through my brain to get to my feet. Anyway, she's ballet trained, or so she keeps telling everyone.'

Susan had no doubt been a nymph in the Dolores Philbrick Dance Academy but now, despite her protestations that she had an hourglass figure, she looked more like a solidly built half-hunter.

'You want to watch 'er, she's a poisonous trollop that one,' said KT, hoovering down a handful of chips dripping with tomato sauce.

I looked disapproving, guilty at my bitchy remark. 'KT, she's fine. She was with you in Grease, wasn't she?'

'Fame. The Middle East tour. She got pregnant by a British Airways air fairy, flew home for an abortion and was bumped up to first class. Has she done the *'I'm in therapy because I used to mistake sex for affection – it's because my dad was a Chippendale'* or some such bollocks?'

'Oh come on, KT, she's all right. She lent me some DVDs. I thought that was really sweet.'

'Give me strength.' He shook his head. 'She's after making herself indispensable to you, you know. The *'I'm the star's best friend'* crap. Reflected glory off you, till she can shaft you. And she's trying to pull Dan, you know.'

Now he had my attention. I was wide-eyed with revulsion and jealousy. The phone rang.

'Bugger. Hallo?'

'Eleanor? Phyllida.'

'Oh, yes, Phyllida. Are you having a nice day? I'm having a lovely day here, on my own.'

'Eleanor, are you drunk?'

'Yes.'

'David said you might go to pieces.'

'Oh yes? When was that?'

'I'm phoning to make sure you've seen to the car.'

'Yes, I've taken its wheels off and propped it up on bricks, smashed the window and stolen the radio –'

'Have you put the anti-freeze in?'

'No – I'm drinking it.' I put the phone down on her and had another glass of Bulbfield Bravery.

I started watching Susan after that, and sure enough, as the days passed, her skirts got shorter and her décolleté deeper. She'd even taken to rolling Dan's cigarettes.

'Oh wow, Dan, I'd so love to be able to smoke but the Voice. I have to guard the Voice.' She stroked a mini-spliff suggestively before putting it between Dan's lips.

It crossed my mind to go into competition with her, but it had been years since I'd felt remotely attractive to anything but the local wildlife, and even they had to be bribed with peanuts and bacon on bits of string.

Before we'd started rehearsals, in an orgy of masochism, I'd looked in the mirror over my shoulder and made excuses for the folds of flesh on my lower ribs. It's only natural, I said to myself. Lots of women have them. But I wasn't lots of women. Soon complete strangers would be paying fifty quid a skull to look at me. Fascinating though its ruin was, my body was unlikely to draw gasps of admiration from anyone but a coach party of pathologists.

Now I rushed home to see the small transformations brought about by the hours of dancing. The breasts had risen sufficiently to accommodate no more than a flip-flop. The bottom, though still as flat as Susan's top Cs, seemed to have inched north. And the under-arms no longer hung like bread dough. To help this transformation I ate only one meal a day – though the intake of full-fat Pinot Grigio made up for lunch and breakfast.

A ray of happiness was penetrating the fog of self-pity. I had a leading role in a new musical and I was looking good. Maybe I should consider an affair; not with Dan obviously, but there must be someone out there who'd give me a fall of soot.

I could hear David's scornful laugh: 'Good God, Nellie, you think fellatio is a character in Les Misérables. It's not enough just to turn up, you're supposed to join in.'

I seemed to remember I'd once been quite good at sex...well, enthusiastic anyway. But as with my cycling proficiency certificate, I hadn't taken it any further. At my age, a lover would expect a bit of finesse.

'How do you give a good blow job?,' I asked KT in a tea break.

'Keep a good tune in your head.'

He proceeded to demonstrate with a banana and Mozart's 40th. I was impressed by his choice.

'It's on my mobile.'

One morning, trying to look nonchalant, I peeled off my jumper to reveal a figure-hugging bit of lycra. The gasps of admiration were more than gratifying. Dan even looked up from his script.

'Eleanor...' He put his hand on my back, the fingertips lightly playing my vertebrae. 'I would not crawl over you to get to Nicole Kidman. You look fabulous.'

Next morning, I was in early and about to put some lip-gloss on when Susan came into the green room.

'Oh Eleanor, after what I went through last night I hardly need a warm-up.' She flopped down with a Starbucks double latte, legs akimbo. 'Dan's doing absolute wonders for my turn-out.'

I felt as if I'd been winded. I tried to tell myself it wasn't because he didn't pick me. I hadn't put myself on offer; why would he? It was just unprofessional – that was it, unprofessional. I caught myself just before I joined the ranks of disappointed middle-aged actresses passed over for newer, younger models.

What made it worse was David. Had he really been chasing chicken-eating spiders in the Amazon basin I wouldn't have given it a second thought. I pictured myself at home during his other trips away. Writing long accounts of the trivia of my life in diaries I never showed him as he never displayed any interest. Relieved to reach three o'clock, so I could turn on the television and watch cosy quizzes until it was time to eat comfort food and enviously watch bad actors in bad soaps.

But my confidence even when sober was growing, though I suspected it would crack with one hard tap from a sharp object. David's tongue, for example.

The anti-freeze remained a symbol of my defiance, until I came home one night to find Phyllida on the doorstep.

'Where have you been, Eleanor? I've been waiting.'

Was I expecting her? I couldn't remember.

'I'm sorry, was I expecting you?,' I asked, opening the door.

'No,' she said, sweeping past me. 'David e-mailed me again about the car, and I knew you hadn't done it.' She went straight to the bowl on the hall table and took out his car keys.

'What are you…?'

I trailed off as she marched out with a large and luminous bottle of anti-freeze. Expertly, she raised the Merc's bonnet and guddled about in its innards.

'Really, Phyllida,' I said, considering letting it drop on her head, 'you should have married David, you're so much better at these things than me.'

She turned and looked up at me. 'No Eleanor, you're the perfect wife for David. He wouldn't want anyone…like me.'

'I suppose not.'

It could be an accident, the shattering of her skull as the bonnet crashed down, severing her spine.

'There. That's done.' The bonnet slammed down on empty air. 'Any message for David if he e-mails again?'

'Just…' I tried to think of something stinging and witty. 'Send him my love.'

NINE

Next morning, I went in to rehearse my songs with Karen and share the knowledge that God didn't wear underpants – and she wasn't there. We'd developed a friendship based on mutual respect, professionalism and a passion for fried-egg sandwiches. I trotted round the building but there was no sign of her.

In the strip of garden, Dan was smoking and working out the rehearsal schedule with Flossie.

'Have you seen Karen?'

Dan looked up. No smile, his eyes as hard as David's topaz cufflinks. He handed me his tobacco pouch. Though I didn't like smoking, Susan had turned making a roll-up into an advert for her manual dexterity. I wanted to show him what my fingers were capable of, even though sharing an ounce of Golden Virginia seemed about as intimate as we were likely to get.

'She's gone home.'

'Oh. Is she ill?'

'No. She hasn't been paid.'

'Oh no, not her as well.' I sat on the edge of the bath. 'Is it just this week?'

'The creative team doesn't get paid by the week, we have three payments and the first one was due on the first day of rehearsal.'

'But that was a month ago.'

'She'd been working for three weeks before that.'

For the first time, Dan showed something other than laid-back good nature. This was Karen's smiling tiger. 'He hates confrontation but he's not afraid of it,' she'd said.

'So she's had nothing for seven weeks?,' I bleated incredulously.

'That's right,' said Flossie. 'She's missed a mortgage payment. Her husband's ill and can't work and she's very slightly desperate. So she slipped away at lunch-time. Didn't think anyone would notice.'

'So what are we going to do?'

They both shook their heads. 'Nothing we can do,' said Flossie. 'It's between her and the management.'

The management was now an inexperienced general manager, an expensive firm of accountants and an even more expensive firm of 'lawyers', as Izzy called the firm of solicitors famously known as The Axis of Evil. From Izzy, through this complex triumvirate, a thin trickle of cash was filtered, and despite rafts of receipts there was always an excuse for the lack of money.

I felt something like a taut elastic band snap inside me. It took me aback. I was angry. I was so unused to the feeling I almost mistook it for indigestion.

'Right, can I call a company meeting, Dan?'

He looked surprised. 'Sure.'

By the time I'd assembled everyone, my small campfire of fury had flared into a fine blaze.

'Um… Er… I'm sorry to call you all together like this, but…' I didn't feel it was a very convincing start. I looked at the expressions on the company faces around me and saw everything from open good-natured trust from two of the girl dancers, to the tight-lipped *so impress me* look that Susan habitually wore. Though, to be fair to her, it could just have been her make-up. Underneath she may have been gazing on me with the adoration of a besotted nun.

'Karen hasn't been paid for seven weeks and she's left the building…' Oh God, did that sound ridiculous? Shades of Elvis? I needn't have worried; only two of the cast were old enough to recognise the phrase and one of them was deaf. '…as she feels unable to continue working without payment.'

There were nods of approval, Lee's the most emphatic of all, which surprised me. Had I judged his all-consuming self-interest too harshly? I'd save the guilt that caused till later.

'And, personally, I don't want to continue rehearsing until she is paid. I'm not asking for a strike, but may I put it to you that we tell Izzy unless her money is in her account by five o'clock today, we won't be in tomorrow. I just feel, if he does this to her he can do it to any of us, and we need to nip this in the bud now.'

I needn't have added the justification. When I asked for a show of hands they were unanimously in favour of supporting Karen.

My head was above the parapet. As I went to telephone the general manager, I knew it would only be a matter of time before someone took a shot at it.

'Hallo, Jonty?'

The general manager answered in his Leslie Phillips 'Well, hello' voice. I was precise and polite; he was surprised and unprepared.

'Well, Eleanor…I don't know what to say. I put the paperwork through. Um…I'd better call Izzy.'

I rang off and found Dan standing beside me, proffering a roll-up.

'Well done,' he said. Approval. I glowed. 'Going to the pub after?'

I needed to do my roots, to brood on betrayal, to practise the dance routines in the bathroom mirror…

'Yes, sure.'

'Good. I've got a production meeting but I'll see you after.'

I felt my face getting hot and beads of sweat on my upper lip. I hoped it was excitement, not the onset of the menopause. It hadn't occurred to me he'd find a shop steward attractive.

My mobile rang. I answered it as Dan turned away.

'Hallo…? Oh, Izzy.'

Dan turned back.

'Hi, pal.' What on earth had given him the impression I was his pal? 'I can't believe what Jonty has done. You know, he's a nice guy, I gave him a big chance with this job, he's young, maybe a little cocksure, but I can't believe he's done this. You know I've been a producer and a businessman for forty years and no one has ever accused me of not paying what I owe.'

'Well, Izzy –'

'See, this is the way it is, pal, this is the bottom line. Karen hasn't signed her contract.'

I knew that wasn't true, she'd borrowed my pen. I told him.

'Are you saying I've got her signed contract? Is that what you're saying?' His blustering rage was intended to see me off, but he didn't know he was speaking to a woman scorned.

'No, no, Izzy, I'm just –'

'If Jonty has it, I don't know. How should I know? I can only do what he tells me. That's what I employ him for.'

His voice was getting louder, distorting in my ear.

'Yes, but Izzy –'

'I can't do things if I don't know what hasn't been done. There's things that haven't been done that I know haven't been done, there are things that haven't been done that should have been done, there are things that haven't been done I don't know haven't been done and this guy, a guy letting me down, not doing what I paid him to do. I had a guy like that in New York, big-shot lawyer. You know what? I just went into his office one day and fired him. Like that. No comeback. That's the way I am.'

Trying to interrupt him was like trying to throw a pebble through the spokes of a moving bicycle.

'Izzy.' I raised my voice over his. Three years at the London Academy had given me the lungs of a sea lion. 'When she turned up for work she was employed by you. The ink on the line is a secondary consideration. She's been working for you for seven weeks and hasn't been paid. And, unless she is, we don't feel able to continue, because she is as much a member of this company as I am.'

He backed down at this display of decibel feminismo, but immediately went into suspicious mode.

'Did she complain to you? Is this her?,' he hissed. 'If she had a problem she shoulda called me. I tried calling her, you know that? And her agent. But they won't take my calls. You know she can't play salsa, she just can't do it, no rhythm, it was Dan wanted her –'

My unwillingness to be bullied or bullshitted into a compromise gave me courage, and in the face of his American Producer act I became more and more British – Edith Evans haggling with a totter.

'Izzy, I'm sure this misunderstanding is absolutely nothing to do with you. And I'm equally sure you'll sort it out before five o'clock this afternoon if you want rehearsals to continue tomorrow morning.'

I rang off, shaking. Why couldn't I face Phyllida like that?

The young union representative was standing beside me. He was ashen under his spiky red hair.

'Eleanor, I phoned Equity, they say they can't back us if we come out on strike.'

'It's not an Equity matter,' I said tersely. 'It's self-preservation.'

The lad subsided, fearful of losing his job but torn by his desire to do the right thing. I put my arm round him, though he was head and shoulders taller than me.

'Don't worry, Izzy's a school-yard bully. It'll be all right.' I was surprised at how convincing I sounded.

Fifty-five minutes later, Karen called Dan to say the money was in her account.

Fifty-five minutes. I didn't feel triumphant, I felt disgusted. Word got round the company and I was a heroine. But, as always, mistrustful of popularity, I ran away, leaving a note for Dan saying I'd be in the Red Lion rather than our usual.

I found a table away from the glowing coal fire because David would have said: 'Eleanor, you shouldn't sit so close.'

Why not? Would I really self-immolate if I drank my wine in its fierce heat? And if I did, wouldn't it be worth it not to spend my whole life cowering in the shadows? Today I was brave. I'd had a small victory in the eyes of my small world.

I moved tables, held my hands out to the flames and felt the delicious heat of the wooden bench through my trousers. I wondered if there was a greater sense of freedom than this. It was such a tiny thing, sitting alone in a pub, defying a husband who would have cared only that his authority was being flouted.

Through the window I watched a thin frightened cat quivering on a roof. Had it been wearing a wedding ring it would have been my reflection. I looked down at the smooth gold band on my finger and, with the help of a little oil from the peanuts I was eating, eased it off. The flesh was indented. Bloodless. Not anymore. I wanted to throw the ring into the fire in a fine Wagnerian gesture, but caution and thrift made me put it in my bag. In the dark. Another little triumph.

By seven o'clock I'd lost the flavour of my success and was sure I'd been stood up. By seven-thirty the fire had faded and so had I. Slowly I left the pub, still hoping he would appear. But this was real life and even though it was probably half-over, I still hadn't got used to it.

Indulging my misery, I went home, changed into a shapeless shift and liberated my one remaining soft toy from the top of the wardrobe where David had banished him.

My script was open, poached eggs ready and chocolate on standby when the phone rang. I was reluctant to answer it, but then the thought it might be David propelled me across the room so fast I dropped the receiver.

'Sorry… I'm sorry about that. Hallo?'

'Eleanor?'

'Yes.'

'It's Dan.'

I panicked, as if he could see me cuddling a pink elephant to my bra-less bosom.

'Oh. Yes.' Very witty.

'Sorry I missed you, the production meeting went on for two and a half hours. Izzy.'

'Ah. Yes. Izzy.'

'Do you fancy a pizza?'

'Well…yes. Where are you?' What if he was on the doorstep? What would I do? I dumped the pink elephant behind the sofa.

'At home. In Russell Street, by the British Museum.'

I started to make excuses, I lived the other end of London.

'I'll send a cab for you.'

I put the phone down and ran to the bathroom. Apologising to pink elephant, I propped him up on the lavatory cistern and jumped into the shower. Life had gone from grey to technicolour. Why would he want me to go to his house at this time of night if he didn't want to…

I raided my knicker drawer for the packet of condoms KT had given me as a joke. David didn't think that sort of thing funny, so I'd hidden them. I prayed they weren't luminous green with tentacles.

Still damp, I threw myself into the taxi and had forty minutes to make up my face by the dim interior light and Braille.

TEN

His building was one of a terrace facing the side of the Museum. The old, wide front door, painted shiny black, bordered by a fence of wrought iron railings, was an imposing entrance to the four floors of flats inside.

More excited than a woman over halfway through three score years and ten had a right to be, I pressed one of the illuminated bells. Number four.

Behind me I heard a voice.

''Scuse me.'

I turned as Dan answered the intercom. 'Hallo? Eleanor?'

'Er, yes. Hold on a sec.'

It was the taxi driver. 'Aren't you her off the telly? With the dog?'

'Look, I'm just –'

'It is you, isn't it? I don't know who you are but my mum never missed you. Sign this for her, will you?'

I put my name of the back of a receipt, smiled and nodded and did all the things expected of a 'celebrity'. I had to be nice. If I told them to bugger off, they'd be on to the News of the World before I'd ordered a four seasons with extra mushrooms.

Smiling and waving to the driver, I pressed the bell again. This time there was just a buzz and click. I pushed the door and went into a bare stone-floored hall. In front of me was a school-style staircase with a plain black, painted metal banister, which rose from the basement flat and disappeared up towards a rose skylight. I climbed to the fourth floor, my shoes echoing off the worn wooden steps. By the top my legs were shaking, and not just with altitude sickness.

Dan was standing at the open door to his flat, jazz playing quietly in the background.

'Hi, come in.'

I kissed him briefly on the cheek and went into the small hall. Theatre posters and cartoons hung on the golden yellow walls. The paper was rag-rolled and glossy, edged by dark blue paintwork.

He led me into the living room, which was also in shades of blue and yellow, dominated by a three-seater sofa, two deep, elderly armchairs and a dining table covered in papers and a lap-top computer. The whole of one wall was shelved, overflowing with all shapes, sizes and ages of book. A small cluttered kitchen led off the living room. I could see his Olivier Award propping open the door.

Table lamps glowed in every corner, and the deep blue floor-length curtains gave the room a seductive atmosphere, enveloping me in sensual sights and sounds, not to mention the scents provided by the expensive candles burning on the hall table.

'There's the menu, would you like to order?'

I sank into one of the chairs while he went into the kitchen. I heard a cork being pulled.

'White all right?'

'Fine, thanks,' I called back. 'So how was the production meeting? I'll have a margherita. Thanks.'

He handed me a large glass of wine and put a bowl of olives on the coffee table between us. While he telephoned the pizza company, I looked more closely at him and the room. This was not the kind of environment I'd envisioned for him; it was softer, more feminine, or perhaps less masculine, than I'd imagined.

He sat down opposite me and raised his glass, pausing in a quick salutation. The soft jazz filled the silence until he relaxed back, legs apart and forearms resting on the chair arms.

'God, Izzy Duck is a piece of work. You know what he came out with tonight? Your character's father is so frightening that the painting of him has to be a blank canvas, as no portrait in the world could be as scary as the man.'

'That's ridiculous. What did you say?'

'Well, Izzy's so vain I suggested it should be a portrait of him.'

'And?'

'He couldn't resist it.'

We laughed, but not as fondly as we had four weeks before.

'That didn't take two and a half hours, did it?'

'No.'

Oh, for God's sake, why were we discussing Izzy? He should be running his fingers through my hair. Damn, I still hadn't done my roots – and what about down below…?

'He went on again about what he wanted you to look like.'

'Oh no, not the drag queen.'

'Yes, but I told him there was no way. You don't buy a racehorse and have it pulling a milk float.'

I was more than flattered.

'And then I reminded him I had to be away for a couple of days –'

'Yes. No problem, we've got Flossie. We'll just be running the show before we go down to Plymouth.'

'Izzy said he's taking over the direction in my absence.'

I almost bit through the rim of my glass. 'You're not serious.'

'''Fraid so. So I said, very politely, I didn't think that would be a good idea. He started shouting. Usual rubbish.' He stopped, his lips pursed tight over his teeth, pulling the skin tighter over his sharp cheek bones. He reached for his tobacco and a small blue ashtray. 'I said if he insisted on treating this production like his own personal train set I didn't think I could continue.'

The familiar cold, as if a window had been opened. Few shows survived the departure of a good director. 'He doesn't know one end of an actor from the other. It'd be like my next-door neighbour saying he'd take over from Luciano Pavarotti.'

'What does your neighbour do?'

'He's a butcher.'

'Good analogy.'

'Please say you didn't walk.'

'No, no.' He batted the idea away. 'I just stuck to my guns and said I couldn't stay on board if he continued to try to override my authority.'

'Has he been?'

'Every day. Every day's been a battle against his interference and inability to comprehend that we have to undercut the big players. They've got vast budgets and high profiles. But I've tried to keep it all from the cast.' He took a deep lungful of smoke and leaned forward, flicking the ashless end of his cigarette repeatedly. 'Tonight he said – no he shouted – that only he has any idea of what it takes to make a West End success, and that I was afraid of success because I'm only the penny-ante director of a second-rate provincial theatre.'

My first instinct was to laugh, it was so absurd, but Dan was deeply hurt. I was surprised, but the attrition of working with Izzy Duck was taking its toll.

'What did Viola say?,' I asked.

'Nothing. She just looked like she wished the earth would open up.'

'She usually looks like that.' She wasn't bright, but she was bright enough to see that what Dan had created was better than anything Izzy had to offer.

'Penny-ante director of a second-rate theatre,' Dan whispered.

I stood up and went over to him, squatting down with my hands on his knees. 'You don't believe that do you?'

I was about to rub my hand reassuringly further up his thigh and then perhaps touch his face with my fingertips – you know the sort of thing – when the doorbell rang.

Bloody pizzas. Carrying them back up the stairs it occurred to me he'd only dragged me half-way across London for a bit of sympathy from a mature woman. Something Susan couldn't provide. Bitch.

'Do you want a plate or eat out of the boxes?,' Dan asked, holding up a sharp knife and a fat kitchen roll.

'Oh, boxes. Boxes are romantic.' I ducked past him, blushing. I hadn't meant to say that; it was a Susan line.

We sat down. My skirt had worked its way up too far for modesty. I yanked it down, thinking he was in too serious a mood for that sort of frivolity. He glanced at me.

'You shouldn't do that, you've got nice legs.'

Nice legs? NICE LEGS??

My legs are, without doubt, the finest to grace the West End stage since Evelyn Laye. The Shergar of Shaftesbury Avenue. But he obviously preferred Steinway.

'Do you think you can survive Izzy?,' I asked, hiding my injured pride and legs.

'I don't know. He sacked the PR company today.'

'Not another one. Why?'

'They said they thought the poster was as naff as a lava lamp but not as post-ironic.'

'KT said something along those lines. I thought Izzy might have been listening. Silly of me. Izzy only waits for his next chance to speak.'

We both smiled. Dan got up to pour me another drink. 'Thanks for coming over tonight. Good of your husband to let you.'

'My husband doesn't let me do things, we respect each other as individuals,' I lied. 'Anyway he's...'

I judged the effects of the wine. Should I offload my burden? Dan was using me as a repository for his woes, so why not? Answer: because an actress in need is a high-maintenance nuisance.

'My husband is up the Amazon with a chicken-eating spider.'

Dan laughed. 'Must be difficult for you, being on your own during rehearsals. I've always needed someone there to reassure me.'

'Oh? Who...?' I let the question hang. I didn't know if he was married, though it would account for the décor.

'No one at the moment.'

What about the boastful Susan? Maybe listening wasn't one of her many skills. 'No one?'

'No.' There was a pause which without the alcohol I would have found awkward. I'd told him a lie, maybe this was his.

'I'd better call a cab, I've got to rehearse in the morning and the director's a demon.'

'Is he?,' he asked, not smiling, looking straight into my eyes. I started sweating again. I'm not falling for that, I thought. Men. Little boys lost, the lot of them, I'm not falling for that again. I'm not. Definitely not.

'No. He's a very nice man. And I don't want to disappoint him...by being late.' I thought I could hear David tutting.

'Right,' said Dan, reaching for the phone. I thought the speed with which he capitulated was slightly insulting.

'May I use the loo?'

'Opposite the front door,' he said.

The bedroom door at the end of the corridor was ajar. Blue velvet cover on double bed, Persian rug. Softly lit in a warm glow of light, reflected from the dark walls...

Now, I can't be the only woman who checks the contents of bathroom cabinets. I eased it open, silencing the spring clip. Inside were headache pills, spare razors, soap...and a bottle of Miss Dior. I closed it under cover of the flush and left.

He said goodbye on the doorstep with a kiss on each cheek. His lips didn't linger, nor his body press close. I should have been flattered he trusted me enough to talk. I should have been flattered the famous womaniser respected me enough not to make a pass.

Yeah, right.

I sat back in the cab, steaming with disappointment and indignation. By now it was raining. I reached for my phone.

'KT? Where are you?' I knew he'd been out with the actor playing my son, touting for romance.

'Gerry's.' A drinking club you didn't go to for seduction.

'Want a lift home?'

'Yeah. I've only got two quid left for the night bus.'

When I arrived at the club KT was huddled in the doorway offering a cigarette to an elderly vagrant, who was keen to share his can of Special Brew by way of thanks. KT extricated himself from his new best friend, with great care to avoid a fragrant embrace, and climbed into the cab.

'I thought you were going to kiss him goodnight.'

The filthy bearded face was beaming through the rain at us. KT waved as we pulled away.

'My agent, love. I tell him not to follow me about, but what can you do?'

We decided to have a nightcap at my place and were soon sitting either side of the almost-real coal fire clutching vases of Tia Maria.

'Sorry, I haven't had time to get to Sainsbury's,' I said, explaining the exotic drinks. 'So? How was your date?'

KT looked coy, arching his subtly plucked eyebrows.

'Very interesting.'

'I thought he was Canadian.'

KT dismissed me with a wave of his glass. 'Kelvin's just quiet, you know.'

I certainly did. I'd only managed to get some vague appreciation of Vancouver out of him and the fact that polar bears were common in Churchill. He was abnormally good-looking and, in my experience, as dull as a bollard.

'I'm amazed you lasted a whole evening with him, KT.'

'Oooh, he warms up a treat. Anyway, it seems he's a very good listener. And he likes you.'

Maybe he wasn't so bad after all.

'So he told me what Susan and Lee have been saying.'

I felt that nasty prickle that was the prelude to home truths.

'Susan said, in the pub tonight, that she can't stand you. She reckons you put everyone's jobs in danger over Karen, and that the problem with you is you think you're clever.'

This wouldn't be the only thing she'd said about me. Like vermin, where there's one nasty comment, there's a nest. I made myself sound indifferent: 'Was that in reference to Karen's fee or just generally?'

KT exploded. 'Well, it's everything, isn't it? You've got your name above the title, and she's got a fat arse and a second-rate voice. She hates you.'

While Susan's feelings towards me hadn't been expressed, blown into the air like anthrax, I could cope. Going in every morning, exchanging camp comments about clothes and men, swapping DVDs, complimenting each other on nothing. In her open smiles there'd been no hint of this hatred. She was a better actress than I'd given her credit for.

What would I do tomorrow? When does diplomacy turn into hypocrisy? I reached over, pulled her DVDs off the television and lobbed them into my bag. Pity I couldn't frisbee them into her gob while she was singing. The comments of a jealous and embittered second rate also-ran shouldn't have affected me but they did. To David I was too stupid; to Susan, too clever.

'Silly bitch,' I said dismissively. I wasn't sure if I was talking about Susan or me. 'Want another drink?'

KT was still incandescent on my behalf. 'So what you going to do about her? I'd slap her. I would, I'd slap her from here to Christmas.'

I agreed, but the consqequences of slapping that complacent podgy face would outweigh the sheer pleasure of it. I shrugged.

'There are more ways of skinning a cat, KT. Let's see how she goes on. We're going down to Plymouth next week, maybe the sea air will calm her down.'

KT crunched an ice cube by way of reply. 'The only down that little trollop'll be going is on Dan.'

That was my cue to tell him about my evening. He listened with gratifying astonishment.

ELEVEN

The next morning, out in the garden, I was pathetically grateful for the enthusiastic greetings of the dancers who were having coffee and nicotine for breakfast. Glenda, as she did with men or women, twined herself around me, laying her head on my shoulder.

'You are a lovely person, Eleanor. What you do is nice. We like you.'

I'd never felt the attraction of same sex relationships until that moment but equally, with the slight weight of her perfect body moulded to mine, I felt a twist of envy. How much easier life must be for the flawless. She kissed my cheek and, having rested on me for a moment, flittered off, happy. I wondered if flowers felt envious of butterflies.

Lee, never a bloom of any interest to Glenda, slithered into her place, an arm draped over my shoulders. Susan, wearing jeans that would have stopped an arterial haemorrhage, watched from the pergola where she leaned like Lili Marlene. She waved across at me.

'Hi Eleanor, missed you last night.'

'Yes we were sorry not to see you. You didn't come to the pub – is everything all right?' Lee said this with sibilant concern. As if I couldn't end the day without a drink. As if.

'Yes. Fine thanks.'

'So what did you get up to? Early bed with your script, I suppose. It must be so difficult for you, not having been on stage for so long.'

Should I boast? Reverse the polarity.

'Actually I was with –'

KT slammed through the fire doors.

'MORNING LUVVIES!' – his usual greeting since a gala at Royal Military Academy Sandhurst, where he'd used it to great effect on a roomful of Irish Guards who froze in fear as he pirouetted through their ranks. I heard some time later that, after he'd failed to teach them a box step and kick line, his cry of 'All together or not at all!' had been adopted on the parade ground.

'So… That a bruise on your neck is it, Susan? What did you get up to last night?' He plonked himself down between Lee and me. Susan simpered, her cat's-arse mouth puckering to suppress a smile that was meant to intrigue. KT obligingly took the bait. 'Oh? And what does that mean, Miss Thing? Love bite or close encounter with a door?'

'Extra rehearsals. With our director…at his flat.' She fingered the blue mark below her ear. 'I need a lot of direction. I'm not as experienced as you, Eleanor.'

It was half-past-one when I left Dan's. Where had she been? Hiding in the post box opposite? I saw KT had exactly the same thought.

'Oh,' he said. 'I thought there was a production meeting last night that went on as long as The Lord of the Rings.'

She laughed: 'Yeah, right, whatever. I'm so tired I can't tell you. He's way more than demanding.'

My stomach was knotted but I laughed companionably, girls together. She was flattered. For all her resentment, she still wanted my approval. That, I realised, had been the problem: I hadn't paid court, hadn't accorded her a position above the others. It was so obvious I'd missed it. No wonder she couldn't stand me. Had he really used me as her warm-up act?

'Oh, Susan.' KT stood close to her, inspecting the evidence. 'What's that perfume? I love it.'

She was where she ached to be, at the centre of attention. Her defences dropped. 'This?' She proffered her wrist. 'It's Poison.'

'Why am I not surprised…? It's gorgeous, really suits you. And those jeans. I love them. You'll not get deep vein thrombosis in those, my gell.'

She was like a buffalo lumbering after a cheetah. KT was gone before she realised she'd been hit. He continued his stream of apparent trivia.

'I like Chanel No. 19 too.'

Susan, of course preferred No. 5. It was 'classic' for evening wear.

'Oh and, what's that one in the square, knobbly bottle? Diorissimo.'

Susan was the fount of all knowledge. 'Miss Dior. I know them all, I used to work in Debenhams as a demonstrator. Between jobs.' Adding quickly: 'Of course that was a long time ago.'

'Oh, yes.' KT looked at me. 'I love that one.'

Susan was dismissive. 'No, no. Too sweet. I'd never wear it. I prefer something more sophisticated.'

'I'll have to remember that.' KT twinkled in my direction.

So whose was the perfume in Dan's bathroom?

'Come on, you turns,' called Ruby. 'Warm-up time. Shift yourselves.'

After the mandatory half hour of vocal and physical exercise, done with differing levels of enthusiasm and ability, we were steaming like a barnful of cows when Flossie came in, closely followed by Izzy and Viola. As usual she looked as if she was walking against drizzle, her eyes screwed up behind her glasses, her angular shoulders hunched with anxiety.

'Hi everyone,' said Flossie, his face longer than a wet leg-warmer. 'Izzy would like a word.'

I moved to the back of the room. There was, like a breeze through corn, a stirring, a whisper from the company that sounded like 'shit'. Susan stepped forward into Izzy's eyeline. Lee, as always, was already at the front. He was looking round, arms crossed, trying to catch people's eyes. Catching mine, he looked to heaven in a characteristically extravagant gesture of boredom. Almost at the same time he smiled his icing-white smile and turned back to face Izzy with an expression of rapt excitement.

'Good morning, everybody,' started Izzy, pacing up and down, gesturing with the cigar. 'As you know, Dan's away for a couple of days on a prior commitment...' He made it sound as if it was with the fraud squad. '...So with Karl here to help out, I'm going to take over as director.'

Several pairs of buttocks clenched.

'I have a camera crew coming in for hotel television and they're going to record rehearsals and interview a few people – when are they coming, honey?'

'Oh, around now,' said Viola with a frown of concentration, as if this were a hugely contentious question.

'Okay,' continued Izzy, with no impression of having heard her reply. 'I told 'em we got the best musical London has ever seen, so I'm going to ask you to do some stuff from the show.' Blind to our ambivalence, he rushed on. 'Are you excited? Yeah! Get excited, it's good for the blood. I want Lee's number and Susan's number and anyone else...'

I stayed resolutely silent, although he was staring at me.

'Eleanor? How about you?'

'Um… I'd rather not.'

His eyes were unfriendly but he maintained the cheerleader tone. 'We're selling the show here, Eleanor. And you're part of the show. Big part. The star.'

More like a black hole from the glare he was giving me.

'I suppose I could do my last number.'

I earned a beaming embrace from Izzy. 'Thanks, pal. Then this afternoon we'll do the whole show for a coupla friends of mine – the great singer Julio Maderas and his wife.'

One of the bolder dancers put his hand up, exactly as he had in infant school when asking for the toilet.

'Sorry, Izzy, but who's Julio Maderas?'

'Who is Julio Maderas? Who is…?' Izzy was doing lost-for-words acting. 'My God, you never heard of Juilo Maderas?'

We shook our heads.

'He is the greatest, I mean *the* greatest salsa singer in the world and, I cannot express how much this should mean to you all, he and his wife are sponsoring the first night party, to which – I hope you're all listening to this – to which the Costa Rican government have been invited, along with many members of your own Royal Family. I been told the Elizabeth Two dances salsa.'

The usual suspects were terribly excited at the prospect of the monarch and a day of performing in front of an audience. They'd araldited their performances into place at the read-through, so losing rehearsal time was irrelevant. But for some of us development would not only be arrested but reversed by being forced to display the unripe fruits of our labours.

In front of the cameras, Izzy played the bongos, joined the dance routines, even interrupted my number to demonstrate how the great Maria Montana would do it.

'You gotta sing with your pelvis, Eleanor. You know what they say? A woman's pelvis is a goldmine.' He swivelled his hips with the smooth seduction of a cement mixer. After that I hid in the garden with KT until he was called for Lee's new show-stopper.

Ildefonso and Viola had written it in a hurry to Lee's instructions while Izzy looked on with fond indulgence. The monster was now truly out of the box. Lee had an anthem which he was determined would rank above 'I Will Survive' and 'You'll Never Walk Alone'. Though somehow I couldn't imagine Liverpool's Kop singing 'A Noisy Queen is a Happy Queen'.

I leaned against the door jamb watching, envious of the orgasmic pleasure Lee got from performing. He revelled in having every eye on his expert gyrations. He reminded me of a stripper, confident in and empowered by his audience's arousal. And yet, for all that he was born to sing and dance, and would do so in the light of an open car door, he wasn't and never would be a star. I wondered if he existed when he was alone.

I resolved to be more generous. It didn't last.

TWELVE

Dan returned to find a company tearing itself apart. There was no concept of Company in Izzy's idea of Broadway. There was a group of performers who could be replaced and a faceless chorus behind them. But I was his Fabulous Star. I would have been flattered, but it was like being told you're beautiful by a cephalopod.

Izzy loudly explained how he'd improved Dan's work, with his arm draped over his director's shoulders. Viola looked distressed, but as she usually looked as if her piles were playing up it was difficult to know if her discomfort was only due to her husband's rank insensitivity.

'Okay Dan, here's the bottom line. We're going to go straight from the overture –'

Dan looked startled – there was no overture in his production.

'– into Eleanor's first scene. It's *funny*, we gotta establish *funny* right there.'

It was my turn to look startled. My first scene was short and, unless I fell down the stairs, not particularly amusing. 'Funny' was no way to introduce a Fabulous Star. Then I noticed Susan looking at Izzy, hand on generous hip and chin tilted, as if he were the second coming. Posing.

The penny dropped. My role was comparatively small but showy. Hers was larger but with only one solo number, which Dan had reduced from a six-minute ad for the Noise Abatement Society to a short, quietly touching ballad. By putting my scene first, while the audience was still unwrapping their cough sweets, I would be her prologue. Very clever. I wondered whose idea it was.

'And Susan came to me with some great ideas, so I've put her number back as writ. Full length. With the money notes. Big band sound. Great. You can't have a voice like Susan's in a show and not use it, Dan. See, you gotta understand, I've produced on Broadway –'

'And I've written, directed and produced in the West End. And that's where you've chosen to be.' Dan spoke with a smile. Had Izzy been listening, he'd have heard the warning.

'See, pal, here's the bottom line, lemme tell you –'

'No Izzy, let me tell you. I have the artistic authority on this show. That's why you employed me.'

Izzy hadn't seen Dan angry before. Neither had the rest of the cast, who were riveted to the spot, torn by embarrassment and fascination. He spoke softly but his face was white with fury.

'If you want to be the laughing stock of London, you carry on and I'll go home. This isn't Broadway, Izzy, and it certainly isn't the Broadway of twenty-three years ago when you were an investor, producer in name only, on a revue – a series of old songs held together by rhinestones, which had no dialogue nor any discernible dramatic construction.'

Dan's contempt for Izzy was withering. I watched Izzy's face and saw expressions that included fear and hatred cross it like clouds across a windy sky. Finally a benign smile spread across his rubber features. Arms outstretched, he turned, like a pope blessing the company.

'Say, Dan, pal, you know what I say? The actors are the most important thing. Without them there is no show. Am I right?'

He was rolling over, showing his belly to Dan, backing down, as the textbook says all bullies do. I thought I saw something else, though: the expression of a temporarily defeated hyena. Partly frightened by the vigour of the living prey, but mainly sly and vicious, determined to outflank it, to snipe and snap until it rolled dying in the dust.

I was romancing. Izzy was less like a hyena than a fawning dog as he tried to deflect Dan's fury.

'Dan, hey, c'mon – I'm like you. I just want the best for the show, for the actors. This group of people here, the best there is, these great actors, they're what it's all about, isn't that so, Dan?'

Dan, still angry and less able to turn on a lie than Izzy, looked truculent and ungracious before this onslaught of charm that was winning over those honoured to be called actors.

'So, pal, you carry on… I wanted to help you, share the load… It was only you being away for so long made me want to keep the ship on course. I'm sorry, real sorry if I upset you. Okay?' He paused, his tongue hovering over his lower teeth. 'Come on, Dan… Shake my hand.'

There was a long, ice-heavy pause. Dan knew the popular balance had changed in favour of Izzy. Reluctantly he walked towards his producer and stretched out his hand, as if reluctant to get too close. Izzy grasped it and pulled Dan into an embrace. Dan was rigid in his arms as Izzy laughed and thudded his palms on Dan's back.

I glanced round the room and, to my surprise, saw the Canadian Kelvin was shaking his head, as aware as I was that we were going on with a crack in our infrastructure. Only time would tell if it would open up and sink us all.

Hands clasped in triumph above his head, Izzy disappeared out of the door with his cigar clamped between his deceptively toothless jaws.

THIRTEEN

Once Dan was back in charge and the chickens had stopped clucking, he persuaded Viola, with a diplomacy worthy of the UN, to change Kelvin's character from incestuous transvestite serial killer to a pleasantly deranged psychopath who was in love with my character, rather than determined to eviscerate her. But it took several hours to convince Izzy to cut the song 'I Pulled her Stomach Open and Put my Head Inside'.

'Let's try this run without it,' Dan suggested on our last afternoon in London.

'Dan, Dan.' Izzy was conciliatory, palms raised in surrender. 'You're the artistic director, I'm just the producer. What do I know about you Brits and what goes down here? Do what you think is best. If Kelvin can't handle the material, it's just dumb to go on with it.'

Before Dan's intervention, it was only KT that had stopped Kelvin heading for Heathrow Airport in despair at the thought of making his West End debut as a cross between Freddy Krueger and Danny La Rue. This cut was a major triumph, even though Kelvin didn't like the implication he couldn't hack it.

Izzy went out to make more phone calls while we ran round checking props, lines and dance steps. Suddenly I was aware of someone sobbing. Viola was sniffling and hiccuping into a mound of tissues.

'Oh, my…it's just so moving. The last day of rehearsals here… you've all been just so fantastic…my dream… Izzy's so proud…'

We gathered round, cooing and comforting. Wiping tears of happiness from her mottled face, she chose that moment to share her innermost self with us.

'You know, guys, The Merchant of Venezuela! is more than just a story…its basis is actually the true story of my own family…'

Several of us had to make unexpected visits to the loo when she admitted, in a whine of self-pity, that she'd been murderously attacked by her cousin with a stuffed mongoose, prior to him being put in a secure unit for his own, and others', safety.

When KT said, 'That's all very well but I'm more of a Hello Dolly! boy myself,' Ruby threatened to withhold our biscuit ration. He had been passing Garibaldis out like packets of Charlie, because Izzy had banned refined sugar and saturated fats.

'You gotta have good health to be successful. You get sick, it's what you eat made you that way.' He generously provided industrial amounts of fruit, most of which went to feed Morag's rabbit, while we snorted Tate and Lyle with our tea.

Once Viola had calmed down and Izzy was installed next to Dan, we did a quick warm-up, with Lee and Susan as usual in the front row with the dancers. I watched Susan's elephantine gyrations beside Glenda's svelte undulations and couldn't fathom Dan's interest, especially as he so obviously fancied Glenda. Lee, in his cropped pink top with IF YOU CAN READ THIS, YOU'RE SITTING ON MY FACE emblazoned upside-down on the front, held himself like Bette Davis, fingers sharply splayed, head raised and leg, bevelled down to a size-nine foot, pointed as if teetering on a stiletto. They both looked like female impersonators, but Lee was more convincing.

I lurked in the back row with the two older men in the company. One of them wore two hearing aids, both usually switched off, and the other simply didn't listen, and when he did it was worse.

'Dan, did you say come on stage left?'

'No, go off stage left come on stage right.'

'Are you sure? I thought you said stage left.'

'I did. Go *off* stage left.'

'Stage left.'

'Stage left.'

'Ah…' Long pause. 'Only I've left my glasses on stage right…'

'The problem with him is, he thinks it's enough to be fat and turn up on time,' said Dan, after one particularly frustrating afternoon working on the opening number, during which the old boy stood like a traffic bollard in the middle of a race-track.

Pleasing though it was that Dan trusted me enough to make that kind of comment, it wasn't getting me anywhere nearer being a sex object, for him or anyone else. Until I had the unconditional love of the audience, I was looking for adoration from any quarter.

The run-through, when it finally started, was like a motorway pile-up. Dancers hurtling into each other, furniture being dropped on feet and lines mangled beyond recognition. An air of desperation settled on us as we staggered through Act Two.

I started my big torch song determined to show everyone I wasn't a total liability, having demolished the chorus line before the interval. Satisfaction at my soaring aria turned to embarrassment when Izzy started to cry loudly and clap like a seal.

'Oh, for God's sake, chuck him a fish,' said KT, loud enough to be heard by the entire cast, most of whom laughed. Susan sucked in her already disapproving lips. KT wasn't fazed. 'Oh, darling, that's a good look,' he hissed at her. 'Gives you cheek bones.'

Finally, God and Glenda did a breath-taking five-minute salsa routine, while on the sidelines Susan shimmied and swivelled her hips, hands lifted in ecstasy. Did she know her stomach was rippling like floral custard?

My ungenerous thoughts were repaid by missing my finale entrance. The looks of sympathy from the musicians were worse than the syrup of smug satisfaction that spread across Lee's face. He took my hand and guided me through the number as if I were a beginner in a line-dance class.

After Dan's post-mortem of the run-through, I ran for home. Actors always go on about being 'naked' on stage. What I'd just been through was worse. Naked, yes, but with curiously small genitals, two left feet and a tattoo of the Titanic across my chest. The dark night of the soul was setting in nicely when the phone rang. By now I was actually feeling low enough to welcome David's abuse as confirmation of my uselessness.

'Hallo?'

'Eleanor? Dan. Fancy a pizza?'

Say no. You've been humiliated enough today. Pizza was no more than soggy bread covered in tinned tomatoes, and there was absolutely and categorically no way I was falling for that again...

FOURTEEN

It was a bitterly cold night, but the walk up Dan's stairs left me bathed in sweat. I fished a paper hankie out of my bag and wiped the underside of my breasts. The inside of my bra was damp enough to grow mushrooms.

The door was ajar when I finally made it to the top; the soft light spilling onto the landing as inviting as the opening of a romantic novel. Dan's flat looked exactly the same as before, except that there was a bottle of champagne and two glasses on the table.

'Help yourself, I won't be a second.'

His voice came from the bedroom. I had no doubt Susan would have been in there like a rat up a trouser leg but, I told myself, I was more dignified, I'd wait to be invited. The part of me that was brutally honest made a noise that sounded remarkably like *'Liar'*.

The living room windows were closed and the faint traffic noise mingled with the jazz playing quietly on the elegant Bang and Olufsen. Bowls of pot pourri and scented candles filled the air with cinnamon and rose; beaded and fringed lamps subtly lit the room. There was definitely a femme to be cherched here.

'I thought you looked a bit upset after the run.' Dan emerged from the bedroom, tucking his shirt into his trousers. I was so glad he didn't subscribe to the fashion that dictated a man's shirt should hang lifelessly like a wind-starved flag over his buttocks. He brushed past me and poured me a glass of Laurent-Perrier. David preferred The Widow.

'Thanks for noticing,' I said. 'I was absolutely dreadful. Sorry.'

He smiled. 'We all have off days. Don't worry about it.'

We sat down, carefully separate, me on the blue-striped sofa, him in the light-coloured wing chair. Impractical colour, I thought. Must mark terribly. He seemed relaxed, elegant hands on the upholstered arms, legs casually stretched out, crossed at the naked ankle, feet in cream openwork deck shoes. Nice arches.

I tried to remember what I knew about body language. What signals was he sending out? More to the point, what were my signals saying? No Entry? Humps for 200 metres? I tried to relax.

'I ordered you a margarita. Is that right?'

'Er…yes, Dan, thanks.'

I was ridiculously flattered he'd remembered. I couldn't recall what he'd had, but I'd recorded every frame of how he'd eaten it. It was with this in mind that I ploughed into the calorie-fest in its big white box. Hoping my face wasn't covered in cheese, I said:

'So, why did you take over at Edgware?'

'I wanted to run a building and have a permanent company. I wanted a family, I suppose.'

That was the opening and I dived straight through it. 'I thought you had one,' I lied, hopefully convincingly.

'I have. A daughter. But her mother wanted to go back to Italy. This is her flat.'

'Your wife's?'

'My daughter's.'

Miss Dior! I couldn't wait to tell KT.

He quickly but smoothly turned the conversation back to his plans to continue work on the show, which was still full of incomprehensible sub-plots and lachrymose songs.

'Susan's number rather holds things up, doesn't it? Now it's back in full?' I tried to sound disinterested. He was dismissive, not as electrically aware of her as I was.

'Yes, I tried to explain, the audience will have lost the will to live by the time we get back to the show, but she won't have it. She's not very bright, you know,' he said, wiping his fingers as if of her. I reached for my champagne, trying to look as if I didn't care what the answer was.

'I thought you and she were…are…quite close.'

That was not the right thing to say. The champagne warmth between us chilled to sub-zero.

'What makes you think that?'

My body language went into fluent defensive.

'Well…it's just…she said…I thought…sorry. I don't know.'

'What has she been saying?'

The ice was still there, but for her, not me.

'That you and she had…were…um…an item.'

I once heard a black actress say she didn't like blue eyes, they frightened her. Looking at Dan's now, I could see what she meant. They were still beautiful, exceptionally so, but as lethal as a carving knife. He leaned forward, his long fingers locked round each other, white at the knuckles.

'She came here one night. First week of rehearsal. She was in tears, talking about her family and her abusive childhood. Said she didn't think she was up to doing the show and needed my help to get through it.'

Clever little tart, I thought, the vulnerable card, not many men could resist it, even from a lump like her.

'Ah, yes,' I said in as non-judgemental a tone as I could command. I busied myself with an olive that had gone feral on the carpet so he wouldn't see my jealousy and disappointment. When I looked at him again, he was studying me closely.

'Sorry?,' I said, thinking I'd missed something during my rummage through the shag pile.

'She said she was frightened of you and she thought you didn't think she was up to the job. She asked me to protect her from you.'

'I've got as much chance of frightening her as I've got of shagging a water buffalo. So…what did you say?' I sounded calm, blasé. If only I could act that well on stage.

'I told her not to be silly, that as the leading lady you just wanted the best for everyone in the company and that we'd all work together for the good of the show.' He paused and smiled again. 'Usual bullshit.'

I liked his smile, his full, rather pouting mouth lifting to reveal his idiosyncratic teeth, not perfect but charming. The blue eyes less sharp, though still watchful.

'So what happened?,' I asked. Am I bothered? Look at this face, is it bothered?

'I sat her down and gave her a drink.'

'And a pizza?' That was cheap, Eleanor. You've been hanging round KT too long. Dan looked hurt, the smile evaporated.

'No. No pizza.' He took a mouthful of champagne. 'Would you have minded if I'd given her pizza too?'

That threw me. 'What? No. No, of course not. Why should I mind?'

I was so unused to flirtatious conversation, I felt as I had as an adolescent, trying to unload my cumbersome and unwanted virginity. When I eventually found a taker, I'd fled in a flurry of tears and school uniform – still intact. I could hardly run down the stairs with my socks round my ankles now.

'She wouldn't leave,' he said. 'Said she was having a panic attack, so I made her breathe into a paper bag then let her sleep on the sofa.'

It was an involuntary reaction to look down at it like a suspicious loo-seat. I could see her Marilyn Monroe pout, her exposing of a well-fleshed shoulder as he stood in the doorway saying goodnight.

'And did she sleep on the sofa? Or did you have to handcuff her to the coffee table?'

He was obviously amused by my reaction, but I couldn't see whether it was because he thought I cared about her or him.

'She didn't stay on the sofa.'

I think I said 'oh' but I know I didn't say 'bollocks!', though I must have thought it loud enough to have been heard by the mummies in the Egyptian room over the road.

'So where did she go?'

As if I didn't know. She'd have laid it out like a haddock on a fishmonger's slab.

'I called her a taxi. She went home.'

I was desperate to say, 'After?,' but I stopped myself, and even if I hadn't, Dan's expression would have. Why is it that men of the heterosexual persuasion don't want to talk in any depth about anything remotely interesting? KT would have named the shops where she bought her underwear and given a dissertation on her chosen method of bikini waxing. Withholding emotion or, in this case, information, was just one more element of the male psyche I had difficulty with.

'So you're not having an affair with her.'

Well, I was allowed to say things like that, after all I was married, technically middle-aged and the mother of the company. My reason to ask would only be for the good of the show. After all, internecine relationships were always dangerous for the status quo.

'I'd rather have an affair with an anaconda.'

Not a no, then.

The following pause, during which I searched for something witty to say and failed miserably, was filled by Dan's mobile ringing.

He seemed reluctant to answer it. Naturally, I assumed it was Susan. Naturally.

'Hi, Izzy. No, not busy, just having dinner…'

No wonder he hadn't wanted to answer; Izzy Duck wanted to talk and no excuse like dinner, or the flat being on fire, would stop the blitzkrieg of the producer's creativity. Ruby took an average of twenty calls a day and Jonty twice as many, mainly about getting the Saudi Royal Family involved with financing the show. KT's reaction had been immediate.

'Why would a bunch of Arabs want to get into bed with Izzy Duck and his spectacularly plain wife, who couldn't write her name on the bottom of a dud cheque? I can't see Lee's number, which is, let's be honest, an invitation to ride on the Lavender Bus, going down too well with people who routinely deadhead pansies. Mind you, they might give us a couple of camels for Susan, as long as she doesn't sing.' He paused to take a quick draw on his Superking. 'You know what I think? I think Mr and Mrs Duck haven't got a pot to piss in, and they're trying to get anybody, no matter how ridiculous, to invest.'

Dan paced the flat trying to get a word in as Izzy talked loud enough for me to hear the bee buzz of his voice. After fifteen or so minutes, he laid the mobile down as if it were some sick and exhausted creature washed up on an unfriendly shore.

'What's the latest from Planet Duck?,' I asked, crossing my legs with what I hoped would be a whisper of silk, or polyester at least. Dan didn't seem concerned with my well-turned calves, or indeed the rest of me. He was shaking his head in despair.

'He wants to audition salsa enthusiasts from around the country, then every week we'll put the winners into your big number.'

'And what am I supposed to do?'

'Introduce them, then get the audience to vote on whether they should come back for the finale.' Dan slumped onto the sofa next to me, his face suddenly grey with tiredness. 'I'm not having an affair with anyone, you know, not even Viola Duck.'

I gathered myself and the floppy ruin of his pizza. 'Don't tell me he thinks you're carrying on with her.'

'You see more a my wife than I do, pal.' Dan accompanied his impression of Izzy's rasping, accusatory tone with the waving of an imaginary cigar. 'It's gotta stop. You know she's gone kinda bats being away from home so long, but I haven't, oh no. I'm healthy…'

Dan dropped his hand, and with it Izzy Duck.

'It's just the usual crap but now he's getting paranoid with it. You know, Eleanor?' He punctuated the question by putting his arm along the back of the sofa behind me. 'When we started I thought the guy was just eccentric, but when I said that to Kelvin he said in America there's no such thing as eccentric. Only certifiable. I'm beginning to think he's right.'

His fingers, as if independent of him, were moving against the skin of the nape of my neck, exploring what I hoped was the softness of my hair. Images of unused bottles of conditioner filled my mind, jostling with pictures of Susan laid out on the striped damask where we were now kissing.

It had come quite naturally, a mutual movement together, noses in the right alignment and lips equally ajar. A very good first attempt – followed by a breath-taking second go, which included some triple-tonguing that made me suspect Dan had played the trumpet in the cadets.

Head tilted back, I tempted him to feast of my swan-like neck. While he was buried there, I, hopefully surreptitiously, reached into my bag. Yes, the condom was still there. Luminous or not, it was coming out of its packet tonight. And hopefully so was Dan.

There was also a diaphragm in my bag. I'd had it since coming off the pill but had been too intimidated by the instructions to use it, and David never gave me enough notice to allow me to find my glasses. I blinked the vision of my husband away, not through guilt but in case he inhibited me, and unbuttoned Dan's shirt. A bare half-dozen hairs littered his breast bone – a slight disappointment, but my opinion of his chest was swept aside by a tidal wave of panic that it was so long since I'd done anything but lie like a grateful mattress under David, I might irritate rather than excite.

Were my lips a sensual delight or reminiscent of a sink plunger? While I was worrying about my performance, Dan manoeuvred himself onto the floor between my legs and, to my horror, was preparing to dive in, like one of those lads who launch themselves into holiday seas from sun-baked rocks. I wasn't sure that what he was about to submerge himself in would be as refreshing as a dip in the Med.

I tried to relax and failed miserably.

Dan expertly insinuated his brass-playing mouth parts into places that had for so long only felt the pan-scouring technique of David's fingers, I was afraid they might be as rough as the soles of my feet.

Oh God, what if he wants to suck my toes?

No. Absolutely not.

I braced myself to kick him off as he peeled down my hold-up stockings, but he didn't linger on my feet. With a delicacy which could only have come from years of practice, he licked his way up my calves and inner thighs, so expertly he almost banished my preoccupation with the lingering stubble I'd missed with my 'twelve for £2.50' razor.

I was just giving myself up to the inevitable when the doorbell rang. I think Dan swore, but his voice was slightly muffled. The doorbell rang again, more insistently, and Dan emerged from under my skirt looking as if he'd been searching for a fuse in a blacked out cellar.

'Sorry about this,' he said and went to the intercom.

It occurred to me he could have ignored the unknown and unwelcome guest, but just as quickly the thought he might be relieved to have an excuse to stop depressed me. Before he'd said 'Hallo?' into the wall box I was getting the whip out for a bit of self-flagellation.

I heard a jumble of words come from the intercom, followed by Dan's 'Come up. Top floor.'

There's no dignified way of putting back on clothes removed in the throes of passion. I pulled on my stockings. The left one twisted so badly it cut the circulation to my lower leg. I feared gangrene might set in before I could get home. Retrieving my knickers from a lamp shade, I pulled them on and sat down, hoping my face wasn't blotchy and that the beads of sweat on my upper lip didn't look too much like a moustache.

Dan, without a look at me, buttoned his shirt and ran his hand over his trousers. Whether to check his zip or his erection I couldn't tell. In the endless seconds before the visitor appeared at the door, which Dan now held open, we didn't speak or even look at each other. Englishness raised to a form of Kabuki.

'Hi, pal, thanks for inviting me in.'

Izzy? Dan had terminated the most exciting seven and a half minutes of my recent life to invite in the man who people threw themselves under buses to avoid.

'Drink?'

'You got Diet Coke?'

Among Izzy Duck's host of unattractive habits was his aversion to alcohol and his addiction to fizzy drinks. I'd once got him to try Irn Bru, telling him it was made in Scotland from girders. Despite his soliloquy on the glories of Edinburgh, he did no more than sip it. I took this to be racism, as it couldn't possibly have been more disgusting than Coke.

'Hi, Eleanor! Say, am I disturbing something?'

'No, of course not Izzy.'

As any day wore on, Izzy would become more incoherent and irrational, but I'd never seen him this late at night. He was twitching, between his wide-mouth grimace of a smile and a scowl of concentration caused by his poor hearing. An elderly dog trying to convince prospective owners he was still a puppy. Suddenly, instead of being angered by his inability to listen and repelled by his ill-fitting denims, baseball cap and phallic cigar, I felt terribly sorry for him.

It couldn't be easy gambling your house on a dream, living in a small unfashionable hotel and being away from friends. I tried to imagine Izzy's friends and failed. For all his exaggerated expressions of affection, we were not friends. We were 'you Brits'; he used the words with uncomprehending condescension masquerading as affection. Like Jock, Taffy or Paddy. When he asked, 'Have you guys always been independent?', I understood Uncle Sam's foreign policy with blinding clarity.

But on that night, still damp from Dan's efforts to reawaken my erogenous zones, I felt sorry for him. He was just a gabby old man, afraid he wasn't really the Broadway Producer he'd put on the first night party invitations: BROADWAY PRODUCER IZZY DUCK INVITES…

I stood up, the cheated flesh beneath my pants throbbing with frustration. 'Well…' I said brightly, 'I'd best be off. Long day tomorrow.' I stepped towards the door and my strangulated leg began to ache.

Dan was hurtfully quick to see me out, avoiding eye contact. At the front door, though, out of Izzy's sight, he whispered: 'You don't really want to go, do you?'

He didn't wait for me to reply, which was lucky, as I'd temporarily lost the power of speech.

'Go into the bedroom. I'll get rid of him.' He kissed me with a flick of his tongue on my lips and I obediently tiptoed into the bedroom.

The bedside lights were on, and a second bottle of champagne stuck out of a cooler, flanked by two good quality flutes. It crossed my mind I should be insulted he was so sure I'd go this far – but, as usual when standing on my dignity, I got vertigo and had to sit down.

The bed was welcoming even in this position. I sat there primly for about five minutes, then reached for the bottle and managed to open it without the cork ricocheting off the ceiling.

Napoleon said, 'In triumph you deserve champagne and in defeat you need it.' He didn't mention anticipation. The first glass went down without touching the sides, the second I sipped while looking out of the window. The view was a Disney skyline of London. Ridged rooftops and glowing glimpses into rooms, above them a perfect sliver of moon set in silver clouds on a velvet blue background. A light snow-shower had made the roof slates shine.

I opened the window and, leaning on the sill, listening to the distant music and laughter from a party, revelling in the romance. Very slightly pissed. Squiffy. Perfect. Now was the time to fit the diaphragm.

Like all ideas conceived in drink, it was a stroke of genius. I pulled the box out of my bag, scattering two Tampax and a set of miniature screwdrivers across the floor. Another swig of champagne and it seemed funny. It was funny. I picked everything up, overbalancing only very slightly, then put on the glasses I was too ashamed to wear in public. I unfolded the instructions.

Squeeze spermicidal jelly onto surface of diaphragm. It sounded a bit brutal. Tried at the Hague for spermicide. Now was not the moment to get sentimental. Sitting on the edge of the bed, I put the diaphragm on my lap and unscrewed the top of the tube. The clear gel oozed out. I carefully replaced the cap.

The diaphragm itself was a three-inch disk of tan rubber with a reinforced spring-loaded rim. I gathered the idea was to fold it in half, then quarters, and then insert it into the vagina. No problem. I'd played netball for the school.

I grasped it firmly and folded.

It shot across the room and stuck to a rather nice print of 'The Scream'.

I peeled it off and tried again. It was like juggling soot. Eventually I got it in half but wasn't sure I had the strength left in my fingers to go for the quartering. Then I realised I still had my knickers on.

The momentary lapse in concentration allowed it to make another bid for freedom, and it catapulted under the bed.

Being almost the same colour as the carpet, it took me a few minutes to find it with the aid of the small torch on my keyring and a coat hanger. It was now covered in fluff.

I dunked it in the champagne.

After drying it on my now discarded knickers I reapplied the jelly. With more luck than skill I folded it.

Triumph. I squatted down and guided the missile to the silo.

It shot through the window like an Exocet. Hit the slate roof opposite and slid into a puddle on the flat roof below.

I had one leg out of the window when I remembered the condom. Clambering back into the bedroom, I banged my pubic bone on the window sill – and men really think women find slamming up and down on a horse arousing. However, I persevered with the condom and, despite having to chew the packet open, eventually released it from its silver shell.

It wasn't green.

It wasn't pink.

It was luminous.

With tentacles.

Exhausted, I flopped onto the bed, the champagne floating me like a water lily.

<hr />

'I think he was lonely.'

Dan sat beside me, jerking me awake. He reached across to caress my face. I hoped I wasn't dribbling.

'Has he gone?'

'Yes.' Dan ran his index finger over my breasts. The nipples reacted like a couple of pointers. 'Viola's got 'flu and he didn't know what to do with himself.'

'You should have suggested hanging under Blackfriars Bridge with a brick in each pocket.'

Dan laughed and filled my glass. I gave myself up to the drowsy delights of being seduced by a master.

<hr />

Waking in the early morning wasn't romantic; neither were the three condoms thoughtfully provided by Dan from the bedside drawer, now lying flaccid in the waste basket. The sharp, bright light filling the uncurtained room was unkind on the dehydrated skin above my knees. And it was abundantly clear I wasn't a natural blonde.

Dan slept quietly with his head on my navel, purring gently in the wreckage of the well-made bed. I was not in love, but looking at him, splayed out like a medieval martyr, I felt a twinge of something that wasn't just gratitude for a magnificent rogering. But if he looked like a medieval martyr, I looked like a stone gargoyle clinging to some dodgy brickwork. I saw my panda eyes and chapped lips in the mirror and headed for the door like a scalded cat, panicking to escape before he saw me sober and unflattered by the dark.

'Rough night?,' said the taxi driver peering in the rear view mirror. 'Here... Aren't you her off the telly? You look older.'

'I am older.'

'Ever thought about plastic surgery?'

ACT TWO

Sea How They Run

FIFTEEN

I was packing for Plymouth when the phone rang.

'Hallo?'

'Eleanor?'

'David?'

It hadn't occurred to me that if he phoned, I rather than he would feel guilty. But after sleeping with Dan I did, especially as my spine was rippling like a Mexican wave.

'Oh… David…how are you? Phyllida did the anti-freeze. I would have got round to it.'

I knew he'd been tempted to break cover by a piece on the show in the Daily Telegraph. I should have known, even in the throes of passion he wouldn't give up the crossword. Neither would he countenance the idea of me doing anything that wasn't directly involved with being his wife.

'Where are you?'

He ignored the question. 'I've heard you're doing a show. A musical.' He said this as if I was doing a sex act in public with a Dalmatian.

I laughed, pretty unconvincingly. 'How did you hear that up the Amazon? Is there a South American edition of The Stage?'

David wasn't amused. I could hear he sensed he wasn't in control and In Control was where he lived.

'World Service.' That was a new name for Phyllida. 'What do you think you're playing at, Eleanor? I thought we agreed you'd given up all that silliness.' His tone of headmasterly dismissal reduced me to a naughty child, as it always had.

'I thought the money would be handy,' I stuttered.

'We don't need money.' He was incandescent. 'I pay for you.'

'Pay for me?,' I repeated, stunned.

'Don't repeat everything I say, Eleanor, it's very annoying.'

Not as annoying as seeing your husband humping another woman. Why couldn't I just say it?

'David.' I reverted to silly little wife. 'I'd like some money of my own. To spend. On myself.'

He made a noise which was a combination of a cough and a bark. 'We'll discuss it when I get home.'

'Oh, when's that?,' I asked brightly, with a note of convincing anticipation.

'Tomorrow. You can pick me up at the airport.'

That was the moment I should have said, *No. I'll pick you up from the scene of your adultery. From your bonk-fest with the Bike of Gloucester.* But I didn't. I wanted to see his face when I told him I knew who his chicken-eating spider was.

'Oh, David, I'm sorry, I'm going to Plymouth, we're opening the show down there.'

He wasn't pleased. Not pleased at all, but then he was in South America, and the phones are notoriously unreliable over there.

'Sorry, David, it's a terrible line, I can't hear you… Say again? No… you're breaking up…' And my index finger, ever so gently, rested on the button that ended the call.

I felt as though my hands were shaking, but they looked calm. My mind replayed the conversation over and over again, while every nerve was braced to hear the phone ring again. After five minutes it did. I forced myself to shut my case, then answered it, ready to accuse and admit.

'Hallo love? All packed?'

'KT?'

'Who d'you think it was, Cameron Mackintosh? What time shall we meet at Paddington?'

'I thought you were driving down with Kelvin.' Publicly invisible though their liaison had been, I knew it was intense, every spare moment spent in sexual athletics.

'No, he wants to exercise a bit of discreet in front of the company. Said I was going too fast! Me! Fast! I haven't even made him Mam's Welsh cakes yet and you know I never rim on the first date.'

'What's his problem?,' I asked.

'I dunno, maybe he's a closet heterosexual. Who knows. Anyway, what time?'

'Two o'clock under the main departures board.'

'Right, see you.'

When I arrived at Paddington, KT was chatting up a policeman. It didn't occur to him that a six-foot-two graduate of Hendon wearing a conspicuously new wedding ring might not be desperate for a blow job in the gents, but KT loved a challenge.

Reluctantly, he tore himself away from 'Dave' and we headed for the train, where KT unpacked a feast of sausage rolls, crisps, salads and fresh crunchy bread. He then produced a bottle of wine from a cool-bag decorated with a tap-dancing penguin.

'Well, there you are,' he said, very Welsh. 'My mother's not the Queen, but at least she dresses tidy.'

KT and I sat back in our '*book in advance if there's an R in the month and your granny was a Viking*' bargain first-class seats, and revelled in the illusion of exclusivity. The sparkling wine brought back the sensual pleasures of the night before with a shudder. I squirmed. KT smirked.

'So? Did you?'

'No, of course not.'

He knew I was lying. What he didn't know was why, and neither did I. It wasn't until later, when I was alone in the sea-front flat in Plymouth, looking out at the moon-rippled water, that I unwrapped that night with Dan.

He'd looked down at me as he cradled me in his right arm and said: 'Tonight I love you more than anyone has ever loved you.' And, look as I might, search though I did the depths of his eyes, I couldn't find a lie. Describing the moment would have withered it. I didn't want to know how many times he'd said it – or to whom.

KT watched me, but didn't ask any more.

'So what have you done about David?,' he asked, screwing up my silence with the rubbish and putting it out of sight.

What had I done? What I always did when faced with a dilemma. Nothing. He was probably home by now. He'd left two messages on my mobile, tetchy that I hadn't dropped everything for his homecoming. I wondered what present he'd bought me. These little souvenirs of his travels had always delighted me in the past, but now I wondered how many had been bought in the fairtrade section of Oxfam. Once I'd settled into Plymouth I'd call him, placate him, save recriminations and confrontation until I got back. Maybe by then he'd be over Phyllida and I'd be over Dan and we'd live happily ever after. And maybe green pigs would fly over Clapham Common.

Alcohol and an excess of emotion made me maudlin, easy tears dripped onto my napkin. 'Sorry, KT, I'm just being silly. A lot of people are much worse off than me.'

'That doesn't make it hurt any less though – you can't compare apples with pandas.'

I wanted him to be right, but knew he simply had more courage than me, and far greater strength.

⁂

The route the cab took into Plymouth gave us a tour of the ring road and a good view of the back of Sainsbury's. I dropped KT off at the flat he was sharing with Kelvin, Ruby and Gaffer Gusset, the assistant stage manager, a sweet-natured girl with a fierce amount of body piercings and an unlikely interest in Jonty.

My flat was on Grand Parade, at the bottom of the Hoe. At the top stood the Grand Hotel and stately houses, with the shadows of Victorians promenading, their parasols and top hats challenged by the breeze. I loved to pause half-way down the steep hill to look at the glittering water toying with delicate yachts, or bearing the last crumbs of our once great navy – a battleship, cruisers and once a nuclear submarine, which surprised me, naked, when I opened the bedroom curtains. And at night, walking back to the flat, lights on the water, the multi-coloured blinking of buoys and the luminous sky darkening to merge with the black sea.

There was something so English about the place, not twee or coy, but quietly elegant, with a becoming lack of exhibitionism in beauty or presentation.

'Daahliing!'

The landlady, an eccentric and entirely enchanting ex-dancer who at the age of eighty could still manage an impressive high kick, embraced me, fussing me into the ground floor flat, which was actually eight feet above the ground, level with the imposing front door at the top of a flight of stone steps.

The bathroom was cold, the lavatory a short hike from the bedroom and there was no shower, but the living room made up for all. A huge bay window, the width of the wall, opened wide enough to enjoy the sun, 'when it's warm enough to sit', as she would say, and gave a perfect view of the sea.

We gossiped while I unpacked my case and she was vastly amused by my description of Izzy and Viola, but she lightly laid her red-nailed, liver-spotted hand on my arm with the delicacy of a small lizard.

'Eleanor, darling, this is a vanity project, isn't it? In my experience they always turn ugly. Always. Make sure you're protected.'

I hugged her and assured her this was going to be the exception. She went upstairs to her own apartment unconvinced.

The stage door keeper, Albert, greeted me as an old friend, and I was issued with a swipe card which we both knew would be lost within 24 hours. I took my key too and opened the door of the number one dressing-room. The familiar odour of air freshener and socks hit me in a wave of nostalgia. The stained sofa was unchanged, the fridge clean and empty, and the vast loo and shower innocent of past use. This was the old number one dressing-room, not the refurbished one which looked like an ad for disabled living aids. The old Rolf Harris panto mural was still on the wall, albeit added to over the years so that beside Goldilocks and the Giant from Jack and the Beanstalk, Hedda Gabler cavorted with the Ladyboys of Bangkok.

I considered the star on the door – *look at me, ma, top of the bill!* No roaming the corridors to find an unoccupied loo and no guessing the contents of the plughole in the communal shower. A small warm glow of happiness enveloped me as I laid out my stall on the dressing-table. Small towel, brushes, pencils, powders, creams, cologne, hair grips, wig nets, remover, moisturiser, mascara, liner, eyelashes, tissues, cotton buds, baby wipes, Strepsils, Beechams Flu-Plus, Rescue Remedy and anusol for the bags under my eyes.

Through the unimpressive black door that led to the stage-left wing the technicians were working on stage, the tallescope in the centre, two burly men holding it steady while a stringy youth adjusted a lamp 25 feet above them. Coils of cable littered the floor and a cordless drill sounded in bursts. In the wings, props and furniture were being marshalled by Ruby, prop tables marked out in white tape, boxes labelled GLASS, NEWSPAPER, CUP, CAKES and DON'T EAT THE FUCKING PROPS YOU GANNETS.

In the auditorium, the lighting designer's desk, laden with laptops, anglepoise lamps and the debris of several meals, straddled the centre seats of row G. The sound designer worked a desk further back, programming in 25 microphones, back-up channels and fold-back speakers, which would allow us to hear the onstage band. Television monitors were slung from the front of the circle so we could see the musicians, to get some idea of when to sing and for how long.

The technical rehearsal would start in the morning. We'd be slapped and frocked by ten a.m. and not see daylight as we worked through until eleven in the evening, but tonight there was a relaxed atmosphere in the theatre, watched over by Basher.

Basher, the monstrous veteran production manager, was standing centre-stage, hands on hips, his massive tattooed arms flexing like wings.

'Come on, you talentless lazy cunts, I want to be out of here by midnight. Oh, 'allo Eleanor. Suppose a fuck's out the question?'

As always, he was dressed in knee-length army surplus khaki shorts, a T-shirt emblazoned with CREW on the back and GLYNDEBOURNE: WHEN THE LIGHTS GO OUT THE WALLS COME TUMBLING DOWN on the front. Circumnavigating the generous circumference of his belly was a rigger's belt, from which hung everything from a machete to a bunny rabbit given to him by his infant daughter ten years before.

'So they've got you back, have they? I thought you were in a home,' he said, striding towards me with a grin that revealed a lot of things that didn't look so much like teeth as the wreckage of a neglected graveyard.

'Hallo, Basher. How's it hanging?'

He kissed me – or rather, hit me with his face – and I was embraced by the strong odour of male sweat, cigarettes and beer. He held me at arms' length, his brown-green eyes twinkling, sexy despite his glorious ugliness. 'Fancy a small sherry?'

A small sherry to Basher was a bucket of wife-beater with a whisky chaser. 'I'm meeting KT, but we'll probably be over the Mexican later. I'll buy you a pint of cooking lager.'

He turned away, still smiling, to berate a spotty lad who was trying to drag a flight of marble steps on stage.

'Let the brake off, you great pillock. Fuckin' work experience, you'll experience my boot up your jacksie if you don't get your finger out.'

'Basher,' I said, 'you can't talk to him like that anymore, you're infringing his human rights.'

'Fuck off, Eleanor,' he replied. 'He'd have to be a human fuckin' being in the first place. Look at him – Oi, you, the Top Turn's taking an interest, stay still for a minute – if he had another brain cell he'd be a cactus, so don't you go worrying your pretty little head about him. Go on you lump of pond life, get on with it.'

The spotty boy continued struggling with the steps.

'Good afternoon, everyone.' The doors at the back of the stalls opened and Dan, wearing a short black kimono over black jeans and boots, walked down the aisle. He saw me and came to the front of the stage. I squatted down in the time-honoured way of actor listening attentively to director.

'Where you staying?,' he asked quietly.

'Grand Parade.'

'Me too. I might pop in for a nightcap.'

Excitement made me laugh. 'I'll nip over to Oddbins.'

He ran a finger along the back of my hand so lightly it was like a breath, then called: 'Is the stage ready, Basher?'

Basher sucked the air over the broken tombstones of his teeth. 'Don't be a cunt. What's it look like?'

Dan immediately assumed his most charming persona.

'I'm sorry, Basher, I just want to see a couple of lighting states. Would you mind?'

Basher, like the White Cliffs of Dover, was unaffected by charm. He shrugged. 'I'll give the crew a tea break. You've got fifteen minutes. No more if you want this ballet on stage before Easter.'

'Thanks, I owe you one.' Dan called back to the lighting designer: 'Kill the workers.' The flat ordinary light went off, but the blue backstage light still bled through.

'Hang the blacks,' shouted Basher, indicating a pile of midnight curtains in the wings. I left the stage, musing that we were the only profession in Britain who could say 'kill the workers' and 'hang the blacks' without getting arrested.

Just arriving at the stage door, loaded with flowers, was Susan, with Lee. She was being vivacious and irresistible for Albert, who was looking at her as if she was on day-release. Lee, in a pink lycra vest and satin hip-hugging trousers, was scanning the dressing-room list and carrying a make-up case with enough slap in it to do every model in Madame Tussaud's. He saw me first.

'Darling!' He screeched. 'How are your digs? Ours are fabulous, we'll have to have you over one night.'

I'd rather have red-not needles shoved in my eyes.

'What a great idea,' I said. 'Good for company morale. We can all bring something.' *Ebola Virus, possibly.*

Albert was holding their dressing-room keys, which they took with a great show of nonchalance. But no matter what your opinion of yourself, it was the allocation of dressing-rooms and the order of the curtain call that told where you really stood. Susan had been put upstairs and, even more insulting, was sharing with the young juve lead, a girl of such vacuous stupidity it was easy to believe she was a natural blonde. Lee was even worse off: he was on the third floor, next to the washing machines.

'Well, it's only right. I said to Jonty I didn't want the Old Farts having to climb all those stairs. I mean, I know I've got Billing but it just wouldn't be fair on them...'

Lee's self-delusion oozed over Susan's righteous fury and allowed them each to save at least one of their faces.

'Is Dan in yet?,' Susan asked brightly, to no one in particular. She'd taken to behaving as if I didn't exist unless I addressed her directly.

'He's in the auditorium,' I said.

She tossed her head, presumably in the style of a high-bred filly.

'Great cut,' I lied. She looked like a Cruft's poodle with a bubble perm which had been a mistake in the 1980s but was positively criminal in the 2000s. She ran her fingers through it, or at least as much of it that wasn't the consistency of a rug.

'Dan wants me to look glamorous...' – she paused – '...for the show...' Suggestion hung as heavy in the air as the perfume she was wearing. 'I'll go and find him.'

She wiggled past me. Her bust, in a clinging off-the-shoulder jumper, rested on the inner tube of fat round her diaphragm. She would describe herself as Rubenesque. I would describe her as a lump of lard with an undistinguished face and no chin.

KT appeared as if by magic.

'She shouldn't have her hair so short – it makes her face a feature.'

Lee, scenting the odour of bitching, came over.

'What does she think she looks like?'

'Kate Moss?,' said KT innocently.

'Stirling Moss, more like,' hissed Lee, leaning on the ss.

'Ooh, that dates you,' said KT, a good ten years younger than Lee, despite the latter's dyed black hair and botoxed brows.

'Have Izzy and Viola spoken to you?,' he asked, turning his back on KT and his small, unexceptional eyes on me.

'No. Why?' As I said it, I could feel a small knot of tension under my ribs. A chat with the producer meant trouble – and with Izzy, today's hero was tomorrow's jobseeker.

'Oh, no reason, he just mentioned a few changes…forget I said anything darling… I'll see you in the morning. Ciao.' And off he went, having sown a seed of insecurity in my already over-planted allotment of self-doubt.

'He's just trying to undermine you,' KT later reassured me as we trawled for the necessities of touring: wine, biscuits, chocolate and industrial amounts of Hulahoops.

I threw an organic chop in the basket, even though I knew there was more chance of it singing 'Nearer My God to Thee' while hanging from the Telecom Tower than me cooking it.

'Trouble with Lee is, he thinks he's the leading lady. But then so does Susan.' He paused over the frozen fish. 'Ellie, watch yourself. They're like athlete's foot those two, just waiting for an opportunity.'

After a couple of sherries in the Mexican bar, thoughts of Lee and Susan were as distant as the Wicked Queen in panto. God and Glenda floated in with their usual straightforward good humour, which was only slightly dented by the shock of moving to Plymouth, where their colour and perfection turned heads and stopped cars.

'This is not a place of beautiful people,' said Glenda sadly.

As if to reinforce her observation, Izzy and Viola walked in. This was as unusual as it was unwelcome.

'Hi, guys,' said Izzy, with the relaxed bonhomie of a satellite navigation system.

'Come and sit down.' I moved up on the banquette seat, hoping I sounded convincingly welcoming. God and Glenda, seizing their opportunity, left for the cinema.

Izzy sat next to me while Viola folded into the chair by KT like a step ladder being put away. We made awkward small talk for a while, then Izzy made a break for the monologue. Conversation was effectively dead.

'I gotta tell ya, I'm worried about the direction this show is going. That run we did on Saturday – lemme tell you, Eleanor, you were great. I cried. You saw me cry, right?'

'Did you, Izzy? Must have missed that.' KT kicked me.

'But where was Viola's masterpiece? All I saw was a lot of horsing around. Juvenile jokes, kids running around carrying furniture –'

'I think that's because there wasn't the budget for a big set...' I might as well have tried to speak over Niagara Falls.

'– You know, I was brought up poor, but after I made a million, maybe two, I married good, right? I'm a businessman, yeah?' We nodded wearily. 'But I'm a producer first. I started out with nothing, I learned. You know. I had to.'

He lowered his voice and his head, leaning close enough for me to share his breath. I was shocked at how yellow the whites of his eyes were.

'You know, my grandparents, both sets, they were gassed in Auschwitz.'

He paused for our shock. Mine was not because of the Holocaust, but at the thought that anyone could use such a tragedy to manipulate their listener into acquiescent silence.

'This show is a monument to them. That's why I'm here. To make sure they didn't die in vain. Viola has written what she knows, but putting it on is my tribute to Yenta, Israel, Miriam and Solomon. I think it's difficult for some people to understand this, that I produce with my soul. To some people, some people in this company even, it's just a paycheck and they lack respect.'

My silence wasn't respect but disgust. Izzy was prepared to use a taboo sledgehammer to smash a nut, and it soon became clear that nut was Dan. Viola sat, her shirt collar turned up round her elongated neck, which was reddening as Izzy talked. She looked down into her glass of fizzy water as if she wished it was a lake.

'You know, pal...' Izzy had been talking continuously, interrupted by nothing but my lack of attention. 'I think Dan has some problems... mainly with Susan.'

Now he had my attention. Dan had never shown irritation with her self-absorbed stupidity. 'No,' I heard myself saying. 'Dan...er... admires Susan. She's got a great voice.'

'Sure, kid – I know she has a great voice.' He said it with a look that said I'd come top of the class. 'But Dan doesn't know talent like I know talent. He's not giving her the time and the big focus. She's gotta be seen.'

How could you miss her?

He sat back and glanced at Viola, she was now hunched over, her face contorted. I wished she smoked, drank or took class A drugs, just to give her some rest from whatever demons were pursuing her.

'He's using her.' He stabbed the air with the cigar. 'He thinks she's got a great ass. But he's forgetting she's got a great voice, and I wanna hear it.'

I could only be grateful Izzy was as unseeing of his audience as an actor on a brightly lit stage. Was he trying to bait me? Was he such a control freak he couldn't bear the idea of a relationship that didn't include him? I didn't know what to say, but before I could formulate a reply that didn't implicate me, Viola spoke. Her voice was more strangled than usual. Her eyes unwilling or unable to rise from the depths of her glass.

'Izzy? Izzy I think you're wrong. Dan wouldn't do anything to hurt the show…'

As Izzy continued to conjure up pictures of Dan grazing on Susan's veal-white body, I looked at KT. He was far quicker and more accurate than I was, but we both arrived at the same conclusion – it wasn't me Izzy was trying to provoke but Viola.

KT and I were extras in a nasty little film that, as always, starred Izzy Duck. The plain, unattractive mouse that had been Viola Allen had been saved from barren spinsterhood by Izzy Duck and now he suspected her of infidelity. If Viola hadn't slept with her director, it didn't matter – Izzy inhabited every part of his wife; any thoughts that wandered from him were a betrayal of adulterate proportions.

Perhaps he was right, perhaps she had become infatuated with the man who never put her down and who treated her as if she were an attractive young girl. In retaliation, Izzy was trying to destroy his wife's small, unformed fantasy with images of her hero in the throes of passion with a woman who was her physical antithesis. In a way it was touching that Izzy would think anyone but him could be remotely interested in Viola, but the ruthlessness with which he was combating that suspicion was cruel. However, not cruel enough for me to tell him Dan would rather sleep with the fishes than his wife.

As KT and I walked home from the theatre that night we laughed at the idea that anyone but Izzy and Viola would want to have sex with Izzy and Viola, but there was still something like the faint aroma of rotten fruit that stayed with me as I walked down the hill. It took away the pleasure of the view.

Once in the flat I opened a bottle of wine and waited for Dan.

It was almost midnight when I heard a tap on the bay window. His face was just visible as he leaned across from the steps leading up to the front door.

'Hallo.' He leaned on the wall, a bit awkward, a bit shy, almost formal, after the intimacy of the previous night. He didn't kiss me but that may have been because, suddenly self-conscious, I turned away to lead him into the flat.

'Wine?'

'Sorry Ellie, I didn't have time to get any.'

'No, I didn't expect you to. KT and I did a shop. How's the fit-up going?'

'Basher'll have the set up by the morning. Everything's fine.'

He pressed close behind me as I poured the wine, gently kissing the nape of my neck. What Viola Duck would give for this delicate arousal.

I turned to meet his lips and opened my dressing-gown. We both needed something quicker, less personal than making love and within ten minutes he was rolling a cigarette and I was peeling an Aero.

The night was moon-bright and cold, so I lit the gas fire, almost losing my eyelashes in the process, then sat on the floor with my back against Dan's knees. He played with my hair much as he might have caressed a labrador's ears. Comforting but hardly sensual.

'Izzy said – no, implied – you're having a thing with Susan.'

The hand stopped moving and withdrew. His silence made me turn round. I knelt between his knees. His eyes were in shadow but I could tell they weren't soft with love. 'And what did you say?'

I laughed. 'Have you ever known him to leave a pause big enough to say anything? I got the feeling he was trying to warn Viola off you.'

Dan stood up and went to the table in the bay window where the wine was sitting in a bowl of iced water. The battleship in the bay was lit up like a Christmas tree. Beautiful.

'Watch your back, Dan. You've banned Izzy from rehearsals and he's had to get your permission to come into the technical – I just think he's not one to take any loss of control easily, particularly if it involves Viola. She's the only proof he's got that he's ever been viable as a man.'

'So what do you think I should do?'

This was one of the most attractive things about Dan: when he asked a question he genuinely wanted to know the answer. In rehearsals, he patiently listened to everyone and never dismissed even the silliest or most self-serving suggestion. But he was so bright he was always ahead of us, and I could see from his amused expression he was ahead of me now.

'I think you should try and include him. I don't know, ask his advice maybe.'

Dan smiled and reached for my hand. 'Bind friends close and enemies closer? Good advice from a wise woman.'

His hands slipped inside my dressing-gown again. Outside a group of drunks approached, singing at the tops of their voices. It took a second to realise they were doing the Act One finale from Les Misérables. I looked out of the window and there, looking in, as if through the glass of a fish bowl, was the stage management team, Jonty, a couple of the dancers…and Susan.

Dan opened the window and leaned out, chatting with them, laughing at their jokes about him giving me extra coaching. But Susan wasn't laughing. She could see I was naked under the green-gold silk of my dressing-gown, and that the deep flush across my chest wasn't due to the cold. Her sucker mouth was drawn in and she was staring at me through melodramatically narrowed eyes – Christopher Lee playing Fu Man Chu in a fright wig.

I now had everything she wanted.

SEVENTEEN

The technical rehearsal started at ten a.m. At nine-thirty, as I was putting foundation on my beard-rashed skin, David phoned.

'Where's my blue shirt?'

'Which one?'

'Eleanor, don't be more idiotic than God created you, the one Phyllida gave me last birthday.'

I ripped it to pieces then boiled it in hydrochloric acid.

'It's hanging up in the wardrobe.'

'How many times do I have to tell you, Eleanor, shirts don't go in the wardrobe, it makes them musty.'

'David, I'm sorry but I must get on.'

'No you mustn't. This is more important than your…play-acting.' His tone was contemptuous, but the ears hearing him were no longer tuned to his frequency.

'What do you want it for anyway? You only wear that for special occasions.'

His sigh could have been exasperation, but I suspected it was hastily covered guilt. 'I've got a lunch.' Slight pause. 'With my publisher.' I doubted the blue shirt would be worn in honour of the unmade bed that printed his esoteric pamphlets on old bones.

'Oh, I thought you might be seeing Phyllida.'

'No. Why should I be seeing her?'

'To thank her for the anti-freeze?,' I said sweetly.

He exploded. 'What are you implying? Just because you were too stupid to do it you're going to get jealous… Oh, this is ridiculous. I'll talk to you later.'

What did I care? I had a lover too. He couldn't hurt me. So why was I crying? He wasn't my life anymore, this dressing up was real life – it had to be. The youngsters laughing at nothing, excited to be a day closer to the West End, the rest of us needing gin and Prozac to get through the next fourteen hours of gruelling repetition, frustration and tiredness.

I looked at my all-too-familiar features, the ones I was so tired of trying to transform, and after so many years in so many mirrors I wondered if it was worth it. When I'd started out everything had seemed possible; now only the impossible presented itself. The only way I was going to look like Elizabeth Taylor was with a face transplant. I'd aimed for the stars and had collided with the ceiling like a fly with a windscreen. David infested my mind as I picked calcified glue off my false eyelashes, losing confidence with each piece that hit the bin. Luckily, before I opened a vein, Ruby called everyone to order and the pre-show music started.

'Ladies and Gentlemen, please turn off your mobile phones. Because if one should erupt, the cast are likely to come down off the stage and ram it up your arse. You are also advised to unwrap noisy sweet papers before the end of the overture because you really don't want to upset this bunch of psychos you've just paid fifty quid to watch.' Slight pause. 'Sorry. It won't be fifty quid till the West End.'

Then silence, uninhabited by the audience chatter that would follow in two days' time. A soundtrack of street noises started up and Kelvin's strong tenor soared out. I crept into the wings to watch for a moment. He got through the first verse before Ruby interrupted, slouching onto the stage wearing a headset.

'Save it, Kelvin…' He listened to the voice in his ear, then: 'Thank you. Reset to the top, everyone. From houselights down.'

And so it would go on, stop-go, back and forth until the first dress rehearsal when the show, which had taken two days to put together technically, was done up-to-speed for the first time. By which time we'd all have lost the plot and the will to live.

Back in the dressing-room there was a subtle knock at the door and my dresser walked in. A professional lifetime of being discreet and invisible for leading ladies had given her a nun-like presence. She laid out my first costume, a violet sequined sheath with spike-heeled sandals.

'So glamorous,' she murmured, stroking the glittering material.

'Maybe on the outside,' I said, pulling on my microphone belt, which was attached to a length of broad, black elastic-band around the right thigh. On this was sewn a cotton envelope for the battery-pack. It was like a calico gun-belt. From the dressing table I picked up the battery, larger and heavier than an iPod, with two terminals sticking out of the top. One housed the aerial, which had to be free and dry at all times, the other was the socket for the mike lead. I pushed it into the pouch, clicked the plug into the socket, threaded the cable under my knickers, up my back, under my bra, round the strap and over my head. A toupee-clip held it in place in the centre of the wig net. Over the top, holding the centre of the wig in place on my forehead, went the jet black hair. The tiny mike was barely visible as it protruded from under the flesh-coloured lace of the wig that framed my face, and which I glued to the skin in front of my ears so tightly it looked like a bad face-lift.

The transformation was pleasing, if a little intimidating. The blonde wimp that was me was replaced by a black-haired woman with fierce eyes. I was convinced by her, until I sat down and the aerial stabbed me in the clitoris. I'd put it on upside down.

I walked slowly – and carefully – to the stage-right wing, holding myself like a great and famous beauty, not, hopefully, like someone with intimate bruising. On stage the cast milled about in the bright lights, waiting. The wings were dark and cluttered, a quiet world of obscurity separated from the glare of exposure by a few paces. Nervous for no reason, I waited for my first entrance, a slow walk down the magnificent staircase. Dear God, if I felt like this at eleven o'clock on a Monday morning what state would I be in by seven-thirty on Wednesday night?

To relieve the shortness of breath, the urge for the lavatory, the compulsive pacing and the urge to eviscerate David, I relived the night before.

Dan was unaffected by our being seen together and dismissive of Susan. 'I'll give her a cuddle in the morning and tell her she's the new Elaine Paige.'

But even as I pulled the curtain across the firmly closed windows, I could still feel her angry jealousy. I knew she'd be poisoning the youngsters against me. That sliver of insecurity grew into bleak thoughts of David and certainty that he was right: I was a bad person and a lousy mother. I broke off from a long lazy kiss that I was reciprocating more through fear of offending than pleasure.

'I'd better phone home.'

Dan let me go with no objection and sat down by the fire while I went into the cold hallway.

It was too late for David, he was ratty with jet-lag.

'Yes?' He'd obviously been asleep.

'It's me. Did you get home safe?'

'No. I'm lying in the middle of the M25 with a machete in my head. What do you think? For crying out loud, Eleanor, don't you know I've got jet-lag?'

Very ratty.

'Well… I just wanted to say hallo and tell you I didn't have time to get any eggs but there's stuff in the freezer –'

'Eleanor. It's two o'clock in the morning. I've just traveled non-stop for eighteen hours. I want to go to sleep.'

'Oh, I'm sorry, David. The M4's a bugger isn't it?'

'What?'

'From Heathrow. The M4. From Heathrow. What did you think I meant?' A pause. I could hear him breathing. Pity. 'I'll call you tomorrow, shall I?'

'Why bother?,' he spat. 'You're no good to me in Plymouth are you? If you can't be bothered to be here, you needn't bother to phone.'

And he hung up on me. With no idea of why I'd put myself through that, I went back into the living room and stood defeated and lost in front of Dan.

'You look like a little girl,' he said, putting his arms round me. 'And I like little girls.'

'Well I'm glad you do. My husband prefers boot-faced old bags.'

'Oh.'

'Sorry, you didn't come here to listen to my problems with my husband.'

He didn't contradict me; after all this wasn't a relationship.

⁂

'You loo' fantastic.'

Glenda had slid up behind me, silent and sensuous as a python. She touched my dress and hair.

'You so beautiful. Really, Eleanor. Beautiful.'

This from a girl whose looks could have stopped the charge of the Light Brigade. I glowed with pleasure.

Susan joined us in a fountain of pink chiffon frills, held up by rhinestone straps that cut into her well-upholstered shoulders. On her feet were four-inch-high white sling-backs rarely seen outside Chigwell. I hadn't seen anything wobble like her since my Auntie Rene made a blancmange for my tenth birthday.

'Oh Susan, you look fantastic. That colour's perfect. Such a pretty dress, and it moves so well.'

Had Glenda been so insincere? No. She was gloriously untouched by hypocrisy, but then, like a child, she loved anything that glistened even if it was base metal. I waited for Susan's reciprocal dishonesty. She simpered, looking me up and down, pausing at the wig.

'You're so brave, Eleanor, black's so ageing.'

Then she turned to Lee and cooed over his skin-tight gold lamé trousers, as he minced on stage to laughter and congratulations. He looked 'wonderful', 'perfect', 'so good'. Susan turned to me, as there was no one else to speak to; Gaffer Gusset didn't count.

'You know he had liposuction. In Estonia. Much cheaper than Harley Street. Still looks fat though, no muscle-tone you see.'

That was the pot calling the kettle beige but I did a bit of '*No! Really?*', and I could see she was pleased. Her smirk at my ignorance was intended to put me in my place. Luckily I knew my place. And so did she: slap bang in the middle of the curtain call. And with that between us, there was no possibility of anything more than a wary truce. She didn't have anything I wanted.

———

They didn't get to my entrance until after the morning tea break. Izzy was pacing up and down in the wings, chewing on his cigar and scowling. Viola sat a couple of seats away from Dan in the stalls, poring over the latest version of the script. Karen, the musical supervisor, was on stage behind me listening to the fold-back speakers. There was no tension as I stood waiting for the sound balances to be rectified. Dan was talking to the lighting designer and Ruby was waiting, hand on hip, to restart, when out of the blue-lit dark strode Izzy, straight to centre-stage.

He shaded his eyes from the battery of lights and squinted into the auditorium, cigar pushed deep into his cheek. His yellow face was livid with anger.

'Dan, Dan, I need a little input here.'

The sort of silence that settles on a forest when the predator appears engulfed us. I looked across at Ruby and, imperturbable though he was, his eyebrows rose. Mine did too.

'Yes, Izzy?' Dan's voice was calm, friendly even.

'The door knobs.'

'What about the door knobs, Izzy?'

'What about the door knobs? I don't like the door knobs is what about the door knobs.' He was shouting now. 'This is a mansion, right? No fancy house would have door knobs like that, Dan. You gotta get rid of them.'

Izzy went to pull one, but it hadn't been screwed on and came off in his hand. There were hastily suppressed sniggers from the dancers.

'Look at this cheap crap! You got no class, Dan. This show is about class and you – you got no class, Dan… Look at these, they look like class to you?'

By now he was screaming. About a pair of door knobs.

There was a stunned pause before Dan spoke. The show was being painstakingly assembled, like a gigantic meccano set, and Izzy was hysterical about door knobs? Dan came to the front of the stage. He wasn't smiling.

'Izzy, the ones that were ordered haven't arrived. Morag put these on just for the tech. Now, there's a lot to do, could we get on?'

'I don't like 'em! They're no good, ya hear me? Get rid of 'em!'

Morag appeared at the side of the stage.

'Izzy –'

He rounded on her. 'I don't like the knobs. They're cheap.'

'So is this fucking show, you wee scheister. The supply company hasnae been paid, so I had to go to B&Q in ma tea break and get these out the sale bin.'

This was the cue, the accusation Izzy had been waiting for.

'Are you saying I don't pay? I've never been accused of not paying what's due.' He was yelling into her face, covering her in a shower of saliva. 'You need more money? You didn't say you needed more money. Why didn't you say, you dumb ass?'

Morag was scarlet now, but she stood her ground.

'I've said it so many bloody times I've got repetitive strain injury. You gave me a budget and I've worked damn hard to bring this show in under it, even though it's like limbo-dancing under a snail's belly, but even I can't do anything if the bills aren't paid.'

Unable to intimidate her, Izzy increased the volume of his screaming.

'I pay my bills! Are you saying I don't pay my bills? You're nothing, you know that? You're only on this show cos Dan wanted you. I don't want you, you're not even second-rate.' He strode up and down the stage. 'The bills are Jonty's responsibility. That's what I pay him for. Get me Jonty! I want him here. Now! I've never been accused of dishonesty.' He turned his fury back on Morag. 'You're nothing, where have you worked before? You ever worked on Broadway?'

'This isn't Broadway and you've spent more on bloody lawyers than you have on the sets and costumes, ye wee shite. And don't you dare blame Jonty, he doesn't have the authority to sign off cheques because you won't let him. Everything goes through you, so don't come all the *I didn't know anything about it* bollocks, cos ma head doesnae button up the back.'

I thought Izzy was going to spontaneously combust. He snatched the cigar from his mouth and approached her, stabbing the air in front of her face with it.

'Okay, okay, that's it. You're fired. You hear me? I been doing theatre forty years and I never heard crap like you talk. Get out of my theatre. Are you still here? I told you, you're out, lady!'

'Jesus Christ, Izzy,' she yelled back, not moving. 'Is that your answer tae everything? The only friggin' reason I have nae walked out before now is Dan. Not you, ye wee dictator.'

Viola had come down the stalls to stand next to Dan.

'Izzy, Izzy, stop this. I mean it, honey. Stop this. It's not good for you.' Not good for *him*? He was the only person who hadn't gone into shock.

'Get that woman outta my sight and outta my theatre.' He jutted his jaw towards Morag. 'I'll see to it you never work again.'

I thought Morag was going to hit him. Ruby put himself between them. Dan jumped onto the stage and Viola wailed.

'That's a break everyone. Back in fifteen.' Ruby didn't dissipate the poison, but he did disperse the company. Reluctantly they shuffled away. Morag didn't move.

'Izzy,' said Dan quietly. 'Shouting and bawling may be the way to get things done in America, but there isn't a corner of the British Isles where it works, and I won't have any member of my team spoken to like that. Now...I suggest, if you want this production to open on time, you allow us to get on and save the histrionics for New York.'

Izzy simmered in silence, and Morag, chin up, eyes bright with angry tears, stared at him, waiting for the apology which was never going to come, then said quietly:

'I'll get you new door knobs tomorrow. Here, in Plymouth. And I'm sorry I lost ma temper.'

Izzy couldn't be gracious, even in triumph. 'Okay. Get 'em fixed by tomorrow or you're out.'

Only Dan's hand on Morag's arm prevented her ramming the door knobs down the producer's throat. Izzy stomped off the stage, leaving a bomb crater of shock and hurt. Viola scuttled after him.

'Izzy...Izzy...wait...'

Dan glanced across at me. He looked as if he'd been slapped. It was left to Ruby to sum up.

'Tosser,' he said. 'I'm going for a fag.'

Morag followed him, already lighting a Marlboro even though her hands were shaking.

As Dan wanted to talk to Basher, I went to my dressing-room, hoping Izzy might have caught bubonic plague by the time we were called back. The phone was ringing as I opened the door.

'Hallo?'

'Eleanor? David.'

I'd forgotten about him. For the first time since I met him I'd gone two hours without thinking about him. Now he was back like toothache.

'Eleanor, I'm not angry at you. I just think it was disrespectful that you should have taken this job without consulting me –'

'You were in the Amazon. By the way, did you find out what killed your bodies?'

David ignored the question, perhaps he couldn't bear to tell a lie. 'I've got some bad news, Eleanor.' I was looking in the mirror, thinking maybe Susan was right, my wig was too harsh. 'Gabriel Michael's daughter phoned. He committed suicide last Monday. The funeral's on Friday in London.'

My mind split in two, half skittering through trivia, half struggling to accommodate the death of my first love. The pictures of him so vivid, alive in the past but not the present.

National Youth Theatre. Sleeping in the wardrobe store under Richard II's velvet cloak. The smell of mothballs and damp. His, the first hand on my breast. Laughing at the seriousness of sex. Playing bar billiards at the Monarch. Walking all night through London because I was too frightened to sleep with him but too much in love to let him go. Aggressive, self-destructive, drunk, gentle, funny, kind and too intelligent to survive as an actor. To live, he wrote romantic novels as Olive Tapenade. Always bored with his own company, locked away with his lap-top, he'd get conservatory salesmen to call at his eighth floor flat.

We'd stayed friends through his disintegrated marriage, his self-sabotaged relationships and the growing up of his children. But his life wasn't the one he'd signed up for. He'd never got the hang of the pointlessness of existence and I understood why my Gabriel, my first kiss, my first heartache, had taken pills and died with no audience.

But that didn't make the pain of his going any less. And now, with David rattling through the funeral arrangements, I wanted his smell of red wine and fine soap and Gitanes. I wanted to phone him to hear his naughty boy giggle. But I'd never hear him, see him nor touch him again. Ever.

I sat and cried until David gave up and rang off. The last thing Gabriel had said to me was: 'Eleanor, it's not too late to save me from myself. David is a gold-plated – not even 24-carat – shit. Ditch him and come back to me.'

And he hadn't even known about Phyllida. I was laughing through the sobs, thinking what he would have said, when KT came in and knelt down in front of me.

'Nellie, Nellie, what's the matter? Oh Nellie, don't cry.'

I couldn't speak, I howled, floundering in the pointlessness of constructing shelters against death.

When I finally got control of my voice I asked him not to say anything to anyone in the company. There was nothing worse than the voyeuristic sympathy of people sidling up in the wings asking, 'Are you all right?', while desperately hoping you'll break down and have to be carted off to a secure unit. *Poor Eleanor keeps crying, some story about*

a bloke, but it's really trying to get sympathy because she's not up to it...'
That kind of gossip travelled faster than the internet. Discretion, like full employment, was unknown.

The tech dragged on, passing as if during a heavy period – a mixture of pain and fear of leakage. My red eyes and occasional tears were excused as an allergy and I spent the afternoon being bombarded with sprays, pills and folk remedies rather than tell the truth.

KT tidied me up, repainted my panda eyes and pushed me back on stage, where Izzy was now complaining about the colour of Susan's legs.

'She's supposed to be from Venezuela and she's orange. Look at her calves, they're the colour of a carrot.'

But the shape of aubergines, I thought.

'Where's the designer? What the hell has she done to my actress?'

'Actually, Izzy…' Susan was all big eyes and finger-twisting curls. 'I did it. Did I do wrong? I wanted to look exotic –'

He was brought up all standing by this 'Whatever Happened to Baby Jane?' act.

'Ohh…say…Susan… I didn't realise. What a great thing you did. Isn't that a great thing, Viola? The kid used her own money to help the show.'

Viola clasped her hands to her sternum, and gazed up at Susan. I noticed Viola never came onto the stage, whereas we couldn't keep Izzy off it. He put his arm around Susan – or as far around as her waist would allow anything but an orangutan's.

'You're a star, kid. A real star.'

⚯

The concentration required to get through the rest of the tech put Gabriel out of my mind until my saccharine ballad in the second act. Viola's inane lyrics, rhyming 'love' with 'God above', suddenly had the potency of John Donne, and I sang it so well even the band woke up.

At the end of the evening, after our 'Well done, but still more work to do' speech from an exhausted Dan, Karen timidly put her head round the door.

'Are you all right, Nell?'

Her kind, bright face undid me, but not as much as her words of comfort and praise. I went home to an empty bed and fell asleep staring at the ceiling rose and crying mascara into my pillowcase.

EIGHTEEN

'Eleanor, pull yourself together, you've hardly spoken to the man for the last ten years.'

David drove me to the funeral, not because he wanted to support me in my, to him, overblown grief, but because he deemed me emotionally incapable. I'd taken the sleeper up to London, and a train less aptly named couldn't exist. Finally we rattled into Paddington at six a.m. and I gratefully disembarked, feeling as if I'd spent the night in a tumble-drier. David was already having breakfast when I arrived home, his newspaper propped open on the marmalade. Thick-cut, Olde English of course.

'You must have missed that in the Amazon.'

'What?'

'Thick-cut marmalade.'

'Mmm.'

'But I suppose there were compensations.'

He looked up. 'Like what?'

'Er...fresh fish?'

He said little about his expedition, except that the natives had been friendly, which was unexpected, as they were notorious cannibals. Perhaps the tribes of Gloucestershire couldn't stomach him any more than I could. I made some toast but couldn't eat it.

'You shouldn't waste food.'

'I'm sorry.' I was in no mood for a fight. 'I'll put it out for the birds.'

He exploded at that. 'God, Ellie, you are so stupid.' He didn't even add 'sometimes'. 'You'll have the place crawling with rats. Just put it in the bin for crying out loud. And hurry up. After the fuss you've made about this chap, it would be utterly ridiculous to be late.'

Then, apart from tutting at the amount of tissues I was using, he didn't speak again until we reached the crematorium.

It was marginally more appealing than a Scout hut, and there was an attempt to make it look non-denominational ecclesiastical by putting modern stained-glass windows in the side doors, but this was defeated by the sign saying FIRE EXIT DO NOT OBSTRUCT. Well, I suppose you can't be too careful in a crematorium.

Gabriel's family, including his ex-wife, sat with his children. David and I slipped in at the back and I stared at the pale coffin, unable to believe it contained his body. During the service I concentrated on the peeling ceiling, the pock-marked floor, the shoes of the undertakers, anything but listen to the moving words of his friends or the heart-breaking music played by his nieces on their school violins.

Then my name was called and I walked along the strip of carpet to stand by his coffin, my hand on the wood above his heart. I read with tears fogging my eyes:

Fear not slander, censure rash;
Thou hast finished joy and moan;
All lovers young, all lovers must
Consign to thee, and come to dust.

Then, shaking, I fumbled for the piece of rosemary I'd pulled from the bush in our garden and put it on the warm wood where my hand had been. Rosemary for Remembrance.

'Another Opening of Another Show' played as he disappeared from view, to be burned into our memories.

I couldn't speak or cry as David drove me back to the station, the silence between us dead with sorrow and dislike. He dropped me off with a bare brushing of my cheek with his lips. As I was about to close the car door he said: 'Thought I might come down to see the show.'

I felt surprise through layers of cotton wool. 'When?'

'Some time. I'll ask Phyllida if she'd like to come. She could do with getting out of that house.'

Yes, I thought, *having been on her back for the last six weeks, she probably has bed sores.*

'I can't put her up at the flat. I've only one bed.'

'Ghastly theatrical digs?,' he said, indicating he was about to pull out into the traffic. 'We'll get rooms in an hotel.' Even when he was cheating on me under my nose, he wouldn't say 'a hotel'. Pedantic little shit. 'I'll give you a call,' he said as he drove away. He didn't wave or glance back.

On the train I was like a frozen computer screen, nothing but disconnection would get me moving again. So I slept. Sleep, balm of hurt minds…half dreams of Gabriel and half thoughts of the two shows we'd done in front of paying audiences. They'd wrapped me in a love that needed no reciprocation. After the first performance we had been stunned by their cheers and the standing ovation. Dan's glorious spoof of melodramatic excess was a triumph. Like an old-fashioned seaside postcard, they loved its glorious vulgarity. It was funny, nostalgic and as Broadway-slick as a Hovis loaf.

Kelvin opened the show in a Humphrey Bogart raincoat, chewing a matchstick. He took a huge handgun out of his pocket and shot into the air. A duck fell out of the flies and bounced across the stage – the audience relaxed into appreciative laughter.

'A duck – that's funny. My name's Duck. It's like a Hitchcock moment. A hommage. I like it.'

Dan, though he'd managed to stop Susan playing as if she was Vlad the Impaler doing a Judy Garland impression, decided there was no point in combating Lee's excesses. With a feathered chorus line and mauve spotlight, he brought the house down.

'You see,' Lee pontificated after the first preview, which was wall-to-wall Friends of Dorothy in everything from diamante thongs to leopard-print chiffon, 'Musical Theatre is a skill… It's a lifetime's work. I've dedicated years to my art. You don't pick it up doing telly.'

Nicely placed dig at me. KT changed the subject.

'Izzy's quiet. I don't trust him when he's quiet.'

'He's got his new door knobs. He's happy,' I said. 'Relax.'

Relax. Relax. Relax.

⸻

The word stuck like a faulty CD in my head until I woke up and realised it was my mobile ringing.

'Eleanor?'

'Yes.'

'It's Tizer here.'

The young union rep, Equity Dep. Twenty-one years old, first job, Scots lad from the rough end of Easterhouse. The local lads beat him up when they caught him tap-dancing in the back yard. Now a strapping six-footer, the red-headed prop forward wasn't about to be beaten up by anyone, though he was quivering timid of his new responsibilities.

'Izzy's told me I've got to call the company together at five-thirty.'

'I won't be back by then, Tizer. What's it about?'

'He told us…he said…he wants us to persuade Dan to walk off the show.'

All I could say was, 'What?'

'Dan's not here. He's in Edgware and I don't know what to do. Why would he want us to get rid of Dan? Did he do something wrong? The previews have been great, haven't they? I mean, full houses and cheering every night… Can you help me, Eleanor? I really need your help.'

The cotton wool stripped away as if in a high wind. I sat up. Help him? I was just David's stupid wife. Leading lady? I couldn't lead a peep of chickens across a road.

'Okay, Tizer. Phone Jonty and say, if the producer wants a company meeting, it's up to him as Izzy's representative on earth to call it. Then call KT…he'll back you up, then, well…at this late notice no one has to go. But get KT on board, he'll speak to Jonty if he plays up.'

'Right,' said Tizer, 'I'll do that.' Then his tone changed; he was the insecure first-timer again. 'Will this affect my chances in the West End? I mean, after this.'

'No. No, of course not.' I had no idea, but Izzy Duck was surely never going to be a big enough player to ruin even this neophyte's career, despite his threats. 'And don't worry, Tizer, this is just Izzy throwing his weight about. It'll be fine.' I hoped I sounded convincing. 'He'll be back complaining about the door knobs tomorrow.'

'Yeah. Right. Thanks, Eleanor. See you.'

I tried Dan's mobile but it knocked on to voicemail. Perhaps he'd been arrested for murdering an elderly Broadway producer. If he had, I'd have stood in a court of law and sworn it was self-defence.

At the theatre, the corridors were deserted, no one having water fights, singing or laughing. Just an eerie quiet. KT was waiting for me.

'Izzy's accountants were in last night and they said the show was all right for provincial audiences but it wouldn't hold up in London. They thought it was unsophisticated. God help us if his dry cleaner comes.' He lit a cigarette under the THIS IS A SMOKE FREE ENVIRONMENT notice. 'After curtain down there was a blood-bath. Izzy called a crisis production meeting. Dan refused to go…'

'Listen, pal, my accountant says you couldn't direct piss into the North Sea from the deck of the QE2. We gotta get this mess sorted out but I'm telling you, pal, I'm not sure you're the man for the job. I put in a call to Trevor Nunn, you know that?'

'I don't care if you phoned Mother Teresa,' Dan yelled back. 'This is a work in progress and an accountant knows as much about theatre as you know about Magna Carta.'

'Well, right now, she'd probably direct this show a damn sight better than you. You fucked up Viola's script and the show is a laughing stock.'

'On the contrary,' Dan replied quietly, 'I am trying to prevent it – and you – from becoming a laughing stock, but I think I may be too late, as your idiocy appears to be genetic. You seem determined to listen to anyone but those who know what they're talking about.' He turned his back on his producer and walked out of the theatre, leaving Izzy screaming after him.

'Get back here! I'm holding a production meeting to sort out your fuck-up and you do not walk away from me. Unless you want to walk away for good. Ya hear me?'

Dan was gone and Viola was crying in the corner.

'It was a nightmare, Nellie,' said KT, his veneer of jagged sophistication stripped away. 'We're just a bunch of bloody muppets, aren't we? Go there, come here, don't think and keep your mouth shut. I can't take much more of this crap.'

I tried to reassure both of us that, because Jonty had persuaded Izzy it was too late to call the company meeting, the genie was still in its bottle. Whatever damage had been done could be repaired.

'It's up to you, Nell,' said KT. 'You're the only one they'll both listen to.'

Flattering though this was, I didn't want the responsibility of peace-making or war-mongering. Me bringing peace to our little world? Didn't they also serve who hid behind the parapet?

The phone rang.

'Hi, Eleanor?'

'Izzy. How are you? I've just got back.'

There was a moment's heavy breathing, then, in hushed and reverent tones: 'Oh, right, yeah. I'm so sorry for your loss. Your grandmother, wasn't it?'

'No, Izzy, just a friend.' Too late I realised Jonty must have told him it was dear old granny so I'd get permission to go. The contract said we couldn't stray from the immediate proximity of the theatre lest we were caught up in a nuclear attack or pogrom and missed a show.

Izzy had more important things on his mind. 'Could you meet with me, pal? In the front of house bar.'

'Now?'

'Sure.'

It was half-past-six, I had to start getting ready at five to seven. There was a time limit. Thank God.

*　　　*　　　*

Izzy was sitting in a corner trying to look inconspicuous, despite being the only man of pensionable age sucking a foot-long cigar and wearing a baseball cap emblazoned 'USA'. He was bent over, head in hands, doing, as I soon found out, an Oscar-worthy performance of remorse. His large hair-filled ears seemed to droop and, had he had a tail, it would have been hanging limp within his spacious jeans.

I thought it best to seem ignorant of the previous night's unpleasantness and pulled up a chair opposite him. The bar staff seemed oblivious. The people sipping coffee on the other side of the room were unaware of the seismic shifts in our world. It was just a bit of temperament. Everything would be forgotten by curtain down.

'No Viola? Is she all right?'

'She's in the hotel. She's a little tired.'

Of life? Of you?

'Oh dear. I am sorry.'

Izzy was not a man to come to the point without a tour of every valley and peak of his opinions. I listened for ten minutes, then mentioned I had a show to do.

'Sure, pal. See, let me give you the bottom line, it's like this…'

KT had obviously misunderstood the situation. All Izzy had done was suggest some changes might be made and Dan had lost his temper, sworn, behaved like a crazy guy, and stormed out. What was Izzy to do? He'd shouted back, yes, in self-defence, but he was sorry.

'Can I tell you, pal? I spent my life getting through on bluster but, you know, I learned my lesson last night. I learned the lesson of a lifetime. I shouldn't shout. You Brits don't like shouting.'

'Yes,' I said, almost but not quite putting my hand on his. 'The British do tend to withdraw when faced with bullying tactics.'

He was all contrition. The little boy during his first confession. 'I'm not a bully, I swear, but you're right Eleanor. I'm real sorry. You gotta tell me what to do. How to handle things. What's best with Brits.'

How about throwing yourself under a train?

'You think I should talk to the kids? I want to talk to them. We don't need directors making trouble. Am I right?'

No. You're an idiot.

'Of course, Izzy, but, you see, actors are like horses…' *No more than dog meat if they're discarded.* 'You spook them and it takes a while for them to calm down. Leave well alone for a couple of days. It'll be fine. Just let us, and our director, Dan,' I added, looking away, 'get on with making the show as great as you want…' *Slight pause.* '…and deserve it to be.'

'Sure. I hear you, pal.'

Yes, Izzy – but you're not listening.

He sat forward, our knees almost touching. 'You know what I think? I think Dan's sick.'

Oh here it comes: psychologically damaged. Mentally fragile. Invalided out.

'It's been too much for him. You know he doesn't look after himself, doesn't eat properly, smokes too much. I've seen him drunk more than once. And you know?' He lowered his voice to a deaf man's whisper and raised his index finger to his head. 'It's getting to him. This is making him crazy.' By chance he tapped the A for America on his cap. I doubted he realised the irony. 'You think maybe someone else should take the show into town? I mean, I care about Dan, I don't want the guy having a breakdown.'

Kill off Dan with kindness, you poisonous toad? How sweet.

'I shouldn't worry about him, Izzy, he's tougher than he looks. Oh…' I looked at my watch extravagantly. 'Look at the time. I'm late for the half.' I stood up. 'And you will patch it up with him, won't you Izzy?' I looked down at him steadily. 'For the good of the show.'

Izzy oozed sincerity. 'Sure, whatever you say, Eleanor. Like I say, I'll be guided by you.'

'Promise? And no more fighting. All right?'

'Sure, Eleanor.'

'I have your word?'

'Sure.'

I had averted a small war. Wasn't I the hero? What would David have said?

Walking through the pass door, the first person I met was KT.

'Game on,' I said with a grin.

'Thank fuck for that,' he said. 'You is a goddess. Well done.'

Behind him, Karen was marking up a pile of music. She looked up and said: 'Did you know that's what we call you? The Goddess.'

I didn't ask who called me that. But I was sure if Lee and Susan did, they were thinking of that ugly piece with the arms.

After the show, growing in self-satisfaction and basking in the heat of yet another standing ovation, I was thinking more along the lines of Pallas Athene. I changed into my dressing-gown, poured some wine and joined Dan on my dressing-room sofa. He looked exhausted, grey with tiredness – Byronic to my infatuated eye.

'Ellie, I want you to try the "Leave me. I need to be alone with my urn" line while clearing everyone off the stage. Do it furious. Wave the jar about. Then you can start your number straight-away. Bang. At the moment, the way I directed it, you look like an embarrassed actress wearing a six-egg omlette.'

'Not a goddess…? Karen said the cast call me The Goddess.'

'Really? Mmm…I've never kissed a goddess,' he said, leaning close. 'Ever slept with one?'

'Not yet. But…' He put his hand on my breast, two fingers gently stroking the nipple. We sprang apart as KT marched in, hard on his brief knock on the door.

'You coming to the pub? Oh…you're not shagging, are you?'

'Not yet, KT.' I hoped it didn't show that my breasts were no longer in the cups of my bra. 'Look, I'm knackered, I think I'll go straight back to the flat. Two shows tomorrow and the voice is a bit tired.'

'Right. See you then. Nothing like a melba cocktail for a limp larynx.'

Dan looked blank.

'It's a blow job,' I said helpfully. 'Apparently Dame Nellie...never mind.'

'And Dan, don't you go leaving us to the mercy of Uncle Fester.'

'Fester?,' said Dan, now completely confused.

'Yeah, Fester and Gonzo. Izzy and Viola.'

Walking back to the flat, we paused at a little gazebo which was, surprisingly, uninhabited by teenagers snatching moments of secret sex. Dan took my hand and held it as we gazed out over the sea: two mature people recapturing the romance of their early days. Except these were our early days, possibly our only days, and it was far too cold for any sort of cocktail.

'How was Edgware?'

'I didn't go. I went to see to see Claudia. My wife.'

'Oh.'

'She wanted some money.'

'Oh.'

'So I went to the bank. All my direct debits have been cancelled. And I have an overdraft.'

'Why?'

'I haven't been paid.' He ran his fingers over the palm of my hand. I hoped he wasn't going to ask for a loan. 'So after last night's performance, and I don't mean the one on stage, I'm not feeling very generous towards our producer.'

'You know he tried to get the company to ask you to walk off the production.'

'Yes. And if I did I'd forfeit what he owes me. Maybe it's his idea of economy.'

I tried to reassure him by telling him about my conversation with Izzy, but left out the question mark he'd put over Dan's health.

'You'll stick with it though, won't you, Dan?'

He stood up and pulled me to him. 'For you, Eleanor?'

'No, for the money, you daft bugger.'

'You don't like romance, do you?'

'I'm not used to it.'

We broke apart and walked down the hill in silence. By the time we reached the bottom, the beauty of the night, thoughts of Gabriel, now a pile of cold ashes, David, the whole situation with Izzy and my confusion over Dan overwhelmed me.

I didn't like romance? Oh, I did, but it just hurt too much. Dan stopped and wiped away the tears. Another romantic gesture, ruined by my nose running and no hankie.

'Do you want to come in?,' I asked, sounding as if I'd prefer root canal work.

'No, you're tired –'

'No, I'm not, I –'

'Just for a drink then.'

'Yes. All right. Just for a drink.'

Two hours later we lay back wet with sweat. Dan, the gentle and considerate lover, had persevered until, taking pity on him, I made the expected noises and did the hooked trout impression quite convincingly, allowing him to come in a rictus of gratitude.

He fell asleep, murmuring my name.

I looked at his beautiful pale face and saw, as I had each time I closed my eyes that night, or felt his fingers, or tasted his tongue, Gabriel. Black-bat thoughts flitterered round my mind. What was I doing in bed with my director? What was I doing in this show? I'd had my chance, a moment of television notoriety, and that was it, the carousel of horses was full of new faces now. The rest of my life would be spent circling the country in dubious tours trading on a TV programme name not even recognised by audiences under fifty. And then, after a twilight of anecdotes in Denville Hall, a short obituary in The Stage. An almost-ran. A small talent promoted above its ability. A talent never fulfilled. A performer more than an actor.

How many paracetamol would it take to join Gabriel? But what right did I have to think about death when life had done nothing to offend? Yes, it had. The absence of unhappiness was not happiness. Life stretching ahead as a featureless landscape of mediocrity must be a form of death. Atrophy until it was too late to call upon muscles left too long unused. I longed for Dan to wake up and listen to my misery. Finally, disturbed by my restlessness, he woke at four a.m., but the time for talking was gone.

We padded into the hallway, pausing by the open front door for a last kiss. The lights went on like a PoW camp yard during an escape. The landlady stood at the top of the stairs, holding her walking stick aloft. I braced myself for a telling off: '*No gentlemen callers, Miss Eleanor. This is not a knocking shop.*' She scowled down at us, then her face broke into a wrinkled mass of smiles. We weren't young thieves come to kill her.

'Oh, have you been for a curry? Lovely. They do make me fart though.'

The three of us laughed until we ached. The dirty cobwebs of the night blew away. There were just two shows to go, then it would be Sunday. We'd hire a car, drive to Burgh Island for art-deco sex and Izzy amnesia. Cut off from the world when the tide came in. Just another eighteen hours.

I went back to bed and slept. I was still asleep when aliens started firing thermonuclear shells at the window.

'Nellie, you dozy cow. It's me, KT. Get the kettle on.'

Realising I wasn't about to be vaporised, I staggered to the door, bashing into various bits of furniture on the way, my knees skinned in a way they hadn't been since I was ten.

'N'em mind, love, think of the fun you'll have with the scabs.'

He swept past me into the kitchen where he unloaded a bag of croissants.

'I cannot begin to tell you what I had to do to get these in Plymouth. God, have you been further than the High Street? They've only just started walking upright some of them. Plymouth – so good they named it once.'

We loaded up a tray and went back into the main room. KT barely flicked a glance at the bed, but I knew he'd seen double-occupancy. I pulled the concertina doors closed, and we sat in the bay window drinking instant coffee, eating his largesse.

'You missed a good night in the pub,' KT said, picking flakes off his plate.

I nodded, not really listening, thinking about Dan and the possibility that maybe, when I finally found the courage to face David, I might just have something, or someone, to fall back on. The sun was shining, sparkling on the sea and making a Renoir study of even the ugliest passer-by. Happiness tasted like Nescafé with long-life milk.

'Here, you'd better be listening to this. Susan – that Hag of Hell – surpassed herself. She got pissed on Bacardi Breezers – cos she doesn't really drink, you know – and she said...' KT paused, '...that you were a manipulative witch who was trying to ruin the show by sleeping with Dan. See, because he's concentrating on servicing you, he's neglecting everyone else, to the detriment of the show. Actually, she didn't say detriment, because anything more than two syllables gives her a migraine. Anyway, Lee agreed with her, said he hadn't had any direction at all and, although you needed more help because you're not a musical artiste, it was a disgrace.'

The sun went in and the passers-by were common, loud-mouthed proles.

'What did you say to that?' I made a pathetic attempt at nonchalance.

'I didn't get a chance. Glenda threw a glass of red wine over her and called her a jealous cow in Spanish. God translated – cos his English is getting better, you know. I just added, very nice like, cos you know I'm very nice, that we all thought she, Susan, was sleeping with Dan, and at his age he couldn't possibly be shagging both of you.'

'What happened then?,' I asked, automatically, wishing I was an anchorite on Benbecula.

'Most of the kids were embarrassed, but Susan's been doing overtime with the South African ingénue and she got all hysterical and said we were all jealous of Susan's massive talent. Glenda said she certainly wasn't jealous of her massive arse.'

I wanted to go home. Not to the house with David, but to the place where the school bully didn't exist. What was her name? Sara Harrison. Hopefully now an abandoned failure with the continuing problem of excessive hair-growth.

'So what should I do? Should I talk to her?'

'No, love, that's what she wants, she wants you frightened of her.'

'I am. She's obsessed with me.'

'Do you think she fancies you?,' KT asked in mock-outrage.

'Don't be daft, she's a nymphomaniac, isn't she?'

'Well,' said KT, leaning towards me like Auntie Ida when she discovered who'd nicked her smalls off the line, 'she has been known to dabble. She has been known to do a bit of muff-diving.'

'She's a lesbian?' I yelped, not shocked at the condition but as if a member of the Ku Klux Klan could be black.

'No!,' said KT, shocked. 'She just helps out when they're busy.'

He paused to finish up a croissant.

'Listen,' he said, suddenly serious, his hands shaking. I'd noticed they shook more these days. Nerves? Drink? I was so full of my own problems I gave no more thought to his than to a reflection in a shop window. 'We need Dan completely back on board and in ego-stroking mode. Cos otherwise we'll have a civil war on our hands. There's bitchiness breaking out on all sides, and half the cast hate Glenda and God cos they're never on time and wouldn't know the word discipline in any language.'

'KT, they're not chorines. They think a good company member is God's cock.'

'Well, I've seen it, love, and I tell you, if that went through the Rotherhithe Tunnel, they'd have to repoint the brickwork. Anyway, a lot of the others are falling for Susan's 'I'm a professional, I just want to do my job' act. I tell you, she's taken in quite a few of the youngsters.'

I couldn't believe she was more intelligent than I'd thought. Life with David had taught me to weigh an IQ better than I could a pound of carrots.

'No, you're right, she is stupid,' said KT. 'Stupid but cunning. Watch her.'

KT and I had never been touchy-feely, but as he stood on the doorstep, preparing for the hike back up the hill, I reached out and hugged him. I had no idea how many friends I had in the company but I was sure of him. A foul-weather friend. All the rest are just acquaintances.

TWENTY

The matinée was a riot of demented pensioners with faulty hearing-aids, which whistled louder than a coachload of shepherds. They clapped and cheered and joined in, much to Susan's irritation. During her angst-ridden ballad, one old lady's whisper ricocheted round the stage:

'Blimey, she's got a belly on her, hasn't she? No chance of her starving to death.'

It cheered me up no end, especially as Susan looked as though she was sucking a lemon by the Act One finale. But then no one was looking at her. I was centre-stage. Spotlit. I didn't care that she hated me and the audience – and anyone else who didn't abase themselves before her.

A sense of my own exceptional worth overwhelmed me. My voice soared with the music:

Men of Venezuela,
My emotions are a zarzuela
A mescla of love and hate
But I long to lay myself upon your plate…

The audience roared, clapping along to the clave beat much as Izzy had done on the first day.

I flung my arms wide on the final note – and caught Susan a glancing blow on the ear. To avoid it, she pulled away and overbalanced on her famously weak ankles. They went from under her and she collapsed into a startled sitting position, legs wide open and arms outstretched. The lights went down on a flash flood of applause, cheers and laughter.

Had I lashed out? Was it deliberate? Was I threatened by her? By her talent?

These questions would be argued over for days. Whatever the answers, the result of my over-confidence was Susan behaving as if she'd been brought down by a rocket-propelled grenade.

Tizer and KT half-carried and half-dragged her into the stage-left wing. Gaffer Gusset cleared a chair and Susan was lowered onto it,

149

wincing bravely. Nelson couldn't have suffered more. Ruby called for ice and was handed a bag of frozen peas.

The crowd around her parted as I approached. I could see accusation in several eyes.

'Oh, Susan, I'm so sorry. Are you all right? Can I get you anything?'

The Award for Best Martyr in a Musical possibly?

Her ankle, in front of which I was now kneeling like some Biblical penitent, looked fine – no swelling and only red because Susan was gripping it as if her foot was about to drop off. She looked down at me. A cat staring at an impertinent mouse.

'It's okay, Eleanor,' she said faintly. 'Don't blame yourself.'

Blame myself? There'd have been more chance of me blaming myself for the fall of the Aztecs. Her face contorted in agony as Dan appeared. He didn't look at me as he put his arm around her.

'Sweetheart…how are you feeling? Can you go on for the second half?'

She bit her lip heroically, her head drooping onto his shoulder. 'I don't know. I really don't know. Oh…I think I'm going to pass out.'

Dan gathered her up in his arms; he didn't actually lift her – he couldn't without risking back surgery – but he did cuddle her.

Ruby was less tender: 'Stick your head between your knees,' he said, slapping the peas on her ankle. 'All right everyone, go and take your interval break, we'll let you know what's happening.'

The cast reluctantly drifted away, except for Susan's understudy, who was rooted to the spot, white with fear.

'I think I could get through it, with the book maybe. I could try,' she said quietly.

Susan flicked her a look only I saw; it was surprising the girl didn't vapourise. Ruby looked up from the stigmata.

'No, love, you can't, you haven't had any rehearsals. If Susan can't go on, we'll have to cancel.'

And that's exactly what she wants, I thought, *the power of life or death*. This would make her pivotal in a way her performance couldn't.

'Can you stand?,' Dan asked, pushing her hair from her face with exactly the tender gesture he'd used on me the night before. A streak of jealousy went through me so painful I almost yelped. But Susan's agony was the greater. She winced to her feet, or foot, leaning heavily but delicately on Dan, and they started up the stairs towards her dressing-room. I was abandoned with the peas. Ruby took them from me with barely disguised irritation.

'Stupid cow,' he said.

'Me or her?,' I asked.

'Either,' he said. 'I'd better phone Izzy. He'll go ballistic if we have to pull the show tonight. I'm going to have fun writing this one up for the show report. Hey…' he added, his thin good-looking face and pale black-lashed eyes impassive, '…Wasn't your fault. I saw it.' He rubbed his chin with a long, ringed finger. 'But personally, I'd have made sure she didn't get up.'

That cheered me. Ruby may not be in my camp, but he certainly wasn't in Susan's either.

Twenty minutes later, with the pensioners turning ugly, it was decided that we would – literally – limp through to the end. Susan performed heroically with huge effort, pain-killers and enough tears to fill a fish tank. After the show, KT was waiting for me outside my dressing-room.

'You all right, love? Wasn't your fault, she just slipped, if you'd decked her the silly bitch wouldn't be breathing. Come on, I'll buy you a coffee.'

'I'll see you over there, I'd better go up and grovel some more.'

I walked with him to the stage door and met Izzy and Viola running in. Ruby headed them off.

'Everything's fine, Izzy.'

'What's going on? You called the doctor?'

'Yes, Izzy.'

'She's gotta go on. I have the Schumachers in tonight. You know who they are?'

Major players in American television and film, the reclusive brothers had a fondness for bankrolling Broadway shows. This was the audition for transatlantic glory. Once Susan knew that, she'd be on her feet quicker than a newborn pot-bellied pig.

Viola came and stood rather too close to me, her dull eyes wide behind the windows of her glasses.

'Eleanor, how could you?'

'How could I what?'

'Hit Susan. That was a terrible thing to do.'

'Hold on,' I said, all indignant, 'I didn't hit her, who told you that?'

She reverted to her pained expression and vocal whimper. 'Susan called us.' Ah yes, Radio Free Plymouth herself. Viola's lumpy index finger pointed at me. Pity she'd missed the Salem Witch trials. 'She said you pushed her over.'

As I was lost for words, KT came to my rescue.

'She wasn't pushed, she's got weak ankles and she can't walk in those shoes, let alone dance. And before you blame the designer, she chose the shoes because Susan's got short legs and didn't want to look like a fat corgi in a skirt.'

'We'll see,' said Viola. 'Susan isn't a liar.'

That was the moment I realised Viola wasn't the mentally battered wife she worked so hard to create in our imaginations. She had looked at me like a rattlesnake about to strike.

'She's nasty. Really bloody nasty,' KT murmured, as we followed Izzy and Viola up to Susan's dressing-room. She was stretched out on a camp bed with Dan sitting beside her, stroking her forehead.

'You okay, kid?,' demanded Izzy. 'You can go on tonight, right?' KT and I didn't exist.

'Let's wait and see what the doctor says,' said Dan, standing up. He still hadn't looked at me. Had he decided I had walloped her too?

'Let me give you the bottom line, Dan. I got a lot riding on tonight's show. The Schumachers are in.'

Dan didn't look impressed. 'If the doctor says she can go on, she goes on. If not, we cancel. Simple as that.'

Susan, enjoying being the leading lady of her own production, in which I was sidelined to the position of character supporting-role, smiled bravely and assured Izzy and Viola she would be fine, she was just in shock and pain.

'Eleanor's not really to blame,' she whispered graciously. 'I mean, she pushed me, but I'm sure...no, I'm absolutely certain it wasn't deliberate. It's not her fault, she's not a trained dancer. She was just a bit off her marks, too far stage-left.'

This was a masterclass in lying brought to the edge of truth.

'You're so generous, Susan, we love you,' said Viola, taking her hand and looking at me with even more malice than she'd displayed downstairs.

KT put his hand on the small of my back in silent support. I was pathetically grateful, though I probably looked no more than truculent, unwilling to take responsibility for the perceived grossness of my actions – for my jealousy of this actress who had threatened my position. I had no doubt there were mobiles ringing all over the West End, hot with tales of my monstrous ego and cruelty: *Well, what do you expect from a washed up telly star?*

The doctor arrived as Izzy was repeating that Susan *was* the show and we couldn't perform without her. 'She could sit on stage while her understudy mimes.'

Dan was having none of it. 'No, Izzy. No miming.'

'A wheelchair! Yeah! Great, that's it! Where's it say in the script she's not paraplegic?'

Dan just said no. As difficult to do to Izzy as to drugs. Frankly, if anyone had produced crystal meth cut with cholera at that moment I'd have taken it. Izzy was getting more and more psychotic, while Viola sat in the corner of the small room, tense with anger, whether towards me or Dan, or both, I couldn't tell.

The doctor arrived and cut through the poisonous atmosphere, unaware of or unimpressed by Susan's importance to the future of British theatre. He diagnosed the possibility of that curse of English football – a fractured metatarsal.

'She'll have to have an X-ray. As soon as possible.'

By now I was as invisible and unsavoury as a long-suppressed fart.

'Get an ambulance right away,' ordered Izzy, to the doctor's amusement.

'I think the young lady would be better off in a taxi.'

'Okay, Doc, whatever you say. But she'll be strapped up and on stage by seven-thirty tonight – right?'

Susan hobbled downstairs leaning on Dan, who was being bombarded with instructions by Izzy. Gaffer Gusset, enjoying a low-fat yoghurt and a few stolen moments with Jonty, was summoned from the crew room. Good-natured girl that she was, she climbed into the taxi with the abuse victim and we watched the car go in silence. Viola subsided against the wall by the stage door.

'Ohmygod, ohmygod, this is so terrible. Ohmygod.'

'Viola, shut up,' said Izzy, proving he wasn't as detached from reality as we thought. 'Dan, we gotta have a meeting.'

'I don't think so, Izzy. I need a break, there's nothing we can do until we hear from the hospital. The understudy can't go on –'

Izzy cut him off: 'I say who goes on. It's not up for question, we do the show tonight –'

He was talking to himself. Dan had turned and walked unhurriedly back through the stage door. Izzy followed furiously but found he didn't have his swipe card and that Arthur was on the phone with his back turned.

Izzy started rattling the door, trying to pull it open. He shook himself back and forth against the unmoving slab of wood separating him from the object of his fury. Then the shaking stopped connecting with the door and retreated within him. His knees buckled as he fell…

Viola screamed his name, frightened and angry. KT and I rushed to catch him under the elbows. Viola beat us off, determined to hold her husband up, but she was no match for his weight, and he dropped to the floor, gasping for breath.

'It's his heart,' she said dramatically, holding him in a grotesque pietà. 'He has pills.'

KT started going through Izzy's pockets and found a small silver box.

'That's it. That's it. Put one under his tongue.'

KT was now holding Izzy upright and passed the box to me. I took out a tiny white pill and, pushing aside disgust at his slack mouth and clammy skin, forced one past his invisible teeth. I felt his saliva on my fingers. Whether the pill went under his tongue or not I couldn't tell, nor was I prepared to delve deeper past those flopping lips.

It was a matter of moments before his eyes opened and his breathing settled down. He looked frail, confused and frightened. I wanted to feel pity for him, but then I thought, sod it. Carefully we pulled him to his feet. His cigar had been crushed and lay in dirty brown flakes around us. He looked pathetic, propped up by his fearful wife, whose eyes were now more mammal than reptile – a cornered rat, unwilling to accept help but willing to bite.

'Thank you. Now leave us alone please.'

'But Viola, he's not well, let's help you. We'll get the doctor back,' I said, my hand hovering close to Izzy's shoulder. KT stood ready to catch him too.

'I'm fine, pal,' said Izzy, like a brave but doomed character in a bad western. 'Just fine.'

'Mr Duck?' The glass window of the stage doorman's cubbyhole was pushed back, and Albert, oblivious to the drama that had just been acted out, leaned out. 'Your guests – the Schumachers is it? – are front of house. Michael and Ralph, is it?'

Lazarus couldn't have recovered more quickly. Izzy set off for the foyer so fast Viola almost overbalanced. My hand went out instinctively to save her.

'Thank you, Eleanor.' She paused and looked at me with what, I assumed, was intended to be burning sincerity. 'You know, maybe you didn't mean to hit Susan… Thank you for your help. He'll be fine.'

I resented her grudging forgiveness and really didn't care whether he lived or died. Leaving KT in the bar with a campari and grapefruit juice, my gratitude and a bag of cashew nuts, I made my way to the company office to see Dan, who obviously thought I was Myra Hindley's mother.

'Dan? It's me, Eleanor.'

There was a pause.

'Come in.'

He sat at his desk, his profile to me.

'Dan, I didn't hit her. I didn't push her over. Honestly. It was an accident.' Oh, for God's sake, why did it matter? Why did he matter? Just walk out. Tell him to stuff the job. And the sex.

He still wouldn't look at me.

'I know you didn't.' He stopped. The silence hurt, so I turned to go, my defiance wasted on the back of his head. 'I did sleep with her,' he said, without expression.

'Oh.'

Surely there was supposed to be some outrage on my part. Some expression of betrayal, misery, an accusation of mendacity perhaps. Nothing came. David had used up my stock of unexpressed anger and humiliation. I just stepped into the corridor and closed the door quietly behind me. The faces of the audience came back to me. I'd given them a good time, tomorrow someone else would do the same. What was the difference?

The dull ache of misery was my only companion as I sat in the dressing-room cleaning my make-up brushes. I felt as dirty and ill-used as they were. Why not just run away? Because the gossip that would follow would be even worse. If it's true that there's always someone glad when you die, then there's a legion to crow when you fall. Even if they don't know you. *I never liked her... I can't stand her acting... She's just been lucky...*

I stripped off all my clothes and stood under the hot rushing shower, wishing it could wash away the contamination of accusation and failure.

The soap was a bar of pink delight which foamed with lather, squeezing through my fingers in chains of bubbles. I covered every inch of skin with them. Great gobbets of soapy froth slipped from my shoulders onto my breasts, then dripped onto my feet. My ears crackled with bursting bubbles. My armpits and between my legs were thick with slippery suds when the water slowed to a dribble.

I waggled the hose to the shower head.

I turned the knob to OFF then ON.

I turned the knob round and round.

The water, offended by my aggression, stopped completely but for a forlorn drip.

Then the lights went out.

The moment the power failed I remembered I had no towel.

Hated by my colleagues, betrayed by my husband, despised by my son, discarded by my director in a part I couldn't do, I was standing in pitch blackness, under a dry shower head with a fanny full of soap and no towel. As a metaphor for the nadir of my life, it couldn't have been bettered.

Groping along the wall, I found, two feet above my head, the bottom of the curtain that covered the gun-slits that served as windows. I pulled. Hard. It ripped, leaving me with a handful of threads that wouldn't have dried an anorexic hamster.

Then I remembered the kettle. It was full. The first luck I'd had for several years.

Back in the shower stall, I poured it over myself, dripped back to the dressing table and sat down.

I still had a fanny full of soap.

Huddling in the dark with my dressing-gown round me, questions I should have asked Dan lined up in my mind like a post office queue the week before Christmas.

I shouldn't have walked away, I should have stayed and discussed the situation, sensibly. I mean, had it just been the once? Well, that wouldn't matter, would it, if it was before me? He was trying to be honest, wasn't he? Had he used any protection with her, though? What cross-contamination had I been exposed to? Susan was well known for bolstering her shaky self-image with lavish gifts of sex. How many times had she assured us of the popularity of her generous figure? Generous to the point of giving it away after anything from dinner at the Caprice to a bag of chips behind the bus shelter.

Was I just an exercise in control for Dan? Was it just what he did with his leading ladies, to make them more malleable to his direction? Yes, I knew it was, and I got a thrill from being on stage knowing he was watching me. I performed for him. Stupid, stupid woman. Only existing in the eyes of a man.

What would I do tonight if Susan allowed the show to go on? And what if I went to talk to Dan? To talk. Two words guaranteed to get any man running faster than a herd of lemmings over Beachy Head. What could he say anyway?

But if he didn't want to discuss it, why had he mentioned it? To undermine my confidence? To make me chase his approval all the more? Or because her injury had made him realise her worth?

The thoughts went round inside my head like a sinkful of scummy water fighting to get down a blocked drain.

<hr/>

It was almost seven o'clock when the power came back on and Ruby's bored tones started the evening's announcements.

'Ladies and gentlemen of the company, The Lord said, Let there be light, and there was light, then he created Andrew Lloyd Webber and the rest is history… Right, Susan is on her way back to the theatre so the show will go up thirty minutes late, that is, curtain up at eight p.m. Hopefully the fifty p we put in the meter will last till then. Could we have everyone involved in the Act One finale and the finale to the stage please.'

I rubbed myself down with tissues and, still clammy, dressed. The woman who looked back from the mirror was glamorous, assured and soignée, but beneath the silk and perfume was an intolerable amount of itching, sticking and chafing. Thrush? More like a flock of Canada geese. Walking like a foot-bound geisha I tottered into the wings. Dan stood at the front of the stage.

'Is everyone here?'

How could he not notice my absence?

'Just waiting for Eleanor,' said Ruby, adjusting his head set. Did I imagine the company tutted? Not Lee: he didn't just tut, he cast his eyes extravagantly to the flies and stropped his hand onto his hip.

'I'm here,' I said, hurriedly coming into the light, clutching my dressing-gown across me as if its thin material could defend me.

Dan nodded at me with a tight, impersonal smile. 'Due to the leading lady beating up the soubrette during the matinée –'

Everyone laughed. Including me. What else was I going to do? Burst into tears and run out into the dual carriageway? That's what David's wife would have done, but this wasn't the time for an in-depth character comparison.

'– We have to restage a couple of bits Susan won't be able to do.'

By the end of the session, the only eye contact I'd had with members of the cast was full of over-expressed sympathy. Those who avoided looking at me had either judged me guilty or were waiting to see to whom history, and the popular vote, would give righteousness.

'Thanks everyone,' called Dan as he came on stage.

The cast opened into a semi-circle round him, the dancers stretching as they listened.

'Now, you probably know the Schumachers are in tonight.'

Lee simpered and nodded an exaggerated '*I told you so*' to anyone who was watching. Everyone else looked anxious or ambitious, depending on their place in the world.

'So, if Eleanor will promise to save her right hook for the welterweight title fight, we should give them an evening to remember and hopefully…well, we'll see, eh? If we don't make it to Broadway, maybe they'll book Eleanor for Madison Square Gardens. Have a good one everyone.'

All the awkward shame I'd been inflicting on myself evaporated in the heat of anger. How dare Dan make me a laughing stock? I went after him, jumping off the stage to the undisguised amusement of Lee's little clique, but I didn't care. I strode up the stalls to where Dan was standing talking to the sound operator.

'What the hell was that all about? I feel bad enough without you doing a stand-up routine on it. I really don't appreciate being belittled in front of the company.'

Dan was having nothing of my fury. He smiled, eyebrows lifted in mock-surprise. 'I was joking to relax the kids. Surely they pay you enough on this show to take some of the weight.'

What had I done to deserve this? This was a Dan I wouldn't have kissed, let alone slept with.

'I think you're...rotten,' I said, slowly and quietly, just as it had been said to me as a child. I had no idea if it would have the same devastating effect on Dan as it had on a seven year-old, but it gave me solace to find some higher moral ground to cling to without ranting or swearing. 'Absolutely rotten, and I don't really want to talk to you.'

Did I see hurt in his blue glass eyes? Not a chance. 'I don't remember opening the conversation.'

I raged back to the dressing-room with an expression of such ferocity even KT stepped back as I passed.

TWENTY-ONE

Cleopatra was fêted into the theatre on her barge at the five minute call. Shrieks of relief and welcome echoed round the corridors. The show would go on, albeit another ten minutes late.

There was a knock at my door. Thinking the dresser had forgotten something, I called, 'Come in.'

I couldn't see the door from the dressing-table so it wasn't until Dan stood behind me that I realised who it was. He couldn't have looked more different from the callous wise-cracker of earlier on.

'I said I don't want to talk to you.' I looked at him through the mirror, wishing I had the excuse of going to the stage. He was subdued and apologetic.

'Eleanor, I know this isn't the moment to say this but…I want you to have a good show and I'm sorry for the way I've treated you. Today. And…well, you know what I'm saying.'

Let it go or stretch him?

'No, Dan, I don't. Please explain. Why am I Cruella de Vil? It was an accident, all right? And as for the other thing…well, I don't think much of your taste but you do what you do.'

He stood behind me, resting his hands on my shoulders. I could see those inquisitive fingers between Susan's cellulite thighs.

'Eleanor, please. I'm sorry. Let me in. Please.'

'Why should I…? All right,' I said, turning round and disengaging his proprietorial grip, 'what the hell was that all about? That's bollocks about making the company relax at my expense. And as for your little admission upstairs? What are you trying to do to me?'

'I thought…'

'No, Dan, you didn't think.'

'Sorry. I'm…sorry.'

It was his turn to look hurt and bewildered. I carried on touching up my make-up. He didn't say anything for what felt like minutes, but took his tobacco out and started rolling a cigarette.

'There's no smoking in here,' I said.

'I know.' Another long pause. Then, still concentrating on his roll-up: 'I needed you to hate me for something stupid because when you…if you…'

He breathed out and started again.

'She…Susan…said…she told me she was pregnant.'

My eyebrow pencil hovered in mid-air.

'And that it's mine. I didn't want you to hear it from anyone else.'

I didn't know how to begin saying what I wanted to say. The words came so fast I stopped them and started to laugh, surprise and disbelief fighting for first place.

'Dan,' I said when I was sure I was in control and that he was listening to me, 'she can't be pregnant. Apart from a string of abortions in Fame, Kiss Me Kate, Guys and Dolls and Salad Days, she had an ectopic on Cabaret in Derby about four years ago. She nearly died – they took her fallopian tubes and her ovaries out. KT was playing the MC, ask him, he knows all about it. Christ, get her pissed and you'll hear the whole sorry story. She's been playing the sympathy card ever since. You've only got to show her a baby photo and she's off. Ask KT,' I repeated, as though this was incontrovertible evidence of her lie.

But even as I spoke I realised the Derby story could be the lie, calculated to keep her in the sympathetic bosom of any company. Dan looked as if he'd been slapped with the Complete Works of Shakespeare.

'Are you sure?'

'Certain,' I said, almost so. 'Yes. I'm sure I'm right.'

'Why would she say she was pregnant if it wasn't true?' He sat in the chair next to me, more bewildered than a man of his age and experience had a right to be.

'Oh, come on Dan, why do you think? Did she tell you after she'd seen us in the flat the other night?'

He thought for a minute then said, 'Yes.'

'Well, there you are then. Jealousy.' I looked at him dispassionately, uncluttered by my infatuation. 'When did you sleep with her? Before or during…' – I paused trying to find the word – '…us?'

'Before,' he said quickly. 'The night she came to the flat.' So he had lied to me. 'And once after.'

'You use condoms with me.' I tried to sound light but it came out as an accusation.

'Miss Woodwarde, this is your call please, Miss Woodwarde to the stage immediately please.'

The DSM's voice was hushed but urgent. I had about six lines to get from the dressing-room to the stage for my entrance. I ran, leaving Dan sitting staring into the mirror.

Susan was stretched out across two chairs in the stage-right wing, her extravagantly bandaged leg on Lee's lap. As I hurtled into position, Lee hissed. I ignored him. Susan joined in. Thank God I couldn't hear whatever viciousness they were throwing at me. Lee tried again; I heard him this time.

'Your skirt's tucked in your knickers.'

My look of utter disdain dissolved into embarrassed gratitude. The gauze went out and I was on:

'Bring me a gin, a line of cocaine and a pretty young boy. I'm having a night in.'

My opening line got a gratifyingly solid laugh. All right, so Dan had shagged the company bike, but that was before me and, well, every good meal included a starter.

Yes, but the second time? A sweet you can eat between meals?

The reality was that without Dan everything was ashes. I wasn't strong enough, even with KT, to face life alone.

I kept my gestures to a minimum in the Act One finale and even got a few smiles as I walked off stage. Life was not so bad. Six hundred strangers the other side of the curtain adored me and I'd been to bed with Dan because I wanted to. He didn't owe me anything. End of story.

KT, attracted by the sound of my singing 'Valencia, stick your head between your knees and whistle up your Barcelona' at the top of my voice, came into the dressing-room.

'What you so happy about?,' he asked, helping himself to a Strepsil.

'You remember when you were in Derby? And Susan got pregnant.'

'Oh yes,' he said, adding another layer of mascara to his already over-burdened lashes. 'There hasn't been such a fuss since Bethlehem.'

'And you said she'd had her ovaries out?'

'That's right.'

'You're sure it was both of them, aren't you? And her tubes.'

He paused in his brushing. 'Why?'

'Well – and you're not to breathe a word, right?'

'I swear on my Armani clutch bag,' he said, crossing himself with the mascara wand.

'She reckons she's pregnant again.'

I expected him to fall about laughing. He didn't. 'I know more about the Moscow metro system than women's giblets, but I'm sure she said she'd had both out…or was it just the one? How many have you got?'

'Two. One each side. Like balls.'

KT thought again. 'No, I tell you what, I remember now, she did have them both out cos the other one had blown up like a mango – it was a cyst. That was it, ovarian cyst.'

'Excellent,' I said, but he still looked pensive. 'What's the matter?'

'Well…' He dragged the word round Swansea Valley. 'She had a millionaire boyfriend at the time who'd gone to Spain to pick up a yacht and she couldn't get out of the show to go with him. The pregnancy happened a couple of days later and, if I remember, we didn't know what hospital she was in, we just got messages from her mother.' He paused. 'So I don't know if it was true or just a crock of shit.'

'You mean she could be pregnant?'

'I remember she had a bit of a tan when she came back.' The tannoy interrupted us with the sound of raised voices from the auditorium. 'What's that?'

Puzzled and slightly worried, we made our way to the pass door and opened it a crack. With what was happening, we could have thrown it open and sung the Hallelujah chorus – nobody would have noticed.

Members of the audience were standing rooted to the spot as Izzy yelled at Dan, who was sitting in the centre of the stalls with the design team.

'Listen to me! Ya listening? Act One is crap. You hear me? Crap. You made crap here, Dan. Look at these people, look at them, you gave them crap.' He banged his hand on a seat back. 'And I'm warning you – you hear this everyone?' He swept the cigar around the circle of shocked faces surrounding them. 'I'm putting this guy on warning, if he doesn't sort out this mess he's out of a job.'

'Are you threatening me, Izzy?,' said Dan quietly.

'Izzy, Izzy, listen to me.' Viola was pulling on the sleeve of her husband's jacket. 'The Schumachers –' This was the cue Izzy had been waiting for. The magic name lit his blue touch-paper.

'Yeah, the Schumachers... You call yourself a director? I coulda directed this better. My dog coulda directed this better. This is what you been doing to my show? Shutting me outside, poisoning my wife against me? And now, the biggest producers on Broadway are here and you made me look like a schmuck. Well, let me tell you, mister, you blew it. This was your chance at the big time, your one go at getting out of the Styx and you blew it. You hear me? Those guys didn't laugh once. I watched them. They didn't think your kind of crap was funny. You got that? They sat there like undertakers looking at your show for kids. That's what you made Viola's great musical, a show for kids!'

He was shoving Dan in the chest. I expected him to spring up, fight back, react in some way, but he just sat there, as shocked and appalled as the audience members around them. Morag, Flossie and Karen were looking at the floor, anywhere but at this emasculation. Viola was yelling now, as loudly as her husband.

'Izzy, stop. Just stop, you hear me? Come away. You just come away now.'

Whether he was listening to her or had finished all he had to say, we couldn't tell, but he turned away and slammed through the auditorium doors into the foyer, followed by Viola running on her flat feet behind him.

There was absolute silence.

Then a young man in jeans and a carefully ironed T-shirt said:

'I think it's a great show. Really funny. That's just American bullshit.'

There was a pause, then the remaining audience members clapped. It sounded as refreshing as the applause for a well-placed four at Lord's. We closed the pass door and stood in the dark.

The producer had just bawled out the director in front of a theatre full of people. This was the equivalent of the Prime Minister being called a pillock by the President of the USA in front of the House of Commons. The PM might be a pillock – but he's our pillock.

By the time we got backstage, my attempted assassination of Susan had been forgotten in favour of this new scandal. The whole company and the band were milling about, repeating and discussing the row that had been broadcast throughout the theatre by the show relay and Lee, who'd embroidered the facts into a positive Bayeux Tapestry of outrage.

All but Susan were loudly condemning Izzy; even Lee was spitting feathers, as ever disloyal to whichever back was turned. Susan sat Sphinx-like on her throne, unwilling to speak ill of anyone, 'until,' she said with largely marked prudery, 'we have all the facts'.

We lined up for the second act in silence, ready for the same from the audience. But they yelled their approval as if to prove Izzy wrong. In the centre of their enthusiasm sat the brothers Schumacher, clearly visible from the stage, applauding and very nearly smiling. Maybe our accents were more comprehensible, maybe our sheer unpolished joy won them over. More likely Act Two was better. Who knew?

By the side exit, Izzy watched them like a prison warder and us like the father of the prodigal son. At the curtain call, the standing ovation spread from the stalls to the circle, engulfing Izzy and the Schmachers. All we could see from the stage was a sea of happiness.

'Well, you can't argue with that,' said KT, as we ran off stage back to the pass door.

Izzy, unable to control himself, was pushing past a family of five struggling to collect their belongings to get to Dan. We couldn't hear what they were saying over the play-out music but Izzy thrust his hand out towards his director. It wasn't taken. Again he offered his hand. Dan stood up and slowly walked away. Izzy's voice rose to audibility and beyond as the music abruptly finished.

'Dan, Act Two was great, shake my hand. I want you to shake my hand. Come back here and shake my hand.'

Dan didn't turn round, but continued to make his way to the foyer doors. 'No, Izzy. Not at the moment. You may have decided everything's fine, but I'm going to need a little more time.'

'Okay, pal,' yelled Izzy. 'What d'you want? Let's forget it, let's just shake hands. I get carried away.'

'I wish you would,' muttered KT.

'Dan, this show means the world to me, it's like my child, I was just defending my child.'

At this Dan paused. 'And I'm not a child abuser, Izzy.'

Triumphant now, because he'd made Dan turn and face him, Izzy assumed he'd won. He walked towards him with a swagger of ownership. 'I know that, Dan, sure I know that. We care, that's what's so special about us, Dan. Here, shake my hand.'

The pause wasn't dramatic, just a tired sigh from Dan. 'No,' he said, and left.

The Schumachers watched Izzy's performance with no more animation than they'd watched the show. Even to them, Izzy's unpredictability had become so predictable it was boring. After the briefest of words with Izzy, who became Uriah Heap in their presence, they made their regal exit, nodding. Waving. Inscrutable.

TWENTY-TWO

'I'm exhausted,' I said to KT. 'I just want to get on the outside of a bottle of wine and a pot noodle, and as far as I'm concerned, Izzy, Dan and David can all bugger off.'

'I'll join you if we can have creme eggs for afters.'

'You're on.'

We were leaving through the stage door when Flossie, his face contorted, ran past, stopped, turned, and gasped: 'Izzy's sacked Dan. He's sacked him. Dan's over the pub, you've got to come. We've got to sort it out.'

The words stumbled over each other and Flossie didn't wait to answer our questions.

'Oh, for goodness' sake,' said KT. 'Not more bloody grandstanding.'

We didn't hurry to the pub but sat on the wall and shared a bar of slightly hairy fruit-and-nut chocolate, which KT found in the bottom of his bag.

Did the Schumachers throw the toys out of the pram? No. They even said well done to the usherettes before getting into their blacked-out limousine. KT and I agreed, this was just more foolishness from our megalomaniac producer.

It was a romantic night – clear and frosty, filled with the distant sounds of people enjoying themselves. The sky was loaded with stars and I was sitting on a wall in Plymouth eating chocolate with a homosexual. Life didn't get much better. Finally, reluctantly, we wandered over to the pub.

A wave of noise crashed over us as we opened the door. Saturday night and the place was jumping. It was one of those vast halls of drink created for under-25s intent on alcohol poisoning. Upstairs, the company was scattered about watching Dan, Viola, Morag and Flossie, who were sitting at a table on the balcony. The women were talking animatedly, but Dan just sat holding his drink and staring at nothing but his own thoughts.

'You'd better go and find out what's going on,' said KT. 'I'll bring you a drink.'

I approached cautiously, neck bent as I'd seen wolves do when approaching an alien pack. Viola was speaking.

'Dan, I won't let you go. You can't.' Her eyes were moist and large with pleading as she twisted to see into his impassive face.

'What's happened?,' I asked.

Dan didn't speak, he seemed bewildered.

'That wee gobshite – sorry Viola – has only sacked Dan.' Morag's red-slash mouth was straight and tight with disgust. 'Does the wee nyaff no realise what Dan's done for this show? Without him there'd be no bloody show. Ungrateful scumbag.'

Betrayal, mendacity, adultery all wilted into insignificance.

'Dan,' I said. 'If you go I go. If you're off the show, I walk.'

That woke him up. 'You can't Eleanor, you've got a responsibility to the youngsters.'

'Aye, he's right,' said Morag. 'Look at them, they're shittin' hedgehogs. Most of them it's their first job. Ye cannae make it their last.'

Dan nodded. 'You've got to keep the whole thing together. You're company leader.' I had been catapulted from Medusa to Joan of Arc. Even Viola was pleading with me.

'Eleanor, please, you gotta tell Dan he has to come back.'

Dan was adamant. 'No, Viola. Izzy sacked me, he insulted me in front of a theatre full of people then demanded I shake hands with him, and because I wouldn't, he sacked me. I don't want to work with him. I can't work with him.'

Despite my new role as arbitrator, I couldn't help noticing the hollow shadows under his cheek bones and the tired beauty of his eyes. Then I realised what he'd said.

'Hold on… He sacked you because you wouldn't shake hands. You're joking.'

'D'ye see anyone laughing?,' said Morag.

'It's true… He sacked me because I wouldn't shake hands.'

It took a moment to sink in. 'Where is he now?,' I asked, with some vague idea of going to reason with him.

Viola was dismissive. 'He went back to the hotel.'

Members of the company were closing in around us, their young faces reflecting the fear they felt. I glanced round and noticed a few absences, the minty Scots queen who'd teamed up with Lee, the deaf actor and a few others – fence-sitters and Dan's enemies. And Susan. Hell hath no fury like an actress in the number eight dressing-room. Her non-appearance wasn't simply because of her foot.

Glenda perched on the arm of Dan's chair and put her hand on his back. At any other time, Dan would have purred with pleasure.

'All right,' I said. 'You just tried to blackmail me with my responsibility to the cast, what about yours? Viola is asking you back, we all want you to go on and you're saying no. Why?'

'Because I cannot work with Izzy. I won't work with him. Simple as that. It'd be easier working with a bag of cats.' Dan took a breath, pursed his lips and went on. 'You have no idea what he's been like in production meetings, accusing Jonty of not providing budgets, Morag of trying to rip him off, Flossie of being an amateur, and me of being the greatest genius the British theatre has ever produced one minute, and a jackass the next – it goes on and on. I'm sorry. I've had enough. He sacked me and I'm staying sacked.'

There was a part of me, a big part, that just wanted to agree with him and allow the show to disintegrate. I could go back to David, pretend this had all been a pre-perimenopausal last fling, pretend I knew nothing about his adulterous romps with the cover girl for Exchange and Mart 1976. I could abort the rebirth of my independence and allow myself to sink into the shadowy age of female invisibility, where all that's of interest is in the past. I could embrace neglected muscles, spreading stomach and the dismissal of my dreams. Settle for telling a dwindling audience of what I should have had, the chances that could have been, the parts that would have been mine. A twilight of ifs and buts. In Chile there were the Disappeared, in Equity there were the Disappointed.

Morag gripped my arm. My pasty ambivalence contrasted unfavourably with her blazing loyalty.

'Eleanor, Dan's put everything he has into this, we all have. You've got to talk to him.'

I had no choice.

'All right…' I wished my brain would provide some flash of inspiration. Nothing came. I felt my way cautiously through the only thought that came to me. 'Dan, if Viola could keep Izzy locked in an underground dungeon until press night in London then, as far as I can see, you'd have no reason not to come back.' Not exactly the delicate

Japanese brush-stroke of diplomacy, but he didn't argue. I went on carefully. 'If Viola can absolutely guarantee, and I mean absolutely, that he won't be allowed to interfere in any way with your work – or the show itself – you have no argument, you have to come back for all of us.'

He didn't say anything but held his drink in both hands as if it were a crystal ball.

'Or is it your ego stopping you? You want me to be humble and serve the greater good, but you're not prepared to yourself?'

Inspiration out of desperation had pricked Dan's self-awareness. He looked at me, hurt – by the question or the answer, I didn't know. I turned back to Viola.

'Can you do that? Can you keep Izzy away for his own good and the good of your show?'

'Now's your chance to find out. Izzy's just walked in,' Morag said, leaning over the balcony rail.

Izzy was lost among the tight press of rowdy drinkers who had no respect for a Broadway Producer. Viola ran down to rescue him, then, hanging onto his arm, she guided him up towards us.

His cigar, pushed into his cheek, pulled his slack mouth tight. He was sweating under his baseball cap but wouldn't remove it to reveal his wispy liver-spotted skull. She held him back at the top of the stairs, talking earnestly to him, voice raised over the noise from below. He tilted his head towards her, trying to hear through his deafness while his eyes shifted round quickly, taking in who was there, calculating the strength of his enemies. In Izzy's mind, enemies were everywhere.

Morag and I moved towards them, intending to welcome him and smooth the way for a rapprochement. Izzy swung round to face us like a belligerent bull. At that moment the lights went on and the music cut out. The closing of the pub provided a melodramatic backdrop to Izzy's unfolding tragedy.

'You want I should walk away from my own show?' He spat his accusation at us, then turned back to Viola, unable to comprehend the enormity of her treachery. 'You, my own wife? You? You're siding with Dan?'

Viola was truculent and adamant. 'Yes I am, Izzy. You can't sack him. I believe in what he's doing. We all do.' She looked round at us; surely for the first time in her life dozens of eyes were watching her with admiration and respect. Intoxicated by liberation, she rushed on. 'Dan is right, Izzy, and you are wrong. Absolutely wrong. Now, will you let Dan and me get on without any more interference?'

'Viola, I gotta tell you, you're getting crazy over this guy. I don't know what you two a been doin' but just remember you're my wife.' We were slack-jawed with horror, fascination and astonishment.

'No, Izzy, I'm co-producer and if you don't stand down I'm going to sack you, I will sack you and take over myself. You hear me?'

He waved his cigar sharply to dismiss her. That was it: she drew herself up, a column of flaming indignation.

'You're fired, Izzy. You hear me? I'm firing you.' She was flying now, her collar turned up round her straining neck, her hands determinedly in her trouser pockets. Another Viola facing up to an Orsino become a foolish Lear.

Someone, KT perhaps, started to applaud. We followed him, whooping and clapping, spurring her to greater heights of bravery against her apparently defeated husband.

Izzy slumped against the wrought iron balcony railing, shrunken and tragically old. 'I'm gonna kill myself, Viola. You left me with no choice.' He paused dramatically. 'I'm gonna kill myself.'

And with those words still dripping off the beer-sodden tables and into the beer-sodden actors, he turned and made his exit.

'He's so full of shit,' said Morag decisively. 'Come on, let's go over the Mexican.'

We gathered our bags, settling like a herd of ruminants forgetting upset in favour of the comforts of grazing.

Dan accepted the homage of the young, recently insecure dancers, then went over to Viola, who had deflated and was now riven with self-doubt. He enveloped her in a hug I would have been jealous of had it been anyone else. Gently he rocked her, her face against his chest. I could smell what she smelled, feel on the skin of my face the cotton of his shirt and hear the slow thump of his heart. He kissed the top of her head, then moved her so as to present her to the room.

'Hey, everyone, Viola's coming over the Mexican for a drink, I'm buying.'

I don't know if the cheers were for his largesse or for our new producer, but I heard the words 'Santa Viola' being called not entirely in jest. I had been The Goddess and now we had a saint. Perhaps she'd be more worthy of her title than I was of mine. She was borne out of the pub on a wave of enthusiasm, protected, like a film star, by her attentive director.

KT and I trailed after them. 'Reckon he's topped himself yet?,' said KT. The thought had obviously occurred to Viola as well, because by the time they'd reached the street she was saying she had to find him and refusing all offers of help with admirable new-found saintliness. Dan put her in a cab to take her back to the hotel where her husband was no doubt sucking on an exhaust pipe while swallowing the contents of the bathroom cabinet.

TWENTY-THREE

That night, Dan and I shared my bed, cocooned in alcohol and forgiveness, sleeping together late into Sunday morning. Burgh Island was forgotten, Susan and Viola unmentioned as we coiled around each other. Life was too short.

After getting hammered on tequila slammers, the party had broken up at about four a.m. in the little rat cove on the sea front. We'd all made so much noise going down the dark concrete steps onto the rocky shore that there were no vermin to be seen, but that didn't stop some of the girls, and a few of the less robust boys, shrieking at every suspicious shadow. Bottles, cans and packets of crisps were produced, and Flossie showed his boy-scout roots by making a fire, around which we huddled as if it was mid-February in Norway instead of mid-February in Plymouth.

Relief, alcohol and exhaustion gave the party a manic edge and with another turn of the popular tide Dan and I were crowned monarchs of the company with garlands of stinking kelp. Flossie became the trusted first minister, Karen the Dowager Duchess and KT the Queen Mother. He squeezed my hand as he slipped away early with the Canadian.

'Goodnight, cariad. Don't think we'll be getting up tomorrow.' A brief air-kiss and they were gone. Soon everyone followed, in search of sleep, sex, drugs or solitude. Dan and I were the last, sitting shivering happily on the flat sheet of cement which jutted into the softly lapping water. Velvet-wet weed softened the man-made surface and small-shelled creatures shuffled along it, finding a home on its ugliness.

'You know,' said Dan, gazing out at the winking buoys in the distance, 'I'm not sure I should have changed my mind tonight. Maybe I should have just walked away. For God's sake, it's only a show.'

'Dan, it's never only a show.'

His face was illuminated like a Velasquez by the dying fire. He looked down at his cigarette. 'I'm just glad I've got you, Eleanor.'

'Don't be too sure of that.' I was surprised by how hard I sounded. He didn't look up. 'Tell me about Susan.'

'There's nothing to tell. I slept with her. Ends.' He flicked his cigarette away.

'Why? Why did you sleep with her, Dan?'

Stupid possessive question which he didn't answer, whether because he was thinking about it or because he didn't want to, I couldn't tell. I didn't know him except in bed and in the rehearsal room, neither a place for honesty.

'Why did I sleep with her?,' he said eventually. 'I can't resist an opportunity. Why does a dog lick its balls? Because it can. ' He paused. I smiled to show I'd got the joke. Not that I was particularly amused to be compared to a retriever's scrotum. 'It ruined my marriage – and every relationship I've ever had. But I can't stop myself.'

'And us?'

He looked at me for the first time, very tenderly and with the unspoken regret of an alcoholic faced with an impossible choice. 'Depends what you want, Eleanor.'

What did I want? A happy marriage, an Oscar and a perfect bum.

'I just want to enjoy what we've got. For as long as we can keep it going.' I hoped I sounded easy-going, uninterested in spinning a web of ownership.

'Tonight,' he said. 'And if I walk away tomorrow morning and don't come back?'

'That's cool,' I said, using a word I barely knew the meaning of, let alone whether it was still current parlance. He laughed at my earnest attempt at careless rapture.

'Oh, Eleanor. I do…' – he hesitated on the L of the next word – '…like you. Come on, let's go to bed, I'm getting wet rot sitting here.' He pulled me to my feet. 'I don't want to walk away, you know. Not from you or the show.'

We kissed, and probably would have got further carried away by the romance of the moment, but the rats, encouraged by the quiet, were reclaiming their territory. Had we lain down, or even sat down, we'd have been overrun, leaving two clean-picked skeletons in a carnal embrace.

'What happens if she is pregnant?,' I asked, as we walked along the front.

'You said she couldn't be.' He stopped under a street lamp. The ghastly light was perfect for his expression of horror. What was it like to be told an action very likely forgotten could create a human being who could take your freedom, your name and your wages?

'I could be wrong.'

'Eleanor, I've watched you work an audience. You're never wrong.'

Yes, it was bullshit; yes, it gave him an escape from facing the question, but after so many years of David's rations of grudging approval I didn't care.

That night we made love slowly, with no pressure to perform or reach orgasm or to impress with our versatility – consequently it was a memorable marathon lubricated by the remains of a bottle of port and something very close to love.

In the late morning we were asleep in the dark of the closeted bedroom when Dan's phone rang. It was on the other side of the folding doors, muffled under clothes, the furniture or carpet – we couldn't tell which, as we ran round naked trying to find it. Dan finally fished it out from the back of the sofa, but not before he'd given a coach-load of pensioners a full-frontal view of his impressive manhood. Though quite how impressive they would have found it after the chamfering it had had that night I didn't know.

'It's Viola,' he said, reading the missed-call display. 'Better call her back.'

I wanted to tell him not to bother, but she was the heroine of the moment and probably just needed reassurance, having stood up to Izzy.

I sleepily admired the back view of his body as he waited for her to answer. Neat, small bottom, good thighs, lightly furred, broad shoulders and a comforting rather than unattractive layer of flesh over his ribcage and the top of his hips. There was nothing a younger model could offer except speed and a flashier chassis.

'Hi, Viola, how – ? We'll come over. Eleanor and I.' He looked round at me. We, not I. I liked that, even if I didn't want to spend my Sunday listening to the whingeing Viola Duck. 'Stay where you are.'

So much for a lazy day in bed eating toast and watching television. We bundled out of the house without showering, as Dan seemed to think it was urgent enough to ignore such niceties, arriving at the local hospital reeking of stale cigarettes, alcohol and sex. I doubt Viola would have recognised any of them, even if she'd been calmly drinking coffee rather than pacing up and down the reception area wringing her hands like a Wal-Mart Lady Macbeth.

'Oh, Dan, Dan, Izzy was in intensive care. His heart stopped twice.'

'Third time lucky,' I muttered. Dan pinched me hard on the arm and I yelped. Viola mistook it for an expression of grief.

'It's okay, Eleanor, he's gonna pull through. He took sleeping-pills, aspirin – everything. Because I sacked him. I did that to him...' Pause for expressions of horror to appear on our stricken faces. 'I found him when I got back... He tried to kill himself. He said I hurt him last night, Dan.' She sobbed in a cross between indignation and terror. 'I'm the one who nearly killed him. He says he's never been so humiliated and it was me, his wife, who did it. The one person in the world he should be able to trust.' He'd recovered enough to push the guilt button then. 'Dan, I'm gonna have to bring him back on board. This show is his life. He's upstairs now, in a room; they moved him about an hour ago – and he won't speak a word.'

Dan wasn't finding Izzy's silence as amusing as I was, but then he hadn't gone down the suicide cul-de-sac as recently as I had.

'Viola, you know I can't work with him, or rather he can't work with me. He doesn't trust me –'

'Oh he does, Dan, he does –' Her pitch and tone would have shattered glass. 'It's me, his wife, he doesn't trust.'

'Viola, Izzy is...unpredictable.'

How had Dan plucked that word out of the English language when so many others were more accurate? Viola's face showed a flash of the cornered animal I'd seen before. Overwhelmed by guilt, she'd do anything to appease Izzy. If Dan was going to see the show through to birth, he couldn't afford to alienate her.

'If you can guarantee he won't interfere. Won't come into the theatre or try to change anything, anything at all...' he said, the words filtered through layers of reluctance, '...and if you keep him out of production meetings, then I have no problem. But he is not, absolutely *not*, to come backstage at any time. Is that clear? I don't want him doing anything behind my back. Particularly – and I mean this –' she pricked up her ears and cocked her head to one side, '– on Tuesday.'

'Tuesday?,' she repeated.

'Yes, Viola, I told you,' said Dan, with exaggerated patience. 'I have to go to Edgware. I told you, my administrator is leaving, there's a gala in her honour. I have to be there.'

'Oh, but Dan,' Viola started, screwing up her face in distress.

'No buts, Viola. It's in my contract, signed by Izzy. I won't be here.'

The pitch of her voice was rising again. 'But Dan, it's press night. It's real important.'

'No, Viola. Press night in London is important, and we've made sure by being so far away that none of the nationals will come here.'

'Dan, I have to tell you, the Schumachers weren't sure about the show, we need good press.' Her blind obstinacy was coming up against Dan's determination. Her head went down as she became more truculent, Dan's chin rose with exasperation.

'Viola, they are Broadway producers, real ones.' She didn't catch the reference to Izzy's dodgy credentials. 'They are not going to make a decision about this after seeing an out-of-town preview and reading the opinions of a couple of gardening correspondents. I've no idea why Izzy got them to come so early anyway.'

Unexpectedly that took the wind out of her. 'Oh well, you see, Dan…' She then looked up at him, her eyes horribly magnified by her glasses. 'Izzy's looking for investors.'

That piece of news left Dan and me totally becalmed. Had he, they, really come this far without finance?

Viola rushed to reassure us. 'No, see, Izzy has the money. We have the money.'

'Yes, you're an oil-heiress Viola,' I offered.

'Well…kind of. My grandfather made a billion, but his sons lost most of it. I have a trust fund, but I can't touch that without…'

'Without what, Viola?'

She looked at Dan fearfully, afraid she'd lose her prince if he found she was a penniless peasant girl. 'Without the permission of the lawyers. My grandfather said the only man who'd marry me would be after my money.'

I was shocked at her brutal honesty. Poor woman.

'Izzy just wants to offer them an in on the ground floor. If they want the show on Broadway what could be better for them, huh? It's four times the cost of London, so to transfer the show makes financial sense. Please, please don't tell him I said anything.'

Dan saw his advantage. 'Viola, don't worry.' He put his arm round her shoulders. She reacted as if he'd put her fingers in a three pin socket. He moved to put his hands on her shoulders, pulling her close and placing his forehead gently against hers. 'You want the best for the show. And so do I, you know that.' She nodded. He pressed on with the gentleness of a good gigolo. 'As long as I can go to my theatre on Tuesday and Izzy leaves Plymouth until I'm back, there's no problem. That's my condition, Viola. Izzy must not be anywhere near Plymouth while I'm in Edgware. Do you understand?'

She was pathetically grateful. What he'd asked for was nothing in comparison with what she was prepared to give. 'Dan, that's wonderful. Thank you. Thank you so much. I'll go tell him. We'll go to Cornwall. A little break would be good for all of us.'

She did a little skip towards the lift, her sneakers slapping on the marble floor. Then she skipped back and planted a kiss on Dan's mouth. I think she was aiming for his cheek but he turned as she approached and they came together like two spaceships docking. I wondered how she liked the softness of his lips. Surely more alluring than the soggy dish-clout she was used to. But then Viola was far too rich to know what a dish-clout was.

We left the hospital determined to be positive about Izzy's ultimate blackmail trick. The pay-off, after all, was not prohibitive.

'Do you want to go back to bed?,' Dan asked.

'Would you be offended if I said no?' The sight of Viola's mouth on his had quite put me off. 'We could go to Lewis's do.'

Some of the company were gathering for a meal organised by our oldest member, a charming, immensely generous actor who was invariably rude to me. Early on in rehearsal I'd phoned an actress who'd worked with him before.

'Oh, darling,' she drawled, 'Don't take any notice, he does it to anyone who's not in the chorus. It's just his sense of humour. He's all right underneath, really, he's just a bit, well…'

'Chippy?,' I suggested.

'Australian,' she said.

When we arrived there were about thirty people – actors, musicians, techies and theatre staff – sitting around an immensely long trestle-table surrounded by tall gas-heaters under a striped awning in the garden of a large pub. On a bright English summer's day it would have been idyllic; unfortunately it was cold and grey with a horizontal drizzle, although this did little to damp the air of barely suppressed hysteria. The overwhelmed waitress quickly confused our orders and those who'd asked for beef were given lamb; vegetarians, slabs of steak. Finally Basher gathered anything not claimed and chewed his way through the lot. We were frozen, wet and monumentally drunk.

'Oi, Cornish.'

'Wha's that, Somerset?'

Two of the boys were standing on the table, innocent West Country lads lost in a maze of choreography.

'You wanna do that there bugger of a finale dance then, Cornish?'

'Oi'd rather have me arms cut off with a spoon –'

We banged the table, yelling encouragement. They rolled up their trouser legs.

'Y'ere we go then, Somerset, two three four…' They gyrated to a clave beat heard only in Polperreth. 'Right…now then, this be how it goes… Twist like a Mary…bit of Michael Jackson – no frightening the kids mind…cock yer leg at the lamp post…and big finish…hands up, "Don't shoot I'm just the window cleaner".'

While we cheered, shouted and stomped our approval, Susan arrived, and our cheers for them became cheers for her. She received them graciously but, with her health being so delicate – her limp was so bad I was surprised she didn't have a crutch and a parrot – we moved inside, clearing the bar of civilians in under fifteen minutes.

It was cosy, with a log fire at one end, in front of which we steamed like so many cows in a barn. I was getting a round in when I saw Dan take Susan to a small booth almost out of sight. KT came and stood, blocking my view.

'Lip-reading?'

'No, I'm just…'

He pursed his mouth in disapproval. 'Don't you take no notice of that slapper. And do you think,' he added so quietly I had to lean forward to hear him, 'do you honestly think that she'd be slamming down the large vodkas if she was pregnant? Don't be twp gell, she'd be behaving like this was the second coming – orange juice and folic acid spritzers.'

Not only was she swigging a large vodka, she was reaching out to accept a cigarette from Dan. 'And she says she doesn't smoke,' I said indignantly.

'Let's face it,' said KT. 'She'd burst into bloody flames if it meant Dan was looking at her. There is no way she's having a baby. What's the betting she's telling him she miscarried?' We looked at each other, thinking the same thought. 'Because you pushed her over, you vicious cow. Very convenient.'

I wanted to slap her simpering smooth-skinned face. That skin that looked so tight across her flushed cheeks that my hand would split them open – an over-ripe tomato full of rot. But I just stood there. KT pulled me back.

'Come on, don't you dare buy me a drink, my gel.'

Still hissing with anger and jealousy, I drank too much, laughed too loudly and generally made a fool of myself. Eventually, Dan noticed and came over.

'Don't you think you've had enough, Ellie?'

'The only thing I've had enough of is her –'

'I'm going to walk Susan back to her digs –'

'Why? What's she come up with this time? Terminal cancer?'

I knew as I said it Dan was horrified. This was not unconditional love. He took a pace back, away from me and my lairy drunkenness, smiled and wished everyone goodnight.

What was it he'd said? Tonight? Tomorrow? Who knows? Well, I thought bitterly as I weaved my way back to the flat, bouncing off various landmarks on the way, I was a total prat-magnet. Top Turn I may be, but Top Totty? Not even close. I was in a maudlin stupor of tears and white wine when Dan tapped on the window of the flat.

Too late to pretend I'd sobered up. I managed to get to the front door, open it and allow him in before I fell over. He caught me and barely winced as I hiccuped alcoholic stomach gas in his face. If my tear-streaked face and red eyes didn't give away my state of inebriated misery, the pile of used tissues and hastily discarded pink elephant did. He picked it up, played with its trunk and put it on the bed, where it sat on the pillows like a furry starfish.

'Come here, you silly thing,' he said, holding his arms out to me. Me silly? I wasn't silly. I was offended. Hurt. Treated with a lack of respect. My outrage came out as:

'Oh, Dan, you came back.'

'Of course I came back.' He began undressing me with innocent practicality.

I wanted to talk, but my mouth wasn't working. Once I was naked, Dan guided me to the bed, slid me under the covers and tucked the elephant under my arm. Then he sat and stroked my cheek until I began to doze, aware I should drink water and eat pain-killers.

'Eleanor…? Susan's not pregnant.'

'Mmm?'

'She was pregnant but now she's not.'

'KT was right,' I murmured, not sure if this was real or a dream.

'She wasn't pretending. She really was pregnant, she even showed me the test.'

'She faked it,' I tried to say, but it sounded more like 'fuck it'.

'She lost it. Last night.'

Casualty must've been confused, coming in with a metatarsal and going out with a miscarriage. But I was too close to sleep and too far from sober to say anything.

'They said at the hospital there was nothing they could do, so she came back and did the show anyway – she's been up all night, very upset…it was when you…' He thought better of finishing. 'The fall caused it. I was sorry for her. But when she first told me, I felt trapped and guilty. But then… Shit… I don't know. I shouldn't have taken it out on you. I'm sorry.'

What was he apologising for? She'd taken him for the ride of his life, blamed me and he'd believed her. I passed out before I could analyse anything but the rising tide of nausea that tasted of rioja and roast potatoes.

TWENTY-FOUR

It wasn't the mildest of hangovers but it blew away with the sea breeze as I walked up the hill on Monday.

Dan was gone when I woke up, dehydrated and with a face-splitting headache, but he'd left a note:

SHALL WE START AGAIN?

Yes. Yes, if only as a shield against the pain of David, who'd phoned while I was comatose. Like a Pavlovian dog with a mobile, I called him straight back.

'We're coming down on Friday. Staying at the Grand, could you fix us up with tickets? Four. Phyllida's cousin Melinda and her husband want to come too. They live in some stately pile in Cheltenham so we're going to stop there on the way back.'

Cheltenham was on the way back to London? From Plymouth? Only with a dyslexic sat-nav.

'Pity you can't come but you'd probably find them terribly dull after all your actory friends.'

What was the male equivalent of a bitch? Right, I thought, I'll make sure Dan's around and that I'm all over him like cocoa butter on stretch marks. I couldn't imagine David being sexually jealous, but he'd be seriously pissed off at the thought of one of his possessions being sequestered by another man. Particularly an 'actory' type who, by definition, should be a raving poof.

Although David and Phyllida were the problem that had catapulted me into the emotional quicksands I now inhabited, I couldn't think about them. They and my neglected son had become unreal – my present feelings more vivid in pain and pleasure than anything since Arthur's birth.

'You better bring a peace-offering for Susan.'

KT had been on the phone immediately after David.

'Why? She's the one who should be grovelling to me.'

'It's in the interest of entente cordiale. And that isn't what your granny made you drink in the winter. Just to keep her face straight.'

I bought a bunch of flowers – not the cheapest, a slender sheaf of early daffs, but a gaudy clump of maroon chrysanthemums, ugly funeral flowers, and pinks, those mean cousins of carnations that are more stem than flower. Carrying my peace-offering I wandered on stage at five to ten, preparing myself for her arrival. Composing my face and words into humility and regret was going to be harder than doing Hedda Gabler in Urdu, but it was for the greater good, or so KT had said when I suggested the accident had been forgotten:

'Elephants and West End Wendies, love – they shit big and never forget.'

Morag was polishing the new door knobs. 'Nice flowers,' she said, bending to sniff them.

'Are they? That wasn't the intention, they're for Susan.'

'Och, you wee tinker,' she said approvingly. 'She'll collapse under the weight of them and accuse you of trying tae kill her.'

'And the stupid thing is, half the cast would believe her.'

The red mouth thinned to a line. 'Well, let's face it, if they were that bright, they'd be stacking shelves in Asda.'

We giggled, remembering too late the show relay was on and we were standing under the microphone. Morag shrugged her silk draped shoulders.

'Aye fuck 'em. If they cannae take a joke they shouldn't have joined. Now let's talk about this finale dress. I'm real sorry, I know it's giving you shingles, but Izzy still wants the drag-queen look. Says "you just ain't sexy" – and apparently any argument is likely to put him back in intensive care.' I opened my eyes wide. 'I know, I know, it's the best place for him, but we've got to keep him sweet till London. Dan's orders.'

I should have been thrilled that a man with such an obvious lack of taste didn't find me attractive, but if Izzy was the lowest common denominator so was a significant percentage of any audience. Morag saw my wobble of confidence.

'Morag, isn't Izzy banned from having any input?'

'Aye, he is, but Viola's speaking for him. She's like a bloody ventriloquist's dummy. But don't worry, Dan said he couldn't fancy any woman who looked like a docker in a frock and all you need is a bit more zhush. Wee bit sequin work maybe. Rhinestones for days and a cleavage like the Grand Canyon – you ken what I mean.'

'No problem, Morag. Bring it on.'

'I've already ordered the diamante-encrusted silk satin. Ninety-eight quid a metre – trade. Well, Izzy said he wanted the show to look expensive, it'd be nice to have something that actually was.'

The cast had now filled the stage, sitting chatting and waiting. The dancers, as always, stretching and flexing. Now the show was in performance, the urgency and excitement of creative rehearsal was forgotten, changes no longer a challenge but a chore.

Dan was just calling us to order when Susan arrived – or rather entered stage right with walking stick, jacket thrown casually over her shoulders. She gave a wan smile and sank onto a hastily provided chair with a murmured thanks to Gaffer Gusset. She was pale, with bruise-like marks under her eyes. It looked like a make-up job for a hospital soap.

'All right, everyone, let's get started,' said Dan, giving Susan a vast smile and a little bow. That should have been all the proof I needed there was nothing between them. Well…nothing but hasty sex on a sofa. Twice.

'Er…just a second. Um…' I raised my voice. 'I just want to say something.'

Every head swivelled.

'I'd just like to say, Susan, I'm so sorry about the…um…'

Her eyes flicked to Dan – was I going to mention the miscarriage?

'…what happened between us, Susan, and these are for you.'

I stood with arms outstretched, a child presenting a hideous bouquet to the Queen. She paused for a moment, considering them as if they were dandelions. Finally, with me bending before her, she reached out and placed her face in their noxious odour with a sigh of ecstasy. The cast applauded. The hatchet was buried. But not so deeply I couldn't dig it up in a hurry.

Dan worked us hard, then left Flossie and God to tidy up the dance routines, and the day drifted into the show with no sign of our producers and every sign of success. We all relaxed and Susan was thrilled with the cheers she got at the curtain call.

I gave her a little clap and nod as I came on for my call. My reception was good, excellent even, but not as loud or as long as usual. I glanced round and there she was, grimacing to the audience, indicating her heavily bandaged foot, mouthing her apologies and giggling with half the front row.

I shouldn't have cared, I should have risen above being upstaged.

Instead I screamed, 'What the fuck do you think you're playing at?', tore off stage and slammed into my dressing-room, followed by KT at a safe distance.

'You'd better tell that scrubber I won't be responsible for my actions if she carries on like this –'

'Calm down, Eleanor,' he said coolly, closing the door on the curious and my dresser, who managed to slip in behind him. I was exhausting my meagre stock of expletives, and she was trying to get my costume and wig off without being battered by either my flailing arms or tongue.

From the mirror a foul-mouthed harpy stared back with such hatred I was shocked. It was me, definitely, but nothing like the woman who only weeks before resembled the terrified creature now unzipping me. There was no question it was good I'd found my strength, but my moods were swinging more wildly than a chimp with PMT.

I sat down. 'I'm so sorry, Jenny. I'm behaving like a total –'

'– hell-hound bitch from hell?,' offered KT.

'Oh, that's all right, I just thought it was your period.' Jenny's round blue eyes looked into mine without flinching. 'They all synchronise, you know, when women work together.'

'So, what excuse do you have for being horrible for the other three weeks?,' asked KT, taking off his make-up with my baby wipes.

'Actually, mine is due any minute now. Maybe you're right, it's nothing to do with Susan,' I said meekly.

'You're probably picking up on her hormones,' smiled Jenny, my foul behaviour accepted and dismissed. 'She came on last Friday.'

I didn't register for a minute as I was pulling on my trousers, then realised what she'd said at the same time as KT.

'Friday?,' I said. 'How do you know that?'

'She didn't have any tampons and I always keep a stock in wardrobe. I let her have a couple, then some more after the show to see her through.' She looked at me through the mirror, her eyes huge and innocent.

'Yes,' I said, careful not to seem too interested. 'It must be awful when they catch you out. Mine are regular as clockwork.'

Periods are for women what football is for men. I could never pretend an interest in either until this conversation.

'Oh, so are hers, she just changed handbags that day and left them in the other one.'

'I'm always doing that,' said KT. 'Not with tampons obviously. I've always wondered though, why do they give you a free cigarette-holder with them?'

Jenny laughed and we moved on to general gossip, then wished her goodnight, closed the door behind her, waited a good thirty seconds then shrieked:

'*Friday!*'

She hadn't been beaten to the ground by me and miscarried until Saturday, so KT had been absolutely right, she never was pregnant. I revoked any residual guilt and reverted to my original scum-low opinion of her.

'You've got to tell Dan,' said KT gleefully. 'Where is he?'

'No idea,' I said, reaching for the phone and dialling stage door. 'Hi Albert, could you put out a call for Dan please?'

'He's in Miss Barnard's dressing-room. She came and got him about twenty minutes ago. Looked upset. You got the extension?'

'Sure, thanks. Yeah.' Susan was no doubt telling Dan about my hissy fit.

'You're not the villain, Nellie, she is. And frankly,' he added, with the flourish of a gossiping neighbour, 'I don' care how good a shag he is, he's not much better. He'd fuck a frog if it'd stop hopping.'

'Doesn't make him a bad person.'

'Does if he hurts you, Nellie.'

I was too touched by this defence to acknowledge it.

'It's not a problem, KT. Go and get your bag and I'll see you at the stage door.'

Dan was going straight from the theatre to Edgware for his gala and would definitely say goodnight. Definitely. I tidied the dressing-table slowly, then made my way to the stage door. No doubt Dan and Susan would appear there, and I'd allow myself just the tiniest gesture of possession, a hand on his arm perhaps, an intimate smile. I stood making conversation with Albert until he said he'd better be locking up.

'But Dan's still here, isn't he?'

'Nah,' he said, hefting a vast bunch of keys out of a drawer. 'He left about ten minutes ago.'

KT and I trudged up the frost-sparkled hill to the Hoe while I railed against men, calling Dan a cold, unthinking, manipulative bastard who played nasty mindgames and who I should tell to take a flying fuck at a rolling doughnut the next time he came sniffing round my knickers.

KT didn't disagree.

ACT THREE

Guess Who's Coming to Dinner

Depression and suppressed fury took the edge off my first night nerves, not that performing in front of Plymouth's glitterati and the prospective verdicts of the local press had me gibbering for hypnotherapy.

I picked up a couple of bottles and some chocolates for those not following us to London – and sat in the silent theatre writing their 'Good Luck and Thanks' cards. After distributing my offerings, I returned to the cold, dark stage to start limbering up. The iron safety curtain was still down, cutting off the auditorium. The sound was dead and any magic dormant. Feet parallel, I stretched and hummed, feeling clicks and hearing cracks as my body and voice woke up, neither keen to work, having spent the night howling at the indifferent moon about my real and imaginary hurts.

In the morning, to cheer myself up, I'd decided to buy a new bra. As if in sympathy, the straps of my favourite had finally parted company with the cups, which with age more resembled coronation mugs. While my contemporaries were lining up for Oscars or being fêted at the National Theatre, I was wandering round Debenhams, in Plymouth, flicking through the sale racks of the lingerie department.

I trailed into a fitting room with a selection of cantilevered lace and started to strip off.

'Hallo? Hallo? You in there?'

A female voice, very shrill, called me with some urgency. Covering myself with the curtain, I leaned my head out.

'Yes?'

A vast woman in polka-dot yellow shorts that displayed her dimpled knees was clutching the other end of my curtain, threatening to pull it either off me or the rail. Her varicose thighs were braced against resistance. She stared at me for a full ten seconds, then turned and called.

'Vera, come and have a look. It is her.'

Vera, presumably, waddled out of another fitting room, wearing a skimpy summer dress that was so tight the price tags stood out like aquaplanes.

The two of them observed me.

'She's older than she looks on telly,' said Vera.

'My friend says you're older,' offered Yellow Shorts as if I were hard of hearing. 'But then you haven't been on the box for a while, have you? What happened? You resting? That's what you people call it innit? Resting?'

An hour on Sunday nights in their living rooms ten years previously and I was still their property. I should wither them with contempt. Set fire to their ugliness.

'How sweet of you to ask but no, actually, I'm appearing over the road, at the theatre.'

'Oh, never mind,' said Vera sympathetically. Then, glazing over: 'It's not Shakespeare is it?'

'No, it's a musical. With salsa music.'

They brightened. 'That's all right, I suppose, a musical.' Yellow Shorts nodded, sending ripples of approval through her necks. 'Any free tickets, for the unwaged?'

'I'm afraid not. I'm so sorry. But there are concessions for the disabled. Perhaps morbid obesity would count?'

It took a second for them to understand what I'd said, but then it took me as long to realise I'd said it. Anger replaced their patronising friendliness.

'You cheeky cow. We pay your wages, you know.'

I'd heard this one before, from fans who didn't get their own way. 'Really? When did you last go to the theatre? Or are you talking about your taxes? Well, I have to pay for your kids' education and prison sentences, I subsidise your jobseeker's allowance and I've no doubt I'll be paying for your hospital treatment when you have diabetes, lung cancer or a heart attack. Now piss off. I'm trying to buy a bra.'

I tore the curtain from Yellow Shorts' puffy fingers and pulled it shut.

'We're telling the papers about you.'

And I had no doubt they'd be straight on to the Have You Been Insulted by a Celebrity? columns as soon as they'd topped up their phone cards. But I was so far from what the tabloids would think of as hot they'd just laugh – if they'd ever heard of me. But then again, I thought as I shakily tried on the bra – confrontation always makes me quiver – the PR company Izzy had hired was so useless, maybe the publicity would help the show. Run by a man who snorted fields of Colombian marching powder and couldn't have publicised the Iraq war.

In the mirror, the favoured bra looked like the balcony in Romeo and Juliet, supporting a magnificent one-piece bosom. So, uplifted in more ways than one, I bought it.

Back in my dressing-room mirror, I was admiring my slit-trench cleavage when the mobile rang.

'Eleanor? Dan.'

Be distant. Punish him.

'Hi.'

'I just wanted to say, you were great last night, I'm sorry I missed you. Susan...'

I left the silence.

'She's worked herself into a terrible state. Says she's frightened to speak to you. I'm sorry, I should have come to see you and I meant to call you, but my battery went... Anyway...you were terrific.'

'Right. Good. Thank you.'

I imagined the three bleeps he heard as I rang off. Immediately I wanted to ring back.

Ruby's voice brought me back to the present. 'Iron going out.' The Act One gauze flew in, sound checks had been done and the front of house staff were being marshalled by the manager.

'Ladies and Gentlemen of the company, this is your half-hour call. Half an hour please. The house is now open, please do not cross the stage.'

The bouncy pre-show music. Eyeliner, lipstick, wig, costume. The build-up of voices as the auditorium fills. The hush on lights down. The voices on stage. Laughs. Fighting back nerves, a vague echo of the sickness I'd feel on press night in London, and I'm on, to an enthusiastic entrance round.

Two and a half hours later, the curtain came down on a thrilling wall of noise – applause, cheers, whistles and stamping of feet.

'Bloody hell,' KT said, tears of laughter rolling down his face. 'Did you see her in the front row? Tits like slate-layers' nailbags. You opening the champagne, Ellie?'

'You bet. See you in my dressing-room.' I was hugged and congratulated as I made my way backstage – the beloved leading lady again.

We were a hit. The audience had been even more hysterical than for the previews. And, best of all, they had stood up for me. Not a full ovation perhaps, but certainly an ovum. For Me. Not the show, not the company. Me. Bugger humility. The champagne cork exploded from the bottle in a triumphant salute. This was happiness.

I flung open the door and was about to yell, 'KT come and get it!' when I saw them.

Walking towards me was Viola, and behind her, grinning and brandishing his cigar at two men behind him, Izzy.

'No! Izzy. That's not part of the deal!'

I sounded ridiculous, shocked, the dream broken.

'Not backstage. It's not part of the deal, you promised. You gave your word. Go away. Get out. Now.'

The small group looked petrified, as if I was waving a loaded gun, not a magnum of Veuve Cliquot. In the seconds before they retreated I saw horror, fear and naked hatred on the faces of Izzy and Viola. And behind them? The Leather Queen in the Bandana. The American director of commercials. Dan's predecessor.

The other man I didn't recognise, but registered his round face, cold unblinking eyes and expensive suit.

Back in the dressing-room I poured myself a tumbler of champagne and watched it overflow, already preparing my apology to Izzy and Viola. Always the actor, always the coward.

'Izzy, I'm so sorry. I didn't mean to be so rude but...well...no excuse. It's just...well, you know...' I trailed off lamely when KT and I met them in the street outside the foyer. Izzy seemed as keen as I was to move on. He waved the cigar and did a bit of *'Pal, you were overwrought. Big night for all of us'*, then turned to his companions. Viola was notably silent but staring at me with undisguised loathing; so much for the truce.

'Eleanor, you remember Ricky?' I shook hands. His grip was large, limp and damp. 'And Ricky's agent, Rudolph Vizhnevsky.' I shook the smaller, limper hand of the suited man, whose upper lip curled very slightly. I couldn't tell whether it was me or women in general that repelled him. I gave him the benefit of the doubt and decided he was just a standard misogynist. Pigeonholes weren't just for casting directors.

'Coming in for the drinks?,' I asked, wide-eyed, over-playing the innocence.

'No, pal,' said Izzy, putting a hand on my shoulder and guiding me a little way towards the glass foyer doors; no doubt he'd have liked to shove me head-first through them.

'See,' he said conspiratorially, 'we have some talking to do, Viola and me. I never was so humiliated, humiliated by my own wife. You understand that? In front of everyone. It was a real blow. My own wife sold me out. Can you imagine what that feels like? I'm thinking divorce may be the answer. Divorce... So we got a bit of negotiating to do. Okay, pal? See you tomorrow, and...' – He pulled away from me, still holding my shoulder – '...you were terrific tonight. You're going to be the biggest star London's seen since Marlene Dietrich.'

I thought for a horrible moment he was going to kiss me, so I got in first and hugged him. His breath smelled of three day-old, cold cooked sprouts.

KT was making Viola and the others laugh as Izzy returned to them. I held open the foyer doors, waiting, but Izzy hadn't finished.

'KT, Eleanor, I wanna tell you something, the most important thing I learned in my years of being a Broadway Producer, you wanna know what it is?'

'Yes, Izzy,' we chorused, rictus smiles on both our faces.

'Okay. What are the two most beautiful words in the English language?'

'Dead Duck?,' suggested KT.

'No, KT,' said Izzy, not listening as usual. 'The two most beautiful words in the English language are SOLD OUT.'

We all laughed appreciatively, Ricky the loudest and longest, as the group moved off, looking for a taxi to take them the short distance to their hotel. I'd asked Izzy about the vast amounts they spent on taxis to places so close the drivers were by turns annoyed and ecstatic. His reply had been: 'You gotta show you got class.' I made a mental note to mention it to Prince Charles if we ever met.

Leaving thoughts of Izzy and Viola on the pavement, we joined the company in the upstairs bar. Like a swarm of seagulls they swooped on drinks and sandwiches. There was real joy, relief, happiness. Susan even raised her glass to me; I blew her a kiss. People in attitudes of humble adoration were queuing for my autograph.

Who needed Dan, David, shopping or housework? This was real life.

TWENTY-SIX

Next morning I battled my way through the wind and found a sheltered seat by a little kiosk selling hot carbohydrates. Despite the fine drizzle, the sea was sparkling and the laughing remains of the British Navy were assembled in the bay, grand and grey in the occasional sunlight. I was just settling in to a plate of mini-doughnuts, still hot from the fryer, when my phone rang. Dan.

'Hallo? Eleanor? I think the line went dead last night.'

Tell the truth or lie? Why cut off the nose to spite the orgasm?

'Yes…the reception's terrible in my room. So…how's my gorgeous director?'

'I may not be the person to ask,' he said. 'Izzy has demanded I come back for a meeting. He's read the local review and says it's crap. I think I'm going to be sacked again.' His voice had lost all its confidence. 'Eleanor, would you meet me at the theatre? I need – I'd like you to be there.' This was a Dan I hadn't met before. He sounded almost frightened. 'I don't know if I can control the situation anymore.'

'Sure you can, but of course I'll be there. I'm sure there's no problem.' Should I mention the Leather Queen? No. 'The show was great last night, the crits can't be that bad.'

As I rang off, I thought again about Ricky and his spooky agent. No one flies from Los Angeles to Plymouth because they fancy a night out at the theatre.

As if summoned by thought, there they were coming towards me through the wind-whipped rain. I hoped they hadn't seen me, and they, from the split-second our eyes met, were hoping I hadn't seen them. We assumed our masks.

'Eleanor. Hi. What a great show last night. I am just so in awe of you. You are so talented. I just love what you're doing up there.'

Ricky's torrent of Americana broke round my stiff upper lip.

'Thank you so much. It's an unexpected pleasure to see you again. To what do we owe the honour of your visit?'

Shall we take a turn about the room, Mr D'Arcy?

'Ohmygod! I just love the way you talk. Rudolph and I just came over to see where the Pilgrim Fathers started from. I want to find my roots.'

'Your roots? Surely you should try Ireland. Or Italy?'

I could see myself in his wrap-around sunglasses. He said nothing as Rudolph hurried him away.

Dan was sheltering from a sudden downpour. A solitary cloud was anchored above the theatre. Omens were everywhere. I kissed his cheek. His response was a bare movement of the air above mine. He looked grey with tiredness and reeked of cigarettes.

'They won't let me have an independent witness.'

'What?,' I said.

'If they're going to sack me, I want someone in there. They said I can't have anyone.'

I couldn't believe this was possible. What about the union? It turned out he was out of benefit.

'That's all right,' I said cheerfully. 'You can lapse up to thirteen weeks without losing your membership.'

He flicked his cigarette-end into a puddle.

'It's more like years.'

'I thought you were a Marxist –'

'Trotskyist,' he interrupted.

'Sorry, I thought you Trots were union-mad. Anyway, you'd better rejoin quick if you're right about this meeting. Is that the review?'

He had the local paper sticking out of his coat pocket. 'Yes. It's pretty illiterate.'

He handed it to me as Jonty joined us, grinning, showing both rows of teeth in his wide jaws. What did he remind me of? The theatrical fox in Pinocchio.

'Did you know about this meeting?,' I asked.

He nodded.

'What's it about?'

He shrugged and did a 'my lips are sealed' mime. It was his job to sit on the fence between Izzy and the rest of us, but I was beginning to think he had crocodile clips instead of buttocks.

'They'll be here in a minute, Dan, the meeting's in my office so just go in when you want to. See you later.'

'Will you?,' asked Dan. Jonty smiled and sauntered off. 'I don't trust him. If I go, you shouldn't either.'

A nasty logic was beginning to emerge. After Voila's public humiliation of Izzy, she'd chosen Dan; and despite her immediate capitulation after Issy's suicide and divorce, he was hell-bent on destroying the cause of her betrayal. Only Dan's absolute ruin would satisfy his shattered pride.

And the Leather Queen in the Bandana had arrived to pick up the ball and score the try. Not that rugby similes were apt for one so far removed from the hurly-burly of the loose ruck.

I left Dan and ran to my dressing-room, ransacked the drawers and ran back.

'Here,' I gasped. 'My tape-recorder. It's old and it squeaks, but that'll be your independent observer.' I stopped him before he could object. 'You'll need something if they do try and sack you. They haven't got a leg to stand on.'

Dan was changing the batteries when Izzy and Viola arrived, as always, in a taxi. They didn't say anything as they passed us, so Dan shrugged deeper inside his raincoat and made to follow them through the stage door.

'Dan? There's something else…'

'What?'

'Ricky Ricky, the American's here.'

'In England?'

'In Plymouth.'

'That's it, then,' he said and walked into the theatre.

I stayed outside, wondering if I should have told him and trying to concentrate on reading the review. It was a poorly written catalogue of who did what to whom, with a bit of pretentiousness thrown in, but it wasn't bad – qualified rapture for the comedy and music and a few doubts about the script, particularly Act One.

Izzy was reacting to this lone example of provincial journalism as if it was the verdict of the Butcher of Broadway. It was hard to believe these flaccid paragraphs could be fashioned into a stiletto for Dan's assassination.

Half an hour later, his air of hurt confusion had evaporated when Dan slammed out of the stage door. He grabbed me by the elbow and hustled me across to the Mexican. We chose a corner table with a sofa and ordered a couple of coffees.

'Well?'

'Thanks for that,' he said, placing my elderly Sony on the table. 'Frightened the life out of the buggers.'

I was childishly excited my plan had actually worked. 'Talk me through it. What happened…?'

Izzy told Viola and Dan to sit down, then paced the floor, issuing vague threats and boasts of his invincibility in the face of adversity.

'The critics trashing us is down to your direction, Dan. I told you you made crap and you shouted me down. I trusted you and we got killed. They murdered us.'

'Izzy, it's one newspaper in Plymouth. It's irrelevant, oh, and…' Dan took the tape-recorder out of his coat pocket and slowly placed it on the low table between them. 'You don't mind, do you?'

Dan was surprised at how calm he sounded, how in control; he was even more surprised to see how steady his fingers were as he pressed the record button. Viola, already pale, went the colour of a distempered wall and Izzy stopped dead in his tracks, staring at the revolving tape. He then launched into a bullying tirade.

'You saying you don't trust me, Dan? That what you saying? We have to trust each other, I can't work with anyone who doesn't trust me. I never worked with anyone didn't trust me. Are you telling me you don't trust Izzy Duck?'

Dan just smiled and held his hand over the machine, as if protecting it from Izzy's harsh words. When Izzy finished his rant, Dan said:

'What was it you wanted to say, Izzy? And if this is just another attempt at intimidation, I think I should leave.'

As always when he was confronted, Izzy backed down, spraying out apologies and accusations of misunderstanding.

'…Hey Dan, you're over-reacting, you gotta know we love your work. You've done a great job up to now…but we all need to improve, it's a life's mission, am I right?' Seeing no reaction, he changed tack.

'The greatest story-teller in British theatre, a genius, that's what I called you to the London Times when they interviewed me.'

Dan, with Izzy on the back foot, rediscovered his charm.

'I'm sure you didn't call me to this meeting to tell me how wonderful I am.' He looked at Viola. She looked down, her cheeks flushing so she looked like a badly distempered red-brick wall. 'What did you want to say?'

Izzy didn't like the direct approach and squirmed around the distant edges of what Dan was sure he'd intended to say.

'Well, see, you know what your problem is, Dan?' He paused. Dan waited. 'Your problem is you're a turtle.'

'Sorry?'

'A turtle, Dan. You know a turtle? Four legs, shell, eats lettuce.'

Dan frowned. 'You mean a tortoise.'

'That's right. A turtle. And that's where you're going wrong. You know the story of the race between the hare and the turtle?'

Dan controlled himself.

'Yes I do, Izzy. And the turtle won.'

Izzy looked blank.

'He did?' A pause. 'I didn't know that.'

He unwrapped a new cigar, puzzled by undeterred. 'So, pal, what I wanna say is this, pal, maybe you could do with a little help. You know, fizz up the choreography a little, give it some Broadway *pizzazz*.'

He paused to see what effect his words were having. None at all, from the look on Dan's face. The tape made a soft creaking sound as it went round.

'Okay, Dan, here's the bottom line. Ricky has come over from LA – just passing through, you know? He's seen the show – loves it, loves what you've done, he admires your work.' He almost shouted this last into the recorder. 'But he thought maybe he could come on board, you know, work alongside you, bring in some fresh ideas.'

'Yes,' said Dan. 'Why not? I think that's a very good idea. Alongside, not instead of.'

Izzy was thrown by Dan's agreement. He continued, but with less certainty. 'Of course not. No way. You're the director. You've done a great show, Ricky's just going to add, that's all…'

On the table in the Mexican, Dan flicked open the tape machine and took out the evidence.

'And you believe him?,' I asked.

'I don't know,' said Dan. 'But I've got no problem with Ricky coming in and redoing a couple of numbers. And I know Flossie'll be over the moon – he's not a dance choreographer, that was God's job – and, well…'

Dan didn't say what had been reverberating round the company since the first week: that God, great salsa dancer though he was, couldn't choreograph a line-dance for the Bolshoi. As KT said, *What's the difference between God the Father and God the choreographer? One of them is an unknowable mystery, the other is Jesus Christ's father.* We certainly needed help, and Leather Queen might be just the man. After all, he'd not only directed laxative commercials, he'd choreographed them too.

'So what happens now?,' I asked, relaxing back into the sofa. Dan put his hand on my thigh.

'Well,' he shrugged, 'I think I should let Ricky have a couple of days to learn the show without me breathing down his neck, and we'll start work for the West End when we get to London on Monday. For God's sake, we've got twenty-one previews, there's plenty of time. It'll be fine. In the meantime I'll make myself scarce for a couple of days.'

'No.' I moved closer to him, afraid to lose my security blanket.

'Just tomorrow and Friday, I'll be back Saturday.' He kissed the end of my nose. 'Promise.'

I snuggled in to him, too close for him to see my face. 'By the way, Susan wasn't pregnant. She was never pregnant. Her period started last Friday.' I didn't bother with the complexities of menstrual coordination. 'The day before her miscarriage.'

'Christ. Is that true?,' he said, pushing me away. 'No wonder she's scared of you. You don't miss a trick, do you?'

'No.' I stood up to go. 'And Dan, she's not scared of me. It's just that vulnerable plays better than hard as nails.'

When I arrived back, the theatre was alive with rumour. Dan had walked out. Ricky had walked out. God was the new director. Someone even said Izzy was dead and the whole show was being cancelled. My instinct, as always, was to lead the company from behind, but KT came to find me while I was reserving David's tickets.

'Oi, Top Turn. What you doing hiding out here?' The box office manager looked shocked – he was old-school chiffon scarf and handbag; leading ladies were to be addressed as Miss unless they were Dame. 'You'd better get back in there and tell those twirlies what's going on. They're twitching like a bag of ferrets with fleas.'

I knew he was right. KT was a far better den mother than I was. He herded me on stage and called the cast to order.

'Eleanor's got some parish notices for you, so shut up and take the weight off your sling-backs.' He turned to me. 'Go on, then.'

'Um…well…I'm sure you've heard a lot of conflicting stories but you're not to worry. Dan's still our director and there's nothing to worry about.'

'What's that American in the headscarf doing here then?' It was the bolshy Glaswegian, Lee's sidekick.

'No idea. All I know is Dan's still the boss. Okay?'

Flossie came to my rescue. 'Izzy and Viola want him to fizz up the dance routines and I think that's great. God and I are too close – a fresh eye would be good. I think it's going to be great for the show.'

The cast drifted off, reassured, and I was left with a vague sense of embarrassment. Playing someone else, I was happy to do the dance of the seven veils in bin liners with my bottom painted purple, but standing up as myself always made me squirm. So it was with some relief I pulled my threadbare character around me and went out in front of 600 complete strangers.

By the interval there was a rehearsal call up on the noticeboard:

THREE P.M. CURTAIN CALL. FULL COMPANY.

We had to break at five, so it was going to be a two-hour call. Two hours on the 'who's best?'. That was about an hour and three-quarters longer than Dan had given it. Izzy had always hated Dan's egalitarian shambles, with the chorus having the final bow instead of me. I didn't mind, but Lee had thrown a strop which boiled over into mutiny when God and Glenda were given their bow after his.

'No, no, I don't think it's right. Not for myself, you understand.' The unmistakable sound of gears of crashing into reverse. 'No, really, I don't care where I go. But Susan and the others should come after them. And then there's billing. I've got billing and so has Barry.' The deaf actor cupped his hand round his ear to signify he hadn't heard. Lee yelled: 'I was just saying – you've got billing – on the poster and in the programme after Eleanor – you should come on after Glenda and God. They're only dancers, after all.'

And Nelson Mandela was just an ex-con.

God said, 'Jiliobollas.'

'What did he say?,' asked Lee.

Glenda smiled. 'Dickhead.'

This would probably be Ricky's first 'improvement' but, rather than find out, I avoided the bar after the show. Through the window I saw Lee, Susan and their followers around the Leather Queen and his slimy agent.

'The company call him Rudolph the Brown Nosed Reindeer,' I told Dan when we met in the Italian restaurant that hovered on stilts over the sea. Knowing he could relax for two days, he was pleasantly drunk before I arrived. By the time the coffee arrived, his head had fallen onto my shoulder. This wasn't in the Worshipped Mistress manual.

'Oh, Eleanor. I love you. You're so strong. Amazing.'

He was fantasising me as much as I was him.

But later, in bed, under the influence of exhaustion and alcohol, and at inebriated half-mast, Dan still gave a better account of himself than David, finally falling asleep on top of me, having forgotten what he was there for. I pushed him off and listened to him snoring beside me. This was the real consequence of losing one's virginity. A hymen is just a membrane of illusions.

'I'll see you on Saturday night then,' he said the next morning, when he'd regained the power of speech.

I quivered my lower lip and gave him a moist-eyed look, but didn't argue. A couple of days apart would do wonders for my romantic image of him and, anyway, David was coming on Friday night with his unlikely temptress. Much as I wanted to hold Dan up as my shield, I didn't want him caught up in the sordid disintegration of my marriage, or to witness the inevitable confrontation.

Suffering from his rare indulgence of the night before, he went back to his flat to sleep and rehydrate. I went for a happy aimless wander and sat for an hour, wrapped deep in my coat, looking out towards Drake's Island, dreaming of flying low over the sun-specked sea with the gulls. I'd just decided to go mad and have an ice cream when my mobile rang.

'Eleanor? It's Cedric.' Floppy floral bow tie, Bordeaux breath and public school manners.

'Hallo, Cedric. How's the Street of Shame?'

'Ah, Eleanor,' I could feel his nostalgia. 'Those were the days, before Murdoch, before Fortress Wapping. Before lunch hours. I ask you, what can one possibly accomplish in an hour? Barely time for the wine to breathe.'

Cedric was a rare surviving dinosaur in a backwater of arts reporting, preserved by his newspaper to deflect accusations of tabloid tendencies. His rambling good nature disguised a still sharp hack whom I'd first met when he was sent to interview the latest flavour of the television month. Me. We got on so well, I'd have slept with him if I'd had the courage. Or if he'd asked.

'What can I do for you, Cedric?'

'Well, my dear, I'm hearing some strange whispers about your producer. That he's possibly not top-drawer.'

'Bargain-basement, Cedric.'

'American egomaniac?'

'Broadway producer who seems to have produced nothing but hot air since 1983 when he had some money in a musical of The Texas Chainsaw Massacre.'

Cedric rumbled appreciatively. 'Well, Eleanor my dear, how would you like to pen me a few words about your new show, mentioning, of course, your producer? Something racy, without being libellous of course. You know the house style.'

'I'm not sure, Cedric –'

'I know, I know, darling girl, you don't want to be seen breaking rank.' He was as warm and jovial as Father Christmas. 'You actresses are supposed to be as pliable as geishas, I know that. But just in case you have anything you want to say...you know where I am.'

'Thanks, Cedric. I'll definitely think about it.'

There was no way I was going to be writing a gossip piece for him. Problem shows were like families riddled with child abuse, you didn't tell, you suffered and moved on, talking only between yourselves about what had been done to you in the name of love.

My daydreams of floating on thermals above the bay were now invaded by thoughts of Izzy. I stood up and walked briskly away from them.

<hr />

The second and final sacking of Dan put an end to my determination not to spill the accusatory beans all over the papers. At seven o'clock on Friday evening, Ruby's voice came over the tannoy:

'Ladies and Gentlemen, please make your way immediately to the green room. Full company to the green room immediately please.'

The urgency of his tone ensured we quickly grumbled and shuffled into the upstairs room where smokers had once been welcome. A faint odour of social sin still hung in the air.

Izzy and Ricky were already there. The Leather Queen looked nervous, his pale lashless eyes watching us for signs of dissent. Sweat darkened his bandana and his hands left marks on his shiny calfskin trousers. Rudolph sat behind him like a compliant but watchful wife. Izzy, by contrast, was already grandstanding, pacing up and down, chewing the cigar and flashing looks of baleful warning at those who entered his sacred space with irreverence. Finally we were all assembled. Ruby languidly draped his anorexic frame across a trestle table. Jonty, Izzy's presence on earth, nervously chewed the side of his already well-chewed index finger. He knew what was coming.

'Okay, guys, everybody here?'

Ruby nodded.

'Yes, Izzy, all here,' said Jonty quickly. 'Except Viola.'

As he spoke she came in, head up, chin jutting out defensively, eyes flicking round like a snake's tongue.

'Okay, guys…' Izzy held his breath, building the tension. 'I want you to meet your new director. Ricky Ricky.'

He put his hand on the LQIB's back and presented him as if he expected us to fall to our knees shouting, 'Habem' Papam.' Glancing round the room, I could see only expressions of disbelief and horror. Who would speak up for Dan? Who would defend him? Susan broke the silence.

'I've got to get my make-up on, it's very nearly the quarter. I just want to do my job.' And she flounced out, pulling her self-righteousness round her.

Lee's head was tilted, calculating which was best for him: to argue for Dan or fall in with Ricky. He stayed silent.

'So, you guys are having a company meal tonight?' With steamroller sensitivity, Izzy continued. 'We'll come along and join you.' He turned to Ricky. 'So you can get to know the company.'

They were smiling broadly as they left, trailing Viola in their wake. Lee, thinking no one was watching, slipped out after them as pandemonium broke out. Several of the girls burst into tears, one of them, a pretty version of the young Liza Minnelli, was distraught, unable to encompass or comprehend the betrayal of Dan. As I listened to the cries of distress around me, I realised she was in the minority. Most were simply indignant and angry at the thought of the Ducks and their creature coming to our company meal.

In their anger, most had forgotten Dan. But only because they were young. The old men stayed silent, fearful of backing the wrong horse. I was already mentally accusing them of spineless acquiescence when KT came up. He was wearing grey sweatpants rolled low on his hips and a tight white vest over his slim torso.

'What's you bastering problem?,' he said, broad Welsh, deep-voiced. His right hand, iron flat, was held up against my objections. 'Where's you tongue, my gell? Bastering cat got it?'

His comic outrage jerked my mouth into action, even though my mind was still in shock.

'Let them come tonight,' I said loudly, 'and I'll talk to them. Please, don't let's panic.'

KT took over: 'Just do the show as usual and don't take any of this crap on stage with you. The punters haven't paid to see a bunch of hysterical twirlies. Eyes, teeth and tits, all right? Oh… It was never like this in the fol-de-rols.'

He finished by shooing the cast out. Only I saw his desperation to get outside the stage door to have a fag, to breathe deep and find some calm. He turned to me. 'You better watch Susan and Lee, they'll be up Ricky's arse quicker than a colonic irrigation.' He put his delicate fingers on my wrist. 'You're on your own if Dan goes – they can't stand you, you're cleverer than them, more talented than them and more famous than them.'

'And better looking.'

'Don't push your luck.'

I did the show in a daze between calls to Dan's mobile. Every few minutes a worried cast member came to my dressing-room. Would we get to London? Would the new director want to keep the dancers? I reassured them I'd do what was necessary to keep Dan and the show exactly as they were. By the end of the performance I was seeing myself as a cross between Arthur Scargill and Saint Joan. That they were both doomed egomaniacs was forgotten as I walked to the company meal. KT was with me, spitting pure acid about Izzy and Viola's duplicity. The Leather Queen was beneath his vast contempt.

'That ugly bitch is behind sacking Dan. She's trying to save her marriage to that bloody gargoyle.'

KT's loyalty ran through him like Brighton through a stick of rock, and his deadly tongue was never so poisonous as when slicing into the flesh of the traitorous. The flaky chorus-boy image, swayed by the passing breeze of opportunity, was simply to fit in with those adrift in a sea of insecurity.

'You've got to understand, Nellie, some people aren't happy unless they're making misery – for each other and everyone else.'

At the subterranean Chinese restaurant, the cast were arriving in small groups, ignoring Viola and Ricky, who were deep in conversation outside. Gesturing to KT that he should go in, I gatecrashed their intimate chat with a smile and a deliberate insensitivity to their furtive plotting.

'It's great you're joining us Ricky, fantastic idea,' I said.

A lie so big it lay like a walrus on the pavement beside us. They didn't seem to notice, though Viola looked wary. The Leather Queen was all over me like sunblock.

'Ohmygod! Eleanor, you're just so out there. You are soo beyond... I cannot wait to start working with you. That duet you have with Lewis?'

The intonation of his voice indicated a question, as did his exaggerated expression of humble openness beneath his floral headscarf.

'I see...' His hands created the scene. 'I see four boys waltzing behind you. With each other. You get it? With each other, wearing tutus, like it's totally normal.' I must have looked like a stunned mullet. 'Really play up the comedy. Yeah?'

He didn't think I'd got it. He spoke louder and slower.

'Then, Eleanor...the sofas you're sitting on? We put them on wheels and they push them on...' – he paused to see if I was following – '...towards each other.'

'While we're singing?,' I asked in disbelief.

'While you're singing!' He yelped in triumph.

I couldn't imagine any moment of Viola's script being described as plumbing the depths of emotional realism, but, as my cut-price Evita found true love with the elderly gardener, our duet was as close as it got. And it gave the audience a rest from the high-octane surrealism of the rest of the show. It was a touching little oasis.

Viola was peering up at her new director. I could see she wasn't convinced either, but this was Izzy's revenge. Anything of Dan's would be thrown on the bonfire of his ego.

There was no point blocking Ricky so early.

'Exactly the lines Dan was going down,' I said. 'Build up the comedy. Let the audience know they can laugh.'

My approval was his cue to open the floodgates of creativity.

'Oh, wow, like, yeah. And the beginning? I see silk...I...see...SILK!' The sibilance was painful. He paused, visualising billowing sails. 'I see silk with the title, okay? The Merchant of Venezuela!, big letters, gold – I see gold...then, then...'

His arms were swinging. An old man passing looked at him like Don Quixote at a windmill. 'Bloody queer,' he muttered. Ricky didn't notice.

'Then...the silk disappears under you as you enter on...a ship!'

A ship? The man was psychiatrically challenged. I couldn't wait to see him tell Basher. I could hear the reaction: 'Fuckin' ship? Fuckin' bollocks.'

'See, Eleanor…' He bent towards me conspiratorially. 'You are the Star and somewhere along the line Dan has lost sight of that.' I hoped my eyes were not spinning in their sockets as they looked into his.

'Ah, yes.' My voice sounded rigid against the deceptive flexibility of his Californian tones. 'Dan. I wonder if we might have a talk. With Izzy, perhaps?'

I looked at Viola. She didn't say anything, but let me lead the way into the restaurant.

The company was sitting at a long table, talking and drinking. They appeared relaxed, but every one of them looked apprehensive or hostile as we came down the stairs.

Izzy sat at the bar, knees wide to the corners of the room, baseball cap pulled down low over his watchful eyes. Next to him, Susan perched on a bar stool in a ferment of vivacity. She threw back her head in appreciative laughter; seconds later she was leaning close, biting her lip with concentration as he spoke. She slid off the stool, moving closer to hear him. Her generous curves pushed out into the room as she shifted her forearms onto the bar – you didn't have to be an expert in body language to understand her proprietorial stance. Or to notice the waiters were treating her like an obstacle in a shipping lane.

Viola, Ricky and I sat in a side booth, studied surreptitiously or blatantly by those at the table. Lee, swaying a large glass of red wine before him, uncoiled and sashayed over, a predatory gleam in his small still-mascaraed eyes. He bent over, head up, neck extended, showing Ricky his imaginary cleavage.

'Ricky, I am *so* thrilled you're on board. We are *so* needing you.'

'For the choreography,' I said, cold enough to chill his rioja.

He didn't bother to acknowledge me. To him the king was dead and so was his court. He pursed his lips in a shadow of a blown kiss towards Ricky and twirled away, his buttocks a riot of semaphore.

I waited until we'd been provided with drinks before I started my pitch. Izzy watched from across the long table but showed no desire to join us.

'Look, I don't want to sound racist here.'

That got their attention. Ricky looked startled, but that could just have been his face-lift, and Viola just looked.

'But there's little or no appetite for Americana at present, there's a slight anti-American whiff in the air for obvious reasons.'

I could see neither of them had any idea what those reasons might be.

'If you impose Broadway "pizzazz",' – I held the word at arm's length – 'it may be regarded in certain quarters as riding roughshod over local sensibilities.' They both looked as if I was speaking Aramaic. 'What I'm trying to say is, are you intending to keep Dan on board in any capacity?'

Viola squirmed and looked down at her hands. Ricky saw her discomfort and jumped in.

'Hey, Eleanor, I always said I want to work with the guy. I love him and I have so much respect... You know what my dream is?'

A flock of flamingos in tap shoes, perhaps?

'My dream,' his fingers spread, conjuring the image, 'is to sit Dan down in the stalls, let him see my work, let him love what I can bring to this party and then...massage his shoulders!'

'Pardon?' What else could I say? – besides, *You need locking up*?

'Oh, Eleanor.' His expansive gesture now became a priestly clasp of my hands. 'Dan is so great, I can see you're so into him but he's tired. Exhausted. All I want to do is lighten his load. I do not, you hear?, do not want to take anything away from him.'

'Good,' I said firmly. 'Because without him you run the risk of losing the good will of the company. Saving your presence, Viola,' – I flicked her a cursory glance – 'Izzy has spooked this cast enough. Much more and you'll have a stampede on your hands.'

That woke her up.

'Are you saying people will walk? They can't do that. It would kill him.'

Not all bad news, then...

'Oh, don't worry about that, Viola, I'm sure everything'll be fine if Dan and Ricky work together, and there's no more grandstanding by Izzy.' I could hear a dead horse being flogged. 'Oh, and um...' I paused; the thought had only just dropped into my head. I felt the thump like a satisfyingly large bundle of letters hitting the doormat. '...you do have a work permit, don't you?'

Rudolph, who'd oozed into the booth after we sat down, came to life. 'It's just a matter of filling in a couple of forms.'

'Really? Only if we want to work in America it's all but impossible to get a work visa.' I paused, certain I was on to something the shape of a spanner, which I itched to ram into all their works. 'So I'm right in thinking you don't have one?'

'It's not a problem,' snapped the agent, closing the subject with a look that would have felled an ox.

Viola said nothing but had an '*Ah don't know nuthin' about making work permits, Miss Scarlett*' look plastered all over her face.

'So, am I right in thinking – until you get your paperwork sorted out with the Home Office visa department –' *Listen to me, Little Miss Prim...* '– that when we get back to London, you will be rehearsing with Dan? With Dan as director.'

'Like I said...' Ricky held his palms towards me so I could see his sincerity. 'I really want to work with him. I don't want to do anything to upset the company or the show. Izzy's a great guy, but he was kinda crazy to say what he did; I don't need to have the title, Dan's got that, Dan's the director. I just want to help.'

'Is that right, Viola? Dan is still the director?'

'Er...well... I suppose...'

'It won't take more than twenty-four hours to sort the permit,' chipped in Rudolph.

'Should we talk to Izzy?,' I asked.

'No,' she replied quickly. 'If that's what Ricky wants, then Dan is still the director. Izzy...just made a mistake.'

Was it really that easy? Was I that good? Despite being congenitally mistrustful of success, I allowed myself to swell a little with pride. I got up from the booth and sat down next to KT.

'Well?'

Everyone was straining to hear the answer.

'It's fine. Ricky's going to work under Dan. Izzy was just flying a kite,' I said, with a broad grin of triumph.

It was swiftly wiped away by the sight of David and Phyllida coming down the stairs with the avenging fury of angels entering the fiery pit. Behind them their two friends hovered close to the door, unwilling to descend to our level.

I had forgotten all about them. That in itself was an achievement for a woman obsessed with images of the cogs of her husband's testicles pumping away between the ship's pistons of his mistress's sturdy thighs.

David was an unhealthy shade of furious and Phyllida looked like an ill-tempered dredger. KT flanked me defensively.

'Where the hell have you been, Eleanor?,' David barked, loud enough to be heard at the back of an average-sized parade ground. 'We've been waiting in the street for an hour.'

I didn't bother with contrition.

'I forgot about you, there were more important things to deal with.'

David exploded: 'How dare you speak to me like that? You seriously think playing in the dressing-up box more important...? Phyllida's absolutely frozen. Apologise immediately.'

My voice, so different now from when I had last seen him, ricocheted off the walls.

'I will not apologise to you – or your mistress.'

Mistress? What badly written script had I remembered that from? The absolute silence in the restaurant lasted five seconds before Izzy shattered it.

'Who the hell is this guy?'

David took a breath. I beat him to it.

'This guy is my fucking husband who's been fucking this fucking woman and now he wants a fucking apology. He should be fucking grateful I'm only eating fucking prawn balls tonight. And as for his fucking horse-faced shag, give her a lump of sugar before she passes out.'

I looked round the room. Susan's jaw was scraping the loudly patterned Axminster, and had Lee been holding a fan he'd have been flapping it about like a towel in a breeze.

For the first time since I'd known him, David was speechless. His mouth opened and closed, but nothing came out. Phyllida spoke for him.

'You cow,' she said. 'You ghastly, ill-bred –'

'Oh tell you pedigree chum to shut her fuckin' row.' It was KT riding to my defence, all guns blazing. 'And as for you, Mr Dick-for-brains –'

He turned on David. I'd always admired KT's turn of phrase, but his comparing David with a mange-ridden camel whose hump was standing next to him was one of his best. Left with little alternative, David slapped my face. I was stunned, but not as stunned as I was when KT hauled off and decked him with a right hook.

'I haven't forgotten everything I learned in Swansea Docks,' he said, as David smashed backwards into the fresh fish display.

Phyllida, screaming, crouched beside him, pulling shrimps out of his hair until the manager and four waiters bundled them up the stairs into the street. He wasn't going to eject any of us – we hadn't paid yet.

KT was shaking as he led me to the bar and ordered a bottle of champagne. 'It's on your bill,' he said. 'Here's to your divorce. About time too, you dozy mare.'

Next morning I woke on the floor of the flat, fully clothed, with my arms round a traffic cone. It was clean – where I'd dribbled on it. KT was sprawled across the sofa with my red Jimmy Choos hanging off his toes.

Unable to move because of the pain, I remembered the night before in jigsaw fragments. After the champagne, KT and I joined the table and sold the Leather Queen to the cast, allaying fears on both sides. We reassured everyone, including the waiters. All this, lubricated by five expensive bottles of champagne, which Ricky and his agent drank with no offer of reciprocation.

Uncomprehending of our generosity, yet suspicious of it, they clinked glasses with us. Several hours later, we stood and clapped them out of the restaurant, assured that Dan and Ricky were now Terry and June. A proxy marriage of convenience.

The euphoria I felt at my triumph, and the desire to allay the dread of David's revenge, kept me drinking until KT and I stood on the Hoe welcoming the dawn with a rendition of the greatest hits from The Wizard of Oz. I seemed to remember the traffic cone was the Wicked Witch's hat.

The doorbell rang as I stood in the shower trying to wash away the pain.

'KT, answer that, will you?'

KT, who'd just made coffee, tottered unsteadily to the front door, only to have it shoved out of his hand as a deranged-looking Viola pushed past and barged into the living room, while I emerged from the bathroom wrapped in towels. KT froze behind her as she launched into me.

'Eleanor, you're vicious, vicious! You are trying to destroy us! Ricky's threatening to go back to the US because you didn't make him feel welcome. He says he can't work if he's not welcome. You didn't welcome him!'

All the work I'd done on my diplomatic skills and my prayers for quiet strength went up in a fire-storm of invective.

'What do you mean, didn't make him welcome?'

My friend had committed suicide, my lover had been sacked, I was leading the biggest, best-polished turd into the West End and now this idiot was accusing me of not schmoozing her cuckoo in my nest.

'So what was he doing drinking my champagne till four o'clock this morning? He and that oil-slick he calls his agent were all over me like chicken pox. When they left everything was fine, you stupid, stupid woman! What the fuck are you on about?'

'Oh, you are so aggressive. I'm trying to have a conversation with you. You upset him. You upset Ricky.' She was whimpering now. 'You upset him asking about his work permit.'

I exploded. All the bile in me poured out as I walked round in circles, the better to compose my contempt.

'Well, what did you expect you daft bint? If you work without a permit you are breaking the law. Our law. This is England, not some outlying protectorate of the American Empire. You can't just do what you like here. It may have by-passed your brain cell, but we've been around for more than a thousand years and no pair of fucking jumped up nyaffs like you are going to come over here and trample on us or our laws. Let me say it again – slowly. He cannot work here without it, or is that too complex a concept for you to grasp? Have you ever heard of the Home Office? Of the Home Secretary? Are you aware that you're in the United Kingdom, or do you think this is some fucking theme park constructed to amuse provincial tourists like you with more money than education or sense?'

There was a shocked silence before she said, with a leaden sarcasm which was the hallmark of her writing, 'Well. It's been nice talking to you.'

'I wish I could say the same,' I spat back, and slammed the flat door in her face.

She hammered on it, screaming like a rottweiler having a hot wax. 'Eleanor, Eleanor! You are evil, you are destroying us.'

'Fuck off,' I yelled back. She retreated, still howling.

KT and I were still in shock when the mobile rang.

'If that's Viola, don't answer it, Nell.'

I looked down at the flashing display. 'Hallo, Dan? Where are you?'

'On my way to the theatre,' he said. 'Izzy's banned me.'

'What?'

Oh God, not again.

'Izzy's told Jonty not to allow me into the theatre.'

'How do you know?'

'Ruby called me.'

'But everything was sorted out last night. He can't do that.' Indignation was the cure for a hangover.

'No, he can't, only the chief exec of the theatre can. But he's in London.' He paused. I could hear him lighting a cigarette. The smoke rattled into his lungs. He coughed painfully. 'Can you get your hands on a disposable camera?'

'Er…yes…sure.'

'Come to the stage door. I'll need evidence… I haven't been told I'm sacked officially, so they're stopping me from going into my place of work. That's unlawful.'

'Is that the same as illegal?'

'Apparently not, but it's good enough for a lawsuit.'

'I'll see you there,' I said and rang off. I didn't think it was the moment to ask if he'd missed me or to tell him about Viola.

———

KT and I were in the car-park when Dan arrived. He looked shocking: grey and shrunken in the shapeless beige raincoat he'd retreated into as things fell apart around him. A sudden breeze caught up a black bin-bag and wrapped it round his legs.

'Very bloody symbolic,' said KT, pulling it off.

We walked towards the stage door either side of Dan. He had his hand on the handle when it opened and Jonty came out. Dan immediately made it easy for him.

'Jonty, I know you've got to do this. Don't worry. I don't blame you.'

The company manager didn't look any happier.

'Izzy has instructed me not to allow you backstage or to let you speak to any of the cast.'

KT took the camera from my hand. Taking his cue, Dan attempted to open the stage door and Jonty, with little force, prevented him.

'I'm really sorry, mate,' he said closing the door behind him with reluctant finality. Dan took his arm, which KT didn't photograph, and suggested we went over to the bar.

Jonty, clutching a Red Bull, curled in on himself in a paroxysm of self-flagellation and painfully climbed off the fence. Head down, he admitted he loathed the Ducks.

'Well, when did you get that revelation?,' asked KT amiably.

'When they told me to wait till you' – he looked at me – 'were out of the way at that funeral, then get the cast together to tell them to persuade Dan to walk off the show.'

'What did you do?,' asked Dan, sipping his coffee as if we were discussing wisteria.

'I went to the cinema. But Izzy phoned Tizer. I hadn't thought of that. Poor kid.'

Jonty had finally joined us as 'the enemy', but we could appreciate his reluctance when he told us: the Ducks owed him £25,000.

'Twenty-five grand?,' I yelped. 'How the fuck did that happen?'

Jonty tried to pass it off as nothing. 'Oh…well…it's just that they don't have a bank account here and I've been putting everything through my credit card.'

KT's mouthful of grapefruit juice sprayed across the table. 'You've got twenty-five thousand on your credit card? Bloody hell, you could buy a house in Port Talbot for that.'

'Jonty, you've got to get it back,' I said, almost lost in the enormity of his gullibility '*Now*. You cannot trust those bastards, believe me.'

His public school confidence wouldn't allow me to be right.

'Don't worry, Eleanor, they're not going anywhere. Izzy just has to make a bit of a fuss before he divs up. It makes him feel like the big producer.'

We chatted for a while longer, persuading ourselves that there'd be a happy ending, then KT and I got up to leave for the matinée warm-up. Dan looked up at me, his eyes so sad I wanted to hold him like a child and make it all go away.

'Tell the company I'll be in here for a drink tonight after the show. To say goodbye.'

'Don't worry, Dan, you'll be back next week. Once the Leather Queen in the Bandana shows how crap he is.'

'No, Ellie. This is it.'

I knew he was right. This time there'd be no way back through the barbed wire of Izzy Duck's ego.

⁕

KT and I walked slowly to the theatre. I felt as if I was in shock, insulated from reality by an immovable conviction that everything was unchanged: that Dan would be back on Monday; that what had happened was just my imagination. On the other hand I was worrying about my position with Viola.

'Well you was a bit strong, gell. Vitriolic, one might say.' KT gave me a look of awed admiration. He saw my discomfort. 'Now don't go backing down, Eleanor. I know what you're like, you'll be sending her a box of chocolates and saying it was your hormones.'

'You know,' I said wistfully, 'I never really wanted to be an actress. I wanted to be a forensic scientist.'

KT stopped. 'You? A scientist? A lab rat, maybe. But scientist? Get a grip.'

'Maybe you're right. I just like the idea of working with dead people.'

He put his face close to mine, I could smell last night's excess. 'Do not back down now, Ellie. You is half-way out of the chrysalis.'

'I won't.' It was easy to say. 'Not this time, KT. They can beat me with a copy of last week's Stage, pull my toenails out or fire me – but I'm not going back to being Little Miss Meek.'

My new defiance didn't stop me worrying my way through the matinée. I was praying, literally, that Izzy wouldn't come backstage, and that I wouldn't have to see Ricky and his oleaginous sidekick.

The strain told in the evening performance: singing flat, jumbling words and fighting mutinous feet. The audience didn't seem to care and we finished in Plymouth with a full house hollering their approval. For me, gratifying but undeserved.

I was wiping off my make-up when the dressing-room door opened after a knock that I had no chance to answer.

'Eleanor, pal. I gotta talk to you.'

Izzy was in the room, his baseball cap shading his eyes.

'I'm in a hurry, Izzy.' Was he going to sack me too? I tasted the humiliation. 'I'm driving back to London.' I didn't add, 'via Dan's wake'.

'You know Viola is so upset. What you said to her was bad –'

The split-second it took for me to decide whether to grovel or attack was filled by Izzy continuing, without looking at me.

'But, pal, I understand. Your granny died, I know that. You're upset. Old people get sick and die, I know that, and the show's a lot of pressure on you. Tonight you were down, I could see that, but you're still a great actress. You're a star, the star of my show.'

I was astonished at his magnanimity and for a moment touched. Perhaps he wasn't an alien monster with the brain of a wolverine... I turned to him, ready to put all animosity aside. He was gazing at me with liquid sincerity.

'So, pal, I'm on your side. I just need you to be behind me. Viola's breaking up, you know? She's not strong like you and me.'

If only you knew, I thought.

'I'm looking to you to lead the company. I want us to be solid, you and me, understand? So here's the bottom line.' The soup went out of his eyes. 'I don't want any more talk about Dan. Not one word. He betrayed me, Eleanor, I can't begin to say how much. He's out of the picture. You got that? I can't have a guy like that in the team. I can't trust him. Ricky's the director now and he wants the best for you. You gotta trust him. I never shoulda trusted Dan.'

He was Napoleon surrounded by traitors. I watched him through the mirror, entirely absorbed in the fiction of his victimisation. Dan tried to screw him, the last in a long line trying to screw him – Izzy Duck, the would-be saviour of the moribund West End.

'...They don't know what we're bringing them. This is dynamite, pal. When they see Susan they're gonna see how dumb they were not to spot her before, she's gonna be a star, believe me. And Lee is gonna bring the house down. That boy's got it, pal...like you got it.'

Ah, yes. Me. An afterthought. To be kept sweet until they could afford to lose me. After all, the flyers had my name above the title and the cost of reprinting would be prohibitive. No, by the time we opened in London I'd be little more than a cameo and his creatures would be the well-set gems. Even as he left my room, showering me with florid compliments and saliva, he couldn't meet my gaze, which was by now cold, steady and deeply unfriendly.

When he'd gone I looked at myself in the mirror. What was I looking at? A heroine or a harridan? The problem with real life is, there's no audience to tell you you're right, no nicely constructed story where judgement and justice are one. I had no idea if I was right in declaring war on the Ducks, in being loyal to Dan. Was I the bully? They were paying my wages, so should I put up and shut up? My opinion of my employers' moral code was not only irrelevant but impertinent, wasn't it? Yes, but...

I left the theatre, my mind racing with contradictory convictions and fears.

Most of the company were already surging round Dan when I arrived at the bar. He was laughing with Tizer and Ruby while the Liza Minnelli look-alike cried in his paternal arms. Only Susan, Lee and his acolyte were absent.

'Lee sent a text,' said Dan with a twinkle when I pointed out their disloyalty. 'Said he had a cold coming on and he didn't want to give it to me.'

'Pity it's not rabies. And Susan?,' I enquired sweetly, accepting a bottle of beer from Tizer. He was too young to know that a glass wasn't an optional extra.

'Failure is more contagious than rabies. You have to give it to her, she doesn't sit on the fence.'

'She would have last week if your face had been on it,' I said, and was greeted by an appreciative hiss from Ruby, who seemed to be thoroughly enjoying himself.

I sipped at my beer and watched while maudlin resignation and over-bright optimism took hold of the drinkers around me. With Dan gone, how safe were any of us? All over the world people were being crucified, raped and starved, but in that hour the lives and agonising deaths of millions weren't remotely as important as the prospect of unemployment and the renewed search for a safe wage packet.

There were emotional scenes of alcoholic affection as the bar closed and the staff swept the floor under us. Dan was smothered in loyalty and outrage as we walked to the car-park, but I knew that most, if not all, of those demonstrations of company spirit would evaporate by morning, to be replaced by sheepish hangovers, pragmatism and the relief that Sunday brings in a six-day week.

Dan fell asleep in the passenger seat after a rambling appreciation of 'the kids', his hand on my thigh.

KT stretched out on the back seat of our hire car, eyes closed, and didn't speak again until I dropped him at his front door. The long journey was blissfully silent. I drove, concentrating on the road through veils of rain, unthinking and glad of the relief. We reached KT's in the cold, pitch dark just before dawn.

'You staying with him or me?,' KT asked, leaning in through my window to kiss my cheek. He'd opened his front door before I answered, knowing I couldn't abandon Dan in the state he was in.

'Goodnight, Nellie. And here.' He trotted back. 'Take a door key. See you whenever you need a bed to yourself.'

I virtually carried Dan up to his flat and, defeated by his determination to listen to 'Love Songs of the Seventies' on the hi-fi, went into his bedroom and collapsed, fully dressed, on the bed. Thinking of Henry V the night before Agincourt, I drifted into sleep. Could I rally the troops? Probably not, as no one was sure who the enemy was. To some it was the man diddy-bopping round the living room, singing along with his youth; to others, it was the Jabberwocky with the cigar. To the rest, it was me.

ACT FOUR

An American in Paris

THIRTY

Dan and I spent that Sunday pretending we were young lovers in late-summer, sun-drenched London. Well, we were in London, we were drenched and we were still young enough to have to pay bus fares, but Dan couldn't raise a smile, let alone anything else, so after a silent supper I left him in the gathering gloom of his depression and headed for KT's.

'I'll call you,' he said, closing the door without a kiss but with evident relief.

'He seemed all right last night,' said KT as I dumped my bag in his spare room.

'It's all an act. He'll be on the Prozac by Tuesday, poor sod.'

I wanted to talk, to try to make some sense of what was happening to Dan – and, more importantly, of what was happening to my emotions. While I felt insulated by kapok from the intensity of my confusing romance, the extremes of my everyday feelings were exhausting me. In the space of a few minutes, I was going from happy optimism to wrist-slitting depression via flat-line indifference.

But I realised, having seen his semi-naked form flit into the kitchen, that Kelvin the Canadian was in residence, and KT wasn't listening to a word I said.

He closed the door and went back to what sounded increasingly like an Olympic trampolining event. I sat on my bed, clutching pink elephant between my breasts, all too aware of the irony. Sleep was slow to arrive and dragged me through a night of agitation and anxiety, before departing through the uncurtained window at another unwelcome dawn.

Kelvin went not long after with a great deal of *shsh*ing and *'Ellie's asleep, be quiet'*, followed by a yelp of surprised pleasure. I tried not to grudge them their joy, and failed. I was just giving myself up to self-pity when the door was kicked open and KT came in carrying a ridiculously laden tray of breakfast.

'I'm starving,' he said, shovelling scrambled egg onto toast and then into his mouth. 'Come on girl, get stuck in.'

'I didn't work up quite the same appetite as you did last night,' I said, with just a dash of acid.

'Ooh, Miss Minty,' he mumbled, spraying egg and crumbs over the duvet and my lucky elephant. 'Lucky elephant?,' he screeched. 'You want to burn the bastard. And that husband of yours and all. You going to sort things out with him today?'

I rummaged about for an excuse: 'No, I'll wait till after I get a rehearsal call. I can only do one thing at a time. We're bound to be in tomorrow to sort this mess out. It'll only take that long for Izzy to realise he can't do it without Dan.'

But Izzy was more stupid than even I gave him credit for. When Dan's agent arrived back from a weekend in the Cotswolds he found a fax from Izzy's overpaid and overconfident solicitors. This time there was no doubt. Dan had been sacked in the most ignominious terms.

Dan showed me the fax himself over a cup of KT's Earl Grey. He hadn't slept, although tired beyond the point of sleep. He couldn't walk away from the show without losing the money Izzy owed him, but his notice said not only that Ricky Ricky would replace him as of the previous Friday, precisely dated, but that any attempt to claim monies from the producer would be robustly rebuffed on the grounds that Dan had not fulfilled his contract by 'poor and ill-considered work which was to the detriment of the production and, because of this, had failed to take the aforesaid production through to West End press night, when final payment would become due...'

I watched him reread the insulting words. He looked pathetic. Unattractive enough, but with his unwashed hair and strong reek of cigarettes I should have found him repulsive. He looked and smelt like a failure, not so far from the sad men shuffling through the rubbish-strewn gutter, selecting dog-ends as if they were gold in a stream. And he was weak. David wouldn't have caved in like this. Real men didn't sit staring into nothing with tears in their eyes. But David's resolute lack of vulnerability was precisely what I now found repellent. He had never needed anything I could offer, and had rarely wanted anything either.

Izzy and Viola had reduced this man to an insomniac wreck, and all because he'd worked sixteen hours a day. KT put him in the shower then into my bed, while I phoned the union and Dan's agent. Both were outraged and determined to fight, but there was little more they could do. Dan's humiliation and wrecked health had no value beyond his outstanding fee.

'You daft bat,' said KT. 'Didn't you tell them about the work permit?'

The truth was, I couldn't really believe anyone would be stupid enough to take on such a high profile job without the right papers. A pot-boy in an Albanian restaurant, yes, but someone who was going to be plastered all over the national newspapers? We were still talking when Ruby rang with our rehearsal calls: Thursday for me; Wednesday for KT; and tomorrow, Tuesday, for Lee, Susan and a couple of the others, Kelvin included.

'What's going on?,' I asked him.

I could hear him shrug. 'Beats me. All I know is they've got new script pages and they want to redo Lee and Susan's numbers.'

'So they want me out of the way till Thursday.'

'Looks like it, mate. I'll keep you posted.'

I didn't mind being sacked, but what they were going to do was downgrade and humiliate me. I phoned my agent to sound off.

'But, darling,' he said dismissively, 'you'll get paid the same. What's the problem?

'You're joking, aren't you?'

'Of course, darling, but I'm ashamed to say, I can't really help you – unless you want out.'

I sighed. Tempted.

'Thanks, but not yet…'

I called Cedric.

'Cedric, how do I get hold of the Home Office snatch squad?'

'Dear Heart, why would you want them? Got illegal Chechens in the company?'

'No, Cedric, a big fat juicy American masquerading as a director.'

'Do I smell a scandal?'

'Not yet, Cedric, but if I need the dogs of war…?'

'Oh, my dear, I'll let them slip, for an exclusive.'

'If there is one, I'll give it to you on an embroidered plate.'

There was no such thing as a free contact. Cedric reminded me of the piece he wanted me to write.

'You may consider my paper the embodiment of evil, Ellie, but think of us as a tool that cuts both ways.'

The idea of breaking ranks with the flock still worried me. Actors didn't do that sort of thing. I could hear the clecking tongues and the thrilled outrage my whistle-blowing would cause. Not to my face of course, just a few well-placed pearl handles between the shoulder blades.

But now it seemed worth raising my head above the parapet, even if I knew there'd be plenty wanting to stick it on a pole. Maybe if I wrote about what we were going through, the critics would realise that the mess they were going to see wasn't our fault. Though I doubted Cedric's reviewer, 'Osama' Kim Bardon, would let us off, even if we were being forced to perform at gunpoint…

Cedric allowed the silence to go on, then, judging his moment, said: 'Fifteen hundred words by Wednesday lunch-time all right? Don't worry if it's a bit rough, I'll tidy it up.'

Once I'd said yes, the fears didn't evaporate, but I did feel I had some power, rare for an actor. Mistrustful of it, I phoned Izzy.

'Izzy –'

'Yes?'

'I've been asked to write about the rehearsal and performance process so far for one of the nationals. What do you think?'

'I have to think about this, Eleanor. I have to give it consideration.'

I almost wanted him to say no, to absolve me of the responsibility of being a grass. Snitch. Narc…

'Naturally, I'd let you read the piece before I submit it. You can have copy approval.'

With his usual chameleonic change of tone, he lurched from distant formality to overbearing familiarity.

'Eleanor, I know you. I know you better than you know yourself; you'd never do anything to harm this show. Maybe you and Viola had a little falling-out but, hell, I don't need to read your piece till it's in the paper. You know I'm a journalist myself. Every week I write for the front page, you get that, the front page of Voz del Pueblo. Diary of a Broadway Producer in English. Say, pal, why don't I send you over some of my cuttings? Maybe give you some ideas. See, what you need is to get in touch with your inner perfection. That's what I tell Viola when she writes…'

Another three minutes of psychobabble and then he hung up, satisfied I was back on message and in my box.

Within the hour Cedric called back with a number for the Home Office. I rang it immediately, before I lost courage. A youngish, bored-sounding man answered, but his lack of interest might just have been the result of an expensive education that involved being separated from his family at an early age.

I explained as clearly as I could, until I ran out of confidence.

'Well,' he drawled, 'this Ricky Ricky's American, you say.'

'Yes.'

He went on as if I was mentally challenged. 'Well, madam, we don't really worry too much about US citizens.'

That tilted me from diplomatic supplicant to blackmailer. 'Have you any idea what trouble this would cause the Home Secretary if it got into the press that you turn a blind eye to illegal Americans but prevent teachers and nurses from returning to this country from the Commonwealth if their papers aren't in order?' *No reply.* 'Not to mention the rafts of illegals you're allowing to escape into the community. It really wouldn't play well in the right-wing press. Especially as an award-winning British stage director has been sacked to make way for him.'

I couldn't tell whether or not my impassioned outburst had dented the Voice's patronising superiority, but he did ask me about Ricky Ricky's details: date of birth, date of arrival, port of entry, star sign and inside leg measurement... Answering as accurately as I could, I didn't hold out much hope of a ninja raid on the rehearsal room the moment I hung up.

'There you go,' said KT, slapping a cup of tea and his lap-top down in front of me. 'Better get writing, you got a deadline.'

'Where's Kelvin?,' I asked, as he flopped onto the sofa and flicked the television remote control through twenty channels before settling for a cartoon that seemed to have been made by a deaf psychopath on drugs.

'Having a nervous breakdown in the bath. He's been called in to rehearse "improvements" to his character. Well, that's what Viola told him, anyway.' I put my face in my hands. 'It's all right, I've got his passport. And the razors.'

Three hours later Kelvin was still in the bathroom, but now with a bottle of champagne and KT. I finished off my article for Cedric and, without even spell-checking it, e-mailed it to him. Too late to back out now. The tone of it was light, but it left the reader in no doubt about the motorway pile-up we were about to present.

I sat back, guilty and exhilarated, completely unsure if what I had done was truly for the greater good or simply revenge. Their images in my mind were joined by the floating head of David. It wasn't floating in a canal or a vat of boiling, extra-virgin olive oil; it was simply there, in vivid shades of red and yellow, projected on the interior of my eyelids. That was odd, because I'd never been someone who could conjure the faces of loved ones, or picture scenes of tranquillity during hypnotherapy. Dan's face was a blur of sunspots – but David's smug expression was etched in perfect detail, no matter how hard I blinked or tried to replace him with pictures of sheep, goats or anything else that wasn't my husband.

Finally, unable to shift the infestation, I grabbed my door keys, shoved them in my handbag, ran downstairs and hailed a taxi before I could change my mind. David and I were going to sort this out before I went into rehearsal on Thursday morning. One nightmare at a time.

THIRTY-ONE

The house looked the same. I don't know why I was surprised; I suppose because I'd assumed everything had changed as much as I had.

The four-wheel-drive was nowhere to be seen, though, and more disturbingly, neither was my old car. Was it MOT time? I couldn't recall. I walked up the path and was pleased to see David had remembered to put out the recycling bags. Even with his marriage falling apart, he could be relied on to observe the public niceties, lest the neighbours suspect.

It took me several minutes to realise that my front door key didn't fit the lock. I must have looked like a beached goldfish with my mouth opening and shutting, as I gasped for air and words to express my fury. I slapped my hand on the doorbell and left it there. The ringing echoed round the house.

David wasn't in. I pushed open the stiff letter-box, bending to peer through it. What did I expect to see? Narnia?

Nothing seemed different in the hallway: it was peaceful, silent, a pile of Indian restaurant flyers neatly stacked on the table. The sight of them started an itch in my mind. Hadn't I seen the recycling bags neatly lined up by the bin?

No, what I'd glanced at without thinking was a row of blue plastic bin-liners, bulging under their anally tied necks. I approached them slowly, already sure of what I'd find inside. Carefully untying David's sheepshanks, I found my clothes. In another, my ornaments; in the third, my shoes.

As it started to drizzle, I howled. Sliding down the wheelie-bin until I was sitting with my back against it, feet flattening my carefully planted crocuses, I cried out loud in wordless misery. But no one came; no parental hand pulled me up and wiped away my tears. Not even a neighbour or passer-by witnessed my despair.

Finally, empty and alone, I heaved myself upright, pulling the wheelie-bin over in the process. My first instinct was to pick up the spilled rubbish. My second was to distribute it evenly over the parquet bricked drive. As I scattered food remains and milk cartons across the front path, I remembered one of the few secrets I had kept from David.

Nothing had made him more delighted or more sarcastic than the frequency with which I locked myself out of the house – closing the front door at the very moment I remembered the keys were on the kitchen table.

'Oh, Kipper Feet,' he'd sigh loudly with a sympathy that was not only false but cruelly patronising. 'I'll have to put them on a bit of string round your neck. Maybe they could go on the same one that holds your mittens on your duffle coat.'

So, knowing I could defeat neither my husband nor my stupidity, and knowing the serial-numbered front door keys couldn't be copied easily, I sneaked the back door key down to the Kashmiri at the dry cleaners and had another made in bright gold. Surely David wouldn't have changed the back door lock as well? There was only one way to find out.

I dragged the over-worked wheelie bin to the back gate, clambered onto it, straddled the lintel, grateful for the daily dance classes, then realised there was a seven-foot drop on the other side.

Carefully clinging to the splintered wood, I swung my leg over so I was sitting like Humpty Dumpty. Slowly, tentatively, I manoeuvred my body round to face the door, then, biceps straining with the weight, I lowered myself, face catching on the creosoted door, until I was hanging by my fingertips. My feet were nowhere near the ground.

I let go, banged my knees on the door and bounced back onto my bottom. But I was triumphant – until it struck me that someone may have seen me and would now be phoning the police.

'Sorry, officer, I locked myself out. You see I'm not awfully bright, I'm an actress you see... My husband's always telling me I'm educationally sub-normal, but I do have awfully nice breasts, would you like to see them...?'

The hiding place of the multi-vitamin jar containing my secret key, a space between wall and drainpipe, was black with cobwebs and guarded by a spider the size of a small dog. The arachnid minder was patiently waiting for anything to fly into her web except the broom handle that smashed through her living room.

The plastic of the jar was so wrapped in spider by-products I couldn't see inside, and was squeamish about picking it up. What if the covering of dirty silk was home to the mother's vengeful offspring? I poked it with the broom handle. Nothing moved. Eventually I gathered my fears, locked them in a vacant part of my brain – plenty of space there, David would have said – and opened it. The bright key rattled out into my hand.

I calculated that after the door was opened there was just time to sprint to the burglar alarm control panel before it went off. I put the key in the lock. I couldn't breathe.

It turned smoothly. Silently. How great small triumphs seem.

What if he'd changed the alarm code?

Visions of me, face pressed into the hall wallpaper, my hand wincingly screwed behind my back by a hatchet-faced WPC. Before I could panic and collapse again, I rushed into the house. The indignant bleep of the alarm ticked the seconds before I could get to the buttons and press the familiar numbers. The bleeping continued endlessly. Any second and the wailing alarm would sound…the phone ring…the police alerted…the sirens.

Then…silence.

He hadn't changed the code. Eleanor wouldn't be bright enough to get through the door, so David's great intellect would tell him there was no need to change it.

My rush of happy adrenalin was quenched when I saw how completely he had erased me from my own home. It was as if I'd never existed.

In the bedroom my wardrobe was full of Phyllida's clothes. In the bathroom my frog toothbrush had been replaced by a turbo-powered monster still bearing the marks of her lipstick. Had he done all this in just two days? I was nothing more than a ghost.

Wandering round my familiar and unfamiliar house, looking for memories and finding nothing but shadows where my pictures had hung. What could I do? Set a fire? Cut up his suits? Leave the taps running with the plugs welded in place? I could think of nothing original enough until I remembered the freezer.

David never examined its contents, as this was my territory and beneath his interest. I went down to the cellar and opened the coffin-like repository of my revenge.

A bag of frozen haddock.

I grabbed a hammer and nails from the toolbox, ran upstairs and nailed fish to the back of the wardrobe. One went in the lavatory cistern, one behind the boiler and two under the chairs either side of the living room hearth.

I replaced the hammer and made sure there was no sign of my being in the house, then I called a mini-cab, reset the alarm and left – again via the back gate, this time jumping, then hauling myself up, gripping the soles of my trainers against its rough paint. I collected my bin-liners from the front garden and waited for the car. To fill the time, I called my solicitor and told him what had happened.

'What a nasty little man,' he said, cheerfully. He'd always been gorgeous in my eyes, never more so than now. 'You'd better come in and see me. Lunch, I think, don't you? You do want a divorce I take it.'

'Can it be back-dated?,' I asked, as a clapped out Sierra hove into view. I loaded it up with my world and went back to KT's.

I slept well that night.

THIRTY-TWO

Limbo – the concept rather than the dance – I'd always found unbelievable, even before the Vatican acknowledged its contrivance. But the experience of opening a show successfully out of town, and then having life put on hold before its birth in the West End, characterised the place where unborn souls languish.

Kelvin, suffering in that place between heaven and nothingness, was shooed out of the flat on Tuesday morning by KT.

'If you don't go to rehearsal –'

'I know,' drawled Kelvin. 'They'll fire me.'

'No, you daft tart,' said KT. 'We won't know what's going on; now get going before I slap you.'

There were several distressed calls from Kelvin during the day, describing the lunacy of Ricky, as well as one from my solicitor, promising to take David to Sketchleys. He was far too posh to say 'the cleaners'. But there was no call from our producer to his leading lady.

The only communication was from Jonty, to say the first week of previews had been cancelled – 'to institute improvements…'

Kelvin returned that evening, gaunt with misery. KT sat him down and plied him with industrial quantities of gin, until he relaxed enough to tell us what had happened.

⁕

Arriving at ten a.m. he found Ricky Ricky, Viola and Izzy closeted with Susan in a small windowless rehearsal room lined with mirrors and ballet barres.

'It's so fabulous,' wittered Viola, turning towards Ricky, parroting the latest credo. 'That terrible place Dan had us in had no mirrors. Everybody knows you can't work choreography without mirrors.'

'You can't rehearse a musical in a cupboard under the stairs either. This is way too small, and there's no air con,' said Kelvin, wiping the sweat from his neck.

Izzy waved his cigar dismissively. 'We have three rooms. Ricky knows what he's doing.'

Kelvin kept his mouth shut after that. He'd rehearsed at this very expensive venue before; the studios were all the same size and it wasn't known as the Sauna for nothing.

'Ricky, show Kelvin what you're doing with Susan's number.' Izzy put his arm round Susan's shoulders as she prepared to show off in front of indulgent relations. The song that Dan had cut down and controlled as if it were leylandii had not only been reinstated, but Susan was ornamenting it in a way even Whitney Houston would have found excessive.

There wasn't a note unbent or a vowel untortured. Susan boasted a three-octave range and was buggered if we weren't going to hear every semitone, even if those at the top could only be appreciated by bats and those at the bottom threatened to attract whales. By the time she had finished her pained and passionate rendition, she was emotionally wrung out and near to collapse. Izzy was in tears; Viola stared at her with Marian devotion and Ricky, perched on a table, was flushed with pride.

'God 'elp us.' KT interrupted Kelvin's monologue.

Lee was then paraded before Kelvin with his newly choreographed show-stopper. All Dan and Flossie's gentle wit had been ripped out and replaced by a pelvis-thrusting, homoerotic, choral gyration, with Lee striking a set of unlikely poses with an ostrich feather. This, like Susan's number, ran more than twice the length of the original.

Having shown Kelvin the glories that could also be his, Izzy, Viola and Ricky started on their plans for him. The original psychopath Viola had written was back, and his solo was cut.

'It just doesn't fit now we have Lee in Act One and Susan in Act Two.'

The consolation for this was that he would now sing a longer version of the opening as an escapee from a secure mental unit, finishing with a new verse:

We rape, we sodomise our mothers,
God didn't make us – this is what we are.
We're DNA floating in a cosmos of cruelty.
Ain't no mercy in this world,
And ain't no such world as the next.
What you want you take,

236

Burning the eyes of your grandmother,
To take what you're owed,
To take what you're owed.

Kelvin read the words to us as we sat on the sofa slack-jawed with disbelief.

'It doesn't even scan,' was all I could say.

Kelvin slumped over his G'n'T. KT took the new lyrics from him and stared at them. When he'd gathered the strength to speak, Kelvin told us his costume, a superb double-breasted pin-stripe suit and corresponding shoes, would be replaced by rags. And a bloody axe, just in case anyone didn't realise he was a sociopathic killer.

'Only thing I can do,' he said bleakly, 'is put so much make-up on no one will recognise me.'

'Too late to change your name though,' said KT cheerily, handing me the dreadful song.

'Can't your agent get you out? You didn't sign up to do this,' I said.

Kelvin groaned a *no*. 'I can't afford to walk, Eleanor, I don't have any money.'

'None of us has,' I said. 'God knows no lottery-winner would have signed up for this, it's worse than eating a kangaroo penis.'

I didn't mention my crushed dreams of being hailed as a bright new star in the London firmament. Kelvin sank further into despondency and I was reminded of a mouse caught on a glue trap, alternately resigned to death and struggling for life.

We went to bed that night drunk and hysterical.

<hr />

I was left alone on Wednesday, as both KT and Kelvin were called, so took the opportunity to see Felix, my solicitor. On my way there, KT rang.

'Karen's been fired.'

'Karen,' I repeated stupidly. 'The musical director? Why? We can't do the show without her.'

'Well, we'll have to. She stood up in front of the whole company and asked Izzy what he was going to do about Dan's intellectual copyright.'

That hadn't occurred to me. Everything in the production that was Dan's original idea, including the complex scene-changes, song lyrics and some of the better dialogue, couldn't be used without his permission – or without them paying him. Neither seemed likely.

'So Izzy sacked her?,' I asked.

'Oh no, he disappeared in a puff of smoke and twenty minutes later Jonty told her she was out. As of immediately.'

'How did she take it?'

'She was shattered. I had to pack her bag for her. She went, and no one dared say a word. I offered to have a go, but she said no. I think she was relieved to be out, to be honest. She's got no money either, but she's held onto her sanity.'

With Dan and Karen gone, there was only Flossie left of the original creative team, and his temper was volatile enough to make his presence at the first night party questionable.

Still thinking about the mess we were in I arrived at Felix's office in Lincoln's Inn Fields. It was always a pleasure to spend time in his company – charming, handsome, urbane, he loved the idea of 'actresses' and, in his rather cerebral world, found the idea of me rather racy.

I always felt I was a disappointment.

After lunch he dealt swiftly with the details of disposing of David, assuring me that half of everything would be mine just as soon as the law would permit. I tried not to think of the house I'd put so much into, already stripped of my existence. Half of that, half his money and half his pension...I wasn't really listening. Half my life gone. I hoped my anger with David would burn long enough to protect me from the cold despair of being a lonely middle-aged divorcee with nothing to show for her marriage but a larger bank balance and a prolapsed womb.

Felix's company and largesse buoyed me up until I got back to the flat, where I was faced with the reality of my life contained in a row of bin liners. I reminded myself I had no right to misery. Divorce wasn't uncommon, difficult shows were the norm. What did I have to be self-pitying about?

Knowing I wasn't best, special, the only one for anyone. Maybe no one is after parental death.

I tried to put out of mind thoughts of perfect marriages, soul mates and all the happy endings I'd been brought up to believe in. They really shouldn't teach girls that stuff, handsome princes and the triumph of good. Boys didn't buy into all those fairy-tales and they were happier. Weren't they? I tried to phone my son:

'Hi, Arthur here – leave a message.'

'Hello, darling…um…your father and I are getting divorced.'

KT and Kelvin came home and I knew it wasn't true. Maybe it was just straight men who sailed through life without dreams. Then I remembered Dan and I ripped my thesis up. Everyone was bloody miserable.

'Well, your finale's out,' said KT when he was settled with a drink and a cigarette. 'You now come on, sing one verse of that song that was cut in the first week –'

'Not that dreadful dirge –'

'Yep. "Life Doesn't Dry Up After the Menopause".' He paused dramatically. 'Then Susan does a reprise of her number and after the curtain call the encore is Lee's number sung by all of us.'

This was true humiliation. Singing 'A Noisy Queen Is a Happy Queen' behind Lee…

'What am I supposed to do during all this?'

'No idea, love, you'll find out tomorrow, I suppose. Susan's like a dog with two tails –'

'Susan is a dog with two tails,' said Kelvin, quietly but with feeling.

'And Ricky's put your first scene immediately after Kelvin opens the show.'

'But Dan told them that wouldn't work. The scene's not strong enough. It's not funny. It only works if my character's been built up and the audience is gagging to see me.'

I don't know why I was wasting my breath.

THIRTY-THREE

The sun was bright in a clear blue sky as I made my way to rehearsal. My call was before Kelvin and KT's, so I was alone when I rounded the corner and saw the company sitting and standing on the stone steps outside. They all seemed to be reading newspapers. My heart thumped; sweat covered my top lip. Cedric had run my piece.

'Eleanor, you are *so* bad.' It was Glenda. 'But what means this? "Dan was fired so often we called him Uzi"?'

'I'll explain later.'

'It doesn't matter… I just love what you say about me.'

To show her appreciation of being described as a living Venus, she embraced me in a cloud of scent as potent as her looks. God just smiled, held his hands together in a praying gesture and bowed his thanks. God rarely touched anyone except Glenda, as he was self-conscious about the psoriasis that crept across his skin as we neared performance – a touching vulnerability that undercut his peacock vanity.

The others in the group were equally enthusiastic, thrilled at my naughtiness – at least to my face. I immediately felt guilty for suspecting them of duplicity. They were just kids – Tizer, the Liza Minnelli look-alike – all trusting me to lead them to some sort of salvation.

'Is it always like this?,' asked my understudy, a girl barely old enough to remember my wig being made.

'Only in musicals,' I said. 'It's like childbirth: the final result is supposed to be worth the pain.'

We all laughed, more from companionship than amusement, and I went in to find our new director.

'Ohmygod, Eleanor, Darling.' Ricky Ricky greeted me with air kisses. 'You have to meet Charlie and Brandon, my assistants.'

He was standing with two young men, both in shrink-wrapped black. Each was holding a notebook, in which they wrote their master's inspirational thoughts.

'What are we doing, Charlie?'

Charlie consulted his gospel and replied, with more sibilance than a leaking gas-pipe: 'You're restaging the opening scene with Eleanor first, Ricky.'

'Uh huh.' Ricky considered this as though it were a proposal to invade Syria. 'Right. Okay, while we're doing that you go tell the kids I want all the boys to wear black, tight, I want to see the contours, you got me? And the girls, colours, bright, no leg warmers and full make-up at all rehearsals – and tell them to diet, they gotta be beautiful. It's too late to do anything about their teeth. My God, don't they have dentists in England? Go tell them. And make a note, the ugly ones go at the back, okay?'

Trinny and Susannah dipped an obeisance to their master and wiggled off to tell our rag-tag chorus that they were to be transformed into Broadway gypsies before the afternoon call.

'Ricky, why are we working on the opening scene? I'm not in it,' I said innocently.

His fish eyes observed me with distaste while his mouth smiled and his limp hands took possession of my shoulders.

'Eleanor…' His face now assumed an expression of sincerity that would have been more suited to a bereavement. 'Can we talk?'

He led me to a short staircase, the only one not festooned with dancers eating, changing clothes or queuing for auditions for other shows. We sat down. His bottom, threatening to split the leather that confined it, spread so its heat seeped through my trousers.

'Eleanor, you know I love your work.' I couldn't return the lie so I said nothing. 'And I know I'm going to love you.' I couldn't imagine a Spaniard or Italian saying such a thing. Americans really were foreign. 'I'm going to transform you, and I need your ideas, Eleanor. You're so creative, you've got such a perfect instinct, I want all your ideas.'

'I'm sure you do,' I said grimly. 'But what's to guarantee once I give them to you I won't get fired?' This obviously wasn't in his script, so I cut across his half-formed objections: 'And what's this about the first scene, Ricky?'

He grabbed the lifeline with another rush of enthusiasm. 'Oh, wow, Viola has done such a good rewrite.'

'I look forward to seeing it.'

Having drawn a blank with me, even after he offered the confidence that he'd pulled out of the original production because he didn't trust

Izzy, Ricky didn't see any difference between my earlier surliness and present anger.

'You gotta understand, Eleanor, I had nothing, I mean nothing, to do with Dan being fired, but there's only room for one director. That's what my agent said.' *Rudolph had shown signs of independent thought?* 'He did the deal, believe me, it was none of my business.' Thank you, Pontius Pilate.

The old deaf actor, Barry, was already in the stuffy rehearsal room reading my article when we walked in. He folded the paper fastidiously, put it in his bag and greeted us politely. I saw he already had the new scene. In the corner of the room, huddled on a stool, was Viola. She wouldn't look at me. I was the only person who had no copy of the rewrite, but I wasn't going to ask for one. The petty games had started and I was a grand master after a lifetime with David.

Ricky made a great play of finding me a new script, which Ruby delivered with a private shrug to me. I was just reading it through when Izzy burst in carrying a newspaper. I could see the rest of the cast, now joined by Lee and Susan, through the glass partition, spectators at my lynching.

'Eleanor!,' Izzy shouted, 'this is great! It's the greatest piece of journalism by an artist in a show I ever read. Great publicity. Just great, kid.' I couldn't work out whether he was unbelievably stupid or, having turned down the chance to read the copy, making the most of a hatchet job.

'Thanks, Izzy.' What else could I say?

Through the window I saw disappointment in Lee's eyes. Susan was looking at me down her sharp little nose. Bitterly frustrated that she'd have to wait to see my fall.

Izzy fizzed with excitement as we started the rehearsal. Two things were quickly evident: the first, that the new lines were literally unspeakable; and the second, that Ricky had not a clue how to stage the scene.

Barry tried to help, coming up with suggestions for basic moves, and modifications to Viola's illiterate lines. I simply sat with my face setting into a stone mask of what used to be called dumb insolence. I felt silly and childish, but it didn't change my expression or break my silence. Trinny and Susannah took down Ricky's inspirations, which included: 'Eleanor could fly in on a catafalque,' and, 'Viola, what if Eleanor plays the whole scene behind a screen?'

This latter brought some joy to our writer's sour face, until the deaf actor pointed out the only place for a screen was upstage and he'd be left in darkness with his back to the audience, which didn't altogether suit an artist who'd spent a lifetime playing straight out front.

'You don't have to look at her,' squeaked Viola. Even Ricky could see that was ridiculous, and the idea was abandoned. We were left with Dan's original idea of my being brought on, down the staircase, on Tizer's shoulders.

Viola hated it and screwed up her face to object. I got in first.

'Sorry, Ricky, I don't think you can use that. It was one of Dan's ideas. You'd be infringing his intellectual copyright.'

I thought Viola was going to explode. I hoped she would, despite the mess it would make.

'You shit,' she hissed, as she ran from the room in yet another river of tears. Ricky and his amanuenses followed at the trot. Izzy clapped his hands in frustration, clamped the cigar into his cheek and followed his wife. The deaf actor and I were alone. He said nothing, but turned his back on me in silent disapproval.

'Something wrong?,' I asked, with more challenge in my voice than I'd intended.

'No, no, darling, of course not. Is that the time? Do you think that's a tea break?' He scuttled out, rather than be caught with me.

I waited a while, but after half an hour I wandered out onto the street and sat on the steps chatting with the kids, who had been hanging round since ten o'clock. Ruby came out a couple of times for a smoke, his thin handsome face grey and hollow from a diet of cigarettes and Izzy Duck.

'He couldn't organise a piss-up in my local. And as for the Leather Queen in the Bandana, he has to have smelling salts every time I mention the word schedule. Sorry – *skedule*.' He went into a cruelly accurate imitation of Ricky's limp wrists and California lisp: '"Ohmygod, I'm an artist, I've worked with Cher, Elton, Madonna… I don't deal with this kind of crap." I tried to get sense out of Trinny and Susannah, but they're so coked up they're bouncing off the ceiling. So the LQIB goes, "Well, just call everyone in at ten a.m., that's what they're paid for."' Ruby took a long drag on his Marlboro Light. 'Stupid cunt.'

The cast mooched about, in and out of the building, half-heartedly practising dance steps and getting more and more irritable, until Jonty arrived in a taxi and, with the briefest greeting, rushed into the rehearsal room.

Shortly after, Viola, Izzy, Ricky and Rudolph shot out and tumbled into the cab. We watched, neither interested nor surprised. Had they been on fire, it wouldn't have raised more than an eyebrow anymore. Jonty came out a few minutes later and stood pensively polishing his sunglasses and watching the traffic, as if expecting the cab to return.

'Well, I was only called for the morning so I assume I'm done for the day,' I said. 'Are you going to the theatre?'

Jonty paused, then said, 'Yes,' drawing it out through a couple of Ms and a few inches of Ns.

'Mind if I come along?'

We may not be previewing for another week but that was no reason to neglect the dressing-room. A free en suite pied-à-terre in central London was never to be neglected: so handy for dumping the shopping.

The cab was filled with companionable silence, apart from a couple of monosyllables when Jonty answered his mobile. Afterwards I could see by his cheese-eating grin he was bursting to say something.

'What?' I obliged.

'I don't think there'll be any more rehearsals today,' he said.

'Why not?'

'Someone from the Home Office has left their card at the stage door – for Ricky Ricky's urgent attention.'

<hr/>

That evening, I sat in the stage door pub with Ruby and Basher. Jonty joined us, sank a pint of Guinness, lit a panatella, sat back with a sigh and said:

'Izzy Duck and party boarded the Eurostar for Paris at four o'clock this afternoon.'

We were so astonished no one said anything. Finally, Ruby broke the silence. 'Fuck me, so he really didn't have a work permit.'

'Nope, and no doubt that'll be my fault,' said Jonty, not obviously worried by the prospect of another unjustified bollocking, nor about his twenty-five grand, which was now sitting on the other side of the Channel.

'You were right, Eleanor.' Ruby looked at me with something approaching admiration. I shrugged modestly. Being right was a novelty.

'So when are they coming back?,' I asked.

'The day after tomorrow…?'

Ten days later, Ricky Ricky and Rudolph were still on the run and Izzy had returned to threaten both the union and the Home Office. Now he was preparing for the verdict on the work permit appeal hearing.

'They don't come through, I pull the show. You know how many Brits that'll put outta work? How stupid are these people? I'm trying to help their theatre, for Chris'sake.'

The stage was ready, the technicians idle, the actors aimless and the production haemorrhaging money every day no audience came. The focus of the Ducks' ire was Dan, who was single-handedly sabotaging their life's work. It didn't occur to them they were at fault, or that their arrogance had brought the Nazgûl down on Ricky Ricky.

'I'm a businessman,' repeated Izzy on his first day back. 'Dan's scum. That scummy guy is stopping me doing my business.'

To prove Izzy's anger was no rattle of an empty vessel, his lawyer fired off letters to Karen and Dan threatening to sue them for the entire cost of the production. Three and a half million pounds. Each.

Karen, beyond desperation, consigned the letter to the bin. 'I don't even own my own teeth,' was her only comment.

Dan, though, closer to breaking-point and desperate for money, collapsed. At his flat, I found him unshaven, gaunt and tearful; petrified of bankruptcy. The turbulence and sheer viciousness of the fight with Izzy had defeated him. And that was precisely what Izzy was counting on.

'It's the way they do things in America,' said Dan, handing me the lawyer's letter. The brash phraseology and paranoia in the words was un-English, despite the smart London address. 'If he sues me, I'll have nothing. I couldn't even afford to defend myself.'

Izzy's bullying and relentless cruelty blew away any vestige of compliance left from my years with David.

'Right, Dan, you're going to see Felix, my solicitor.'

'I can't afford it. I'm so broke I don't know how I'm going to live. I owe money everywhere.' He looked utterly defeated.

'I'll buy you an hour's worth.'

Felix gave me a good rate when I promised him champagne in the dressing-room. 'And may I sip it from your slipper?'

'Felix, I'll buy a pair specially – size ten, wide-fitting.'

'Tell your director friend to write down everything so we don't waste time telling the story.'

Dan was nervous when we went in with the bullet-point list. Felix might be my fantasy flirt, but he was pretty intimidating with his hanging judge half-glasses and impeccable vowels. He gestured us to sit while he read the catalogue of woe. Dan looked round the room, at the ominously ticking clock, then at the boxes of papers stacked along the wall.

'Have you been here long?,' he asked, to break the ice.

Felix glanced up. 'Three hundred years.'

'Ah,' said Dan, sinking into his raincoat.

A couple of minutes later Felix started to smile, then laugh out loud. 'Mr Duck sacked you, then Mrs Duck sacked Mr Duck?'

We nodded.

'…Then Mr Duck threatened divorce? Followed by attempted suicide?'

We nodded again.

'Then Mrs Duck reinstated Mr Duck, following which Mr Duck fired you again?' He was fighting to catch his breath now, barely able to speak for laughing. 'Well…this really is a canard.' That set him off again. 'Or a pair of canards, should I say?'

Eventually, wiping tears of mirth from his eyes with an immaculate white handkerchief, Felix delivered his verdict.

'First, Mr Cawdron, we'll stop the clock at half an hour, there is no case for you to answer here. It's my opinion Mr Duck has absolutely no grounds on which to sue you. Indeed you would have every right to consider suing him for your outstanding fee. However,' – he looked over his glasses, to continue his judgment – 'you may have to pursue him to the rainforests of Costa Rica for that pleasure, if that is where his assets are. And the costs involved may be considerably more than you are owed.' Felix turned to me. 'I take it Mr Duck has no assets in this country?'

'Only the show. The company manager's paying for a lot of stuff on his credit card, then reclaiming it.'

'I hope he knows what he's doing,' said Felix drily. 'As for this letter, I shall reply to it or ignore it as you wish. Mr Duck's solicitors and my firm have enjoyed skirmishing for many years. Of course not three hundred in their case, they are comparatively nouveau. Which, of course, would suit Mr Duck, being –'

'A parvenu?' I suggested.

'American,' he said smoothly.

I left Felix with a brief but heartfelt kiss on his well-shaved cheek.

Dan was still on the brink of penury, but was so relieved, he took me to the Savoy for a glass of champagne. I paid.

'So what's happening about rehearsals?,' he asked, spearing a rugby ball of an olive.

'Well…while Izzy and Viola were AWOL, we didn't do any. But now they're back, and we're rehearsing on stage, they call Ricky in Paris and he directs us down the phone.'

I thought Dan was going to choke. 'You're not serious.'

'Problem is the dance numbers. He counts the band in, but there's a one-second delay – three people fell off the stage yesterday and the drummer went out and got so drunk he was arrested.'

'Is he back?'

'Yes, but only because the police refused to deport him.'

⁂

I went into the theatre the next morning, after a passionless night with Dan. Sex hadn't survived the chaos and I wondered if friendship would when we finally crawled out of the wreckage. The balance of attraction had changed between us and I didn't want a child any more than he wanted a mother.

KT, having a smoke in the urine-soaked alley by the stage door, greeted me as I arrived.

'He's only gone and thrown the toys out the pram.'

'Who?'

'This week's director, Nokia Nell. Stupid tart's run out of ideas so he's thrown a hissy fit and slammed the phone down. We could hear him screaming "I'm an artiste – the natural successor to Bob Fosse. I cannot, repeat *cannot*, work like this!"'

Above us a window rattled up; Ruby's head appeared as if beneath a guillotine.

'All right you two, this is not a place of entertainment, get yourselves on stage for the Crazy Frog's next trick.'

Viola and Izzy stood with their backs to the auditorium, Susan between them. She was wearing a look of smug satisfaction. It didn't suit her.

'Hi, everyone. I have good news. Great news!,' called Izzy to his Happy Campers. We braced ourselves. 'I'm real pleased to announce that this morning we persuaded Susan to take over the direction of the show.' Several jaws dropped and a whisper of *'shoot me, shoot me now'* was clearly audible to everyone except Izzy. 'It's just until Ricky gets back with us, which should be in the next thirty-six hours.'

'Oh, does that mean he's got his work permit?,' I piped up.

Viola chewed her lower lip, Izzy waved his cigar as if I were a late-summer wasp and Susan sucked her cheeks in so far I was afraid her lips would rupture. What was the cure for collagen poisoning?

'She has great experience as a director so we're real lucky she's agreed take the show on.'

She simpered and said, in a little girl voice, 'Of course, I'll do my best. I just, well, I just want to be here for all of you.' Lee tutted, but she was on a roll. 'If anyone's got any problems, just come to me and I'll try to sort them out. I've had fifteen years of getting shows on –'

'Where's that then, Susan?,' chimed in KT, all innocent enthusiasm. She paused, then went on with no awareness of her inadequacy.

'The Brenda Thorn Theatre. I've done eighteen shows with them. As choreographer and director.'

'I've never played there,' said Lee, frowning with confusion. 'Is it a producing or receiving house?,' knowing full well it was a corrugated-iron Scout hut on a traffic island in Croydon.

'It's non-professional,' she replied regally. 'I always draw a line between non-professional and amateur, which is a state of mind.'

'Oh…well that's all right then,' said KT with such sincerity Susan was flattered. 'And, just one other thing. What shows have you done there?'

'Bugsy Malone, Jack and the Beanstalk, Aladdin –'

'Fab,' interrupted KT. 'We're in safe hands.'

'So if everyone's okay with me taking over…?, we'll work through from the beginning.' Then, as if remembering a sexually transmitted infection: 'Oh, Eleanor, is that all right with you?'

She was expecting me to be spitting broken glass. Her saccharine smile and quick glances towards Izzy and Viola spoke more eloquently of her satisfaction at my discomfort than any words.

'Frankly,' I said, 'I think it's a great idea for you to take over, especially with the experience you've had. I can't think of anyone better qualified to work with Izzy and Viola.'

She draped her jacket round her shoulders and clapped her hands, quite the Ninette de Valois. 'Okay, people, let's start – and please, no talking, this is going to be really hard for me, my voice is tired, so I need you to be focused one hundred per cent. I'm only doing it to help all of you –'

In the wings Lee vented his feelings in a poisonous whisper. 'Non-professional theatre? Oh per-*lease*. All she's done is panto, looking after the under-tens. She's not a director, she's a fucking classroom assistant. Well, I'm telling you, I'm not being directed by her.'

His outpouring was interrupted by Susan's voice: 'Lee, can you come on stage please?'

'Yes, darling, I'm here.' He walked into the light and shaded his eyes, looking out to where she sat in the stalls. 'I think it's fabulous you're doing this, Susan, so brave. We're all so grateful.'

In the half-dark of the wings, KT shook his head and Kelvin mimed slitting his wrists.

<hr/>

In the ten days of uncertainty before Izzy's Home Office appeal hearing, more previews were cancelled. The Ducks consulted their Parisian Muse and more outrageous requests for set changes were relayed to an increasingly grumpy Basher.

'Listen, Izzy. Ah'm going to say this dead simple, so you'll understand. If you want silk, ships, catafalques, a flying moon or a firework chandelier, the specifications have to be in yesterday.'

'Talk to the director. I'm just the producer,' said Izzy, intimidated by Basher's enormity.

'How can I?,' he rumbled. 'I can't get the big jessie on the bloody phone. And when I do he talks bollocks. So…' He heaved his rigger's belt further up his impressive belly. 'You'll have to do Dan's production. No bloody choice you dozy yank. Cos you've bolloxed about till it's too bloody late to do it any other way.'

Izzy and Viola, in that moment, realised there was a price to pay for their imperial idiocy.

'Right, you two, I'm off for a cheeky pint. If you want me, I'm in the pub.'

Now Dan had them over a barrel: they would have to pay. He could close us immediately if we performed his version. His rejoicing was muted, though; there was enough that wasn't his in the show to allow for a mighty perversion of what was. His original thinking, wit and humour were being swamped by over-zealous acting, ludicrous dialogue and perverse changes. And, despite Susan's surrogate care, Izzy and Viola were obsessed with Ricky's unique ability to save their baby.

Miraculously, Dan's cheque arrived the next morning, but now Izzy was totally out of control. Imagining plots and conspiracies behind every curtain, he suddenly burst in on a call that Flossie was taking and accused him of leaking stories to the press that made him, Izzy, look stupid.

'You don't need me to do that,' said Flossie, with unmistakable clarity.

'I never liked you!'

Flossie, unwilling to be baited, moved to leave.

'Stay where you are, fella. You walk out that door, you walk out of a job.

Flossie kept his temper. 'Excuse me, you think I'm going to stand here like a seven year-old till you give me permission to leave? Fuck off.'

Izzy's voice rose, triumphant, the cigar stabbing towards his prey. 'You're not an actor, you can't dance and you sure can't choreograph shit. And now you're telling the papers about this show. That's disloyal and you know what I do with disloyal people like you? I fire them.'

Flossie, who'd only been holding on through loyalty to the cast, blew: 'You can't fire me, you disgusting gremlin. I'm walking out. I'm walking out on you, your talentless cow of a wife and this whole pile of dog mess. The best thing you had on this show was Dan, and now you've let him go you've got exactly what you deserve – a cack-handed vanity project with absolutely nothing to recommend it. Except a cast working their arses off to try and save your concrete balloon of a show. But oh no, every time someone tries to float it, you blow another hole in it and you have the gall to blame them. Well: Good, Fucking, Luck.'

He'd reached the auditorium doors. He kicked one of them open and was gone.

Susan looked satisfied. Lee examined his nails. The rest of us realised we were on our own.

Izzy was madly triumphant. 'I didn't fire him, he walked out. You all saw that. You saw it. He walked. I'm going to sue, believe me, he'll be left with nothing.'

'Oh, I shouldn't do that, love.' It was KT. Every eye turned towards him. 'He hasn't got a pot to piss in. He hasn't been paid for the last month.'

If he'd thrown a grenade at Izzy, it couldn't have caused a greater explosion.

'Okay, pal. You're out. I watched you for weeks, you're like some kinda disease, but I kept you on and now you're accusing me of not paying wages?' He stabbed the air at us all. 'Anyone of you not been paid? Anyone else accusing me of dishonesty?' We shuffled and looked anywhere but at him or KT. Izzy was screaming now, sweat running from under his baseball cap, staining his shirt collar. 'See? See? You're on your own, pal. And here's the bottom line: you're no longer in this show. Get out of my theatre. Now. You're fired. Goodbye.'

KT was ashen, but he'd been in the business too long to expect anyone to defend him.

'Izzy…' I thought he hadn't heard me. 'Izzy, may I say something?'

'No, Eleanor, you may not. You've said enough on this show. I don't want to hear any more outta you.'

I thought Susan was going to die of pleasure; sadly I was wrong. Izzy beckoned her over and whispered into her hair. She nodded with an overdone look of resignation, then, as Izzy and Viola left the stage, she clapped her hands.

'Okay, people. Let's take five. Then we'll pick up with Lee's number. We'll have to respace it without KT. Oh, and Eleanor, you'll have to learn the words – Izzy wants it to be the play-off number in the finale.'

'We'll discuss that later,' I said, dismissing the cocky little madam.

She didn't even look at KT as she swept out after her masters. Once she was gone, everyone, even Lee, crowded round KT, offering outrage and condolences.

'They really are mistaking me for someone who gives a fuck,' he hid behind the traditional bravado phrase. 'I'm off to the pub.'

I caught up with him as he was clearing his dressing-room. He was trembling, and when he looked at me his eyes were red.

'Sorry KT. I'm really sorry.'

He tried to speak, but his throat had constricted. I knew that agonising ache, the sharp pain under the ears, the stab at the root of the tongue. I wanted to hug him, but that wasn't his way; nor was it mine.

'It's just…' He almost lost control. '…anger and frustration, girl.'

Kelvin came in a couple of minutes later and brooked our reserve. He put his arms round KT and held his stiff body until KT disengaged himself, squeezed Kelvin's arm and left, his bag slung over his shoulder. Dick Whittington – but there'd be no turning again, neither from him nor Izzy.

⁂

We went on rehearsing for rehearsal's sake, parrots caught in a nightmare of mindless repetition, unable to prevent disastrous changes and with no one qualified to polish what we were in – Carry On Costa Rica, as performed by the cast of the Marat-Sade.

Susan continued to call us at ten a.m daily.

'I need to nail the laughs. Comedy is accuracy.'

'She couldn't get a laugh with a kipper pinned to her minge,' said KT, a couple of nights after his exit. He, Kelvin and I were shovelling mounds of pasta into our faces. KT had taken on the role of cook and mother with alarming alacrity, and he provided a refuge as our balsa-wood raft tossed on the tricky tides of Izzy Duck's ego.

'So, Ellie,' said KT, dolloping tiramisu into our bowls, 'Izzy's not going to sack you then. Not with a week to go to press night and no sign of Ricky.'

'No, much as he'd like to lever Meryl Streep into my sequined basque, no one with half a brain would touch it now with a sterilised bargepole.'

Where I had been vague about Izzy and Viola's behaviour, the papers were now joyfully rummaging through their past and turning up all sorts of juicy gobbets of tittle-tattle. And none of it had come from me – I'd had to make a public promise about that:

'If I take over directing this show permanently –'

'Susan, you're only baby-sitting till Ricky gets back.'

'Eleanor, you're not making this easy. I'm risking my career taking this on. If word gets out that I've taken over –'

'But you're not taking over.'

253

'I don't want people getting the wrong idea about me.' Susan clutched her jacket round her, arms crossed on her breast. I thought she was going to launch into the Dying Swan. 'I'm just a company member who wants the best from the show.'

'Don't you mean *for* the show, Susan?,' I enquired sweetly.

'That's what I said,' she snapped, with a quick clench of her sphincter-lips. 'And I don't want anyone, I mean anyone' – she was looking only at me – 'leaking my presence as director to the press.'

The ego of the woman. As if Max Clifford would be hammering on the stage door to sell her life-story to the News of the World.

'Well,' I said, humbly, 'If they get to hear of it, I swear it won't be from me.'

'I don't want my name appearing in the papers. Do you understand? You have the ear of the press and I really don't want you making things difficult for me.' She was loving it. As fey as Garbo. 'I want to be left alone to do my job.'

'I assure you, Susan…' *How could I phrase it?* 'Your name won't be printed anywhere if I have anything to do with it.'

'That's the point, Eleanor,' she said, waiting for us to appreciate her cleverness. 'I don't want you to have anything to do with it.' She paused like an infant school teacher in front of the new intake. 'Do you promise?'

'Of course, Susan. I promise.' I dipped my head and stared at the newly painted floor-cloth. Susan sucked her cheeks in and turned her massive intellect to the problem of getting Lee off the stage without giving in to his demand for a solo encore.

That was about the last thing that had happened to make me laugh. After KT's departure, the company fractured, with several of the younger girls, including the South African juvenile, falling into Susan's exclusive clique. As a form of defence, other groups and pairs started to form alliances of self-interest. Most of them fell silent if I appeared. Some, like Tizer, Glenda, God and the Liza Minnelli look-alike, because, in their misery, they didn't know what to say. Others, like Lee and his group of carrion-eaters, complacently certain of my fall, whispered in corners: I was responsible for all the ills of the show; I was keeping Ricky out of the country, endangering all their jobs; I knew I was crap in the show, so didn't want it to open; I was scared of eight shows a week, scared of nodules on the vocal chords, scared of being found out.

The longer it went on, the closer I came to the edge of reason. Maybe Ricky's work permit was irrelevant and his replacing Dan was no bad thing... Maybe the new script was a vast improvement... Maybe I was afraid of being trashed by the critics...

I pressed a mental nail into my flesh and clung to the truth. As I saw it.

THIRTY-FIVE

Eventually the 'tenth day' arrived. Ricky and Rudolph were poised at the Gare du Nord ready to be back for the evening rehearsal. At two-thirty we gathered in the auditorium to hear the Home Office's verdict. The atmosphere was poisonous. Some of the brighter twirlies had realised Ricky's return would be a disaster after Flossie, in a guerilla raid on the stage door pub, told them Ricky had announced his intention to replace them.

'They have to go! My God, they're so ugly.' Did this man not possess a mirror? 'They can't dance, they can't even walk across the stage. They just have to go. I have to have dancers, real dancers, not that chorus line of sweating cabbage-patch dolls.' He waved his jewelled hand under his nose as if he could smell them.

'And neither Izzy nor Viola said a word to defend you,' finished Flossie, with no sense of revenge. 'I'm sorry, kids, but there's no one who can protect you.'

The last group, the fence-sitters, led by the deaf actor, kept their heads down and changed with whichever wind was buying them a drink: all things to all men, except a spine.

In my corner, I was glad to have Kelvin, who had been befriended by Lee, with whom he shared a dressing-room. Lee underestimated the quiet Canadian and assumed his silent acceptance of all Lee's bitching was approval. Most of it Kelvin reported back over carb-heavy dinners at KT's.

'You know that website, theatreblood.com?'

'Oh, yes,' said KT, slapping a dollop of sponge pudding on each of our plates. 'It's run by that one-eyed female who was an assistant director on Annie, remember her? She shagged the lead in Jesus Christ Superstar and he got scabies.'

'It wasn't scabies,' said Kelvin lazily. 'It was herpes.'

'You never hear about that these days, do you?,' said KT.

'She stalked him all the way to Australia. He had to get an injunction out against her.'

'Whatever. Anyway, what's the haglet been up to now?'

We waited until Kelvin was ready to speak. He looked awkward, embarrassed. Finally, concentrating on his spoon as it pushed clots of custard round the plate, he said, 'Lee has been posting messages on theatreblood's message board, anonymously. About you.'

He was looking at me.

'What sort of messages?' KT was all for logging on.

'I don't think so,' I said. I didn't want to be infected by seeing the words. 'So what's he said?' I hoped I sounded relaxed about it, but knew I didn't.

'That you're out of your depth with real musical theatre people and you don't want to be shown up as not being able to sing, dance or act… That you've done everything you can to ruin not only the show but Izzy and Viola's dream. That you're unprofessional and should be sacked for jeopardising everyone's jobs, and that you know you're no good in the part, which is why you're trying to sabotage the show.'

'I can't believe Lee could spell either jeopardise or sabotage,' I said, too shocked for outrage.

Kelvin smiled. Lovely teeth. 'That was my sanitised précis.'

'See?,' said KT to me. 'Classical education. I don't go for no rough trade. So…what you going to do, Nellie?'

Kelvin hadn't finished.

'He also said you'd deliberately hit the one person who was going to show you up for the sham you are in an attempt to get her off the show, and that she miscarried because of your attack on her.'

I was standing in a sewer. Rats feeding on the filthy by-products of human malice.

'Nellie, you can't let this one go.'

I nodded to KT, unable to speak. This was the real death of David's wife. Where, only weeks before, I would have crumbled, cried, revelled in victimhood, now instinct was to wade in and let the past weeks out in a river of bile.

In bed, I planned revenge that ranged from the sadistic to the murderous. Instead in the morning I called my agent.

'I'll have a look at it,' he said. Twenty minutes later he called back. 'Darling, it's libellous. What do you want me to do?'

'I don't know, but if someone doesn't stop him I'm going to tear his head off and shove his script down the hole in his neck.'

The agent was entirely on my side, gratifyingly defensive. Finally he asked, 'Who's his representation?'

'The Great White Shark.'

'Ah,' he said. Lee's manager had earned the name, but mine was no mean barracuda himself. 'Leave it with me, darling, I'll tell him what his client's up to and call you back.'

Later, alone in the backstage corridor, Lee and I squared up, ready for a fight as I thought. But, to my astonishment, he treacled charm over me. Would I like a coffee? What did I think of Susan? Didn't I find it an insult what she was doing? After all I was the leading lady. Oh, and by the way, Eleanor, you're going to be *sooo* fantastic in this part, I've learned *sooo* much from watching you. We *must* have lunch. *Darrr*ling.

'That'd really cheer me up, Lee, after these awful things on the internet about me.'

'On the internet?'

'Yes, Lee. Someone in the cast is posting vicious lies about me on theatreblood.com, and if I were to find out who it was I'd make sure their name appeared not just on that silly cow's website but in the press as well. And, of course, there'd be a more personal revenge.' What that might be I had no idea, but I hoped I sounded convincing.

We looked steadily into each other's eyes. An observer would have thought we were lovers.

Lee looked away first.

I thanked Kelvin with a silent kiss on the cheek and phoned KT.

'I'll get the wine for dinner tonight. Oh, and does Kelvin like chocolates?'

<hr />

So…two-thirty on the tenth day.

The auditorium.

Silence.

Viola sidled in and scuttled to Susan's side, as if for protection. A minute later, Izzy came through the same door and stood with his back to the stage, facing us as we sat scattered in the stalls.

I had expected a triumphal entrance, the cock-crow of a victorious general, but he sagged, tired and miserable, a sad figure whose jeans were too big and whose baseball cap was pathetic on his tortoise head. The fight had gone out of him, but his limbs still twitched.

'Okay, so here's the bottom line.'

How many bottom lines were there in his life?

'Ricky Ricky is…not going to be rejoining us.'

There was a group exhalation, like a breeze through leaves. Some were relieved, some despairing, a couple optimistic that Dan might return. Izzy then ripped into a monologue about the imbeciles in the Home Office, the traitors in the union, led by an outside force 'of pure evil' that I could only assume was Dan.

'…These people are trying to destroy this show. These small-minded provincial nobodies are frightened to have Broadway standards here. And Jonty…Jonty let me down. It was Jonty's responsibility to fill in the visa forms. He didn't do it. I didn't know. He didn't do the job I pay him for. I can't have that.'

They'd been easing Jonty out for about a week, but this must surely be the death-knell. I only hoped he'd cleared his credit card. Izzy was rambling and ranting, anger giving him new life, when he said something which electrified us all:

'They think they've beaten me, but I'm telling you, if we can't have Ricky Ricky, the greatest director in Los Angeles…' – he teetered on the precipice, then jumped – '…I'm gonna direct the show.'

Pause.

'I will direct the show myself.'

He didn't have to repeat it; we heard him the first time. With universal horror. Even Susan jerked out of her complacency for that one.

'Er…Izzy?' I put my hand up hesitantly. He didn't want to be interrupted, especially by me. 'Izzy?'

'What?' It was not a friendly enquiry.

'You can't direct the show.'

Several necks cracked as they strained to look round at me. Izzy went dark with anger.

'Whaddya mean, I can't direct the show?'

'Well, I'm sorry, Izzy, but you can't…' I paused. Timing. 'You haven't got a work permit.'

If it hadn't been for Viola grabbing his arm, I swear he would have run up the aisle and ripped my face off. The expression 'to go ballistic' hadn't had much meaning for me until that moment. He shouted. He threatened. He screamed. He slapped his head in disbelief and rage. He was as impressive, as pathetic and as impotent as Willy Loman but, ultimately, less real.

Susan and Viola managed to get him out of the auditorium and, stunned, we wandered back to our dressing-rooms. Ruby winked at me, but to almost everyone else I was a disease not worth catching.

I sat in my dressing-room, a grim windowless box in the abortionist's waiting-room style, and stared into the liver-spotted mirror.

It was Monday and we were due to start previews on Friday. My costumes hung glittering on the rail. I only wished my performance was draped next to them, as I had no idea what I was going to do when the audience, hyenas all, were finally allowed in to see the carnage.

I murmured Dan's name, but that spell, even when repeated, no longer had power. He had thrown himself back into the life of his own theatre and was rarely available when I rang. He'd put a barrier between himself and everything to do with the show. I couldn't blame him, he'd gone close to breaking and his self-image couldn't accommodate that kind of weakness – nor the witnesses to it. He didn't want to talk to me – it was over, whatever 'it' had been. I should leave him alone.

If you love it, let it go; if it loves you, it'll come back. Bollocks.

'Hi, Dan, it's me.'

The air between us was cool.

'How's it going?' He sounded as if he was in a hurry.

'Sorry, is it a bad time?'

'No…no…not really. I've got a meeting in five minutes. Local MP, great supporter of the theatre. We're trying to get a new rehearsal room built and he could help.'

The water had closed over my head. 'Sorry, I won't keep you long, it's just, the man at the Home Office, he say no…'

Dan was silent, listening out of politeness. 'Well…good.' There was a pause, then tenderness and regret in his voice. 'You'll be fine, Eleanor. You're strong enough to cope, whatever happens… Take care.'

'And you…take care, my –'

He'd gone.

I put the phone down slowly. Was it too late to run back to David? Was it too late to become a model mother to my stranger of a son? Was it too late to retrain as a tampon packer?

Ruby's voice called us back to the stage and roused me from a slough of despond that was becoming as well-frequented as a municipal lido. The reluctant prisoners shuffled into place and were told Susan had graciously agreed to see us through to press night. Lee produced a bunch of flowers so fast he must have nicked them off a passing funeral cortège.

There were cheers, and a speech from our reluctant directress, filled with emotional pauses and an appeal for us to be a united company under her proud but diffident leadership. Viola stood limply crying with relief. Izzy had his way: he was the director, and his face was plump, over made-up, with a mouth like an inflamed cat's sphincter.

THIRTY-SIX

We ran the show twice a day, but now the high comedy had been confined to a bungalow of earnestness. Bland mediocrity had flattened individuality so, desperately clinging to the character Dan had created, I stuck out like an Alp in Norfolk.

Kelvin, the singing psychopath, had gone to Fox's theatrical make-up emporium and bought every bit of false hair in the place. Unfortunately, the stress had put him back on the Silk Cut and, nipping out to the stage door for regular cigarettes, he went through three sets of eyebrows before the first preview. But that night we had more to worry about than the stench of burning hair.

The audience was made up of ticket agents, a few tourists who'd come in out of the rain and a scattering of Mesdames Defarges. This group of ambulance chasers went to previews for only one thing: to see a disaster unfold, the nastier and gorier the better. Each of them had tales of dance routines like bloody abattoirs and cat-fights in the chorus line. At the end, they grudgingly applauded our dreary curate's egg, no longer fun, no longer camp and definitely not funny.

There followed days of chaotic lighting, sound and music changes from Izzy through his presence on earth, Susan. Occasionally she nodded or shrugged at me – I assumed these cryptic signs were notes on my performance as we lurched towards press night.

It finally arrived, not with a bang but with a whimper of dread.

KT, in his pinny, waved us off as if we were going off to the Somme.

Thanks to him, Karen, Flossie and our composer Ildefonso Campi, my dressing-room was so full of flowers it looked like Golder's Green Crematorium. Dan sent a single yellow rose; David, a solicitor's letter accusing me of malicious damage.

I propped the bouquets up in the shower and stuck a bottle of champagne from my agent in the lavatory cistern, as the fridge was broken, then set about writing sincere messages in cards which, as there were 34 people to buy for, had been selected more for their low price than aptness for the occasion. For each performing member of the company there was a decent bottle of wine, the minimum expected from the leading lady. For the stage management, scotch and port. Some stars distributed Tiffany trinkets or engraved crystal. But they were on footballers' wages.

Susan left more ostentatiously expensive bottles of wine outside each dressing-room, an inappropriate gesture from the soubrette but perfect for the anointed heir to Trevor Nunn. There was no hint of a note or gift from the Ducks, not just for me but for anyone – as shocking as the monarch not bothering with Maundy money. All we had to show that they existed was a card on which were written the words

IZZY DUCK, BROADWAY PRODUCER INVITES YOU TO...

the first-night party, to be given at a nightclub more famous for fighting supermodels than sophisticated theatrical soirées. At the bottom it said:

FROM 9.15 P.M.

The show didn't finish until ten to ten.

Outside the front of the theatre, a baroque conceit of gilt and plaster cherubs, a small huddle of paparazzi waited for celebrities. The few who had any idea who I was hosed me good-naturedly and wished me luck as I walked past to leave two free tickets for my agent at the box office. This traditional largesse towards the company had been incomprehensible to Izzy, until it was pointed out that the theatre would be empty if he didn't cooperate. I'd offered mine to KT but he said he'd rather eat his own leg.

The youngsters, like virgins, rushed towards their deflowering filled with excitement – the possibility of disappointment incomprehensible. Trying to ignore the mounting hysteria in the corridors and the violent butterflies in my stomach, I joined Kelvin on stage, quietly warming up while the crew hoovered round us. The spotty lad was diligently polishing Izzy's door knobs.

I stretched, sang a few scales, wished Kelvin good luck, then went to my dressing-room to calm my convulsing bowels and pray for a miracle. Morag put her head round the door.

'D'ye want me tae wish you luck?'

'No, I want a miracle. You going to the party?'

'No. Sorry Eleanor. This is me. I'm off. I cannae stand any more. I'm catching the eight o'clock to Glasgow. Going tae see ma mammy. Get a wee bit sanity. I'm sorry.' She came towards me, arms outstretched. 'Goodbye wee yin. All ra best.'

We hugged long and hard, then parted with tears in our eyes.

'Bye Morag. And thanks for everything.'

'Aye…bye.'

I felt her loss acutely.

***

Sometimes the only thing keeping the audience upright is rigor mortis. But on this occasion we got a mob of whistling exhibitionists, most of whom seemed to be related to Lee.

He dropped any pretence of being in anything but a one-man cabaret after his fans stopped the show with shrieks more suited to a rock star exposing himself than a West End musical.

Susan, seeing the sensitive delicacy of her direction being decimated by his Panzer of a performance, rounded on him in the interval.

'What the fuck do you think you're doing? I have never seen anything so amateur, so vulgar, so destructive on a stage. You are a fucking joke.'

Lee tossed his head disdainfully. He would have tossed his hair, but there was so much product on it it wouldn't have moved if Hurricane Rita had hit.

'Well, if I'm a fucking joke, at least I get fucking laughs, which is more than you could, either as director or in that drag act you call a performance.'

She replied by throwing her water bottle at him.

He flew at her and yanked her hairpiece, which, being anchored with industrial rivets, came away along with a fair amount of her bubble perm. She screamed, burst into tears and slid down the wall, her head thrown back in loud wailing.

Lee slammed into his dressing-room, roaring: 'That witch. That brainless, talentless, fat-arsed —'

Susan hammered on his door screeching. 'I AM NOT FAT. I'm not the one who's had liposuction!'

'Susan,' he shouted, 'you could get it done free in Japan — as part of their whaling program.' Then he opened the door and sprayed her with deodorant, sound and fury signifying nothing but the smallness of minds and largeness of the mouths of those involved.

Kelvin joined me, carrying two glasses of champagne, one of which he handed to me. 'First time I've ever agreed with Lee. Here.'

I tried to look shocked as he handed me the glass.

'Oh, come on, Eleanor, you don't seriously think I'm going to do this shit sober, do you?'

I saw his point and took a large swig. Immediately I felt much, much better.

The second act saw Susan deliver her number with such overblown emotion and at such a decibel level that people were pinned to their seats, the skin of their faces blown back as if in a high wind. At the end, she hit the money note, flung her arms wide and collapsed to her knees, heaving chest raised up to the gods.

There was a stunned silence, then a voice from the stalls:

'Bloody hell, I haven't heard anything like that since they decommissioned Concorde.'

I peeped through the masking flats and saw the faces of the audience. Many were open-mouthed, whether at the comment or Susan I couldn't tell. Reluctant applause broke out, but Izzy was shouting and whooping as if she'd just ridden an unbroken bull round the circle. Before I looked away, I saw the critic from the Independent. He was sitting, slumped, head moving slowly from side to side.

He wasn't smiling.

'Osama' Kim Bardon looked like a trapped rat. Further down the aisle, one famous hatchet man was busy scribbling on his programme with a twisted smile of pure wickedness on his thin lips. The only critic I could see who was enjoying herself was a well-known alcoholic, who probably had no idea where she was.

As if in the grip of a hideous nightmare, I made my final entrance and looked down into the audience. They looked back as if I was a Rampton out-patient. I opened my arms to them as I sang and caught the eye of the Independent critic. He was still shaking his head. But this time it was personal.

The re-choreographed curtain call was as long as Tannhäuser, and several of the audience looked as if they were suffering from dehydration, but Susan was triumphant.

'We got a standing ovation. They stood up.'

'They were trying to prevent deep vein thrombosis,' spat Lee, incandescent that only his claque had stood up for him. Two people had indeed jumped to their feet, shouting bravo for Susan alone: Izzy and Viola. The rest were critics stampeding to get out.

It was too much for Lee. He kicked his dressing-room door off its hinges. Susan blew me a kiss on her way up the stairs, smugly sure she had been launched into the firmament of stars.

My agent opened the bottle from the cistern.

'Well, darling, what can I say? I'd better look around for something else. They're looking for a rape victim in The Bill.'

Even though I knew it was a disaster, I was still upset. I had hoped so much I was wrong. Hope: what a waste of human endeavour was in that four-letter word.

'What did you think of Susan and Lee?' I intended to sound casual.

'Well, darling, she's got a career scaring the pigeons out of Trafalgar Square if she wants it, and frankly, dear, for all the glitz and glam, he couldn't carry a tune in a bucket. You're in quite a different league, dear, quite different.'

'Better, I hope,' I said, relaxing.

'Well, of course. Otherwise I wouldn't represent you, would I? By the way, has he had liposuction?'

I arrived late and reluctant at the party, in a rickshaw pedalled by a Peruvian chemistry student. Two bouncers standing on a patch of red carpet inside a deserted rope cordon inspected my invitation, then waved me down the balloon-covered staircase.

In a swirl of blinding lights and deafening music, Izzy and Viola were in the centre of a group paying court to Susan.

'Izzy,' I shouted. 'Thank you so much for the first-night present, it was fantastic! Amazing! I've never had a first-night present like it. Neither have the rest of the cast.'

His mouth opened, but nothing came out that I could hear. As I walked away, several people asked him what he'd given us.

'Tinnitus,' I called back over my shoulder.

The food had all gone, unsurprisingly, since the party started 35 minutes before we got off stage, and there were no clean glasses for the sour wine that was being circulated by irritable waiters.

Kelvin was getting drunk with serious dedication at the bar. I joined him, leaning on the luridly tiled surface. The place was packed with rejects from Big Brother and a Romanian double-act from the Eurovision Song Contest, who were effusive about my performance. Apart from them, no one had the bad taste to mention the show.

'I have to see my therapist,' was all Kelvin said, before sliding to the floor.

On the dance floor, Susan was rippling like a vast jelly in a spray-on, slit-to-the-thigh, green satin sheath. One bosom, making a bid for freedom, she rounded up and shoved back, as if it were a recalcitrant sheep.

God watched with fascinated revulsion. 'The problem with you white people dancing,' he sighed, 'is you move too much.' He and Glenda stayed aloof, bemused but smiling.

Lee, wearing a pale lavender suit, was talking animatedly to Viola. I caught the words 'my encore' and 'new costume'. You had to admire him – even on a sinking ship he was trying to upgrade his cabin.

All around me, the company bubbled with the certainty that triumph had been snatched from the jaws of the reviewers. How could they not love a show that had been greeted with such wild applause and screams of delight?

Sitting with Tizer and a couple of the other chorines, I was ashamed of being a bitter old bag, with my cynical certainty that Izzy and Viola were shysters, my gnawing loathing of Susan and Lee, and my contempt for the ruin they'd made of the show. And what was worse, as I peered inside myself, was the twisted disappointment that perhaps I was wrong, that it hadn't been a disaster.

As the wine took hold, I thought vaguely of publicly abasing myself by apologising to Izzy and Viola, of trying to befriend Susan, even of telling Lee I thought his performance was wonderful. *Dar*ling.

'You all right?' Tizer broke into my thoughts like a puppy through toilet paper.

'Sorry. Yes. Fine… What the heck's Izzy up to?'

Wearing a new, tweed flat-cap with his jeans and jacket, Izzy, cigar in hand, was clambering onto a small round table. Viola hovered behind him, her raised hands flapping feebly, presumably to catch him if he fell. Once he was upright, she folded her fingers under her chin, gazing up at him with devotion. I was surprised no one gave her a bone.

Izzy clapped loudly to bring us to order, but stood like Canute before the waves of sound until someone persuaded the DJ to silence. Reluctantly, the party came to order.

'Hi, guys. I'm Izzy Duck.' There was a huge cheer. How short memories were, when faced with free vol-au-vents and Croatian chardonnay. 'And I have here the morning newspapers.'

Another cheer; whoops; whistles. Izzy brandished the Daily Telegraph, the Daily Mail and the Guardian with the satisfaction of Neville Chamberlain.

'So here goes, guys.' He opened the Telegraph, unused to its size, crumpling the large pages as he folded it open. A chant started up.

'Yes! Yes! Yes! Yes!'

Stomping. Clapping.

Izzy's sallow face gleamed with sweat. The shouting subsided. An uneasy silence settled on the room. Izzy threw down the broadsheet and snatched up the Mail. Smaller, easier to handle, he flicked it open and broke its spine, folding it back to reveal the verdict.

Again he read.

Again he threw the paper down.

The Guardian he opened even more violently. He couldn't have read more than the headline when he threw it down. The Independent was ripped in two and flung across the room.

He made a sudden and dramatic exit, forgetting he was on a table. Viola reached up to him, but he slipped, tipped, and toppled, crashing to the floor, with the bright, festive cloth-covering from his plinth over him. The table shattered into a pile of grubby chipboard.

There was a spot of blood on his temple, and his cap had fallen off to reveal the mottled skin beneath. Embarrassing in his indignity, he rushed at the stairs like an incontinent for a bathroom, followed by Viola.

No one spoke.

Jonty bent slowly and picked up the verdicts. He scanned them quickly.

'Jesus.' He said it quietly, with respect. Then he put the papers down carefully and walked out. Within minutes the room was empty.

The papers lay on the floor, sad rags after many hands had touched the words that hailed the most monumental flop of the year.

This hideous vanity project is entirely the responsibility of husband and wife team, Izzy and Viola Duck. One can only regret that duck-shooting is illegal in this country.

… The lachrymose sentimentality of one song, sung by a sumo wrestler in a chiffon mini-dress, made me feel physically ill…

… They say it isn't over till the fat lady sings – and that's exactly what she did last night – loud, flat and for far, far too long.

… There is no director credited with this horrifying spectacle. If there was, I would file for damages.

Well, Susan got her wish – no one mentioned her name in the press.

Those that came out in the following days and on Sunday were no less decisive.

Viola Duck has created, seemingly with the assistance of her husband, an evening unrivalled in my experience for sheer awfulness…

…If we can deport clerics who threaten the nation's security, surely we can kick out two Americans who threaten our sanity…

A vanity project with nothing to be vain about.

If this is Broadway, give me Southwold.

Rush to see this show! It won't be there long…

Here we have caricature homosexuals, a torch-singer who deserved to be shot and Eleanor Woodwarde, who I must take to task for writing about this show. What she said was dreadful. But she lied. What I saw was much, much worse...

... There should be a law against those with more money than talent cluttering up London's stages with drivel like this...

...Produced by the Ducks. One can only hope bird-flu is on the way.

It was a total, undisputed disaster.

Sunday afternoon, surrounded by the papers, Kelvin and I were watching brain-dead television with KT when the doorbell rang. None of us moved. Eventually, on the third ring, I hove myself out of my chair and answered it. Dan stood there with a bottle of champagne in each hand.

'I read the reviews.' He kissed me with some force. 'How do you feel?'

'Depressed, knackered and guilty for being right.'

'Eleanor?'

'What?'

'I've missed you. Third time lucky?'

Why not?

THIRTY-SEVEN

When I arrived at the theatre the next day, I had a hangover and a post-coital glow that could have lit up Blackpool.

The air backstage was heavy with gloomy foreboding. How could we survive such a trashing? The house was tiny, made up mostly of the sort of people who like public hangings, but by the end of the show there was no sign of Izzy, nor, more importantly, of the piece of paper on the noticeboard that would announce our closing.

Susan, devastated by the demolition of her dreams, those ambitions which had been so public and so publicly destroyed, was weepy and subdued on stage and off. Lee, angry and defiant, went so far over the top he was interfering with the Heathrow flight-path. The kids were depressed, and we took all sharp objects out of Kelvin's room.

'Are West End musicals always so…so…awful?,' Tizer asked during the interval, bewildered by the disintegration of the company and his illusions. Now the panic calls to agents would start, any job chased, rumours of castings seized upon with desperate hope. We were all preparing for the end. Dead men dancing – though limping optimism could be heard in the goodnights as we left the theatre. Perhaps we could become a cult hit? Other productions had survived bad press…

KT, ministering spaghetti bolognese to Kelvin and me at midnight, was philosophical:

'Oh well, you've fucked up better shows than this.'

On Tuesday morning, the phone rang early.

'Eleanor?'

'Jonty? What's up?'

'Izzy's just phoned.'

'Is the notice going up?'

'No. No, of course not.' Of course not? What did he think we were doing? The Mousetrap? 'No, Izzy rang me from the airport…'

'I didn't have him down for a plane-spotter.'

'He and Viola have gone back to Costa Rica…'

'You're not serious.'

'...to release more funds.'

More chance of them releasing Rudolf Hess.

'What do you mean, "release more funds"?'

He went into a complicated and superficially convincing explanation of the running-costs of the show. Izzy Duck had to go home to sign papers in person to release monies that would be used for a big publicity drive – and to cover a few small outstanding bills.

'Not to pay the wages, then?'

'Well...er...'

'Oh, Jonty, don't tell me...hang on, they owe you money, don't they? Have they given you anything?'

'A bit.'

'How much?'

'Nine thou.'

I couldn't believe it. 'So they've stiffed you for sixteen grand?'

'Um...yes. But it's all right, they'll be back on Thursday with the money.'

I couldn't control my frustration with the poor lad. KT and Kelvin came out their bedroom to see what I was shouting about. 'You dozy tart.' I'd definitely been around KT too long. 'You stupid sod, they are not coming back. Don't you understand? They've done a runner...and you're not the only one owed money, are you?'

'Well, no, actually.' He sounded completely different from the cocky, public school boy I was used to. 'The first night party hasn't been paid for.'

'How much?'

'Twenty grand. He told them that salsa singer was paying – he didn't even turn up.'

'Bloody hell. Anything else?'

'The sound company, the lighting company, the PR company, not that they've done much, the prop-makers, the printers, the hire company, the set-builders, the costume- and wig-makers.' He paused, then in the voice I was used to, added, 'But they'll be back. You really mustn't be so cynical, Eleanor, negativity is the enemy of life.'

'No Jonty, Izzy Duck and his Cro-Magnon wife are the enemy. See you at the theatre.'

I sat in exhausted silence after I'd repeated the details to KT and Kelvin, who, having indulged in a fountain of vitriolic fury, started checking flights to Vancouver. He would be gone as soon as the final curtain came down.

'Well...,' KT said to the back of Kelvin's head, as he trawled the internet, 'I'll make a pie, got a few blackberries need eating.'

Hurt and upset, his hands went ice cold. Perfect for pastry. I followed him into the kitchen, ignoring the tears on his cheeks and the cigarette burning by the rolling-pin.

'KT, what's your agent doing about your money? They had no grounds to sack you.'

'Jonty never took me off the payroll,' he said, through a cloud of flour. 'I was never officially fired. They've been paying me to sit on my backside.'

A small silver lining in the gathering clouds.

'You're not broke, then...you could jump a flight to Canada.'

KT stopped his furious attack on a block of margarine.

'He hasn't asked me.' He thought for a moment. 'And, you know, Eleanor, a West End fuck stops at the end of the Northern Line. No... it was good. Leave it at that.'

⁂

That night, the serious rumour squad had been working overtime. We were coming off that evening. Izzy and Viola were transferring the show to a smaller theatre, then on to Broadway. They'd been arrested for drug smuggling. They were definitely on the Wednesday overnight flight, and Susan had been assured by Viola that everything was fine. The show would go on. After all, it was their baby.

I tried to get into the stage door with my double latte foam-backed coffee without being seen by Susan, who was posing with a cigarette under the outside light like a 1950s hooker. She didn't speak, but gave me a look that when we started rehearsals would have left me whimpering and unable to go on. Now I gave her a cheerful good evening and asked her if she had a migraine.

'They will be back, you know,' she hissed, with a ridiculous overplaying of the *will*. 'And you're going to be shown up for the destructive bitch you are. What you did to those people was vicious, just plain vicious. They're just trying to make their dream come true and you stopped them.'

I considered rising above this and sailing past in dignity, but then I thought, what the hell...

273

'I helped stop those two crooks from breaking the law, yes, and I stopped this show being taken over by a talentless egomaniac who knows as much about theatre as you know about singing. And if I have any part in stopping them ever putting another show on in London, my life will not have been lived in vain. And if that means I've stopped you becoming a star then frankly, Scarlett, I don't give a flying fuck.'

I'd like to say I ducked the punch she aimed at me and danced laughing into the theatre, but it landed messily just above my left ear and bounced me off the door frame. I didn't have time to think or feel pain, as I hurled the vat of boiling coffee over her. She screamed, not just from shock and outrage, but from real pain, as a pint of scalding brown sludge smacked her in the face. Her hair flattened under the weight of the liquid and drops dripped from her false eyelashes.

I couldn't help it. I laughed.

I roared with laughter. She started to slap me around the head screeching incoherently, and I couldn't stop laughing until Ruby came out and separated us, when I subsided onto the ground holding my ribs.

'What the fuck's going on?' It was the first time I'd seen him abandon his dynamic lethargy.

'She thinks they're coming back. That stupid great hippopotamus think Izzy and Viola Duck are coming back with the contents of their piggy bank. That Viola's Cinderella and I'm the Wicked Stepmother.' I stood up, not laughing anymore, and put my face threateningly close to hers. 'They are not coming back, you dimwit. You backed the wrong fucking horse. But that's the story of your career isn't it? Also-ran and not placed.'

She tried to kick me, but Ruby stopped her. As I staggered into the theatre, the last words I heard from Susan were:

'She thinks she's so fucking clever.'

'I don't think, Susan, I know,' I yelled back.

The only smiles that night were on stage. In the bleak corridors and dressing-rooms were fear, confusion and anger. We were waiting to be put out of our misery.

It would be neither swift nor humane.

At three o'clock on the Wednesday, during the matinée, Jonty put up the notice, as the only thing to come from Costa Rica was silence.

No money. Nothing.

We would play for two weeks on the wages lodged with the union. Then the nightmare spiralled into Thursday. The technicians, with no union buffer, weren't to be paid at all. Our pot of Izzy the Fool's gold didn't cover them. But it did cover cast members who, through meanness or stupidity, weren't union members, to the fury of those who'd paid their dues. I longed for the return of the closed shop.

Jonty called us together.

'Due to funds not being available to pay the staff, we will close this Saturday. In three day's time.'

Pandemonium broke out. The show had lasted nine days. All that work and heartbreak for nine days. Twelve shows.

Jonty raised his voice. '…If – and only if – the staff will consent to work until then. It means that, should there still be no funds by Friday morning they will do three shows, Friday, Saturday matinée and Saturday evening, without pay, and they may well refuse. In which case, we close tonight.'

A simian boy, Lee's unshaven and uncaring sidekick, shrugged. 'That's all right by me,' he said in his loud Glasgow voice. 'We still get two weeks' money.' He had been equally vocal in refusing to join the union.

The cast dispersed. Impotent at the unfairness of life. 'It's not fair,' I'd say as a child. 'What's not fair? A dark horse?,' would come the impenetrable reply.

Enemies I didn't know I had would be laughing at my name – above the title – on the ridiculous posters hanging in shreds from neglected hoardings. A public humiliation. A famous flop. I'd barely climbed the ladder and was hurtling down the snake.

On stage that night, we looked no different – bright, beaming, brainless, servicing the punters. Off stage, the atmosphere was leaden with unspoken recrimination.

⁘

Everyone agreed to stay on – some were in denial, some because they believed there would be an eleventh-hour reprieve, some because they felt a loyalty neither the producers nor the fates reciprocated.

The last performance came and went with no word from Izzy or Viola. No thank you, no regrets or goodbyes, and definitely no money.

At the curtain, I stepped forward. The cheers of the few to witness our demise died away.

'Ladies and gentlemen…'

Susan made to stop me. I covered my mike. 'Fuck off back in line. Now.' Maybe it was the ferocious wig – she obeyed.

'Ladies and gentlemen, you may have heard our producers have returned to Costa Rica to spend more time with their bank account.' Gratifying laughter. 'So I would like you to give your applause to the technicians and staff of this theatre who have not been paid and have worked since Wednesday out of loyalty to the cast and to those of you who have come to see us. Thank you.'

We clapped and shouted for the unseen heroes. Even Lee and Susan.

———

The wardrobe mistress held a sale of the costumes to pay the dressers, whose collective wages didn't amount to one of Izzy's solicitor's letters. The washing machines, driers, irons and sewing machine were looted. Everything of value was taken in lieu of what was owed. Even the padded coat hangers.

KT came down to the theatre and the two of us wandered onto the empty stage. The flat grey light of the workers threw shadows on the great house.

'Here you are, gell. Thought you might need this.'

He produced a screwdriver.

We took Izzy's door knobs. A souvenir of the best and worst months of my life. The rest of the set would be dismantled and thrown in a skip. But Izzy hadn't even provided money for that. It was two weeks before a producer paid a pound for it and took it away on a 36-week tour of The Merry Widow.

We said our goodbyes with that false merriment that protects at times of bereavement. We would grieve and nurse our wounds alone, the hastily exchanged phone numbers never used.

Susan and Lee, elaborately ignoring me, swept out with their entourages. I leaned out of my dressing-room window.

'Oi, Susan.'

She turned, mouth sucked tight.

'Let's meet for a coffee sometime, you can tell me where I went wrong.'

She gathered her dignity, turned on her impossibly high heels, tripped and fell into the bottle-filled crates that lined the entrance to the stage door.

'Mind you're not still there on Monday morning – that lot's for recycling. You might come back as an actress.'

'Or a singer,' chimed in KT.

We looked at each other.

'Nah…,' we chorused.

CURTAIN

KT and I are sitting by the sky-blue pool of a deserted hotel in Tenerife. Izzy's money paid for a cheap holiday in the sun and, between the chip shops and sports bars, we've found an oasis of peace. The British holiday-makers know nothing of what we've been through, and simply consider me to be a star in their midst, overwhelming me with drinks and requests for autographs. Their adoration is comforting if occasionally irritating, like Savlon on cracked skin.

They surround us as we lie on the tiled terrace under a palm tree, watching us with undisguised fascination. KT is next to me on a sun bed, his thin – too thin – body desperate for the warmth of the sun. His hands don't shake as he picks up his Sco and Co on the Ro. He removes the violet umbrella from it with steady fingers.

My winter pallor, with liberal basting, is turning a shade of gold that contrasts nicely with the white of my bikini line. We've been asked to sing at the Karaoke tonight. KT thinks we should do 'I Got You Babe'.

God knows we've neither of us got anyone else.

Kelvin's in Toronto doing Carousel, and Dan's in Edgware doing his leading lady.

Well, it wasn't a relationship, it was simply an interlocking of needs. I'm grateful to him for making me feel attractive and for reawakening my passion for sex.

Speaking of which, the hotel manager's just walked past, a bear of a man, built like a rugby player, black trousers, white open-necked shirt, thin jumper tied across the shoulders. Barcelona chic. He looks across the swimming pool at me. Almond eyes, strong jaw. So Spanish. So different. He doesn't smile. Just looks.

The past comes back as he disappears into reception.

Izzy and Viola have plans to mount the show in New York.

'Over their dead bodies,' says KT.

No one's been paid. The sound guy asked for his money and Izzy replied with a solicitor's letter threatening to sue for a fraudulent claim.

Thinking about them churns up feelings I wish I could have left at Gatwick, but they won't be silenced. As if I have to go through them in detail to purge them. Left unexamined they might rot and fester in my subconscious. As it is, my nights end in anxiety dreams and the occasional nightmare.

But some things I didn't allow in. Viola's vitriolic seven-page letter of attack on Dan, Jonty and me went unread. Apparently the debacle was our fault, we had destroyed them, their faith, their show and almost their marriage.

I sent Izzy his door knobs in reply.

But for all that I feel as if I'm trying to get dog dirt off my shoe, I'm in better shape than Jonty, who's working in IT to try to pay his credit card debts. It should take him ten years, or three if he goes into voluntary liquidation.

Glenda and God are in Viva Latina at the Trocadero, Blackpool. Tizer's in Jesus Christ Superstar. Lee's doing the Latvian tour of La Cage aux Folles.

And Susan? Who knows. Maybe she never existed...

David is fighting my claim for half of his worldly goods. He'll lose, and that should give me enough money not to have to take the first thing that comes along, even though no job offers have come in. Also, I'll be able to pay KT a good rent. Oh yes, we're going to live together. We've neither of us given up looking for the Great Love, but in the meantime we have a better marriage than some, and Arthur, my son, has said he'd like to see me when he returns to live with David and Phyllida. He might even grow to like me, now he can't bully me anymore. No one can.

KT's looking forward to having him stay. 'Public school boy his age? Ooh, love... he'll have a season ticket on the lilac bus.'

'KT, he's got a girlfriend.'

'She's just a beard, love.'

He interrupts my thoughts, hitting me with his paperback.

'He fancies you.'

'Who?'

'That manager.'

Well, maybe he doesn't, but I'm up for a challenge. We've got ten days left.

'Let's face it, Nell, sex doesn't mend a broken heart, but it does the rest of you the power of good.'

I can't disagree, particularly as the manager is coming towards us with a bottle of wine and three glasses.

'Hola, buenas tardes.' What a voice. Marinated in cognac and Ducados. 'My name is Jose Luis Diaz, do djou mind if I sit here? I am tol djou are a very famous actress. As manager, I am honoured to have djou here at the Hotel Che Pepe.'

He's opening the wine.

My mobile's ringing.

'Excuse me... Hallo?'

My agent. 'Eleanor? I've got you a meeting.'

'Great. What is it, a movie?'

'A new musical, darling... Set in Puerto Rico...'

'Thanks, but I'd rather eat my own leg... Oh, just a small one Jose Luis, I can always come back for more.'

Lights fade to black.

DRAMATIS PERSONAE

Eleanor Woodwarde *The Leading Lady*
Susan Barnard *A Soubrette*
Lee Smilie *A Musical Theatre Perfomer*
KT *Dance Captain and Friend of the Leading Lady*
Kelvin *A Canadian Tenor*
Glenda *A Salsa Dancer*
God *Salsa Dancer and Choreographer*
Barry *An Elderly Deaf Actor*
Lewis *An Older Character Actor*
Tizer *Chorus and Union Rep*
And Others

BRITISH TEAM
Dan Cawdron *Director*
Karl (Flossie) *Non Salsa Choreographer*
Karen *Musical Supervisor*
Morag *Designer*
Jonty *CSM / General Manager*
Basher *Production Manager*
Ruby *Male Stage Manager*
Gaffer Gusset *Female Assistant Stage Manager*

THE AMERICANS
Izzy Duck *A Broadway Producer domiciled in Costa Rica*
Viola Duck *His Wife. A Writer. Also domiciled in Costa Rica*
Ricky Ricky *Choreographer and Director. A Californian*
Rudolph Vizhnevsky *His Agent*
Charlie and Brandon (Trinny and Susannah) *His Assistants*

THE CIVILIANS
David Mertons-Mills *Husband to the Leading Lady*
Phyllida, née Bosanquet *A Member of the Minor Aristocracy.*
Friend of the above
Cedric Owen *Arts Editor of a National Daily Newspaper*

MUSICIANS
Ildefonso Campi *Composer*
Jimmy Fuentes *Percussionist*
Samson Quarenton *Pianist*

A SHORT GLOSSARY
of Theatrical Terms

Mike   Microphone

Float Mike   Microphone on the floor at the front of the stage where 'floats' (a row of lights) used to be

Head Mike   A small microphone taped to the forehead or cheek

Mike Pack   The battery, aerial and connecting wire, usually on a belt under the costume but also on the inside or outside of the thigh. Down the back of a corset, under the armpit. In America, in the wig

Stage Left   Auditorium Right

Stage Right   Auditorium Left

Prompt Side   Stage Left

Bastard Prompt   Stage Right

OP   Opposite Prompt

USC   Up Stage Centre. A Nice Place to be

DSC   Down Stage Centre. A nice place to be if facing the audience

Centre   The best place to be. As long as no one's USC

Wings   The bits either side of the stage where actors wait to come on and leave their throat sweets as they enter. Nothing to do with Red Bull or sanitary wear

Flys / Flies   The place the crew go to have a chat during the show. In the roof of the theatre accessible by a vertical ladder

Grid   A mesh that forms a floor above the stage. Newcomers are often asked to 'sweep the grid'. It is a joke

Sightlines   The angles from which the audience can see the whole stage. Difficult in a house where the auditorium is wider than the stage. It is thought hilarious to ask newcomers to 'Paint the sightlines'

Lighting Rig   The stage lights (lamps), which hang from bars, the circle, the wings or any available hook, depending on the lighting designer

Brace   A bit of wood which holds up a flat

Cleat   A bit of metal sticking out of the back of a flat

Cleat Line   A bit of string

Set The world inhabited by performers on stage. Minimalist, Surrealist, Drawing-room or Box, invariably littered with actor traps

Flat A painted canvas on a wooden frame which makes up part of the set

Masking Flat Black material on a wooden frame used to prevent the audience seeing into the wings

Stage Weight Square or round lump of metal of some weight. Used to steady braces. Also to prop doors open. Often put by stage management into a prop-suitcase just before an actor picks it up thinking it's empty. Also often put by actors into furniture the stage management have to move during a scene change. They were often used as ashtrays in the past

Trap Hole in the stage with a lid on it. Used for entrances and exits

Star Trap Small hole with a lid on it through which actors enter very rapidly. Usually in panto

Cyc (Cyclorama) Painted cloth at the back of the stage

Backcloth Cheaper painted cloth at the back of the stage

Skip A large cardboard box, originally basket, for storing and transporting anything except actors

Props Any object used by an actor that's not nailed down

Talking props / Software Actors

TLC Talentless lazy c∗∗∗s (usually the actors)

Prop table The table on which props are kept. Can be anywhere depending on the room available backstage. Normally in the wings

Workers Lights used on stage when the show lights are off

Blacks / Drapes / Tabs Various curtains

The Rag The Curtain

The Washing Line The song sheet flown in during panto or the Ring Cycle

Fourth Wall Through which the audience observes the actors in straight plays. Non-existent if the actor plays direct to the audience. This is referred to as 'breaking the fourth wall' 'playing out front' or an 'absolute disgrace' depending on whether you're doing Brecht, Cooney or Ibsen

Hemp House A theatre where the flying of flats and curtains is done by hand with hemp ropes. It is not a West End theatre where the crew are mainly Rastafarian

Iron The Safety Curtain

Forestage What sticks out beyond the Iron or the pros

Pros / Proscenium Arch The frame round the stage going from floor almost to grid

Pasaralle A semi-circular runway from the stage, often surrounding the band – to keep them out of the pub

Vomitorium A tunnel entrance from the auditorium

Sitzprobe When everyone sits and probes what's going on just before opening a musical. Very Royal Shakespeare Company term

Treads Stairs on stage

Tallescope Ladder on wheels

Riggers' Knickers Varies from place to place

Gaffer Tape The DNA of theatre. Without it nothing works

LX Electrics

Sound Irritating people who think the show is all about them. Often to be found under women's skirts adjusting their mike packs

Prince of Darkness The Lighting Designer

Chorine Chorus member

Lahdy Straight actor   .

Turn Musical theatre / comedy, non-Shakespearean actor

Twirly *see* Walloper

Dance Captain The person who makes sure the dancers perform the choreography correctly. Often rehearses new members of cast who have joined after the show has opened

Walloper Dancer (does not include Rudolf Nureyev or Margot Fonteyn)

Swing Dancer who knows the 'tracks' of every other dancer. A universal understudy. Can go on for anyone at a moment's notice. Paid very little extra. Needs psychiatric help

The Band More than one musician

Who's Carving? Who is tonight's condutor?

Follow Spot What we all want

Blonde / Basher / Limes Old terms for lights

House Lights Lights in the auditorium

FOH Front of house and its staff, including House Manager, usherettes, bar staff etc

Crew The people (mostly men) who work for the theatre as scene shifters. They build and dismantle the set. Not usually vegetarians

Stage Management Team Consisting of Stage Manager, Company Stage Manager, Deputy Stage Manager, Assistant Stage Manager(s). SM is most senior on stage and backstage after curtain up, outranking all including director. CSM deals with money as well as egos. DSM is on 'the book': sits in prompt corner with the script and 'calls' the show to lighting and sound operators. Also provides prompts if needed and calls the actors to the stage during the show in time for their entrances. This is a courtesy not an obligation. ASM spends life running round getting props, making tea and doing everything no one else wants to do. Often to be found in tears during the Technical Rehearsal. All but Company Manager wear black

Read-through the first reading, seated round a table, of the script

Technical Rehearsal A nightmare that can last between two days and four weeks. It does what it says on the tin. Everything of a technical nature is rehearsed and the actors are no more than the software

Tannoy / Show Relay Speaker through which the perfomance is heard in the dressing-rooms. Replaced call boys

Interval When the theatre owner makes their money

Entrance Round Applause when a famous actor comes on. Now confined to theatres where the audience is of an age

Exit Round Applause as an actor leaves the stage. Usually to show appreciation of a fine performance or a brilliant exit line. Often started by the actor himself

The Who's Best The Curtain Call

SADS Severe Acting Deficiency Syndrome

Notes Interminable sessions in the stalls when the director attempts to improve the show by telling the actors where they're going wrong. Some directors visit the dressing-room and give notes privately. This is often done rather than embarrass leading artists in front of the company. The late great Ken Hill wrote them out in different colours and nailed them to the wall for all to see

Cattle Call / Audition / Meeting   Methods of getting work, depending on how high up the tree you are

Offer   High enough up the tree not to have to do any of the above